"WE DID IT. . . . WE KILLED HER."

Officer George Coelho swallowed hard, and asked the teenage girl to start at the beginning. He was still having trouble believing that these two kids had slaughtered eighty-five-year-old Anna Brackett in her own home.

With very little prompting, Shirley, 14, described the murder, taking great care to include each terrible detail. The seasoned cop found it creepy. He had to keep reminding himself that this sweet little girl sitting there smiling at him was a vicious murderer.

After she'd finished, Coelho went into the next room to collect the girl's blood stained clothes and found the small flowered diary she'd mentioned at the end of her confession. Thumbing through the book, he was shocked to read the final entry, written in her own, juvenile hand:

Today Cindy and I ran away and killed an old lady. It was lots of fun.

LITTLE GIRL LOST

JOAN MERRIAM

PINNACLE BOOKS
WINDSOR PUBLISHING CORP.

To Karen,
who helped me find the courage and strength
to begin this project eight years ago . . .
and to Jane, Jan and Pam,
who helped me learn how to use that courage
and strength to complete it.

This book is also dedicated to the memory of
Anna Eugena Brackett.

PINNACLE BOOKS

are published by

Windsor Publishing Corp.
475 Park Avenue South
New York, NY 10016

Second printing: November, 1992

Printed in the United States of America

This book is the result of eight years of investigative work and background study into a murder, the two killers, and the events and circumstances in their lives which may have played a role in propelling them toward that scarlet fourteenth day of June in 1983. It is intended to be neither an apology nor an expiation. It is rather a journey through two young lives corrupted and mutilated by the violence and depravity surrounding them in their own families, and forsaken by a system designed to save them.

All of the material within these pages is taken from my own records and observations of people and events, from personal interviews, or from authoritative transcripts and documents provided me both officially and confidentially. Where incidents and conversations have been reconstructed or recreated, or thoughts of individuals inferred, every effort has been made to ensure the greatest degree of fidelity possible, based upon my knowledge and understanding of those events and the people involved in them.

All of the characters portrayed in this book are real, although the names and descriptions of certain individuals have been changed to protect their identities.

NOTES OF GRATITUDE

The idea of using a leaden, dispassionate word like "Acknowledgments" for this section can't begin to express the depth of my feelings for the many individuals who have made the difficult and painful eight-year process of creating this book both possible and bearable. I do not choose to simply "acknowledge" these friends, associates, and invaluable sources—rather, I offer them my deepest and most heartfelt gratitude.

First to my beloved father Cliff and my dear aunt Jane Merriam-Wrightsman, who have given me such wonderful gifts of love and support, guidance and understanding, throughout all the days of my life.

Next, to those who have stood beside me with unyielding affection and encouragement through these latter years of my journey toward wholeness: my two Nancys—Nancy Bloom and Dr. Nancy Otterness, who show me in different ways the power of genuine love; therapists Susan Coit, Linda Farley, and Bonnie Serratore, and Reverend Jackie Kortright, all of whom taught me the freedom of revealing my own dark secrets, and then poured their loving compassion on my searing wounds like waters from cool mountain springs; my beautiful "daughter" Christi Crosby; "Doctor Gary," who remains special in my heart despite it all; and my precious friends Ron Howard (no, not *that* Ron Howard), Tom and Linda Cox, Barbara and Alan Deal, Gary Reid, Gloria Beverage, Joe and Eddie Sandven, and Evelyn Deane.

There are also those without whom this book would not have been possible: my wonderful editor Paul Dinas at Pinnacle Books, and my agent Hal Lockwood at Penmarin Books, who took a chance on an "unknown," and Hal's acquisitions assistant Carol Smith, who first brought my work to his attention; KXTV reporter Mark "Hondo" Hedlund and former News Director Rick Kavooris, who unknowingly started me on this journey during my internship at KXTV; Dr. Roland Summit, Dr. Richard Paul Mahoney, Steve Healy, and Ron Henke, who so generously shared their personal and professional insights into the ravaging effects of child abuse and family dysfunction; and all those who entrusted me with their personal remembrances of Anna Brackett as well as Shirley and Cindy—Audra Wilson, Shirley's uncle Michael and aunt Anna, Gladys Thompson, David Carver, Christine Falkenstein, Richard Steffan, Marie Hubbard, Ann Wagner, Tammy Kell, writers Pat Murkland and Cheryl McCall, NBC News Producer Polly Powell, and all those who have spoken to me under the promise of anonymity over the past eight years. For their special kindnesses to me during my research trek through New York City in 1990, my thanks go to Eddie, the New York Telephone repairman and to my ever patient driver, Robert.

Nor can I neglect the many professionals who spent hours—sometimes weeks and months—helping in my quest for information and a better understanding of Shirley and Cindy as well as the crime: former Placer County Deputy District Attorney and now Judge Larry Gaddis; Judge J. Richard Couzens; D.A. Investigator David Brose; Detective George Coelho, Sergeant Ray Mahlberg and Inspector Johnnie Smith; Court Reporter Ann Bothello; former Probation Director Ted

Smith and staff Pat Brown, Mick Barnes, Tom Hoffman and Ken Englund; John Bixler and counselors Kathleen Williams, Liz Maher, Mike Rains, Gail, Dave, Dennis and Mike; Placerville Police officers Bob Ewing and Howard "Tom" Carroll; Bertha "Bert" Jackson; Principal David Baker, former Vice-Principal Janeene Coleman, and teachers Richard Huff and aide Susie DeCamp, Marie Hubbard, Dennis Price (and his wife Sherry), Don Schaefer (along with his wife Harriet and her sister Tina Beaulieu), Richard Payton, Scott Anders, James Coate, and Pat Vogel. From the California Youth Authority, former Director James Rowland, C.A. "Cal" Terhune, Welby Cramer, Peter Zajac, Sharon English, Elaine Duxbury, Roslyn Harris, Dr. Edward Daube, and Lance Curtis; at the California State Department of Corrections, Tip Kindel; at the California Women's Institute at Frontera, Lieutenant Floyd Huyler; and at the Central California Women's Facility, Lieutenant Edna Miller.

For their endless patience with me during the completion of this book, I say a grateful thank you to my Board of Directors at the Child Abuse Council.

To all those I have failed to mention — not out of disregard but simple memory lapse — who provided me help and support during the creation of this book, I extend both my apologies and appreciation.

And finally, in some ways most importantly, for sharing their pain and joy and grief with me in person and through their writings, I offer my prayers and loving thanks to the countless victims and survivors whose lives have been shattered by the dark shadow of child abuse, yet whose gentle voices of faith and encouragement have helped me bring the dream of this book into reality.

Preface

All art is a kind of confession, more or less oblique. All artists, if they are to survive, are forced, at last, to tell the whole story — to vomit the anguish up.

— James Baldwin

In many ways, that act of vomiting up the anguish has characterized much of my last eight years. More than once during the blackest and most hopeless days of those years, I found myself poised on the jagged edge of that terrible yawning chasm, peering into the darkness beyond with an agonizing certainty that there was no way out other than into the void. Sometimes I stood there alone, sometimes with others who were on their own journeys through the scattered debris of their lives to wholeness. Most of us, I am glad to say, made it back.

The story of how I ended up on that fearful edge of nothingness is hardly unique — although for most of my years I lived in a state of total emotional alienation from the rest of the world, certain that no other living human being had ever been where I'd been, felt what

I'd felt. I wore a myriad of pretty masks which concealed a past twisted by dark and shameful secrets — secrets which I knew no one would ever understand, much less believe.

My mother's raging alcoholism, which endured for more than twenty years after my birth, was one of the first of these secrets, made even more insidious because of our family's social status. We had a reputation in the community, an image to protect: to that community, we (especially we three children, who inherited our blessings without having to suffer for them) were viewed as upstanding and exceedingly fortunate, favored by comforts if not luxuries, living a near-perfect life. The fact that the perfection and good fortune didn't extend inward past our front door was something all of us knew better than to tell. Even to ourselves.

Another secret was even larger and more potent — so potent, in fact, that I tucked it away in the farthest and most inaccessible recesses of my unconscious memory, where it festered for more than four decades. What emerged after all those years was the terrifying memory of my mother's acts of uncontrolled hatred toward me as a youngster: a hatred born of her own self-abhorrence and unspoken pain which simply became focused on me . . . a hatred that reached its zenith when she attempted to choke me to death in my crib. So began the years of physical abuse, hidden from all eyes but mine and hers, which didn't end until I reached my late teens.

Yet there remained one final secret for me to keep: at age eight I was molested by someone I loved and trusted — an abuse which continued for the next five years. I, of course, remained just as hushed about this latest and darkest secret, having learned well the lessons of my past.

My own circle of silence began to take shape out of

10

the muteness we all maintained over my mother's drinking; then connecting to that first arc was the crescent curve of her incomprehensible violence and hatred toward me; and finally lay the dark, concave line of my sexual molestation, completing the toxic wreath of silence.

June 14, 1983 was the catalyst which would ultimately break that circle. Late that summer afternoon, two girls barely into their teens took the life of an elderly woman in my hometown of Auburn, California. Cindy Collier and Shirley Wolf were captured and taken into custody within eight hours of the slaying.

At the time I was working toward my Master's degree at a Sacramento university and doing an extended internship at KXTV, the CBS affiliate television station in that city. A series of fortuitous events landed me at the murder trial on behalf of the station. It was there, during the first days of the hearings, that a tiny voice began to nag at me: *There's a lot more here,* it cautioned, *than just the story of two girls who went crazy one summer day and stabbed an old lady to death.* As whispers circulated about Shirley's history as a victim of abuse, my own hidden memories began to emerge like skeletons from a coffin-strewn basement.

I hadn't asked for any of this — and I certainly wasn't prepared to look at it — and most of all, I didn't want to believe what I seemed to be remembering. But even in the midst of all that denial, I simply couldn't deny the feelings that were overwhelming me.

By now my mother had been sane and sober for a decade and a half: after far too many long and painful years, we had finally established a bond of love and mutual respect. But before I found the voice to tell my secrets to her or anyone else, she died. Over the next five years, with the help and love of countless people, I managed to slog through the noxious swamps of my past. During the last of those years, I also worked toward my Master's degree and my thesis, which delved even further into not just Anna Brackett's tragic murder, but the tragedy that made up the lives of her two young murderers.

Strangely, the more I researched and learned the truth about the massive psychological wounds suffered by both Shirley and Cindy as victims of child abuse, the more I began to breathe and see and speak again. As the months rolled into years, I discovered I was far from alone in my suffering and grief; soon, some of those old, gangrenous wounds began to heal.

Slowly but steadily (and for the first time in my life, not alone), like a sojourner seeking some ultimate truth, I began to face the monsters in my closet and the rattling skeletons in my own basement chamber of shadows — and one by one, to banish them. I admit there are a few that still keep me in their chilling company during those nightmare darknesses that haunt from time to time . . . but I envision the day when they, too, will disappear into the mists from which they came, leaving me far more whole and free and at peace than I have ever been.

So, in many ways, the journey I speak of in describing Shirley's and Cindy's descent into darkness is also the story of my own journey toward the light.

There are, I believe, lessons to be learned from them all.

Auburn, California
April, 1992

Part One:

Blood Sacrifice

One

A huge scarlet clot splattered onto the side of the gleaming steel basin and oozed slowly down the outside edge. Soon more droplets appeared on the glossy surface and began to trickle toward the mouth of the drain, leaving behind little crimson slug trails which disappeared into the gaping hole. By now the mirror and a nearby wall were dotted with red, and tiny flecks were scattered on the yellowed linoleum floor.

"Shit!" Shirley tried to catch a glob of the stuff that had begun to dribble down her left cheek, but she only succeeded in smearing it even worse. Glancing at her reflection in the bespattered mirror, she grinned widely. Her cheek bore an evil-looking slash of red, and both arms were speckled here and there. A large rusty red splotch was on the side of her neck, and another on her shoulder.

"Don't get that shit on your jeans or you'll never get it out," cautioned Cindy. "It's even worse than blood."

The big girl idly poked at a gelatinous puddle of the mixture that had dropped onto the side of the sink, drawing swirls and figure-eights in it with the tip of her finger. Two canary yellow plastic bottles of

15

Miss Clairol Loving Care (Covers Only the Gray) in Red Ginger lay askew on the countertop, drooling out the last of their contents.

Suddenly the door to the bathroom burst open and a stick-figured blond girl rushed in. She stopped dead in her tracks when she saw the two amateur beauticians with their waterlogged burgundy heads.

"Oh! I . . . uh . . . I didn't mean . . ."

She looked from one girl to the other with wide-eyed astonishment at their appearances, then slowly turned her gaze back to Cindy with a look of recognition that verged on horror. Her pallid face seemed to shrink.

"Oh," she repeated dully, taking an involuntary step backward. "Cindy." Flaming spots of color began to rise on her cheeks.

When she'd dashed into the room she'd needed to go to the bathroom so badly she didn't think she could hold it one minute longer, but suddenly it felt like her bladder was absolutely empty. She was clearly afraid of the girl she was facing.

Cindy stared at the intruder for a few seconds as if trying to place her face, then nodded her head almost imperceptibly and grunted a name. "Stephanie. Right?"

The blonde's dry lips stuck together as she wordlessly opened and then closed her mouth several times, while her head gave a series of little birdlike nods. Cindy looked at Stephanie's reflection in the red-smeared mirror, then asked if she was at the pool alone.

"Huh-uh. Tiffany and me are hangin' around the pool together."

Saying that made Stephanie feel somehow a little safer, just to have Cindy know she wasn't by herself.

16

She couldn't tell yet what kind of a mood the big ninth grader was in, but with Cindy it was always smart to be on your best behavior right away so if the fireworks *did* start up, they wouldn't be aimed in your direction. Even though she didn't really know her very well at all, she knew enough to give the older girl a wide berth. Cindy had a short fuse — and she had a real rep for being tough and mean. Word was that even the boys didn't want to mess with Cindy Collier when she was pissed off.

Squeaky voices drifted into the bathroom through the half-open door. Kids hollering and splashing in the pool, wet feet smacking on concrete; then the raspy voice of a disinterested and frustrated mother bellowing out, "Okay you guys — I've just about had it!" The screeching died down a little.

Suddenly struck with an overwhelming desire to urinate, Stephanie hobbled back and forth from one foot to the other and wished she and Tiff had gone to pool number Two instead of this one. Her long ivory hair, which by the end of summer would be tinged with pale green from so many days spent in the heavily chlorinated water, swung damply to the rhythm of her foot-to-foot shuffle.

It never entered her mind that she could easily go ahead and use the toilet while the two teenagers were at the sink. Being in the same room alone (or, almost alone — the other girl hadn't said a word so far, just stood there staring with those weird eyes) with Cindy Collier was bad enough. To be in the same room alone with her with your pants down . . . well, that just seemed like too much of a risk. Twelve was too young to die, Stephanie figured.

The three teenagers stood facing one another in the sour-smelling coolness of the bathroom for what seemed like hours, no one saying anything, until suddenly Cindy mumbled something that sounded like "shit," under her breath, bent down, and stuck her soggy hair under the faucet. Shirley quickly followed her friend's example and began to rinse the color from her hair as well. It looked like cheap red wine as it gurgled down the drain.

At the sound of the water Stephanie began to squirm.

Finished, Cindy wrung her hair out as best she could, then flipped her head back, ran her fingers through her hair and appraised herself in the mirror. At the same time, Shirley combed her fingers through the sopping strands of her own deep brown hair, grabbed a handful, and held it away from her scalp. She leaned over the sink toward the mirror until her broad nose was almost touching the glass, then backed away a step or two, shaking her head blankly. Her hair was simply too dark to take much of the color at all, too much like her mother's.

It didn't take a lot these days to conjure up an image of her mother in Shirley's mind's eye. There was the raven-haired Katherine, diddling around the house with a cigarette stuck in her mouth, trying to keep the boys from killing each other and everybody out of their dad's way if he was in one of his black moods. The vision shifted to her darkly handsome father, and Shirley felt that old familiar flip-flop in her stomach. Thinking about him made Shirley so confused sometimes, especially at times like this when she was with a bunch of strangers in a strange place, and when it had been so long since she'd been with him or seen him. Sometimes—especially during those nights when the moon sliced through her window like a blinding silver white laser beam—she

18

couldn't quite figure out if what she felt was love or hate. If she stared at the moonbeams for a while, she could even begin to feel herself being lifted away far above everything, where once again she could almost recreate the smell, the sound, the sight of him, the feel of his huge dark hand against hers, and once again the poisonous fear mixed with longing burbling down deep in the pit of her stomach.

Her reverie was interrupted by the sound of a voice. Cindy, who had noticed Stephanie eyeing Shirley curiously, figured she'd better introduce the two girls, and started to say Shirley's name. Earlier, she agreed to pretend Shirley was her cousin, just so no one got suspicious—after all, as of ten o'clock that morning Shirley *was* a runaway. Cindy was, too, for that matter, but that fact really didn't concern her at all. She'd been in trouble too many times to let something as minor as being a runaway get to her.

Shirley stopped her before Cindy could finish saying her name to the younger girl.

"Melissa," Shirley corrected. "My name's Melissa."

It was a name Shirley particularly loved. It seemed to have a kind of musical quality that her own down-to-earth name lacked. She had even started to write a book she called *Melissa's Choice,* based on her own life. It was the story of a young girl who had a lot of problems, but whose "choice" was that she would have a good life in spite of what had happened to her. The problem was, in the book—much as in Shirley's own life—things just didn't seem to be working out that way.

But as far as today was concerned, she liked the idea of having a new identity. Becoming someone totally new and different, with a whole different life. Maybe it would be a good omen.

Cindy threw a quizzical look at Shirley, then shrugged her shoulders.

"Yeah," she said. "Melissa. This's Stephanie."

"Hi." Stephanie bobbed her head in acknowledgement, not really knowing what else to say.

In the commanding voice of a drill sergeant, Cindy suggested they all go back out to the pool and go for a swim.

"Well, the two of us're just layin' around," offered Stephanie tentatively, afraid of arousing Cindy's anger by contradicting her order, but at the same time unwilling to brave the chill waters of the unheated pool. "Water's too cold."

Cindy snorted acidly, muttering something about Stephanie being a wimpy jellyfish, and headed out the door.

Finally. Finally they were leaving and Stephanie could go to the bathroom in peace. She plopped onto the cold white seat and peed for what seemed twenty minutes straight.

When she got back to the pool, Cindy and the girl she'd introduced as her cousin were huddled together on the edge, their feet dangling in the water and heads bowed in intense conversation. Cindy seemed to be doing most of the talking.

"Hey, where've you been? I started to think you drowned in the toilet!" Tiffany looked at her friend Stephanie to see if she was all right. Stephanie motioned to the two girls sitting on the side of the pool.

"Cindy Collier's here," she explained. "She was in there with that other girl and I had to wait till they finished. They were dyeing their hair."

"They were what?"

20

"Yeah, can you believe it? In the pool bathroom! It's really gross in there." Stephanie kept her voice low.

"What's she doin' here at Auburn Greens anyways?" Tiffany asked. "I thought they moved away."

"She said the other girl's her cousin. Melissa."

"Melissa who?"

"I dunno—she never said." Stephanie ran a wide-toothed comb through her hair as she talked, her eyes never leaving Cindy.

Tiffany also turned her gaze to the broad-shouldered girl lounging at the side of the pool with her cousin. She'd known Cindy for about a year, ever since the girl's family moved into an apartment in the Greens. What she knew, she didn't much like . . . but like Stephanie, she had no intention of crossing the older girl.

As she watched, Cindy slowly raised her head and swiveled toward the two younger girls. Her eyes locked onto Tiffany's, and then she smiled warmly, raised her hand in a wave, and motioned the two friends over to where she was sitting.

Tiffany and Stephanie walked uneasily across the warming concrete to the edge of the pool and sat down next to Cindy and her friend.

Introducing the dark-haired girl, Cindy said, "This is my cousin, Melissa."

Glancing back at Tiffany, Cindy asked, "How ya' doin', Tiff?"

"Okay," she replied, trying to figure out why Cindy was being so nice.

"You wanna go swimming?"

"Uh, I guess so," Tiffany said. She'd really rather just lay around and work on her tan, but when Cindy asked you to do something . . .

21

"You coming in, Steph?" Tiffany asked her friend hopefully.

"Uh-uh," Stephanie replied with a little shiver. "Too cold."

Cindy laughed, but with no trace of her earlier rancor. "Then you can keep an eye on our stuff."

Stephanie watched as the three girls dove in and began to lap the pool. She noticed that Cindy was a pretty fair swimmer. A little heavy, but a lot of muscles in her upper arms. The other girl — Cindy's cousin — was quite a bit slimmer than Cindy and already had a nice tan for only the second week of June. Either that or she was just naturally dark. Italian, maybe.

It was almost four o'clock. Stephanie still had a couple of hours before she was due home. She turned her face into the waning glare of the sun and closed her eyes. Around her floated sounds of churning water, a laugh she recognized as Tiff's, further away a child's angry wail at not getting *Just five more minutes Mom please*, at the pool, and the ever-present hum of traffic along the highway a block away.

Cindy pulled herself up over the edge of the pool and stood beside the motionless figure for a moment before Stephanie opened her eyes.

"Borrow your towel?"

Stephanie jumped to her feet and handed Cindy her beach towel. Little rivulets of pink-tinged water dribbled from her hair into the ample cleavage of her purple swimsuit.

Cindy would have been a big girl anyway, even without the extra weight she was carrying. She stood 5'9" and weighed a little over 140 pounds, but every ounce was as solid as a football linebacker. Broad-shouldered and full-busted, she appeared much older

22

than her fifteen years—a distinct advantage whenever she ditched school in the middle of the day and took off hitchhiking. Unless she bumped into one of the cops that knew her, most of them never even looked twice.

Her shoulder-length dark brown hair hung loosely around her squared-off face, which in the past couple of years had taken on a tight, hard look. Her brows were usually pinched together in an angry scowl at the broad bridge of her nose, and her trademark impenetrable layer of murky eye makeup only added to the callous, forbidding image. Yet it wasn't really all that difficult to see Cindy was essentially a pretty girl—especially when she smiled and her dark eyes lost some of their snapping fierceness.

Stephanie watched as Cindy dried her hair with the towel—which as a result now featured pale splotches of muddy red hair color that obviously wasn't all that permanent—and dropped it in a heap at her feet.

"We're gonna go change," she said over her shoulder, as her cousin padded after her toward the restroom.

A few minutes later Cindy was back, zipping up a pair of skintight faded blue Calvin Klein jeans with a devil patch on the back pocket. "You guys gonna hang around here for a while?" she asked the younger girls, who'd settled in a sunny spot near the pool's edge.

Tiffany and Stephanie exchanged apprehensive glances. "Uh, I guess so."

"Great. You can watch our stuff till we get back, then. We gotta . . . we're gonna go make a phone call and see some guys. Okay?"

Grudgingly, Tiffany agreed. "Okay, but we gotta

be home by six."

"Fine. No problem," Cindy said.

By now they were nearly alone except for a grandmotherly-looking woman with silver blue hair and a purple swimsuit with huge orange flowers on it. "Melissa" was still back near the bathroom, tugging on the laces to a ragged pair of Adidas. When she stood up, Tiffany could see that the blue corduroy pants the girl wore were filthy. She was tying on a lavender headband, and she had a jacket on over her black flowered swimsuit that was pinkish lavender and made out of some shiny material.

"Umm, I've left my journal over there," she said as she joined Cindy. "It's really important to me, so don't let anybody steal it, okay?"

Stephanie wondered why anyone would want to steal some dumb journal, if that was really all it was. As the two girls walked away, Stephanie saw that the jacket Cindy's cousin was wearing—now she could tell it was satin—had the words Roller Disco on the back.

Tucked off to one side of the little square building that housed the women's restroom, just near the fence, there was a fairly nondescript jumble of personal effects left by the two girls. A black purse, an orange football jersey with white stripes, a pair of ratty brown deck shoes with Garfield shoelaces. Off to one side was a pink flowered journal laying half-open, pages fluttering in the gentle summer afternoon breeze. Really, nothing anyone *would* want to steal. Nothing anyone would even care that much about.

"Oh, God, Tiff—it's gone."

"What's gone?" Stephanie's dismayed comment had come out of the clear blue sky.

Tiffany pointed toward the entrance to the pool restroom, where Cindy and her cousin had left their things. The spot was empty. A look of concern — or, more aptly, horror — had darkened her freckled face. *Did somebody come by and pack everything off while we went running after that stupid ice-cream truck?* Sensing that her friend was beginning to panic, Tiffany put on her best show of bravado. "Hey, I bet Cindy and that other girl just came back for it all. After all, who'd want to rip off a cruddy T-shirt and some shoes?"

"What about the purse?" Stephanie pressed the point. "And the diary or whatever it was?"

"Cindy told me there wasn't nothin' in the purse anyways except her comb and a bunch of other garbage. No money or anything like that. Besides, nobody'd want somebody else's diary, would they? 'Specially if they didn't know them." Tiffany concluded her argument, thinking to herself: *At least, I sure hope that's the way it was. The idea of Cindy Collier coming after me 'cause I let some creep steal her stuff is a real nightmare on wheels.*

Stephanie sighed with relief. "Yeah, I guess you're right. They probably came back just a minute or two after we left."

She and Tiff had left the pool a little after five to catch the ice-cream truck that came through the huge Auburn Greens condominium complex every day around five-thirty. But they'd started talking about something or other and let the time get away from them; by the time they heard the familiar music-box melody from the little silver truck, it was blocks away and on its way out of the complex. They ran after it for a half-block or so, but then gave up, puffing and giggling.

Instead of going back to the pool, the two girls meandered around that part of the Greens, doing nothing much and going nowhere in particular. Just hanging out and talking. By the time they decided to go back to the pool to pick up their towels, it was a few minutes past six o'clock.

Suddenly the scream of a siren shattered the late afternoon calm. Whipping around toward the sound, the girls saw a white ambulance, its lights flashing wildly, racing up Quartz Drive. A minute or two later a white rescue squad truck shot by, sirens shrieking.

"Cripes!" gasped Stephanie. "What's going on?"

"Maybe some old lady had a heart attack," offered the other girl. "Wonder where it is?"

Stephanie craned her neck in the direction the vehicles had taken, but she couldn't see anything. She shook her head, then glanced down at her watch. "Oh my God!" she said excitedly. "It's way after six! I better get home or my mom'll have a shit fit!" The alarm and fascination the two friends had felt at the wailing sirens quickly vanished as they turned to more pressing matters such as making sure they got home in time for dinner.

They picked up their towels, still damp and smelling faintly of chlorine, and skipped down the stairs to the sidewalk, walking and talking together for a while in the incandescent evening air that carried the mingled scents of freshly cut grass and barbecuing hamburgers. Then their paths parted. It had been a pretty ordinary summer day for the two fresh-faced youngsters, all things considered. Nothing really all that earth-shaking happened, nothing

26

that would normally stand out all that much in the memory of a twelve-year-old. Yet unbeknownst to these two young friends, the events of that single day in June would soon change their innocent lives forever. From then on, nothing would ever be quite the same.

Two

All things considered, it's a fairly ordinary town. Squatting solidly in the low foothills of California's Sierra Nevada mountain range, Auburn used to be the kind of place where kids grew up and left and gnarly old-timers passed the days until it was time to die. It was a town untouched by the harsh shock waves of modernism, content to amble through time at its own tortoiselike pace. Today, however, the story is quite different.

Today, getting there means joining the urban exile weekend nature-seekers in their silver BMWs and white Volvos, and polyester-clad senior citizens in belching tour buses bound for Reno, as they roar eastward on Interstate Highway 80 out of San Francisco toward the rolling hills and majestic mountains beyond. From the steel-girded outstretched span of the Bay Bridge it's only ninety miles, more or less, to Sacramento—the Big Tomato, California's capital city, which rests in the lap of the huge Central Valley. Continue westward on the modern superhighway (a legacy of that 1915 intercontinental auto route linking the nation's East and West Coasts for the first time) for thirty miles, through a region literally exploding with rapid-fire growth, until the ancient Southern Pacific Railroad trestle and the curiously pigeon-laden utility lines that crisscross the highway come into view at the first freeway exit to Auburn. Above it all rises the stately, golden-domed Placer County Courthouse.

Auburn is the seat of Placer County, which stretches some 150 miles from the floor of the fertile Sacramento Valley to the rim of pristine Lake Tahoe in the high Sierra Nevada Mountains. Only 120 miles from San Francisco and barely 80 from Lake Tahoe and the Sierra wildlands, the city has also become a mecca for urban malcontents fleeing to "the hills," who marvel at a life that marches by at a slower pace and revel in the fact that the grass on the local high school's football field is still a product of nature rather than DuPont Chemical.

For those who quiet themselves long enough, these hills can evoke a childlike sense of wonder: the crystal brilliance of star-spangled night skies, the pungently sweet, clear air, the cry of a red-tailed hawk or the gentle chirp of a tiny wild canary, the fields upon fields of brilliant golden poppies and purple lupine dancing in warm spring breezes. In winter an occasional dusting of snow turns the foothill cities into Currier and Ives prints, while in the distance the brilliantly white Sierras glimmer in the late afternoon sun. Summer brings its own special magic as frogs thump and thunder in rhythm to the rasping chirp of crickets, and the intoxicating scent of hundreds and hundreds of roses perfumes the air.

Yet the last decade's massive changes have blurred some of that dreamlike vision: while pockets of undeveloped land still exist, every year more and more is swallowed up in the mad rush to provide

29

homes and shopping centers and auto dealerships and restaurants and office complexes for the hordes of upwardly mobile émigrés pouring into the area. Today, the once-sleepy Auburn area is home to almost forty thousand people, while new settlers keep arriving daily, lured by the promise of their own slice of the American Dream in the golden California foothills.

This frantic onrush of civilization and progress has been for the most part restricted to the easily developable valley and low foothill areas, leaving untouched the high country where life tends to take on a much more basic, elemental quality. Scattered throughout the mountains between Auburn and Lake Tahoe, where the counties of Placer, Nevada, and El Dorado melt into one another, there are dozens of remote enclaves with names as eclectic as their residents: Yankee Jim and Iowa Hill, Dutch Flat and Emigrant Gap, Lotus and Fresh Pond and Rough & Ready and Fred's Place. Some are actual towns with post offices and murky country and western bars and general stores with creaky oiled floors, and some are simply wide spots along the side of the road where a dusty trail bumps and grinds its way to a rough-hewn log cabin on fifty or a hundred acres, and perhaps another beyond. Here one is just as likely to find a long-haired leftover from the drugged-out sixties smoking a joint and practicing yoga with his three or four housemates, as a bearded woodcutter in a battered pickup with a bumper sticker that reads: I'M THE N.R.A. — AND I VOTE!

Yet for the visitor or newcomer there is an undeniable aura of being on the outside — *far* on the outside—looking in that pervades these unsettled mountain lands. These are the places where asking the wrong question of the wrong person can mean a hurriedly closed door or a wordless, intimidating stare, and where breaking the unwritten code of honor can bring swift retribution at the end of a .45 or the bottom of a canyon. Meanwhile, in those more accessible communities like Georgetown and Foresthill, where developers have managed to carve out one or two rural subdivisions from the forest-lands outside of town, resident loggers and rednecks and outlaws mingle a little uneasily with the invad-ing yuppies and social security retirees, wondering what the future may hold.

The remote placidity of this high hill country stands in sharp contrast to the ever-more-urbanized region below. Cross either of the two bridges span-ning the forks of the spectacular American River as it crashes westward toward the lakes and dams of civilization, follow the roads as they curve and drift upward out of the canyon, and you will find your-self rocketed forward in time.

Heading northward out of Auburn on the treach-erously overburdened State Highway 49 is an expe-rience which has prompted the creation of a bumper sticker that reads I Survived Highway 49. The four-lane road is perpetually choked with traffic and frequently littered with the remnants of acci-dents caused by too many cars and too little room. About six miles outside town, just past the entrance to Auburn Faith Community Hospital, Quartz Drive juts off to the west. This is the main road through Auburn Greens, the city's first large-scale condominium complex containing nearly five hundred individual apartments. Begun in the late 1960s and finally completed in 1978, "the Greens" was envisioned as a monumental leap into the future for the just-waking city. Over the intervening years, however, that leap has turned out to be a bit shorter than anyone anticipated, as the development has become in many respects just another example of the less-than-successful amalgamation of urban planning in a rural environment. High-density living seems to work much better in cities like New York than it does in small towns like Auburn.

Today, the complex is home to a wide variety of residents, from single mothers on marginal incomes with two or three or four children, to young couples just starting out, to comfortable retirees who enjoy the luxury of living in a managed development and the freedom to go anywhere at any time without worrying about who's going to water the lawn. Generally speaking, the rents are affordable and the neighborhoods are safe — except for the occasional budding juvenile delinquent who makes a habit out of stealing hubcaps or even an occasional car from the open garages at the rear of each building — and at the very least, it provides a good jumping-off point for wanderers in transition.

If you were to follow Quartz almost to the end, to the spot where it intersects with Galena Drive, you would find yourself in front of a corner-lot fourplex, from the outside practically indistinguishable from any of the other 155 quadruplet units in the sprawling development — except for the shiny red-and-black No Solicitors decal glued to the front door. When Anna Brackett lived there, relatively few cars shot by that door compared to the seemingly endless parade that meandered up and down the other streets within the complex, primarily because this unit was among the last before Quartz Drive dead-ended a few hundred yards ahead. To Anna and her friend Jim, it seemed like the perfect spot to get a little peace and quiet without giving up the security of having neighbors nearby.

It was the middle of the morning of June 14, 1983, and judging from the clear blue sky outside her front window, it was going to be a beautiful day. Anna Brackett's son Carl had suggested she and Jim move into the Greens, feeling they needed to be closer in than they were when they lived several miles away on Dry Creek Road where neighbors were much fewer and farther between, and where it would take a lot longer to get to a doctor or the hospital if there was an emergency. Here at the Greens, the hospital was right next door. "For land's sake," Anna used to chuckle, "we're so close we could probably just holler and an ambulance would be here before we'd closed our mouths." But she'd been glad at their decision to move, and grateful for Carl's help in finding such a nice place. He had been as good as gold to her and Jim over the years and so considerate about including them in the things he and his family did. And as far as Carl's wife Geri was concerned, Anna couldn't wish for a better daughter-in-law.

Now that Jim was so ill, they had been even more devoted, always coming down to Auburn from their comfortable home in Meadow Vista to take Anna to see the man she loved as he lay helplessly

33

in that hospital bed, looking so thin and fragile that it seemed even the slightest breeze might blow him away from her forever.

James Wedgeworth was a dapper, short-statured man with an easy air of sophistication reminiscent of European nobility. Not that he was aloof or haughty—but there was a distinctly polished manner about him, a genteel quality in his attitudes and dealings with people that seemed to suggest a background that was anything but common. From the moment Anna first met him, she was quietly but completely enthralled.

For one thing, he was an astonishingly good dancer, as she discovered that first evening when they were introduced. Anna herself was no slouch on the dance floor, so when they whooshed off into the center of the room to the "Blue Danube," more than a few of the other couples took note. To add to his charms, he was an absolutely perfect gentleman to her and all the other women at the dance, whether or not he knew them. He rose from his seat when they approached, pulled out their chairs if their own partners forgot or weren't there, and made sure they had whatever they needed—a glass of wine or ginger ale or a cup of tea—before he got anything for himself.

Anna had noted with some amusement that this charming, slightly rotund little man seemed to take particular delight in the ladies, apparently preferring their company to that of the solo men there at the gathering. What she didn't realize at the time was that this was simply part of Jim's nature: he derived little or no pleasure from those stereotypically male pursuits like hunting and fishing and watching endless rounds of boxing or football on television—and that disinterest didn't bother him at all. If it bothered others, well, then, that was their problem. He was secure enough in his own sense of himself that he didn't need his ego buoyed by pretending to be someone he wasn't. That kind of honesty and self-esteem appealed tremendously to Anna, who was herself a little insecure and withdrawn.

No one seems to know how long Anna and Jim were together as friends before they fell in love. No one is even too sure how they ended up in Auburn, or exactly when: some say they came from Southern California in the late sixties or early seventies, while others insist they migrated to California from somewhere back East—Massachusetts, perhaps—or even the Deep South, which Jim called home. In fact, except for the little bits and pieces of information one or the other of them dropped from time to time, no one really knew too much at all about Anna Brackett or Jim Wedgeworth. They were the kind of people who enjoyed being around others, going places and doing things, but they never seemed to talk a lot about themselves. It wasn't actual secretiveness—it was simply their way.

This was especially true of Anna, whose sweet, trusting, yet sometimes painfully shy demeanor made her appear far more delicate than she actually was. Her soft New England twang and habit of keeping to herself much of the time spoke of a bygone era and culture which valued privacy and quiet reserve above almost all else, where women learned to be seen and not heard, and where the rules of ladylike behavior were absolute and inviolable. A quiet and extremely soft-spoken little woman

35

who seldom spoke without being spoken to first, Anna's fastidious and conservative appearance was a perfect compliment to Jim's, especially when they were in public. Seldom did she go anywhere without stockings and dark pumps and perfect makeup, and of course the everpresent ash blond wig to hide her thinning gray hair. Most of her clothes were pastels—never anything flashy or cheap-looking—or in somber tones of navy blue, which she usually reserved for funerals. Seldom did her friends see her in slacks, although she wore them frequently around the house simply because they were so comfortable and she could get by without having to squeeze into a girdle.

She was thrilled that she had managed to land a man like Jim, who never failed to offer his arm when they walked across the street or open her car door, or show her how much he loved her. They would sit across the table at a restaurant, or next to each other at a friend's home, and pretty soon they would be holding hands and just smiling at one another. It was clear the man was every bit as much in love with her as she was with him.

Audra Wilson had known Anna for the last several years—probably about ten or twelve, she figured—and she always enjoyed the birdlike little woman. Especially once you could draw her out and get her talking, which sometimes seemed to take an act of God. In all these years Audra still didn't know much about the small, sweet-faced person who would often sit across from her in the bright and cheery sunroom of her big Auburn farmhouse.

Shortly after the two women first met at the Senior Center in Auburn, Anna walked through the arts-and-crafts room where Audra was working on a still life with a wine bottle, plate, and two large apples sitting near the edge of a table. The artist looked up as Anna stopped beside her.

"Oh, I like that painting, Audra!" she exclaimed softly, her blue eyes shining.

"You do?" Audra really didn't think the painting was one of her best pieces—the colors were much darker and more subdued than she usually preferred—but she was flattered that Anna appreciated it. "Would you like to have it?"

"Oh, my," Anna stammered. "I really . . . I mean, it's lovely . . ."

"Well, then, it's yours!" Generosity was a hallmark of Audra's personality—and as giving and compassionate as the retired nurse was with strangers and people in need, she was even more so with her friends. Besides, she had a feeling that she and Anna Wedgeworth were going to be friends for a long, long time.

Only years later did Audra discover that Anna and Jim weren't married, and that she simply went by "Wedgeworth" in public to avoid controversy and gossip. Audra was shocked at first, especially considering her friend's primness and propriety—but, she reasoned, it wasn't her place to judge. Before long she came to accept the couple's relationship for what it was, and for the obvious joy they brought to one another.

Several years after she and Audra became friends, Anna left California to go to the East Coast and care for her ill sister, of course taking Jim with her.

During that time the two women frequently kept in touch and always sent one another Christmas and Easter and birthday cards—even though sometimes months flew by before a note or card from her friend would pop up in Audra's mailbox. Looking back, Audra figured it was close to five years before the couple came back to town and settled into the tidy condominium at Auburn Greens. They really seemed to love it in the big complex—*just too many folks there to suit my taste,* thought Audra—and very quickly settled into a comfortable routine of going out dancing, traveling to Reno on the bus for a day at the casinos, playing Bingo, and having dinner with friends. For whatever reason, Jim was adamant about not leaving California again, although if Anna asked, he most probably would have gone without a complaint.

Anna had become quite dependent on Jim for nearly everything. Friends had the impression that she was reluctant to make any decisions for herself, and that whatever happened in their life—even the everyday things—was up to Jim to plan and execute. She seldom took the lead in any conversation and seemed happiest just to sit beside Jim and listen, smiling and bobbing her head like a sparrow while the talk flowed around her. Even when someone was successful at drawing her out and getting her to say a few sentences, when she was finished she would draw back inside her little shell again. She was never known to ask for a recipe or the name of a perfume or where a friend had purchased her new dress, and only rarely did she seem to notice if someone was wearing something new or had a new hairdo. It wasn't that she was unkind or unfeeling—it was more that she was shy about fussing over people and drawing any kind of attention to herself in the process. So her relationship with Jim was perfect: he could be the one out front, the debonair charmer who carried things along, while she was content to simply go along most of the time.

By now, the couple had slacked off a bit as the Fred Astaire and Ginger Rogers of the foothills. There was a time they drove to nearly every dance within a thirty-mile radius of home, from the private Auburn Happiness Club dances to the every-Saturday-night public ones at the Golden Sierra Grange in Nevada City: Anna in one of her many floor-length chiffon gowns in a rainbow of soft pastel colors, and Jim in his immaculately tailored dark suit and crisp white shirt. But although they continued to attend the Happiness Club events at Auburn's Veteran's Hall, in recent months they'd been taking to the dance floor less and less often.

Smiling, Jim would explain, "Anna's not really up to dancing all that much anymore. Her feet bother her quite a bit." On the surface it made sense—after all, Anna was somewhere into her eighties and a decade or more older than Jim, although she never acted it. Underneath the smiles and reassuring words, however, lay the fact that it was Jim, not Anna, who was having health problems. Just how serious they were would only become public several months later.

So while the smiling couple appeared less and less frequently on the social circuit, they still managed to get out fairly often—especially if it involved Bingo. "Don't worry," Jim would say with a twinkle, "just like always, we'll be there to beat you at Bingo!" Playing Bingo and visiting with Carl and his family had become Anna and Jim's primary passions of late, now that they had pretty much given up dancing. At the same time they would occasionally go out with friends or take the bus to Reno or spend time with Audra and her husband in their rambling, two-story home where the heady scent of roses in bloom sweetened the air and the pungent odor of compost and freshly tilled earth wafted in from the immense vegetable garden.

Three

At a few minutes before five that afternoon, two young girls knocked on the door of Anna Brackett's apartment.

"Excuse me, ma'am," one of them said. "Could we come in and have a drink of water and use your phone? We're tryin' to call my mom to come and pick us up, and I think there's some guys chasing us."

"Of course, girls. Come on in." Anna stepped aside and let Cindy and Shirley into the living room. "You said you needed a glass of water?"

"Yes, ma'am. And the phone." Cindy began to scan the room, swiftly assessing its contents to see if there was evidence of anyone else living there. It was important that the old woman live alone—or at least *be* alone right now.

"This is a really pretty apartment. Do you live here all by yourself?"

"Well, right now I do. Umm, let me show you where the phone is. Then I'll get you children some water." She looked toward the second girl, who had been completely silent through this interchange. "Sit down, honey." Anna gestured toward one of the two beige naugahyde overstuffed chairs.

41

"My name is Mrs. Brackett. What's yours?"

"Shirley . . . uh, Melissa. Well, Shirley Melissa." She nodded her head and grinned widely.

Anna smiled, then directed Shirley's companion to the beige telephone mounted on the kitchen wall, directly over the bar dividing that room from the dining room. As Cindy dialed, Anna filled two glasses with water and ice and took one over to Shirley, who sat primly in the chair, still smiling.

"Thank you."

"You're welcome, dear."

In a few moments Cindy hung up the receiver and turned toward Anna and Shirley. "No one answers," she shrugged. "I can try again a little later, if that's okay."

"That's fine, honey. I've put your water glass on the counter there. Uhh, what was your name?"

"Cindy."

"Okay, Cindy . . . well, come and sit down. It's kind of warm outside and I'm sure you'd like to cool off a little."

Cindy gulped some water and set the yellow-and-green-flowered glass back on the edge of the tile bar, then settled easily into the other leatherette chair in the living room. Again she glanced around her.

"Mmmm, so you live here alone?" She wanted to make absolutely sure. "Don't you have a husband?"

Anna smiled and sat down across from her two young visitors. "Well, I have a husband, but I'm afraid he's not feeling so well and he's in the hospital. He's been there for quite a while." Out of habit, Anna almost always referred to Jim Wedge-

42

worth as her husband. It saved a lot of embarrassing questions.

"What's wrong with him?" Shirley asked.

"Oh, he's got cancer."

Shirley said how sorry she was.

"That's OK, honey. But he is pretty sick, and the doctors just don't know. . . ."

For the next twenty minutes or so the two girls and the old woman chatted with each other, sharing tidbits about their lives and families. Anna ended up talking quite a bit about Jim and telling stories about their travels and adventures together over the years; she also told the girls about her own children, grandchildren, and even great-grandchildren, and how much joy they brought to her life. Shirley frequently interjected with comments and stories of her own.

Cindy was another story. Although she started out as the spokesperson for the pair, she had lapsed into a peculiar silence broken only occasionally when Anna asked her a direct question. She didn't appear nervous or upset—just preoccupied.

The jangling of the telephone startled Cindy out of her self-absorption and she jerked her head toward Shirley. Anna pushed herself up out of the chair and made her way toward the phone.

It was her son Carl on the other end. "Oh, hello, son." She paused and listened, nodding her head and then turning to look at the clock. "Mmm-hmm . . . Okay . . . that sounds fine." She listened again, and then in a moment she smiled into the receiver. "Hi, Geri." Clearly, someone else had come onto the line. "Yes, Carl told me. I think that'll work out fine. I'll be waiting." There was another brief pause, then Anna said good-bye and hung up. As she walked back into the living room, she explained her call to the two girls.

"That was my son, Carl. He and his wife are on their way over here to pick me up to go play some Bingo."

Cindy stood up. "How long will it be before they get here?"

"Oh, I'd say about twenty minutes or so. They have to come from Meadow Vista." Meadow Vista was a small village about ten or twelve miles east on Interstate 80.

Cindy just nodded and said nothing. Then she turned slowly toward Shirley, who was still seated happily in the armchair, her legs curled up under her. "It's time," was all she said.

"Huh?" Shirley looked blank.

"It's time to do it. Now. We do it *now*." The command in her voice was unmistakable. Shirley recognized the tone instantly and sucked in her breath. The old warning bells inside her head began to shriek and suddenly the room and everything in it began to spin away into dark nothingness. She wasn't sure anymore where she was, whose voice was reaching out to her, or what that voice had told her to do.

"Don't just sit there starin' at me! DO IT!"

Nodding silently, Shirley uncoiled her legs and stood. It was time to obey. To do her job.

In an instant she was standing next to the dumbfounded and increasingly frightened elderly woman. Shirley grabbed her around the neck in a carotid choke hold, her muscular arm slowly cutting off the flow of air to the woman's lungs. Anna's pale blue eyes were glazed with a mixture of terror and what looked like astonishment. Unable to speak because of the horrible pressure against her windpipe, the only noise she could make was the screaming inside her own head.

Shirley, too, was silent at first, only making low grunting noises as she attempted to wrestle Anna to the floor. They were near to the same size—though their heights were similar, the older woman was heavier than Shirley—but Shirley was in superior physical shape. Of course Anna's fear had generated an enormous surge of energizing adrenaline, but she was simply no match for the athletic, almost robotlike, teenager.

Somewhere in the background Cindy ordered, "Tighter! Squeeze her tighter!"

Battling with every ounce of strength, Anna grabbed for a handful of Shirley's hair, but the girl jerked her head back and Anna lost her hold. She felt the sting of jagged fingernails raking her neck, then a barrage of blows pummeling her head and arms. At some point during the struggle, her lower denture popped out onto the floor.

Shirley still had her forearm around Anna's throat, pushing her face down on the rug with one knee on her shoulder blade.

"I'm gonna kill you . . . kill you . . . kill you . . ." She kept repeating the words over and over.

Cindy pulled the telephone receiver off the wall, then rummaged in the kitchen. A moment later, she'd returned with a small knife in her hand. It looked like a steak knife or a paring knife that you would use to cut up an apple. "Here!" she barked, and tossed the knife to Shirley. It landed blade-down in Shirley's open hand and made a tiny cut. She didn't feel a thing.

All she felt was this enormous need to release the septic venom churning deep within her—and to hurt something, to inflict punishment on something. She smiled, the same smile she had seen on her father's face a hundred or maybe even a thousand times before. Clutching the knife like a talisman, Shirley swung her arm up in a slow arc and brought it down into Anna's back. The girl gave a barely perceptible jerk as the blade sliced through Anna's skin and down into the yielding, pink flesh.

The woman's scream of pain was muffled by the carpet and Shirley's choke hold. Then suddenly Anna began writhing like a snake in Shirley's grasp, throwing her off balance and forcing her to momentarily relinquish her grip. Gasping for breath but still unable to do more than whimper, Anna struggled to her knees while Shirley tried vainly to reassert her hold. Cindy realized they could be in big trouble if the woman started screaming or managed to get out the door. Looking around the room, she spotted a large plastic brush in the chair where Shirley had been sitting. She moved like a panther, grabbing the object and turning swiftly toward her prey.

"Sorry, lady," she smiled humorlessly, and smashed the handle down several times against the left side of Anna's head. The makeshift club made soft, plopping noises when it hit, and Anna tumbled to the floor again, dazed by this new attack. In an instant Shirley pinned her once more with her knee and began to stab and slash at the woman with renewed energy.

But if Anna Brackett was anything, she was a fighter. She'd fought cancer and won, she'd fought a heart attack and won, she'd fought poverty and despair and soul-crushing grief and won. She had regained some of her voice, although when she spoke it came out as little more than a harsh, loud whisper. "You're not going to get away with this," she rasped. "You can't do this and get away with it!"

Shirley continued her attack with the knife, hoping she could just make Anna shut up.

Cindy, on a mad hunt through the house for a gun, heard Anna's cries as well, and they made her every bit as nervous as her companion. She had to find a way to shut the old broad's mouth, and fast. Rummaging swiftly through the bedroom dresser, she pulled out a light blue nylon nightgown. Rushing back into the living room, she tossed the gown at Shirley. "Stuff it in her mouth!"

Shirley did as she was told. Then she tried to stab Anna again, but something was wrong. She looked down at the knife in her hand and cocked her head in puzzlement. When her eyes focused, she saw that the blade was bent at a ninety-degree angle. She threw it down in disgust. "Hey," she cried out, "it's broken! Get me somethin' better . . . and you better hurry!" She could still feel Anna moving and breathing, and was afraid she

47

might get a second wind and start acting nutty again.

Cindy ran back into the kitchen and began another frantic search of the drawers. She emerged, smiling victoriously, with a large, black-handled butcher knife. The blade was at least eight inches long.

Picking up the knife from the floor where Cindy had tossed it, Shirley resumed her monstrous job. Again and again she hacked at Anna, that odd, zombielike smile once more on her face. Once or twice she felt the thick blade sink into the old woman's back, but most of the time she was totally unaware of just how deep the wounds were. All she knew was that somehow there was an enormous, almost orgasmic release in the act she was performing. In spite of the strange thoughts that kept seeping through the dark crevices and canyons of her mind, she was beginning to feel better. Much better. It felt so good to finally be able to let it all go: all the anger, the pain, the hatred, the humiliation, all of it. With every thrust she felt more and more free. With every penetration, she focused more and more on the power of being so much in control, of being the Deliverer.

Shirley remembered reading some satanic books—"devil-books," she called them—that described different ways to kill people, and different ways to tell when they were dead. The voice in her mind reminded her of what she'd read: it only takes twenty seconds for a person to die once their throat has been cut. Responding to the voice, she mechanically drove the blade of the knife through

48

the soft tissue of Anna's neck, just below her right ear where her head was turned sideways on the carpet.

"I'm dying," Anna said in a barely audible voice.

"Good." Shirley spat the word out like it was poison.

Then there was nothing.

"Is she dead?" Cindy came back into the room, carrying something in her hand.

"Yeah, I think so. Blood's coming out of her mouth and nose." That was something else the book had said. Another way to tell if somebody's dead.

Cindy bent down for a closer look and shook her head violently. "No, she's still alive—I can see her breathing!" There was an almost imperceptible rise and fall to Anna's blood-drenched back. She ripped the knife from Shirley's hand and cleaved two or three more wounds in Anna's neck and side. Then she knelt down and felt for a pulse. Nothing. The old lady had stopped breathing, too, as far as Cindy could tell.

For a moment the two executioners stared at the body that lay motionless on the carpet before them, watching as the viscous trickle of blood that had oozed out the side of Anna's mouth began to congeal on the floor. If there had been an observer there that day to chronicle it all, he would have been struck with one thing more than any other: the staggering indifference of these two near-children to the horror of what they had done. Throughout the entire blood-drenched experience, there was not a single moment of regret, of loathing; not an instant where a stomach churned or a hand trembled—not even now, at the end of it all.

It was as if the act had no meaning for them, no relationship to the essence of who they were. They had killed—not out of mercy or duty or fear or even love, but out of something so dark and malignant inside both of them that it could not even be named.

Now tiny smiles played at the corners of their mouths.

Cindy handed the bloody knife back to Shirley and stepped over to Anna's white purse on the floor next to the chair where she'd been sitting. She unceremoniously dumped the contents out on the chair, grabbing a set of keys and a wallet.

"Let's get the fuck outa here." Cindy opened the front door cautiously and looked to see if anyone was nearby or watching. "Come on," she whispered, and began trotting back toward the carport. Shirley followed, slamming the door behind her and sprinting past Cindy toward the old brown Dodge they knew belonged to Mrs. Brackett. The passenger door was locked, so she vaulted over the hood and clambered in on the driver's side, shoving the butcher knife and the rag she'd picked up to wipe her hands back under the seat as she did. *Can't have that knife layin' around the old woman's house. My fingerprints are all over it!* It never entered her mind that her prints were also probably on the door, the water glass she'd drunk from, and the paring knife she'd left on the floor near Anna's body.

Cindy climbed into the car next to Shirley and

stuck one of the keys into the ignition. Rather, she tried to. No matter how she twisted or turned it, it wouldn't fit. With mounting frustration and apprehension, she tried every other key on the ring, even the ones she knew weren't car keys.

Cursing Anna's ghost, she angrily jerked open the door and threw the useless keys toward Shirley. It was clear that they were going nowhere in that car. She began to run down the back alley toward the highway, several blocks away.

Shirley absently grabbed the keys and stuffed them in her pocket, then scurried after her friend, worried that she'd be left behind. "Hey," she puffed, catching up with Cindy, "are we gonna stop by the pool and pick up our stuff?"

"Yeah, okay," Cindy grumbled, turning quickly down another alley that led toward the south side of the pool. They were still running when they got to their little pile of belongings near the back fence surrounding the swimming pool. Everyone had left the area by now, and as the two girls gathered up their things they were both smiling. Breathing heavily, Cindy turned to Shirley and stared into her dark eyes for several seconds. Then once again, she burst into a huge smile.

"What a kick!"

"Yeah, a real kick!"

"Come on. Let's head down the freeway."

Down the freeway? thought Shirley uneasily. *I thought I was gonna get to go home to Placerville.* There wasn't any doubt in her mind that Placerville wasn't *down* the freeway at all. In fact, you didn't even have to take the freeway to get there. *Oh, well,* she shrugged. *Sooner or later I'll get home. For now, I'll just stick with Cindy, 'cause she and I are friends. Best friends.*

At this point, the two girls had known each other for all of seven hours.

Four

The sun was setting as Carl Brackett swung his car onto the highway toward Auburn Greens for the second time that afternoon. He and his wife Geri already stopped by his mother's modest condominium ten or fifteen minutes before to pick her up, but she didn't come out to meet them as she usually did.

Because they were early anyway—Anna wasn't expecting them until six o'clock and it was only five forty-five or so—Carl decided to give her a few more minutes while he and Geri drove over to check on Anna's companion Jim Wedgeworth at the convalescent hospital just a few blocks away. They'd talked about taking his mother along, but Jim was so ill that Carl thought it might be too hard on Anna to see the man she loved that way. Jim was dying of cancer . . . in fact, it didn't really look to Carl as if he would last the night. His mom was really going to miss that man. He was, too.

Now, driving back toward his mother's place from the hospital, Carl lowered the visor to shield his eyes from the glare of the descending sun and glanced at his watch. Several minutes past six. She should be outside waiting for them by now, Carl figured. Signaling to turn onto Quartz Drive, the main drag of the Auburn Greens condominium complex, he noticed a couple of teenagers trying to hitch a ride up ahead on the highway. He shook his head and remarked gruffly, "Can you believe it: two young girls like that, hitchhiking. They're so stupid. Either that or they're a pair of real toughies." Geri agreed, glad they didn't have daughters that age to worry about.

Carl pulled up in front of his mother's unit, but the door was still closed and Anna wasn't outside. He thought it was odd.

Geri walked up the concrete steps leading to her mother-in-law's front unit. The lawns were green and freshly mowed, and the large flowering plum in the front yard was in full leaf. The front of the shake-roofed fourplex was attractively trimmed with red brick, and low-slung shrubs lined the footpath leading to the two side units. As she paused at the door, Geri smiled at the neat sign underneath Anna Brackett's apartment number. No Solicitors, it read in bold red-and-gold letters on a black background. She knocked and then automatically reached for the doorknob.

Carl followed his wife up the front stairs, puffing a little from the exertion and his rising level of concern. That concern only intensified when Geri turned to her husband with a puzzled look and said the door was locked. *Locked. Locked? That doesn't make sense. She never keeps the door locked when she knows we're coming. It's one of her little habits that she never, ever varies from.* The drapes on the living room window to the left of the door were partially open; not knowing what else to do, Carl stepped into the narrow flowerbed that ran along the front of the unit beneath the window, where he could take a look inside of the condominium.

His eighty-five-year-old mother was lying facedown on the floor of the living room, her head turned to one side. There was something light blue — a sweater? — lying near, almost under, her head. She was wearing white polyester slacks and a cheery blue-and-white-flowered tunic top with the sleeves pushed halfway up. One of her white slipperlike shoes was kicked halfway off.

Carl Brackett mentally processed the entire scene in a matter of seconds, and yelled to his wife that they needed to get an ambulance. They ran around the side of the unit to apartment number 3 and knocked furiously.

"I need to call an ambulance!" Carl screamed to the startled woman at the door. "Or the Sheriff! Something's wrong with my mother! *PLEASE!!*"

The neighbor opened the screen door and let the distraught man use her telephone. He barked a few terse words into the receiver, then slammed it down and dashed out the door without saying another word to the increasingly terrified neighbor.

Back at the front of his mother's apartment Carl tried the door, momentarily forgetting he couldn't get in that way unless he battered it down. Scrambling through the plantings along the walkway again, this time he went to the smaller window to the right of the door. Only aware that he had to get inside to see her, to help her if he could, Carl Brackett smashed his mother's dining room window and climbed in.

The shattered glass crunched icily under his feet as he stepped over to where his mother lay. Her face was so covered in blood that Carl could barely recognize her, as she lay in a spreading pool of red that had already soaked into the carpet beneath her. A tiny trickle was drying at one corner of her mouth, which was locked in a grimace of pain. Blood had begun to soak through the silver blond Eva Gabor wig that lay slightly askew on her head, revealing tiny strands of thinning gray hair underneath. Her age-speckled hands, one of them clenched in front of her as if in defiance against her attackers, were smeared with crimson.

Everywhere he looked there was blood. It wasn't easy to see where it all had come from, but something had impaled Anna's neck a half-dozen times, and her broad back was a mangled mass of stab wounds. Some of the gashes, ragged and inches deep, still oozed onto her once-gaily-flowered tunic.

The gold Timex watch on her left wrist was still running; if Carl had looked closely enough he would have seen a long brown hair caught in the band. He also missed seeing three more hairs clutched in her right hand.

As he raised his eyes from his mother's ravaged body, he noticed a white handbag turned upside down with its contents dumped on the seat of the large stuffed chair that sat along the dining room wall. His gaze suddenly caught something shiny on the floor, next to the tan Naugahyde recliner. It was a bloody paring knife, the blade bent at a ninety-degree angle. The room began to swim. To the right of Anna Brackett's lifeless body lay a partial set of false teeth, grinning insanely on the rust-colored carpet.

Carl Brackett was standing numbly in the middle of the living room, staring at his mother's mutilated corpse, when a loud knock came at the door.

"Open up, please—it's the ambulance company." A man's voice boomed through the closed door. Carl shuffled across the room and let in the two paramedics; they quickly took in the scene and rushed over to where Anna Brackett lay. On the back of their jackets was the name of the ambulance firm: ETS. Emergency Transportation Services. They were headquartered less than a half-mile away from the Auburn Greens complex, in the same center where the Sheriff's Department was located. Another whooping siren announced the arrival of the Rock Creek Fire Department Rescue Squad at the front of the residence.

The attendant who had called through the door felt for a pulse, while his partner expertly sliced open a section of Anna's blouse to attach the heart monitor. With all the blood he knew the woman had been attacked somehow, but when he saw her back he realized she'd been stabbed—and not just once. It was a real mess. The first paramedic went outside to the ambulance to call the Sheriff's office; by now the rescue team had come into the apartment to see if they could help. It was beginning to get a little crowded in the tiny living room, what with everyone trying to stay away from walls and furniture so nothing got touched or disturbed. It was clear to all the men that this was a crime scene, not just the apartment of some old woman who'd had a heart attack or stroke.

In a few seconds the monitor buzzed to life, but the screen remained empty. Flatline. The attendant looked toward Carl with a sympathetic shake of his head.

"I'm sorry, sir. I'm afraid she's dead." The young man looked at his watch and noted for his report that the time was 1815 hours, June 14, 1983.

Carl knew she was dead, of course, but somehow hearing the words made it even more real.

Another siren broke the summer evening air. By now a crowd had gathered across the street, while other neighbors peered inquisitively out their windows. A Placer County Sheriff's Department car pulled up, its red light flashing madly; Sergeant Bruce Johnson hopped out and began to mount the front steps, two at a time.

He approached the nearest member of the rescue team and introduced himself. The man said it appeared the woman inside the condominium had been stabbed to death. The sergeant walked inside and took in the scene with a practiced eye. As he approached the body lying on the floor, he could tell she was dead. Time to bring in the big guns.

Closing the door partway with a handkerchief, Johnson strode back down the steps to his cruiser and called in a quick confirmation of the murder to the Homicide Division, Sheriff Donald Nunes and the Coroner's Office.

Within two minutes, still another screaming siren announced the arrival of Homicide Deputy George Coelho. Coelho, an eighteen-year veteran of police work, was no stranger to murder. He'd worked for twelve years in southern California—Newport Beach, a trendy beachfront playground for the rich that was far from immune to violent crime—and a good portion of that time he'd spent in the Investigations Division, then later on a specialized crime suppression team. He moved his family to Placer County four years ago to get away from southern California's hectic, rat-in-a-trap lifestyle and find a better place to raise his four children. In the interim the four had become five, and there would probably be a sixth before it was all over. A good Italian Catholic, George solidly believed in the virtue of family—and the bigger, the better.

After getting some sketchy details from Sergeant Johnson, the deputy swung open the door to Anna Brackett's condominium and the two officers walked inside, Coelho's senses on the alert for other victims or anyone lurking inside who shouldn't be there. He didn't really think the perp would still be there, but there was always a chance he'd gotten interrupted by the arrival of the woman's son and hidden in a closet or under a bed. (The "he" came naturally to George: a crime like this was almost always committed by a male, and the officer had no reason to think that this murder was any different.) Instinct told him the motive was probably burglary: drawers ransacked in the bedroom and kitchen, the contents of the dead woman's purse scattered on a chair, evidence of a struggle—it all fit. It might not have fit so well if the deputy had realized at the time that Anna had been stabbed some twenty-eight times, but until the coroner's autopsy, no one would have a concrete idea of just how extensive her wounds were.

Back outside, Coelho began to gently question the dazed Carl Brackett and his wife Geri. He realized the timing was terrible to try to talk to the grief-stricken man, but he desperately needed more information, and Brackett was the only one who could provide any. From the looks of the body, the murder hadn't happened too long ago—and every minute that passed was another minute's head start the killer had on them.

Slowly, Coelho pulled the story out of Brackett: how he called his mother around five-thirty that afternoon to say he and Geri were coming by; how when they arrived the first time the door was closed and they assumed Anna wasn't quite ready yet, so they went to Hilltop Convalescent Hospital less than a half-mile away to see how his mother's friend Jim Wedgeworth was doing; how they came back to Anna's apartment, by now beginning to feel some uneasiness at her absence out front; and how after Carl looked in the front window and saw his mother's blood-spattered body lying there, he ran next door to call an ambulance, and then came back and smashed the window to get in because the door was locked.

Toward the end of the interview a woman approached the deputy and introduced herself as Anna's next-door neighbor in the fourplex. After extending her sympathies to Mr. Brackett, she told Deputy Coelho that around six o'clock she had heard a short series of loud thumps coming from the victim's apartment. Did you hear anything else?

Coelho asked her. Any screams, cries of distress? No, replied the woman. Nothing but the thumps.

Starting toward the apartment building directly across Galena Drive from Mrs. Brackett's, Coelho was stopped midway by two residents of that unit, Pete and Mabel Fredricks, who came outside when the first officers arrived. Mrs. Fredricks was extremely distraught and just kept repeating how awful this whole thing was, that she couldn't believe such a thing had happened, and that it could as easily have been her. Every time the elderly lady made that last statement or one like it, her hands began to tremble and her already pallid complexion turned even more ashen. Coelho was afraid she might pass out before he had a chance to get her story.

"Oh, dear," she sighed heavily, shaking her head and wiping a tear from under her thick glasses. She looked over at her husband, who put a protectively encouraging arm around her shoulder. "Well, it was around five o'clock when my doorbell rang; when I went to see who it was, there were two teenage girls standing there. I asked them what they wanted, and one of them said they needed to use our phone, because a man here in the Greens had been chasing them. They were going to call this one girl's mother.

"So I let them in, then the other girl asked if she could have a glass of water. After she finished, the first girl hung up the phone—she said something about not being able to get through—and then my husband walked into the room. They thanked me and walked out the door, and I walked outside after them to see if I could see who might be following them — but there was no one there."

"Excuse me, Mrs. Fredricks," Coelho interrupted. "I wonder if you or your husband could describe these girls for me?" His mind was racing already: he remembered seeing two half-full water glasses in Mrs. Brackett's apartment, and there was something about the kitchen phone that caught his eye. Oh, yeah: there was no receiver. The receiver was missing. But the thing about this being *girls* didn't make sense. Who knows: maybe the girls were the setup, the hook, and then when the victim let them inside their male accomplices would come in and finish the job.

Mr. and Mrs. Fredricks were both talking at the same time, giving their impressions of what the girls had looked like.

"Well, the first one was about eighteen or nineteen . . ."

"No, no," broke in Mabel. "She looked older, but I'm sure she wasn't much more than sixteen or seventeen. The other was about the same age . . ."

"A little younger, I think."

"Well, maybe. Anyway, the first one had long brown hair, about to her shoulder . . ."

"No, Mabel, that was the other one. The one that came in to use the phone had shorter hair."

"Mmmm — yes, I guess that's right. But I know she had on old faded jeans, and some kind of dark-colored top that tied behind her neck. And she was barefoot. That much I'm sure of."

"Yep. The other one was a little shorter than the first . . ."

62

"I thought they were about the same size . . ."

"Well, close, anyway," demurred Mr. Fredricks. "She had this purple headband on . . ."

"Lavender. It was lighter than purple."

"Okay. And she had on a pink jacket, real shiny material like . . ."

"Satin . . ."

"Satin, and it had some white writing on the back. I didn't get a good look at what it said."

"Neither did I."

"I also noticed," said Mr. Fredricks with an embarrassed shrug, "that they were both pretty . . . uh . . . well, they seemed pretty well-developed for their age, if you get my meaning."

Deputy Coelho had been scribbling away on his field notepad. "Okay, folks, that's great. Did you see anything else? Or hear anything?"

"We most certainly did," said the woman, smoothing her gray hair absently. "Tell the officer, Pete."

"Well, it must have been thirty minutes or an hour later—I don't remember the time exactly—and I was sitting at the dining room table eating my dinner. Something outside the front window caught my eye"—he pointed up toward the living room of their second-floor apartment, which had a clear view across the street to the Brackett apartment—"and I looked out. It was those two girls again, and they were running like something—someone—was after them. They ran around the side of Mrs. Brackett's house, and then disappeared through the side door into her carport. I never saw them come out. Of course, if they came out the main garage door I wouldn't have been able to see them."

The deputy took down the couple's full names and address, and told them someone else from the department might be by later to interview them. Then he walked over to the fourplex where the Fredricks lived and knocked on the door of one of the two downstairs apartments. A middle-aged woman in shorts came to the door, and proceeded to tell Coelho that she too had seen the girls that afternoon as they walked by her apartment window toward Garnet Way. She had also seen them earlier in the day, she explained, in front of the Greens pool number One. In describing both girls, she said one of them was wearing a pink satin jacket with white lettering on the back that read something like "Rockettes" or "Rock and Roll." She couldn't be sure.

Before Coelho could move on, he was approached by a young woman who lived in the adjacent building on Garnet. Her mother, she said, had told her two girls came to their house to use the phone a little before five that afternoon; one of them was wearing a dark halter-type bathing suit top, and the other had on a pink satin fluorescent jacket. She told her daughter she'd seen the same two girls running south through the alley, toward Highway 49, around six o'clock.

Backtracking, Coelho returned to the Brackett condominium to find it swarming with personnel from the department, including the officer in charge, Senior Sergeant Raymond Mahlberg. Mahlberg, a tall, Nordic-looking man with cool gray-blue eyes and thinning blond hair that had probably darkened somewhat over the years, was intently examining the victim's apartment. He looked up when Coelho approached, but didn't smile. Ray Mahlberg didn't smile much at all, period. Only recently assigned to the Crimes Against Persons Division, this was the first homicide he'd ever been called to—and because both of his more experienced partners in the division were out of town, he was having to handle this case all by himself. It would be enough to make even the most jovial and self-assured cop a little nervous and tight-lipped.

But Ray Mahlberg was an experienced officer, and knew enough to holler for help when he needed it—which is exactly what he'd done here. In addition to all the departmental regulars out scouring the neighborhood for clues and leads, Mahlberg called in two criminalists from the state Department of Justice to dust for latent prints and gather whatever evidence there was. He wasn't about to have this case blow up in his face just because of something he'd overlooked out of his own inexperience.

"Learn anything, George?"

"Well, Sergeant, I've located a couple of possible witnesses who saw two girls running from the victim's apartment around eighteen hundred hours, another witness who said these same two girls stopped by her apartment for a glass of water, and one couple who let the girls into their place around seventeen hundred hours to have some water and use the phone. Sounds like we could have some solid leads here."

Mahlberg nodded silently, then told Coelho to go back to the Fredricks's and obtain the water glass and telephone receiver as evidence. He could see a connection, too—but like the deputy, he hadn't yet begun to think that these two mystery teenagers were the actual perpetrators. It was just so far outside the realm of normalcy to think that *girls* might be involved in a crime like this, that no one even questioned the presumption that at most the only thing these girls might be was material witnesses.

It wasn't long before Coelho came back, empty-handed.

"You won't believe this," he said in spite of himself. "She says the girls were so dirty-looking, and they made her so uncomfortable, that after they left she immediately washed out the glass and wiped down the phone with alcohol!"

Mahlberg missed the humor at the moment—although later on he would chuckle a little about Mrs. Fredricks's fastidiousness.

Around seven-twenty that evening the department's photo technician, Bonnie Norman, arrived to photograph the crime scene. A few minutes later one of the officers reported to Mahlberg that he'd discovered a brown, 1970 two-door Dodge Dart in the Brackett carport, and that there appeared to be footprints on the hood. A Department of Motor Vehicles inquiry showed that the car was registered to a James Wedgeworth, listed as living at that address. Mahlberg assigned the deputy to guard the vehicle until the Department of Justice criminalists arrived, and to make sure no one went inside the car. By now, more reports were coming back of witnesses in the complex who either saw the girls or who were approached by them, asking for water and the use of a telephone. The M.O.

fit, the descriptions fit—the only thing that didn't fit was that they were females.

Sheriff Nunes issued a special press release about the murder and their search for the two girls in connection with the crime. Local radio station KAHI-AM broadcast the bulletin immediately and reaired it several times over the course of the early evening before their mandatory sundown sign-off.

Shortly before nine o'clock that night, Nunes got a telephone call from a young girl who identified herself only as Donna. She'd heard about the murder, she said, and had some information about two girls she saw that day at the Greens. After several minutes of coaxing, Nunes convinced the girl to come into his office for an interview, along with her mother.

It was almost ten-thirty by the time they got there, bringing a friend of Donna's with them who also saw the possible suspects.

"Umm, well, we were driving up past pool number One with my friend's aunt, and I saw a whole lot of kids and people there. Fourteen, maybe fifteen of them, all just hanging around and swimming and stuff. I looked and saw a girl who used to go to Cain . . ."

"Cain?" interjected the Sheriff. "You mean E.V. Cain School?"

"Yeah. Anyways, I saw this girl, and I remembered meeting up with her last summer sometime, and that she was Cindy Collier. She was lyin' on a towel next to another girl I'd never seen before, and the other girl was wearing this pink, silklike jacket."

Sheriff Nunes asked Donna to describe Cindy Collier for him, which she proceeded to do. Then her friend spoke up.

"Tonight, oh, about eight or so, a friend of my mom's comes runnin' over to the house, bangin' on the door and hollerin' for us to let her in, that she has somethin' important to tell us. Well, she goes, 'This old lady up on Quartz got murdered, and they're looking for two teenage girls, 'cause some people seen them runnin' down the alley after the murder.' Well, that made me remember what me and Donna seen, and Donna remembered, too; she says to me, 'Remember those two girls we seen off the balcony at your house this afternoon? I'll bet it's those same two girls.'"

"Okay: now, tell me what you saw from the balcony of your house."

Donna picked up the conversation again. "We saw Cindy and the other girl, walking really fast down the alley of Garnet; you know, toward the highway. They kept looking around them, behind them, all over, like they were worried somebody was following them or somethin'. They looked real suspiciouslike."

"Donna, are you absolutely positive that this was the same girl you saw earlier at the pool?"

"Absolutely!"

"And are you certain she's the same Cindy Collier that you met last year?"

"Yep. It was her."

"Can you tell me anything else about her?"

"Umm — well, I know she goes to Placer now . . ."

"Placer High School?" Placer High was Auburn's only high school, except for the continuation school north of town.

"Umm-hmm. She's got a brother, too—he's about ten. Maybe twelve. I don't know. Oh, yeah: Cindy used to live here at the Greens, maybe about a year ago."

"Would you know Cindy if you saw her again?"

"Oh, sure. Any day. She's somebody you don't forget."

By now the two state criminalists were on the scene, busily collecting evidence and dusting for fingerprints. The Dodge was impounded and towed to a body shop on Nevada Street, where it would be examined the next morning. Word identifying Cindy Collier as one of the two girls had filtered down to the Sheriff's officers milling around the Brackett apartment, who fanned out to canvass the neighborhood once again with the new description.

Deputy Gerald Thompson had been listening all night to the calls over his car radio about the murder. As soon as dispatch broadcast the bulletin about two female juveniles possibly being involved, the deputy decided to head on over to Auburn Greens. For some time, Thompson had been assigned to the specialized Placer Law Enforcement Agencies Special Investigation Unit, which was a coalition of law enforcement personnel from throughout the county whose job it was to investigate illegal drug activity. Naturally, he came into contact with a fair number of teenagers during the course of his job, and he figured he might be able to help the crime scene investigators with some information.

When Thompson got to the Brackett apartment and talked with the sergeant, Mahlberg told him about the positive ID on Cindy Collier. It was a name Jerry Thompson knew well. More times than he could count he'd been called out to the girl's residence at Auburn Greens to conduct drug investigations and probation searches of various members of the household. He also remembered that Cindy was currently on probation herself, and that as a part of that probation she was subject to mandatory search-and-seizure—meaning that any time they suspected the girl of something, the authorities had the right to search her home or personal belongings, and seize any evidence they found. No special search warrant was necessary when someone was under search-and-seizure orders.

Talk to George, came the command from Mahlberg. When Thompson mentioned Cindy's name, Coelho's ears perked up. He knew her, too. He'd taken a couple of reports on the girl over the years, and in fact in the past couple of years he had handled a few cases where Cindy's name came up in connection with some burglaries at Auburn Greens.

It was now almost eleven o'clock, and Coelho was already halfway into his second shift of the day. He was desperate for a cup of coffee, so he and Jerry Thompson headed for departmental headquarters and some serious conversation about Cindy. Within half an hour they were relaying their thoughts to Sheriff Nunes. The three men agreed that Coelho should contact the county Probation Department and talk with Supervisor Tom Hoffman about Cindy's probation status and the terms of that probation. Yes, Hoffman confirmed after a midnight search of the records, Cindy Collier was in fact on probation *and* under search-and-seizure. He gave the officers authority to conduct a probation search at Cindy's home on the outskirts of downtown Auburn.

By this time the Coroner's Office had removed Mrs. Brackett's body and transported it to Auburn Faith Community Hospital for X-rays. From there she would be taken to the morgue to await an early morning autopsy. Sergeant Johnson, the first officer on the scene that evening, was among the last to leave at one-thirty the next morning. After nailing a piece of plywood over the broken front window and making sure the door was securely locked, Johnson carefully pasted the county Coroner's seals over the doorjamb.

Ray Mahlberg, George Coelho, Jerry Thompson, Sheriff Don Nunes, and Auburn Police Department Officer Steve Cash were seated in the Sheriff's Department conference room. It was nearly two in the morning, and every man gripped a cup of steaming coffee in his hand.

After he and Thompson had brought the group up to speed on their conversation with Tom Hoffman, Coelho concluded that Cindy was on probation, was under search-and-seizure, and that they did have the authority to proceed. He went on to say Cindy formed a friendship with a girl from the Fresno area when she was in Juvenile Hall last time, and she might have fled there. Fresno is a medium-sized agricultural city in the central San

Joaquin Valley, some two hundred miles south of Sacramento on Highway 99.

Steve Cash spoke up. "Uh, you guys should be aware that we have an officer on the Auburn force who's pretty familiar with Cindy Collier. He knows the house where she lives now—and he's on duty tonight."

Sheriff Nunes stood up, signaling the others that the conference was over. He told his own men to head out for the Collier house with Steve Cash—meanwhile, he'd ask the Auburn Chief of Police to mobilize some additional officers to help with the stakeout and search. As the senior officer, Ray Mahlberg was designated to be in charge of the operation.

After eight hours, the adrenaline had begun to pump again.

It was deathly quiet in the little canyon neighborhood; the only light that shone was from a porch fixture somewhere across the street that had been left on all night. The evening breeze that acted like a natural air conditioner for the foothill town, even when blazing daytime temperatures sizzled at over one hundred degrees, was briskly stirring the huge oaks and pines that decorated the hillside.

An involuntary shiver marched up George Coelho's spine and tickled the back of his solid neck. It could get downright chilly in these canyons at two-thirty in the morning, even in the early summer. Coelho and Deputy Thompson had posted themselves on the east side of the house, near the basement window, along with Auburn Police Department Officers Steve Cash and John Strahan. Sergeant Mahlberg and Auburn Police Department Sergeant Richard Nelson were making their way through a tangle of weeds and overgrown vines to the dilapidated front door; in a moment Coelho heard the hollow knock of Mahlberg's knuckles against the wooden door frame.

While he waited for Mahlberg's signal to enter the house, Coelho shone his flashlight through the basement window. The scene left him momentarily awestruck.

The two girls were sound asleep in a pair of bunk beds, Cindy in the upper bunk and Shirley below. Their hair tousled and the covers pulled up to their chins, the teenagers looked like children from a Norman Rockwell painting. *Well,* thought the deputy, *we've sure got ourselves a dead end here. There's no way these two kids, sleeping there like innocent lambs, could have been involved in something as brutal as this murder.* Coelho continued to stare at the sleeping girls. *This is just not going to pan out at all. From now on, all we'll be doing is going through the motions. And we'll have two kids and at least one parent madder than hell at being rousted at two-thirty in the morning by a bunch of cops, for nothing.*

The next sound he heard was the front door opening, and the muffled voice of Ray Mahlberg talking to someone inside. Then there was a gasp, and a woman's voice crying, "Oh, my God!"

In short order, George Coelho would find out the evening wasn't for nothing after all.

Part Two:

Pilgrimage to Hell

Five

A newborn baby's indignant screams echoed off the glistening tiled walls of the delivery room. "It's a girl, Mrs. Baumgartner," announced the doctor, his voice muffled from behind the white cotton mask. "And a little mite of a thing, too," he added. When they weighed her, she tipped the scales at only four pounds, seven ounces.

Linda was glad it was over. It had been a fairly easy labor—only two hours—but even so, it hadn't been a picnic. Barely nineteen years old, she had already been through this twice before, and wasn't all that anxious to do it again. Three kids was enough, especially when things were as crazy as they were in her life right now.

Linda was born in Michigan in 1948. Her family moved to northern California when she was only a child. Her father, Harry Peabody, worked for years as a truck driver, barely making enough to keep his and the family's head above water. Things were tough for Linda from the beginning: to add insult to the injury of being poor, of never having the nice clothes and things so many of the other kids had, Linda also had a learning handicap that set her apart from the mainstream at school. In those days, the classes for kids like Linda were called "slow classes," and those in them were branded by some of their crueler peers with ill-deserved nicknames like "dummy" and "retard."

Linda Peabody was far from stupid. She just had a hard time understanding the words sometimes, and making the numbers come together and make sense. The problem didn't resolve itself as she got older, so in frustration Linda coped the only way she knew how—by keeping herself as far as she could from school as often as she could. At sixteen she met a man named Jim Baumgartner and before long he asked the young girl to marry him. Within two years she had borne him two sons, Keith and Jeff. However, unbeknownst to Linda until after their births, Reuter, not Baumgartner, was their father's real name. Because he used an assumed name at the time of their wedding, the marriage was considered illegal, meaning that under California law, Linda's first- and second-born children were illegitimate—not a condition that met with a great deal of public acceptance in the mid-sixties.

In January of 1967 Linda moved in with David Collier, even though she stayed "married"—in name only, of course—to Reuter/Baumgartner. Collier, an unemployed millworker, was three years older than Linda, with an even more troubled history. Raised in Indian Valley, California, he dropped out of high school in his sophomore year and joined the army. His service record was dotted with problems and minor infractions that became less minor as time wore on; in 1964, he was thrown out of the military "under other than honorable conditions." Lean and scruffy, Collier was essentially a loner and drifter who was no stranger to trouble, and who knew how to handle himself when things got rough—later, friends would hint that he also knew how to get rough with Linda. But that was already something of a constant in the young mother's life. It was simply the way things were.

Cindy was born on April 18, 1968, in the old and dismal Placer County Hospital in Auburn. The hospital is gone now, a victim of suburban growth and "mall-itis": near the spot where Cindy came into the world, a huge Long's Drugstore sells everything from acne medications to adding machines and condoms to caramel corn; across the parking lot, where the bladder green walls of the threadbare hospital lobby once stood, Wells Fargo Bank customers wait in line to use the automatic teller machine.

Like her mother, Cindy had problems from a very early age. She was born with misaligned hip sockets, and had to wear a heavy metal brace until she was two years old. By that time the doctors realized the child had a slight hearing problem, and soon after she began to suffer what was to be a history of bronchial and upper respiratory disorders. Even though their life at home was far from harmonious, in May of 1971 Linda gave birth to her fourth child, another son. Less than two years later the pressures of domestic life finally got to Collier, and he abandoned the family. Linda was left alone to raise and provide for three sons—eight, seven, and eighteen months—and a five-year-old daughter.

Alcohol, drugs, and violence were never far from

their lives, and David Collier's abrupt departure did nothing to change that. Linda tried her best to be a parent, but lacking the skills and knowledge to provide the kind of structure and discipline needed by young children, she failed dismally. When she wasn't out working, she was out doing other things, while men of various temperaments and moralities came and went, each one leaving his telltale mark on the children and their impressionable psyches.

In the best tradition of dysfunctional families, many of the secrets of those early years remain buried. No one will say, for example, just what kinds of things may have happened in that house under the cover of darkness or behind their tightly closed doors. No one will talk about what, if anything, may have happened when Linda had to go to work, leaving a strange man in the house with her four children.

And for many years no one would talk about the fact that when he was only ten, Linda's oldest child, Keith, began molesting his pretty little stepsister. At barely seven years old, Cindy was already learning the hard and humiliating truths about power and weakness.

In 1974 Linda married Wilson Osborne; four years later she divorced him, and the pace of the family's decline picked up. Thus far, only Keith had made any discernible ripples on society's waters, although his younger brother seemed to be showing a similar propensity for finding trouble. In less than two years, their twelve-year-old stepsister Cindy began to make her own negative presence felt. Cindy recalls having spent the last five years of her life being sexually victimized and assaulted by Keith and a number of other men; those experiences, along with the general climate of decay and hopelessness which surrounded the family, began to eat at Cindy's fragile sense of self-esteem. Like a ravenous swarm of insects, they gnawed at her image of the world and the people in it, mutilating it beyond all recognition.

By 1980, Linda and the children were living in Roseville, a medium-sized agricultural and industrial town midway between Auburn and Sacramento, where one of the largest employers at the time was Southern Pacific Railroad. From its genesis, Roseville was branded as a rough-and-tumble city, similar to many of its sister "railroad towns"; in recent years, however, a huge population surge—sparked by the migration of several multinational electronics companies into that portion of the county—has mitigated that reputation somewhat.

November of that year marked the first of Cindy's serious brushes with the law. She got into one of her by-now legendary fights with another girl at school—only this time, the fight escalated into something much more serious. The police were called, and eventually Cindy was charged with assault and battery. Because of the overwhelming backlog of juvenile cases, her case wasn't even adjudicated until the middle of June; at that time she was declared a ward of the court and sentenced to sixteen hours of Work Project. Despite its seriousness, because this was her first offense she was released from probation when she finished at the Project, and she returned home.

By then the family was back in Auburn, where Linda's mother and father lived in a two-bedroom condominium at Auburn Greens. It was a sweltering mid-July day in 1981 when Cindy and two friends decided to hit the local PayLess Drug Store, located in a large shopping complex less than a mile from the Greens. Inside half an hour two of the three—one acted as lookout—shoplifted hundreds of dollars worth of cosmetics and personal toiletry items. An alert security guard caught them the minute they left the store—much to the chagrin of Cindy, who had convinced her cohorts their heist would be virtually undetectable. Obviously, it wasn't. This time she served ten days in the Juvenile Hall, was sentenced to two hundred hours on the Work Project, and forced to pay five hundred dollars restitution to the store.

Two months later, Cindy was hauled in for failure to attend school; the very next day she was picked up for loitering. Both times she was released from Juvenile Hall to her mother's custody, with the understanding that Linda would have to assert more control of her daughter in the future. At her review hearing a few weeks later, her probation officer noted that Cindy "appeared to be maintaining in home and fairly well in school."

But barely a month went by before the teenager was in trouble again, this time for skipping out without paying from a hotel and restaurant in Roseville. Four days later she was arrested for shoplifting at a large department store in the same city. In

82

frustration over Cindy's intensifying delinquency and her mother's admitted inability to control her daughter when she was home, the Court ordered Cindy to be placed in a group home; within a week she was gone, on the run. By now, juvenile authorities in Placer County were very familiar with the name of Cindy Collier. She had been a thorn in their side for months, and yet in spite of the aggravation she caused to everyone around her, still they tried to do everything possible to help her straighten her life out. Clearly, that wasn't about to happen. Cindy was on a roll, and God only knew where it might take her.

When her mother came in to tell her it was time to get up, Cindy was already awake. There was no missing the grimace of pain on her daughter's face.

"Cramps?"

Cindy groaned in response, her eyes clouded with pain and lack of sleep. This was her first night home after spending thirteen days in Juvenile Hall, and as much as she'd been looking forward to sleeping in her own bed again, last night was a real bitch. The damn cramps had plagued her on and off since the early hours of the morning, and Cindy was none too happy a camper.

Every month, the cramps got worse and worse no matter what the doctors did, and no matter what kind of medication they gave her. Even the birth control pills they'd put her on to see if they could regulate her periods a little better didn't change things—they only made Cindy feel sick to her stomach half the time, on top of the torture of the cramps. Plus the bleeding was getting worse: this month, she'd been going at it for nearly twenty days without stopping.

The teenage girl still lay curled in a fetal position on the upper mattress of the two bunk beds. A faint hint of musty dampness hung in the subterranean room, which was illuminated only slightly by what little daylight could filter through the grimy ground-level window. Clothes were strewn here and there, and cardboard packing boxes littered the floor; it appeared as if someone had either just moved in, or was getting ready to move out.

Clearly, Linda had to do something about her daughter's medical problem, but that day was not the day. As a condition of Cindy's release from Juvenile Hall the day before, the Court had ordered her to spend 150 hours in the Probation Department's Work Project, headquartered at the county's administrative center just off Highway 49 north of town and less than a half-mile from Auburn Greens. She had to be there by 9:00 A.M.

Cindy hated people telling her what to do. All her life, people had been forcing her to do things she didn't want to do and getting on her ass whenever she tried to do things her own way. She hated the idea of being inferior to anyone else, so she worked hard to cultivate not only an aura of personal power and control, but also the ability to use that power to get what she wanted. She didn't always win—especially when the cops got involved—but even when she got busted for doing something out of line, she knew how to manipulate the system and the people in it to her own advantage. This time she was pissed off that they'd ordered her into that stupid Work Project—after all, 150 hours was almost three weeks, and here it was the beginning of summer. She had no intention of doing what they wanted.

But Cindy was a master at putting up a front. This morning she agreeably got dressed and climbed into the car beside her mother for the ten-minute drive out to the Project site. She maintained a moody silence for most of the ride, lost in her own thoughts of what she would do once her mother dropped her off. When she'd been on probation before and ordered into the Juvenile Day Treatment Center, she could walk out pretty much any time she wanted, because it wasn't a lockdown facility—but this was a little different, and security was tighter. Better not to risk showing up at all if there was any chance you couldn't run.

Linda dropped her daughter off and watched in the rear-view mirror as she stood on the sidewalk waving good-bye. The Court had set down a 9:00 P.M. curfew for Cindy, so when her daughter asked that morning if she could go swimming and "fool around" after Work Project, and that she'd get one of the supervisors to bring her home, Linda reminded her she needed to be back inside the house by nine.

Smiling, Cindy watched as her mother drove down the street; once she was out of sight, the girl ducked around the corner of an adjacent building and waited. She needed to make sure no one from the Project saw her get dropped off, and came outside nosing around. No one did. Ten minutes later Cindy was poised on the shoulder of the busy highway, one thumb stuck out at a cocky angle in an appeal for someone to give her a ride.

She eyed each car that whizzed past without stopping, knowing that sooner or later someone would stop. The idea of what it would be like to be free—*really* free—had always teased at her like a dandelion puff caught on an errant spring breeze. Especially after these last few chaotic years, it was little wonder that she might be intrigued by the thought of no one telling her what to do and how to do it, no one dictating her life anymore, no one messing with her head and trying to make her into someone she wasn't, no one doing anything with her unless she wanted them to. There in that wonderful new world of freedom, she'd be able to have it all. Do it all and have it all, and nobody could say anything at all about any of it. It would be like a whole new life.

A new life. It sounded wonderful. Like being born all over again, only without having to go through all the dung heaps she'd had to go through in the last fifteen years. Without having to go through all the pain, the crushing loneliness, the abuse and abandonment and toxic shame that had been her companions all her life, and that had molded her into who she was now. Yet no matter how enticing the vision of that golden future, there were always the dark shadows of the past that crept in like malignant fingers of fog, obliterating the glittering dream.

* * *

It was enough to make any mother frantic. Cindy had disappeared from the group home in Auburn almost a month before after stealing Linda's car, and since then there had been total silence. As if that wasn't enough, her two older sons were creating their own brands of chaos; hardly a week went by that the cops weren't banging at the door of their apartment at Auburn Greens, questioning the boys about drugs or vandalism or burglaries in the area.

But this was different. None of them had ever run off for this long, simply vanishing without a trace. And what made it worse was that no matter how brash and independent she might seem, Cindy was still just a fourteen-year-old girl, out in the world alone and unprotected. The danger was very real.

Then out of the blue, Linda got a call from the authorities — not in Placer County, but in Monterey, almost two hundred miles away. The Monterey County Sheriff's officer told the relieved young mother that they'd found her daughter. To put it more precisely, she'd found them. Two runaways, one of them Cindy, had turned themselves in earlier that day, with the request that they be taken home as soon as possible.

When Cindy arrived at the Placer County Juvenile Hall, she was a mess. It looked as if she hadn't showered in days, her clothes were filthy and torn, and she was considerably thinner than she had been when she'd left home a month before. A routine medical examination revealed something else: she had contracted gonorrhea. Under questioning, Cindy finally admitted that she had acquired the disease from her older stepbrother Keith, who had been forcing sex on her for the last seven years. At first the authorities were relieved to have something solid and substantial to pin on Keith; but their joy was short-lived when Cindy angrily refused to cooperate. No, she wouldn't testify against her stepbrother, she said; and furthermore, she wouldn't even press formal charges. Her words to the investigating officer at one point were something like all of them could take a flying fuck if they thought she would ever do anything to help the cops. Her hatred of authority figures was even stronger than her hatred of her own victimization.

During the ten days she was in Juvenile Hall awaiting sentencing, Cindy met and became friends with a girl named Jana Jarvis—a meeting that would have momentous consequences six months later. At the juvenile hearing to determine Cindy's fate, the judge made the following statement:

"It is clearly evident that the minor cannot function adequately in the mother's home. The minor leaves the Court with no other alternative than to place her in a suitable foster home—a recommendation the minor was aware of at her last court appearance only two months ago."

On December 29, 1982, Cindy arrived at a large group foster home in the Sierra Nevada mountains. According to the social worker on her case, Cindy's first six weeks passed in relative harmony; she was attempting to get along with the other girls in the home, her school attendance was excellent, and her academic reports above average. There was every reason to believe that she had a chance of making it this time.

But by mid-February the staff at the home began to spot signs of trouble. Cindy's volatile temper was out of control more often, and reports from school indicated she was missing classes more frequently. There was also some suspicion that she might have been involved in petty thefts from other students at the school, but until March those charges stayed unfounded. On March 2, all hell broke loose, for reasons that are still unclear: Cindy manipulated her way into another student's locker at school and stole forty dollars from her purse, plus some jewelry and makeup. Then she simply took off.

Four days later she was caught, ending up once again in the Placer County Juvenile Hall in Auburn. After her arrest, staff at the group home discovered she had stolen several items from the facility as well as from other residents. One of the counselors drove down to the Hall to talk with Cindy and see if she wanted to go back, but more than that, to see if she would be willing to abide by the rules and start working on her issues with an eye toward making substantial personal changes. At first, Cindy was contrite and agreeable—until the counselor confronted her about lying. In a split second, the sweet little girl who'd been promising to be good and do better next time turned into a raging panther, hurling insults at the counselor and slamming out of the room in a seething fury. It was agreed that Cindy should be sent somewhere else.

In late April she was placed in John and Ann

Wagner's foster home in Shingle Springs, a small community a few miles outside of Placerville on Highway 50. Cindy arrived at the Wagner's about six o'clock in the afternoon and spent an uneventful night. The next day Ann took the girl shopping for some toiletries and personal items, then returned home to make them both some lunch. After returning from taking a lunch to her father, who lived in the mobile home on the back portion of their property, Ann noticed Cindy was gone, but presumed she was just in her room. About an hour later Ann opened the door to the garage and discovered her car was missing. Back inside the house, her purse had also disappeared.

This time it was only a matter of hours before Cindy was picked up by the authorities and charged with receiving stolen property. On May 17, she was continued as a ward of the court but placed back into her mother's home and ordered to undergo psychiatric counseling and attend the Probation Department's Juvenile Day Treatment program. It was her probation officer's hope that intensive family therapy might help Cindy resolve some of her long-standing resentment toward her stepbrother Keith and her mother. In Cindy's mind, she was the one who'd had to pay for what Keith had done to her, and for all the other craziness in the family. She was the one whose life was totally screwed up, she was the one who kept being shuffled from foster home to foster home, and nothing ever happened to Keith. Her mother hadn't even thrown him out of the house.

She stuck it out at the Day Treatment program

for six days—only three of which she actually stayed in class. The other three days she simply walked in the front door and out the back; because it wasn't a lockdown facility, all the staff could do was call Linda and tell her what happened. Well, Linda would respond, I dropped her off there this morning like I was supposed to. On May 26, a petition was filed with Juvenile Court accusing Cindy of failing to attend her court-ordered day treatment. She was ordered to serve twenty days in the Juvenile Hall, with credit for seven days previously served.

On Monday, June 13, 1983, Cindy walked out of the Juvenile Hall after serving her time. By nine-thirty the next morning she had defected from her court-ordered Work Project, and was standing on the gravel shoulder of Highway 49—trying to hitch a ride away from Auburn and her life.

Six

"Jesus Christ, Lou—you're gonna kill us all!" The car was weaving wildly in and out of traffic along the busy Brooklyn expressway. *You'd think he'd never had kids before,* she chuckled softly to herself. *I'm the one gonna have a baby—my first baby—and he's the one acting like a crazy person!* Katherine was barely eighteen years old, in many ways not much more than a child herself. Despite the pain and ragged edges of her own life, she retained an air of innocent naïveté that made her enormously attractive to a man like Louis Wolf whose sense of masculinity was based in large measure on his ability to dominate and control the people around him. Katherine was, for all intents and purposes, a perfect foil.

Jamaica Hospital swung into view before them. Today, there is virtually nothing left of this old hospital, which was supplanted in the late 1980s by a sparkling new concrete-and-glass structure, and finally fell to the wrecker's ball in 1990. But in the spring of 1969 it was a large, boxy, four-story red brick building that faced north onto the buzzing Van Wyck Expressway, which slices uneasily through the heart of Brooklyn. Tall double columns of matching brick marked the building's main entrance, through which tens of thousands of the borough's ill and infirm had passed over its lifetime. In the back, just outside the hospital's maternity wing, a sooty brick chimney raised its head toward the sky in mute testimony to countless years of smoke from the coal-fired furnace.

It was to that fourth-floor maternity wing that Katherine Guiliano was wheeled on that seventeenth day of April, 1969. Since this would be the young woman's first baby, the clinic staff was in no hurry to prep her—experience taught them that labor frequently went on forever with first-time mothers. This would be no exception: Katherine's labor lasted for almost twenty-four hours.

During those hours, before the contractions got so strong and close together that they were all she could think about, Katherine pondered this new life that she would soon be giving birth to, and how she was determined that her baby would have a very different—and much better—life than her own had been.

Katherine's early years were spent with her mother, Muriel, and her father, Santo Guiliano, in Babylon, New York, on the south shore of Long Island. The beachfront house was unkempt and dilapidated, more of a shanty than a real house, with a broken toilet in the basement. By the time her youngest brother turned four, Santo and Muriel divorced, leaving Muriel to care for four children as best she could. She struggled by for a while, but all too soon it became apparent that they were in very deep trouble. It wouldn't be long, Muriel realized, before the state came in to take her children away from her—not necessarily because she was unfit to be a mother, but because she just couldn't provide for them.

Rather than see her children separated from one another in foster homes all over the city, Muriel decided to place them at the Mission of the Immaculate Conception on Staten Island, a Catholic mission home that was commonly known as Mount Loretto. Some time later, Muriel married Rudy Kettering; Santo, meanwhile, had also remarried, to a woman whose own children—eleven of them in all—were also at Mount Loretto.

Young Katherine Guiliano stayed at the mission home for about a year, until her father's elderly mother took her in. She remained there with her grandmother until she met Louis Wolf at sixteen.

There were times she wished she had been able to stay at Mount Loretto. Not because it was such a wonderful place: it was far from that. But as kind as her old grandmother usually was to her, she desperately missed her three little brothers, and her mother. And there was more to it than just being lonely for her family—the insecure and frightened Katherine, not yet even ten, had also begun to be regularly and sometimes violently molested by her father and her uncle, both of whom spent a fair amount of time in their mother's house.

Her father Santo was an alcoholic, passionately dedicated to his gallon jugs of Thunderbird wine. He was also a renowned womanizer who frequently cheated on Muriel during their marriage, and on his new wife Hazel as well. Muriel herself had not exactly been a saint during their marriage, with her own roster of extramarital flings. One of them was back in 1946, four years before Katherine was born, with a man whose ghost would ultimately figure prominently in her daughter's life.

In a quirky, unexplainable twist of fate, Santo's second wife would also end up having an affair during their marriage—to that same man Muriel had slept with in 1946.

It had been an insane, emotionally ravaging life for Katherine. The only security she ever knew was with an old woman who looked the other way while her two sons were molesting her granddaughter. She had grown up with a pernicious sense of worthlessness about herself, and a twisted sense of what it meant to be a woman, much less a wife and mother. At the same time she learned how to distance herself from intimate relationships, how to protect herself from the agonizing pain of abuse and abandonment that sometimes felt as if it would swallow her, and how to surrender her self and her own needs to those around her. When Louis Wolf swaggered into her life when she was sixteen, she was enthralled by his potent magnetism and imperiousness, as if he were the master of his—and everyone else's—universe. She was totally and irrevocably hooked.

Louis Wolf sat chain-smoking in the sulphur-colored maternity waiting room, waiting to hear what was going on with Katherine. It had been hours, and no one had said a word. Only that she was still in labor. Still working on popping the kid out. He didn't recall if it had been this hard for his first wife when she had their son and then the other two. Somehow, he didn't think so—but time has a way of playing tricks on the memory, so he wouldn't have bet his life on it.

He got up from the ratty yellow plastic-covered armchair and stretched, letting out a loud yawn. He was a big man, right at six feet, with a full chest and bronzed muscular arms, one of which sported a fairly new tattoo that read Kathi. His dark hair curled lazily over his ears, and his deep brown eyes glittered with a hard sensuality that was reflected in his full mouth. When he smiled, it was easy to see how, like a gorgeous but sinister spider, he could easily ensnare a woman in his silken, deadly net before she even realized she had become his victim. Louis Wolf was an extremely attractive man, dark and sexual and more than a little dangerous.

Louis Wolf was born in Queens General Hospital in Queens, New York, on August 1, 1944. From the beginning, there was trouble in the family. Most of it was his father, Louis Sr., whose violent temper frequently left the little boy's mother, Dorothy, bruised and bloody. He never did understand why his mother didn't do something—stand up to him or ask somebody for help or at least run, but she never did. She simply tried as best she could to pacify her husband, and to keep the kids out of his way when he was on one of his rampages. Unbeknownst to her at the time, however, her husband's violence didn't stop at beating up on her. He had also begun molesting her oldest daughter, the product of an earlier failed union.

And then there were his women. Dorothy had no idea of how often her husband cheated on her, but she knew it was a lot. One of the most blatant episodes came just days after his second child, a daughter, was born in 1946. In a plot twist worthy of *Peyton Place*, Dorothy had just come home from the hospital with her new baby, and she asked Louis to go pick up a prescription at the drugstore several blocks away. He was gone all night; when he finally stumbled in, it was without the prescription. Apparently he had run into Santo Guiliano, a fellow worker at the Canada Dry bottling plant, and they spent the night with a couple of women. The name of the woman Dorothy Wolf's husband slept with was Muriel — the same Muriel who later married Louis's friend Santo, and ultimately gave birth to Katherine.

Louis Jr. spent most of his childhood in the Ozone Park neighborhood of Queens, on Ninety-ninth Street near Woodhaven Boulevard. That was where he started school, and where he started having trouble almost right away. He suffered from dyslexia, and as a result was always falling behind in his schoolwork. Unlike some children who suffer from disabilities and other conditions that make them different from their peers and who respond by becoming withdrawn and passive, Louis covered up whatever insecurities he felt with an ever-thickening veneer of sullen aggressiveness and bullying. The lessons he had learned at home by watching his father were taking hold.

Then Louis Sr. was killed in a freak traffic accident when the Long Island Banana Company truck he was driving collided head-on with another truck on a narrow bridge. Dorothy had no option but to go to work right away, even though she had three children at home. It would be three years before she remarried—three years of grinding poverty and deprivation from which there seemed to be no escape. Little Louis's problems escalated, only magnified by the arrival of a new stepfather and shortly thereafter, a new baby brother.

By the time he was eight he was such a problem in school and at home that Dorothy took him to a child psychologist; yet despite the weekly counseling sessions his behaviors continued to worsen. He had become physically violent by now with his sisters and other children and was beginning to seem overly preoccupied with sex. One day he drew an obscene picture of his teacher orally copulating a man, and Dorothy threw up her hands in despair and sent him to a special home for troubled boys and girls on Staten Island. The name of that home? Mount Loretto. The same Mount Loretto where Lou Wolf's future wife Katherine spent a year of her own childhood.

Some years later Louis told stories of being beaten with electrical cords at the school and being physically abused in other ways by one of the priests. He also said that same priest took nude pictures of him and many of the other boys. When he came back to his mother's home in Queens, very little had changed. In fact, according to him, things only got worse, with an escalation of the savage batterings he says he received over the years at the hands of his alcoholic stepfather (although there are

98

those in the family who maintain the beatings never occurred at all). Regardless, there can be little doubt that somewhere during the course of his life—most likely at several points—Louis Wolf was subjected to extreme emotional and probably physical abuse that was a major factor in his developing personality. And true to form, as with his disability at school, he did not turn the anger and pain of these experiences inward upon himself, but outward toward the world and the people in it.

Soon his violence took on sexual overtones, and he raped his youngest sister—a fact she only admitted many years later. He began carrying a gun to school, drinking, and using drugs, until the beleaguered school authorities finally had enough and transferred him to a "600" school in Brooklyn, which specialized in youngsters with behavior disorders. It didn't take long before Dorothy's husband had also had enough of Louis and threw the boy out of the house at the tender age of sixteen. With his mother's blessing, Louis entered the Air Force, only to discover he was unable to fly because of chronic nosebleeds. He returned home, had his nose fixed, and signed up for the Army.

Shortly afterward, he left for Germany, where he met Shirley Duvall, who was also in the Army. Within months they were married, and soon afterward had a son. But even the Army couldn't tame Louis Wolf—he was constantly in fights, being disciplined for infractions of regulations, and being demoted in rank because of his actions. Longing for the freedom of civilian life, Louis left the military, taking his wife and two children to California.

From there the family, now with a third child, moved to Ohio, near Shirley's parents; but the problems the couple had been suffering for years didn't diminish with either move, and so Louis left and went back to New York. According to him, Shirley hadn't fallen in love with him so much as with his uniform; when he no longer wore one, she promptly fell out of love.

Back home in Brooklyn, Louis met young Katherine Guiliano. By now, Katherine's father Santo had divorced Muriel and married Dorothy Wolf's sister Hazel, further intertwining the two families. Katherine was completely swept off her feet by Louis, who lavished her with attention and gifts and affection. Here was someone, she thought, who could take care of her: who could get her out of the house, take control of things, and give her a better life. On his part, Louis was taken with the young girl's dark-haired beauty, her rapt admiration for him, and her willingness to subvert all her needs to his. They made the perfect match.

Soon the couple was living together in a tiny apartment above a laundromat on Liberty Avenue in Queens, and Katherine was pregnant. She registered under the name of Katherine Wolf at Jamaica Hospital where she struggled through twenty-three and a half hours of labor, giving birth to little Shirley.

Katherine gave birth to two more children—boys, Louis Jr. whom everyone called L.J., and William—within the next four years. By now the family lived in a small ground floor flat at 230 Etna Street in Brooklyn. The modest brownstone had two bedrooms, one bath, a living room, and kitchen, and a small yard in back. In front, a black wrought-iron fence ran the length of the building. It was no worse and no better than a hundred other flats in Brooklyn lived in by a hundred other families. A few blocks to the south, the behemoth clattering elevated railway known simply as "the El" bisected the borough; in its shadow, huge trucks vied for space with belching buses and a tangle of cars and taxicabs on the narrow Liberty Avenue, and the air rang with the perpetual urban symphony of screeching brakes and blaring horns.

This portion of Brooklyn was then, as it remains today, a slightly shabby neighborhood of storefronts that reflected an eclectic mix of races, cultures, and lifestyles, from Chinese laundries and Jewish delicatessens to tattoo parlors and musty hardware stores. From morning to sunset, a steady stream of people choked the sidewalks along the street—businessmen on their way to appointments, withered old grandmothers with fishnet shopping bags out to buy a loaf of black rye bread at Harvey's Bakery, small children on their way to Public School 65 just a few blocks away, and vagrants and misfits of every description looking for a handout or a park bench to sleep off their hangovers. On one side of Liberty, the giant Eldee Warehouse Outlet lured customers in search of a bargain with huge window signs promising We Won't Be Undersold!, while a few blocks away ripe fruits and vegetables gleamed in the midday sun in front of the decades-old Liberty

Fruit and Vegetable Market. Both Louis and Katherine felt very much at home here, in the middle of the most populous city in the nation.

They scraped by on a fairly tight budget most of the time, although sometimes Louis came home with large amounts of money that his job as a carpenter and remodeler couldn't account for. Of course, no one dared to question this sudden wealth, even though many harbored the secret suspicion that Louis hadn't exactly come by the money by working overtime. During those times of affluence he spent lavishly on the children — especially his firstborn, who they named Shirley Katherine, an incongruous blending of his first and second wives' names — and on things for the house like stereos and new furniture. Then things would go back to the way they were before, with the family barely squeaking by from month to month. During these years of the early 1970s, work wasn't all that easy to find; but as a carpenter Louis Wolf did excellent and painstaking finish work and was seldom without a job. He wasn't the easiest man to work with, however: demanding and rigid, he expected absolute perfection as well as loyalty from the men he worked with. There were also times he would fly into black rages for no apparent reason, while the people around him scattered like flies.

The furies weren't restricted to his working environment. They were cropping up more and more often at home, and the tension was beginning to build. The loyalty and obedience he demanded from his coworkers was insignificant compared to what he demanded from his family; when they failed to measure up, they paid the price in pain. More than once he lashed out at his daughter, leaving ugly black-and-blue marks where his huge hand connected with her little girl's body. His suspicion of people and their motives, always present in his psyche, was also more noticeable. I don't trust nobody, he would say—and he didn't. He insured the family's isolation from the rest of the world by sabotaging every friendship Katherine tried to establish and by insisting that his children spend virtually all their spare time with him and the family. Their world, such as it was, revolved around Louis Wolf, the king and master of the clan.

By the time she was three, little Shirley had already become a victim of her father. She was also a victim of her mother, although Katherine never saw it that way. All Katherine did was to live her life the only way she knew how, which meant running her family the way her own family had been run, and raising her children in much the same way as she had been raised. When Louis went off into the night with other women, she simply sighed and let it be. When he started hitting Shirley or L.J., she cowered in a corner and waited until it was over. Then when, out of her own frustration and inexpressible pain, she, too, lashed out in violence against her children, she simply justified her actions to herself and tucked it all away in the little box in the corner of her mind where she kept those things she didn't want to touch or see.

And when things started happening that Katherine was afraid might point to something dark and depraved going on between her husband and her daughter, she looked the other way. After all, she reasoned, she was powerless to do anything anyway.

On Monday, September 9, 1974, five-year-old Shirley Katherine Wolf walked through the door of Mrs. Steinberg's kindergarten class at New York's Public School 65, a big three-story rusty red brick building on Richmond Street in the heart of Brooklyn. Periodically, the Fulton Street El roared by just a half-block away.

Shirley was never a particularly shy child, although for the first few days of school she did seem a little quiet and withdrawn. One of hundreds of other children at the imposing grammar school, she felt isolated and alone and as if she simply didn't belong with all these strangers. She felt so very different from everyone else, and in fact she was. Already her life experiences had matured her well beyond her years and conferred upon her an ever-hardening shell of cynicism and mistrust of almost everyone.

Shirley sat in the noisy classroom, alone on her own private island, staring out the window at the snowflakes whirling through the afternoon sky. She had been sitting there for several minutes, oblivious to the childish pandemonium around her, when suddenly she felt, more than saw, a presence standing in front of the window, blocking out the gray-bright winter sky. She gave a little gasp of fear and cowered defensively in her desk.

"Shirley?" Aware of her surroundings again, Shirley realized that the monster in the window was only her teacher.

"Yes, ma'am?" she replied with a wide, gap-toothed smile.

The pretty young woman who spoke Shirley's name so softly looked at the child sitting before her and wondered. Wondered what on earth was going on inside that five-year-old mind, what was happening in her life that was turning her into such a strange, unpredictable creature. One minute Shirley would be laughing and playing with the other children, then as if someone had flipped some secret master switch, she would turn dark and sullen and unreachable. It had happened enough times in these first months of school that the teacher was worried. Something wasn't right.

"Yes, ma'am?" Shirley repeated, the smile that seemed somehow a little vacant still on her face.

The young teacher reached down and patted Shirley's shoulder. Shirley Wolf was one of the strangest kids she'd run across in her teaching experience, and yet there was something about the skinny little girl that tugged at her heart so fiercely she felt like crying sometimes. She didn't think she'd ever seen a kid so anxious—no, it was more than just anxious, it was almost like she was *desperate*—to please the adults around her. Most of the time Shirley didn't give a damn for the other kids, but she'd do almost anything for a teacher.

That was the puzzle, and it was something that really worried her and a couple of the other teachers she'd talked to. There were always children that were more reserved than others, that didn't join in class and playground activities as readily—but Shirley was different. She was a complete loner, isolated behind a wall so high and thick it was almost visible. It seemed she didn't have the vaguest idea of what it took to get along with her peers, and furthermore, she couldn't have cared less about learning. It was as if she hated the other children.

Those two things together—Shirley's inability to get along with other kids coupled with her insatiable hunger for affection and approval from adults—were what led the discerning kindergarten teacher to contact Shirley's parents. It was a pleasant enough conversation, Mrs. Steinberg recalled, but at the time she got the feeling that they hadn't really heard a lot of what she said. They listened, but they didn't hear. At least that was how it seemed.

She was right. Somehow Louis and Katherine Wolf never quite got around to taking any concrete action on the suggestion that they might want to take their daughter to a child psychologist for evaluation. Eventually, the frustrated and overworked teacher became involved with another more deeply troubled child, and little Shirley Wolf began to slip through the cracks in the system.

In May of 1975, Katherine gave birth to her fourth child, Brian. Five months later, on October 20, while standing on an outside ledge installing several windows, Louis Wolf lost his balance and fell. He'd been hurt before in construction accidents, but this was the worst: when he fell, his left leg plunged like a battering ram through the fifteen sheets of plate glass leaning against the wall below him. He was rushed to Elmhurst General Hospital, where he underwent several hours of emergency surgery to repair his lacerated knee, femoral artery, and nerves in his left leg. The following month he was back in surgery again for more repairs to the damaged nerves.

Nothing, however, seemed to diminish the constant pain. They gave him a prescription for Percodan, a powerful narcotic painkiller, but even that didn't help all that much. He could barely stand, could only sit for brief periods of time, and was completely unable to go back to work. By the time he underwent a lumbar sympathectomy to surgically remove the offending nerve fibers in 1976, Katherine was scrambling to make ends meet. Their Welfare assistance check just didn't go very far in feeding and clothing a family of three growing children and a new baby.

As the months dragged on, Katherine's hopes for her husband's full recovery dimmed and then died altogether. He didn't seem to be getting better at all—in fact, in some ways he was getting worse. His bitterness over his deteriorating physical condition grew into venomous anger, which he used as a cudgel against his wife and children to keep them in line. Never one to let an opportunity for personal gain pass him by, he also began using his injuries to manipulate people into accommodating his needs and desires. This worked particularly well with physicians, whom he could cajole into prescribing more and more drugs to help him cope with his pain and the resultant stress. All it took was finding the right doctor, one with a reputation as a "pill pusher." With Louis Wolf's connections, coupled with his uncanny sense for sniffing out people with ethical weaknesses, the search didn't take long at all.

But the drugs were affecting his mind in ways he hadn't counted on. What were once mere suspicions turned to paranoia; the three or four days of insane fury a month became triple that; and his uncontrollable impulse to strike out physically at someone seemed to mutate into something more like a morbid need to hurt and punish. Things were completely falling apart and there wasn't a thing that anyone could do about it.

Seven

Sometimes it seemed as if he would end up killing her. She heard the sonic boom of the front door smashing closed, the leaden footsteps coming her way down the hall, and the tiny hairs on the back of her neck would stand up as if they were electrified.

There were really only two possibilities as to what would happen next, and Shirley didn't want to think about either one. Both had been played out many times before in the dark-haired girl's life, even though one was a little clearer in her mind than the other. Nevertheless, the thought of either scenario made her feel like she wanted to throw up. Or run like hell and never stop. Of course, in reality neither option existed for her, and Shirley knew it. Somewhere deep within her, in that place that lives within us all where the diamond hardness of truth shatters our mythic illusions and false hopes, Shirley Wolf understood there was no escape.

There was no telling what his retribution was for. Maybe it was because she'd brought home another bad grade on a test. All she had to do was try harder next time—that was what the teacher had said, and it was what Shirley promised she would do; it was what she always promised she would do, only it never seemed to work out quite that way.

Or maybe it was because of a glass of spilled milk that morning at the breakfast table, or a rip in the skirt of her favorite red dress when she fell down in the playground, or a spot on her shiny new patent-leather shoes, or the fact that she'd talked back when someone had asked her to do something she didn't want to do.

Or maybe there was no reason at all.

Sometimes it just happened like that. It didn't really matter, after all, what the reason was—the outcome was always the same. Well, maybe not exactly the same every single time, but close enough so that one time just sort of blurred into another.

In fact, you could almost invent a scenario, and it would probably have enough elements of reality in it that it wouldn't really matter. You could say they were driving home, and Louis Wolf was in one of his black moods from something—or nothing—his daughter had done. No matter how long it took to get there, all the way home he might refuse to speak, with the tension in the car growing like some evil, malignant thunderhead. Shirley would begin to feel as if she couldn't breathe. Once they got home, he would just stand there like a huge dark mountain, his brown-black eyes filled with venom and fury, hands clenching and unclenching as he decided what his next move would be.

It had happened like this so many times Shirley couldn't even count them all.

Slowly and deliberately he would stand to his full

towering height, menacing eyes staring as if to incinerate her; then in a scene reminiscent of Scrooge's encounter with the macabre, black-hooded ghost of Christmas Yet To Come, one huge hand would rise with a single finger outstretched toward his victim like a portent of doom.

After so many years of practice, Louis Wolf's techniques of psychological and physical intimidation were tuned to a fine and perfect pitch. Underlying it all was his motto, unspoken but perfectly understood nevertheless, that the only way to correct behavior was to inflict pain—physical or emotional. He was an expert at both.

That day, just like so many others, he stood before her, wordless and almost motionless, his black eyes boring into her like a laser; his tongue darted in and out from beneath his front teeth, making the habitual little *thsk, thsk* sucking noise that meant he was contemplating doing or saying something. Shirley felt like a wispy little creature trapped in his ominous shadow. No matter how many times it had happened before, the effect on her was always the same. Too terrified to speak or even move, mouth drooping open and deep brown eyes wide and staring, recoiling from the intensity of his mere presence, she simply waited for the reign of terror to begin.

Just let it come. Let it come so it can be over.

She touched her left arm where the bruise had finally begun to fade from deep purple-black to a sick shade of green. There would probably be another to take its place all too soon.

Finally he would speak. "There's no excuse," he

might say, his voice smooth as oil and poisonous as hemlock. "No excuse. You know what needs to be done."

Then suddenly he would explode into the rage that had been festering there for most of the day. While his terrified daughter stood frozen to the spot like a helpless deer blinded by onrushing headlights, Louis would reach to unbuckle the thick leather belt around his waist.

Shirley's mother had witnessed scenes like this often enough. Her breath came in shallow little gasps as she watched, but like her daughter she said nothing. She understood, as everyone in the family did, that to intervene or even utter a word in Shirley's defense at times like this would be to bring Louis Wolf's terrible wrath down upon herself as well. No one—not even your own child—was worth that price.

Spinning his daughter around, he would pull down her white cotton underpants and begin to lash at her back and buttocks with the uncoiled belt. The brutality of the attack would force the child to double over in pain, although she barely even uttered a whimper. All the while, a small, tight smile played across his lips.

Shirley didn't recall a time when she hadn't been afraid of her father. Even in what she thought of as the "good" times, when she was just a little girl in New York, he frequently seemed perched on the edge of some sort of catastrophic, lethal explosion.

The strange thing was he could be incredibly kind and sweet to her, too. Some of the memories were sharp and clear as a crystal icicle—memories

112

of being just a little girl, and of her father giving her a stuffed bear and a doll that cooed and pretty dresses with matching shoes and warm caps with fuzzy flaps you could pull down over your ears when the December wind whipped through East New York. She even remembered seeing a picture of herself standing on the sidewalk in front of their brownstone on Etna Street in Brooklyn, grinning from under one of her favorite furry hats. So that much was real, she knew.

Other memories, though, seemed more like dreams than realities, as if she'd been told the stories so many times she had come to own them for herself. It was almost like some other voice were telling her the story from inside her head.

And so now Shirley dreamily remembered that which had never been: of being younger, being nurtured in a happy and loving family where they had everything a family could ever want, and where their backyard bulged with elaborate jungle gyms and play sets, a complete replica of Sesame Street—about the only thing missing was a real-life Cookie Monster—and what seemed like dozens of bikes and scooters and wagons and doll carriages of every description. All for her, just her.

Well, for L.J., too, she grudgingly admitted—but in those days Shirley was the real apple of her father's eye. She was his princess, and most of the time she could have almost anything she wanted. The only thing her father asked was that she please him. It didn't take her long to learn what pleasing him meant. After a while she also came to understand that if she could make him happy, things

113

would be much easier for her and for everyone else, too—at least for a while.

In Shirley's eyes her father was the handsomest man on earth, with his broad shoulders and thick black hair and a smile she knew could probably melt an entire city block of snow, even in the middle of a blizzard. Sometimes he would sweep her up into his huge arms and whirl her around and around and around until she thought the whole world was going to sail off into space; then he'd pull her so close she could see every pore on his bronzed face, and stare into her chocolate colored eyes for what seemed like an eternity. Afterward he'd give her a gentle kiss that tasted like cigarettes and tell her how she was his girl, his very best girl in all the world.

"You're Daddy's princess, you know," he would say softly, and she would nod her head.

Sometimes it wasn't so bad. . . .

Shirley Wolf was an olive-skinned child with a long, thin face; as the years progressed, the shallow cleft in her delicately pointed chin would become even more prominent. Uncurled hair the color of walnuts hung limply just above her shoulders, and a long fringe of bangs covered her brows. Her dark eyes stared out into the world as if hypnotized, bottomless pits of near-blackness that seemed devoid of light or life or feeling.

During those early years she seemed to have an almost desperate need for attention, affection, and approval. Family friends recall her as a sweet and outgoing little girl, yet with needs so deep and powerful that they threatened to overwhelm anyone who became close to her. She would see a favorite neighbor coming and run down the block calling her name over and over and over like a homeless kitten crying out for shelter. She desperately craved attention and approbation and was willing to do almost anything to get either. There were times she tried so hard to please, to be loved and accepted, that she ended up driving away the very people she wanted to bring closer.

What no one knew was just how much little Shirley wanted to please. Just how much she *needed* to please, in order to safeguard both a pernicious secret and at the same time the strongest source of love she knew. For by the time she was three years old, her world had already begun to fall apart. Only a child, Shirley Wolf already knew that the monsters who lurk in the dark of night truly do exist. Her soul had already begun to die, annihilated a piece at a time by those who were supposed to keep her universe safe and free from harm.

Katherine rolled over, numbly aware that her husband was shaking her shoulder and calling her name.

Louis Wolf's voice was thick with . . . was it sleep? Or was he out of breath from something? Katherine's dream-fogged brain began to stir into awareness. She struggled to prop herself up on one elbow, peering at her husband in the darkness. *Something's wrong. Funny, I didn't hear the phone ring*

. . . and there's no cryin' from the kids' room. Maybe Lou is sick.

"What's wrong? What happened?" She reached across the nightstand and clicked on the light, squinting painfully in the sudden brightness. Her husband's hair was disheveled, and his cheeks already bore the hint of what would be a merciless stubble in a few hours. His ebony eyes looked a little glazed, yet somehow angry at the same time.

"It's Shirley. She . . . she was in here. . . ."

Katherine glanced around the shadowy room for her daughter, then turned back to her husband with a puzzled expression on her face and asked what on earth he was talking about. He reached across her and grabbed a half-empty pack of Kools lying on the wooden nightstand. After lighting one, Louis took a deep drag, closed his eyes for a moment, then started to talk.

"I been asleep for a while," he said, "when all of a sudden I'm dreaming. At least, I think I'm dreaming. Anyways, I was dreaming that I had this terrific hard-on because you were givin' me a blow job. It was really something. . . ." He smiled thinly as Katherine wondered why the hell he woke her up in the middle of the night just to tell her about some screwy wet dream. Then he scowled, paused to flick the growing ash off the end of the cigarette, and breathed a deep sigh full of what seemed to her like sadness.

"But then—then everything gets all confused and I don't know if I'm asleep or awake, and I open my eyes and it's not you givin' me a B.J. at all. It's Shirley."

Katherine felt like someone had punched her full-force in the solar plexus. She struggled to find the words to respond to what her husband just said, but the thoughts were racing through her head in incoherent fragments, like crazy pieces of a jigsaw puzzle someone had thrown up in the air all at once. Her mind was screaming, but nothing came out of her mouth. *I DON'T UNDERSTAND I DON'T UNDERSTAND I DON'T UNDERSTAND. This has to be a dream. A horrible nightmare. Just make it stop . . . make him stop.*

But Lou Wolf's words didn't stop.

"Hey, I'm not sure what happened." Louis's voice was stronger now, more in control. " 'Cept she was here, for sure. Right here on top of me, and I couldn't help myself. After all, I was asleep—how was I to know it was my little girl and not my wife doin' that to me? The point is, I'm pretty sure I might have come, and I figure you oughta go and check on her. You know, clean her up. Just in case some of it got on her." He crushed out the last of the cigarette and looked at his wife.

Katherine was half sitting, eyes staring numbly into space, the sheets pulled up tightly under her arms. For a minute she said nothing, just once or twice gave an almost imperceptible shake of her head. Then, as if emerging from a deep trance, she turned to her watchful husband and repeated the bizarre tale he'd just told her. She needed to get the whole thing clear in her mind.

"You was asleep . . . and Shirley comes into the room, and . . . and she. . . ." Katherine stopped, letting the pieces of the puzzle fall into

117

place. She tried again.

"Okay: Shirley comes in, crawls into bed and starts in on you. Only you don't know it was her, and you don't know you was awake. By the time you realize this isn't no dream, it's too late. Right?" It sounded as crazy out loud as it had in her head.

"Well, yeah . . ." He didn't sound quite as self-assured as before.

Katherine nodded, got out of bed, and pulled on her flimsy robe, shivering in the night air. Somewhere, far down Euclid Street, a police siren went screaming by. She thought about stopping in the bathroom on her way to Shirley's room to get a towel or washcloth, but by the time her brain registered the idea she was already standing outside her daughter's bedroom. She opened the door as quietly as possible and padded across the floor to where the little girl lay. *God, she's just a baby! This is impossible. Lou must have been dreaming after all. There she is almost three years old, still tucked into her little bed like I left her hours ago and sleeping like an angel, nothing wrong at all.*

Except that Shirley wasn't asleep. She turned her face toward the door at the sound of her mother's approach, her eyes wide and staring.

"Shirley? Honey? You okay?"

Shirley was silent.

"Hon, Mommy needs to check you for a second, okay?" Katherine looked at her daughter's face and hair, but both were completely clean and dry. Her tiny hands were equally unsullied. Finally, she pulled the child's bedclothes down, and saw what she hoped she would not. There was a large sticky-wet spot on the front of Shirley's pajamas, covering her entire groin area. Gently, she removed Shirley's pajama bottoms and examined her panties underneath. They, too, were soaked in front.

As she changed her little daughter into fresh panties and pajamas, she began to reenact the whole scene in her mind. Yet one bewildering question was conspicuous by its absence: *if it had happened the way Lou said it had happened, how did semen get on Shirley's crotch?* The logical answer was one that would have probably made Katherine feel as if she were going insane, so both the query and its answer were obliterated from her consciousness before they could even arrive.

Katherine looked down at her daughter, by now asleep again in her little bed. Shirley moaned softly, and her mother tucked the pink-and-yellow striped blanket up around her shoulders. "Sleep peaceful," she whispered to the child. *And when you're older, we'll all laugh about this.*

Only, the laughter never came.

By this time Shirley had already been betrayed by another member of her family.

According to Shirley, she was less than three years old when her father's step-brother Artie and his girlfriend agreed to babysit one night. She didn't know him very well, but he smiled at her and told her she was pretty and that they'd have a lot of fun together, so she didn't mind.

The three of them spent the early evening watching television and eating pizza, and then it was time for Shirley to go to bed. "Uncle Artie was

119

gonna help me brush my teeth," she explains. He went into the bathroom with the little girl, telling his girlfriend he'd be out in a while.

About what happened next, Shirley says with bitter irony in her voice, "He brushed my teeth all right. He gave me a full physical with a toothbrush." Unbeknownst to her uncle Artie, standing there in the cold bathroom with his compliant, vacant-eyed little niece, oral sex was nothing new. She had already been down that twisted path many times before, and knew precisely what to do. Later, she says, she told her father what Artie had done, and he nearly beat him to a pulp.

After all, as a loving father it was the least he could do to protect his little princess.

By the time she entered first grade at P.S. 65, Shirley was more and more withdrawn and self-sufficient. Her class picture reveals a sullen child in the center row who seems somehow completely separate from the twenty-seven other classmates that surround her. She had a certain air of aloofness and self-determination about her which created a very effective barrier between herself and the other children. The more she grew, the more distant she became from everyone.

She seldom developed any real friendships, preferring instead to play and spend time with her brother L.J., only a year younger than she, or in solitude. Besides, most of the time she was discouraged from having outside relationships with other children her age: "You're better than they are, princess," her father told her. "You're special." And Shirley would reach up and take hold of his rough, strong hand and believe his words.

Then in October of 1975, her father — and her world — changed. No longer was he the powerful, strong man he once was, a kind of Superman figure capable of, if not leaping tall buildings in a single bound, then almost anything else. In a single instant her father became like the fallen Goliath, a once-mighty giant now powerless and defeated. The serious injuries he sustained when he fell through those fifteen plates of glass left Louis Wolf a near-cripple, increasingly addicted to the narcotic drugs that helped control his constant pain but only added to his depression and volatility.

Things weren't much easier for the rest of the family. Although in the past there were times Lou seemed to have an inexplicable abundance of ready cash, most of the time the family finances were shaky at best. After the accident, their shoestring budget became even more stretched. Gone were the days when Katherine took Shirley shopping to try on dozens of outfits and choose the one she liked best. Instead, the only shopping they could do was in secondhand stores.

For Shirley, however, one thing hadn't changed because of her father's terrible accident: his insistence that she was the only one who could bring him that special care, that special comfort that fused them together and that would forever remain their own inviolable secret.

* * *

121

Mrs. Chambers called for quiet in the classroom. It was five minutes before the bell would ring announcing the end of another school year, and she still needed to pass out report cards. Starting with the As, she called out the children's names to come forward and pick up their cards.

"Shirley Wolf." Finally. She was usually the last to be called, and she hated that. Everybody was always looking at her, whispering and snickering, and she was sure most of it was about her. Not about to let anyone know she felt uncomfortable, Shirley threw back her shoulders and marched forward, giving her teacher a wide smile.

Mrs. Chambers pressed the stiff card into Shirley's outstretched hand and said, "Have a nice summer, Shirley."

Shirley's momentary elation at being recognized by the teacher was quelled as soon as she saw the black printing "REPORT TO PARENTS" leap off the page at her. She had tried to do her best—she always tried—but it seemed like she could never do well enough, never be good enough. All she ever wanted was for people to love her, to tell her she was okay and that they wouldn't go away and leave her if she did something bad or wrong. But everybody was always judging her, criticizing her, blaming her, telling her she needed to try harder . . . didn't they understand that she was trying as hard as she could? Didn't they understand she was doing everything in her power to make them like her, to make them approve of her, to make them happy with her?

She shuffled down the stairs of P.S. 65, the stiff

card gripped tightly in her hand. A block or two later she got up enough courage to look inside and see just how bad it was.

The left-hand side of the report was for the academic subjects: reading, oral and written language, math, social studies, and science. On the right side were the ratings for music and art, plus personal and social development, work habits, and health. Shirley scanned the first section and breathed a sigh of relief. No "Unsatisfactory" marks. No "Excellents" either, but she hadn't expected any. Out of the twenty categories, she'd gotten nine "Good" marks, and the rest were either "Fair" or on the line between the two.

Her heart dropped when she looked at the right-hand side of the report card. No better than the last two times. There were "Unsatisfactory" check marks all over the page.

"Gets along well with other children." Unsatisfactory.

"Shows self-control." Unsatisfactory.

"Homework." Unsatisfactory.

And on and on.

In a rage of shame and guilt, she started to throw the card into the gutter, but stopped as her eye caught the writing on the back side under "Teacher Comments." She liked Mrs. Chambers well enough, but why did she have to pick on her? Why couldn't she understand? It was the same old thing as the two times before: "If Shirley controlled her behavior," the teacher had written, "her work would improve. She is capable of doing much better!"

Then Shirley reread what her mother had plead-

123

ingly scrawled under "Parent Comments" after the last report period: "Please write a little note each time Shirley doesn't finish her work, or waste time. I wish to know what she is doing wrong the same day she does it. I am really hurt to see Shirley is doing so badly. I know I am asking a lot of you. Please."

In truth, Katherine Wolf didn't know what else to do. Every time Shirley brought home a note from the teacher or a bad report card, she sat down and tried to talk to her daughter, tried to find out if there was a problem somewhere. Sometimes she would get angry and yell at the child and maybe even hit her, but who could blame her? It was frustrating as hell to keep getting these reports month after month, and never see any improvement. Besides, Shirley never said anything. Just that there was nothing wrong, and that she'd try to do better.

Of course, even Katherine had to admit that ever since the accident things hadn't been exactly easy for any of them at home, and that could be part of the problem with Shirley. As time went along Lou had become more and more difficult to live with, his moods swinging wildly and unpredictably from sympathetic benevolence to maleficent abuse. Katherine wondered if some of these emotional roller coaster rides might be the result of the narcotics and other drugs like Valium, Percodan, and Dalmane the doctors prescribed for his pain and sleeplessness — and which Lou seemed to be using in greater and greater quantities, even as their effectiveness diminished. But questioning him — or worse, challenging him — about the drugs or anything else was asking for trouble, and Katherine figured she already had enough of that, just trying to live with him the way he was. She had no intention of doing anything to aggravate him more: her husband had always had an unpredictable and violent temper, but it was getting steadily worse.

Many times his fury was aimed at Shirley, but bewilderingly to Katherine, instead of coming to hate her father, Shirley only seemed to grow closer and closer to him and idolize him more and more. Once again, it crossed her mind that there might be "something funny" going on between her husband and daughter—but as she usually did, Katherine pushed the idea away before it became persistent enough to really upset her.

As a result, she failed to recognize just how "close" her little girl and her husband were becoming. Louis would tell her daughter things sometimes, things he said she shouldn't tell Mommy she knew. Of course, at seven she didn't really understand a lot of what her father told her, except that for some reason he didn't think her mother loved him. Not enough, anyway. Not the way Shirley loved him. He told her that he could tell she loved him because she would do the special, secret things with him; he said that doing them made him happy, and that if he was happy, then he would make her happy too.

What Katherine also failed to realize was that Shirley had discovered early in life how to do whatever she had to do in order to survive. Much of that survival, the little girl learned, was dependent on her ability to please her father, no matter what she herself wanted or needed. In order to be his princess, she had to allow him to be king. It was as simple as that.

Eight

It was the summer of 1978, and the car was like a can full of sweaty sardines with the whole family jammed into it, heading for California. They drove day and night, and everybody was getting sick of being cooped up together for so long. Some guy named Mike came along with them to share the driving with Lou, since Katherine had never learned. In the middle of New York City, she didn't need to know how to drive a car.

It was a miserable trip, and as far as nine-year-old Shirley was concerned, a miserable place they ended up in. Her parents insisted that living in California would be easier, that it would give her father the chance to start all over again, and that she would love living in the country. Shirley hated it. She had grown up with the jet-propelled New York pace of life, and rural California seemed like a graveyard by comparison.

"Give it a little time," people would say. "You'll see: things will get better."

But almost as soon as the Wolfs began to settle in, things got worse.

* * *

Fall had arrived in the Sierra foothills, washing the hills and canyons with an unrestrained exuberance of iridescent colors from crimson to tawny copper. On Placerville's Main Street, the svelte and perpetually smiling mannequins staring out from the windows of Combellack's Department Store were already outfitted with down parkas and wool turtleneck sweaters in anticipation of the coming season. And along the Highway 50 corridor which bisects the town on its way east to Lake Tahoe, sports shops packed away the hiking boots and backpacks and tennis rackets in favor of the newest models of downhill skis and snowmobiles.

The air had a decided crispness to it, especially in the mornings and after sundown; in the dilapidated house Louis and Katherine Wolf rented there were times it got downright cold. The wall heaters scattered throughout the house helped, but the one in the bathroom had suddenly gone on the fritz. Louis figured he'd better fix it before winter really set in and somebody ended up freezing to death in the shower.

He was engrossed in trying to free up a stubborn screw that was clinging to the heater's faceplate. Shirley stood silently next to him, holding the rest of the screws in her hand. Her cat, Mr. Peter — no one seemed to know how little Shirley had arrived at that particular name for the animal — rubbed against her faded jeans, purring noisily.

It wasn't long after this that Lou stood up again, brushed his dusty hands against his pants, and announced he needed a part for the unit. Probably just a fuse, he explained to his wife, but he needed

128

her to go to the hardware store across town to pick one up.

Always eager to find a reason to get out of the house for a while without having to drag four kids along, Katherine was happy to oblige her husband. A minute or so later Shirley heard the car's engine cough into life and then the crunch of tires on the driveway. Louis walked into the living room where the boys were milling around.

"You guys get outside and play. NOW." His tone made it perfectly clear this was not a request but an order. L.J. and William started to protest, but then seemed to think better of it and headed out the door, little Brian and Mr. Peter the cat bringing up the rear. Lou closed the door solidly behind them and turned to Shirley.

"Come on, princess," he said, and led her back to the bathroom.

When they were inside he closed the door, then turned and began washing his hands. Shirley watched the water gurgle down the drain as her father talked. He talked about school and the kinds of things they teach you in school, and the kinds of things they can't teach you there. He used words like "special" and "secret" and "love," and kept on talking.

Shirley was a little confused about what this was all about, but for some reason she was beginning to get that half-sick feeling in the pit of her stomach that she got sometimes at night when she heard the heavy footsteps in the hall. Her father threw her a look over his shoulder as he was rinsing the soap off his hands, then went on.

"You know I love you, don't you?"

Shirley nodded mutely, feeling a warm glow suffuse her whole body.

"And because I'm your daddy, I know you love me, too, Shirl. That's why I want us to have this really special thing together. Special and secret and ours alone, okay?" He didn't wait for a reply, but pressed on with his somewhat oblique soliloquy to his nine-year-old daughter.

By now Louis was facing Shirley, his own dark eyes locked onto hers. She felt trapped, like a small animal cornered by a hunter in the forest—only she didn't really understand why she felt that way. After all, this was her daddy. Not somebody she should be afraid of. He took her places and did things with her and smiled at her and said he loved her more than he loved her mommy. She tried desperately to slow the insane pounding of her heart.

Watching his daughter intently, Louis began to weave a romantic verbal tapestry of seduction, explaining how wonderful it would all be and what fun they would have. Several minutes later he stopped and somberly asked Shirley if she was sure she really loved him. As she had done before, Shirley nodded wordlessly.

Good, he replied, because the only real way she could prove absolutely, positively that she loved him would be for her to never tell anyone about what they were about to do. No one at all, ever. Especially not Mommy. Finally, after he was sure she understood it would be their Very Special Secret together, he told her to take her clothes off.

As his daughter slipped out of her little-girl jeans

130

and T-shirt, Louis Wolf reached over and locked the bathroom door. The sick feeling in Shirley's stomach was worse than ever now, but she knew she didn't have a choice but to do what her daddy said to do. It would make him happy, he had said. Maybe that would mean he wouldn't be hateful and cruel anymore. Maybe, if she did very, very well at this other special thing her daddy was telling her about, it might even make him love her more.

Shirley stood naked in the little bathroom, arms hanging passively at her sides and toes curling against the chill of the floor — an anxious child-waif waiting to begin her twisted rite of passage with the human monolith that was her father. Louis began to stroke and fondle her undeveloped breasts, which he insisted were "getting bigger" as she grew toward womanhood. Like a fragile doll he lifted her up and sat her on the countertop next to the medicine cabinet. Tiny beads of sweat appeared on his upper lip as he unzipped his pants. As the siege began Shirley gave a gasp of pain, but something in her father's eyes, now glazed and nearly unseeing, told her she didn't dare cry out.

Suddenly she felt as if she'd been ripped apart, and for a moment the room swam, flooded with brightly colored dots and splashes of light. She gagged as her morning's breakfast surged acidly into her throat, but she managed to fight it down again. Shirley noticed the smile on her daddy's face had twisted into a kind of grimace.

Then all at once the initiation was over. Frightened and bleeding, she sat staring at her father, wondering what was next.

"Okay, get dressed now and get outa here." Louis Wolf's voice had turned hard as steel, and his eyes still had their faraway look. Trying to ignore the now-excruciating pain, Shirley dressed hurriedly and left the frigid bathroom; a few minutes later her father walked out as well, brushing by her without a word or even a smile.

She didn't understand. He was supposed to love her.

One year later, the Wolfs moved into another rented house on Grand View Drive in Placerville. This lower part of Grand View is, however, quite inappropriately named: from the Wolf home the grandest view is of the county Welfare offices across the street, and just below them, polluted Hangtown Creek. While the remainder of the neighborhood is dotted with towering oaks and firs, the only tree gracing the house at the bottom of the hill is a lone, sickly pine that arches across the slightly ramshackle dwelling.

Unlike its neighbors, most of which boast lawns and lush landscaping, the Wolfs' old house sits only a few feet off the paved roadway, bereft of any front yard at all.

Everyone in the Grand View neighborhood was terrified of Louis Wolf. With an M-16 submachine gun strapped across his shoulder, Wolf was an ominous figure as he strode up and down the street searching for his children who had been out playing too long, or who had unknowingly broken some unwritten household commandment. The .357 Magnum revolver tucked into his belt helped insure

132

absolute and total compliance.

Although the Wolf house was relatively isolated from the others in the neighborhood, the picture window of the home directly above had a clear view into the back yard of the house below. Standing in that window one day, young David Carver saw Louis beating Shirley and L.J. with a savage-looking whip that reminded him of an electrical cord. It wasn't to be the last time the young boy witnessed Louis Wolf's violence against his two oldest children.

There was, after all, the matter of the thing out at the back of the house.

Lou and a friend of his, a man named Tom Biggs who the local police had arrested countless times on drug charges, had built it, and when it was finished they put it on the screened back porch.

David Carver couldn't figure it out at first. It was made of blonde wood, probably pine, and had a huge latch that one might use on the door to a dog's pen. Unbeknownst to the young boy, who had only seen a paragraph or two about these contraptions in his American history class and promptly forgotten what he'd read, this "latch-thing," as he called it, had a somewhat illustrious — more aptly, nefarious — ancestry, dating back to sixteenth century England. Its proper name was a pillory, or stocks. The victim's head and wrists were placed between two boards with round cutouts for the arms and neck; then the boards, attached to a wooden framework, were locked together so that escape was impossible.

The Carver boy's puzzlement was short-lived.

One stifling summer day, as he was playing outside with a friend, he saw for himself the reason Louis Wolf had built the thing out on the back porch.

"I heard some noise from the house and looked down there," David later recalled. "I figured it was just the same old stuff—you know, L.J. or Shirley gettin' into it with each other, or maybe getting yelled at or beat on by Mr. Wolf. But then," he said with a shudder, "I saw Mr. Wolf hauling L.J. out onto the porch, and he put him in that thing so he wouldn't get away. Then he pulled down L.J.'s pants and whipped him bare with the electrical cord. I watched him do it. He whipped him and whipped him and whipped him until he got tired of doing it, I guess. L.J. was screaming, trying to get away. But it didn't do any good."

Days later, David said, he saw Shirley in there too, getting beaten by her father in the same way. Over the next several months, until the Wolfs moved to another house in another part of town, the scene was repeated many times.

Louis Wolf's sadism and violence continued to mount as his children grew. Somewhere he managed to acquire a cattle prod, which he seemed to take particular joy in using on them all as evidence of his displeasure. Throwing his children against a wall, or slamming their heads into one, was another favorite. Depending on his mood and the degree of discipline he felt it necessary to impose, his vengeance took on different hues and patterns. Frequently it was like a shotgun blast, spraying anyone within a certain radius with indiscriminate fire;

other times, it was more like a cannon shot directed at a single target.

One of Louis's favorite ways of instilling discipline and reinforcing her subjugation was to force Shirley to stand with arms outstretched, holding an empty glass five-gallon bottled water container, for a quarter of an hour or more. When her arms and shoulder muscles began to cramp and the bottle started to droop below its initial parallel position, Wolf would deliver one or two burning blows to the tender spot at the back of his daughter's knees with his black wooden cane.

Even when he wasn't punishing her, even when everything seemed just fine and they were all having fun together, his humor could take on a brutal twist.

It was a beautiful, sunny day, and everyone was excited about the new motorless go-cart the family had acquired. The precipitous Grand View hill was a perfect spot for Shirley to test out her fearlessness and prove herself to her father. But Louis had another idea: why not, he suggested, tie the cart to the back of the station wagon and let me pull you down the hill? Talk about goin' fast . . . your eyes'll be buggin' outa your head!

While that wasn't exactly what Shirley had in mind, she wasn't about to subject herself to the humiliation of telling her father she was a little bit afraid. She would make him proud of her by going along with his suggestion, and keeping a smile on her face the whole time. Everything was fine at first, with the warm wind whipping through her hair and the acceleration tugging at the corners of her eyes like it did when she rode the roller coaster at the fair. Then suddenly she felt one side of the cart begin to lift off the pavement. Instantaneously, she knew it was going to tip over, and there was absolutely nothing she could do to stop it. Shame began to burn her face even before her arm touched the black roadway beneath her.

Inside the car, Katherine saw her daughter, still holding tight to the handlebars of the go-cart, spilling onto the street. She screamed at her husband to stop, that the cart had toppled over and Shirley was being dragged, but it was several seconds before Louis even touched the brake pedal. Finally Shirley let go, and rolled end-over-end down the hill for several yards before coming to rest in the middle of Grand View. It felt like hours before they came to pick her up; luckily, the street was unusually devoid of passing cars, any one of which could have accidentally hit the motionless child lying in the road. When all was said and done, Shirley ended up with a compound fracture of her arm, and a gnawing sense that her father might have intentionally ignored Katherine's warning, simply out of the desire to punish his daughter for her failure.

Imperfection was one thing Louis Wolf did not tolerate.

Louis's intentional acts of cruelty often extended to animals—particularly those animals with which Shirley had established a special bond. Her cat, Mr. Peter, her special friend for years, was one of those creatures. The two of them presented a curious and humorous sight, marching down the street together

136

like a two-member army contingent, Shirley leading the charge with her head held high and shoulders back, and Mr. Peter bringing up the rear, his fluffy gray tail held aloft like a flag. Invariably, when you saw Shirley you saw Mr. Peter: on the way to school (Shirley trying in vain to shoo her pet back home), down at the creek, climbing a tree, or just lazing in the shade of an oak tree in the midst of a summer heat wave.

One day, however, it all came to an end. Her mother's dog had picked up a bad case of worms, and Louis was anything but happy. It was Mr. Peter's fault, he declared, because the dog had gotten into the cat's litter box and picked up worms from the feces. His solution was simple and immediate: in front of his pleading, crying daughter, he grabbed Mr. Peter from her arms and took him away to be killed. Shirley still has dreams of her beloved pet, holding fast with his claws to her blouse and mewing forlornly, while her father wrestles him out of her arms and disappears.

The young girl also became a frequent if unwilling witness to her father's pitiless slaughter of other animals. The vision of him looming above one of their quivering, terrified rabbits with a hammer in his hand is one Shirley can never erase from her mind. The family raised the animals for food, and the senior Wolf was naturally designated as the one to slaughter them when the time came. But rather than making the kill cleanly and humanely, Wolf crushed the animal's head with several methodical blows from his hammer or a rock, then unemotionally watched for a minute or more as the mortally injured creature vomited and convulsed and finally died.

Shirley's beatings continued unabated — although they seemed to take on a new flavor with each passing year. Sometimes he would barely leave a mark on her; at other times she found herself bleeding and with massive bruises all over her body after his attacks, which seemed to come and go with little or no reason or provocation. One day a classmate spotted a huge, spreading bruise in the middle of Shirley's back while they were dressing for gym class. When asked what happened, she replied flatly, "My father hit me."

Yet Louis Wolf wasn't the only one venting his rage at his daughter and the other children. On the surface, Katherine Wolf gave every impression of powerlessness and weakness. She was a virtual captive of her husband, most of the time able to do things and see people only with his consent, which was seldom given. At the same time, he had installed himself as the sole potentate in the household, undermining his wife's authority and competence at every turn. "They don't listen to nobody but me," Louis had boasted. "And they don't rely on nobody but me, either. In fact," he would add maliciously, "I even fix most of the meals around here, 'cause she's such a lousy cook and they hate her cookin'."

Looking inward, Katherine must have realized only too well that the powerlessness she had known all her life, and now the powerlessness she felt living under the dominion and control of her husband, extended to her relationships with her children as well. Infuriated with this impotence, Katherine lashed out uncontrollably against those children with a violence that sometimes equalled that of her husband. Her tongue had an edge like a carving knife, and she was more than capable of letting any of the four of them feel the savage back of her hand across their mouths or the backs of their heads. When her fury was great enough, she used a ceramic trivet—a Christmas gift handmade by Shirley for her parents—as an instrument of punishment and retribution, until the day it broke during a beating. Once, Shirley remembers, her mother rammed her brother's head into the ground because of something he said or did that set her off; another time, Shirley made the mistake of turning her back on her father during an argument, and her mother grabbed a butcher knife out of the kitchen drawer and screamed, "Don't you *ever* turn your back on your father!"

Shirley says her mother even threatened to kill her if she ever found out her daughter had been "doing things" with her father that only Katherine should have been doing. Since Shirley had never told anyone about the incest, she assumed that what Katherine meant was that her father shouldn't be taking her places where her mother should have been going. Like the times he would tell his wife that he was just going "out" with Shirley—her mom, the girl figured, was pissed because she probably thought they were just going someplace together to have fun or eat dinner or whatever.

But Shirley knew what she didn't think her

mother knew, and that was that those outings were anything but fun and games. What they were, according to Shirley, were drug deals. Louis would leave Shirley in the van with a .38 pistol and instructions to shoot anyone who ventured near, while he went off to make a sale or a drug pickup. When one day she protested and questioned why he was dealing drugs, his answer was simple. "You want new clothes, don't you? You want to go roller-skating, don't you?" Just like everything else, it was her fault that her father did the things he did. And, he would add with that odd smile, it was simply because he loved her.

Experienced far beyond her years with the corrupt underbelly of life, by now Shirley was also experiencing more than beatings and verbal abuse from her parents. After the incident in the bathroom when she was nine, Louis Wolf had sex with Shirley more and more often. He would choose a time when they were alone in the house, or as he had done before, he would send his wife on an errand and his sons outside to play. There were other times when, with Katherine gone for the day, Louis would take his sons to school and leave Shirley at home with strict instructions to stay there until he returned. She knew very well what would happen when he got back.

But sometimes it was more than just sex Louis wanted. Sometimes he would brush her hair and tell her he was going to make her all pretty for him, then he'd tell her to take her clothes off. By now Shirley had learned to submit — silently and unquestioningly—to anything her father asked. Besides, she knew what he wanted and what he was going to do. At the same time, she knew what was expected of her. While he focused and fiddled with the elaborate camera in his hand, he instructed his naked daughter in how she should pose. Where she should touch. What she should do with her legs, with her lips, with the things he gave her. She was never sure what he did with the pictures—he never told her—but years later after she saw her father's collection of child pornography magazines, she suspected he might have been sending her pictures off to these publishers. Louis Wolf's very own princess, in glossy black-and-white for all the world to see.

Occasionally, Katherine flew back to New York to visit her family there. She never understood why Shirley got so upset when she had to leave. As Katherine reasoned it, Shirley was too old to need her mother there with her all the time now anyway.

But Katherine's vacation days were anything but a vacation for Shirley. On top of being stuck with the housework, there were days on end when Louis prohibited his daughter from going to school so she could be there for him.

"I really need you to stay home and help me today, princess," he would say, a smile curling the corners of his mouth. "I have something for you to do."

The only good part was afterward, when he bought her a new dress or shoes or maybe even some makeup. The next day she would show up at school dressed to the teeth, in stark contrast to her regular little-match-girl look. Sometimes the clothes, although new, made Shirley even more of a target for her schoolmates' derision than her regular outfits. Sauntering onto the school yard in the morning dressed, as one teacher put it, "like a two-bit hooker" in some tight-fitting, low-cut dress or blouse that was totally inappropriate for her age, the other kids would hiss and sneer their taunts all day.

No matter, because the clothes made Shirley feel special. They were her proof that her daddy really did love her, that she was his princess.

But there were times the price she had to pay to be his princess was much higher than she expected. Sometimes what really happened turned out to be a lot more, and a lot worse, than what had ever happened before.

One morning while her mother was in New York, Shirley woke up sick to her stomach. At first she didn't say anything, fearful of what would happen if she stayed home alone with her father; but as soon as she sat down at the breakfast table she knew she couldn't keep up the act of feeling fine. Louis insisted she get back into bed, gathered the boys into the van, and headed for school.

She was in a half-asleep twilight when she heard the sound of her doorknob turning. *No, please,* she thought, *not today.* But no amount of pleading, silent or aloud, could keep Louis Wolf from his daughter's bed when he wanted to be there. Smiling, he walked over to her and put his hand on her forehead.

"How ya feeling, princess? Better?"

"A little, I guess." It was a lie, but then, Shirley figured it wouldn't make any difference either way.

Either way he would do whatever he wanted with her.

When he looked down at her, he had that look on his face: the one she'd come to know so well over the years, the one that reminded her in a language stronger than words that he needed her, desired her, loved her. A whispered voice inside her kept trying to say that something was wrong, but she could usually silence it by saying over and over again to herself that she was loved, that she was her father's most precious possession. That knowledge was worth whatever price she had to pay.

Standing at the foot of the bed, her father undressed and pulled back the sheets. As it usually was, the sex was quick and, for Shirley by now, fairly painless. The best part was when it was over and he left her alone for the day. It was about the only time she allowed herself to relax.

But this particular day things were different. After he'd finished with her, he turned over and fell asleep. Shirley felt even sicker than she had before, and the sticky pool beneath her seemed worse than usual; but because he hadn't left her bed she was afraid to move, to get up and clean herself off.

She lay there for some time, wondering what to do, when Louis rolled over and opened his eyes. Unbelievably, he reached for her again in renewed desire.

"No, Daddy, please . . ."

But her father ignored her whimpering cry, pushing her head down between his legs and letting out a moan of pleasure. Then for the second time that day he raped his ten-year-old daughter, and calmly got dressed and left her with her thoughts.

Shirley hated what her father did to her, and there were times she hated him, too, for doing it. But it was all so confusing: he said that if she didn't do it, it would mean she didn't love him—and worse, that he wouldn't love her. She was convinced that if she ever lost his love, if he ever decided he didn't love her after all, then she would simply die. The only way to prove to him that she would never betray that love was to do what he wanted. Soberly, Shirley also realized that it was also the only way to defuse his deadly anger—and if it kept everybody safe for a while, plus if she could get a little something like a new dress or a trinket out of it once in a while, then maybe it was worth it. Whether it was or not, she thought, it was simply her lot in life.

Dennis Price looked at the lanky, dark-eyed girl sitting in the back of the fifth-grade class he taught at Placerville's Sierra School and recalled what he'd been told about her. It had been months before, right when school started in early September, and one of the fourth-grade teachers pulled him aside. "This kid," the woman said soberly, "is really going to be something else." She spoke with a certain degree of wisdom, as she'd been Shirley Wolf's teacher the previous year. At the time Dennis wondered exactly what that "something else" was.

He'd heard of Shirley, of course—everyone in school had. The ten-year-old had managed to establish a real reputation for herself in the brief time she'd been at Sierra School, even though most of the teachers were pretty supportive and concerned in talking about her. It seemed that everyone knew something was wrong, even though they couldn't put a name to it.

Part of it was probably her family — her father, really — but even that was tough to get a handle on. He'd heard about Mr. Wolf wandering around town with a .357 Magnum on his hip, how he'd tell people he was affiliated with the Mafia in New York. Then, too, there was the matter of his "disability" from that accident he'd had a few years before. Sometimes you saw him in a wheelchair and he'd say he was a paraplegic, then the next time he'd be up and walking with only a cane. Someone told him not too long ago that they'd even seen Wolf out dancing.

Now, months after his first encounter with her, Dennis Price was sure something was happening to Shirley, that something was very wrong. When one kid made all the other kids sick, when they all talked about her behind her back and virtually every one of them openly admitted they hated her, there had to be a serious problem.

Besides the fact that she dressed like a street urchin, most of the time she was just plain dirty. He remembered one day when some of Shirley's peers had been particularly brutal.

"Oh, PEEEE-U! Shirley Wolf stinks!" The small band of fifth-graders whooped hilariously at the comment by one of their classmates, who held her nose in mock disgust as the object of her derision walked by.

Shirley hesitated for a split second, then threw back her shoulders and marched on, her tan face

145

flushed with anger and shame.

Earlier that day they had square dancing in gym, and none of the kids would touch her. The problem was, Dennis realized, Shirley did stink. Perhaps "stink" was too strong a word—but much of the time, she had an indescribable, slightly rancid odor about her. Everyone who spent any time around her noticed it: her schoolmates, of course, the other teachers, even the police department's Juvenile Diversion Officer Bob Ewing who got called in to calm the waters whenever Shirley was in trouble. And increasingly, Shirley was in trouble a lot. Nothing all that serious, really—just enough to shake things up a little and call some attention to herself.

Her problems almost always revolved around her anger and her inability to control it. The previous school year she was involved in five separate incidents at school in a three-week period, from arguing in the cafeteria to slapping a classmate in the face to being so out of control during a game of dodgeball that ultimately, the police were called. Already this year she had gotten herself in some kind of fight with a kid named Tony, and in the process knocked him over a stone wall they'd been sitting on and broke the poor kid's arm. That day, just like the dozens of times before, Louis Wolf came marching onto campus like a Nazi storm trooper, demanding to talk to somebody about why all these people were picking on his little girl. And just like every other time when they saw him coming, the little knots of kids and teachers gathered on the playground for recess or gym would part like the Red Sea. No one in their right mind wanted to be anywhere near Lou Wolf when he was at that kind of explosive level. Dealing with Shirley's anger and frustration was one thing; dealing with her father's was something else altogether.

Shirley in the classroom was no better.

Sometimes Shirley shouted at the top of her lungs at someone or something outside the window. Thirty-two faces would turn toward her, disgusted at the display and irritated at her for once again disturbing the flow of the class. She seemed to have no idea at all that she'd done anything out of line, or that the other members of the class were beginning to despise her for the constant disruptions.

Yet despite all the problems she caused with the other kids—and despite the emotional agony she must have been in as a result of all the abuse she took from them, Shirley never once openly confronted her teacher or showed even a hint of discourtesy. She was so damned anxious to please all the time, always smiling, wanting to help, and yet somehow always missing the mark. Time after time she came up to him during and after class to ask, "Mr. Price, did I do this right?" or "Mr. Price, what can I do better?" There was an urgency in her voice that bordered on desperation.

"In all that time," Price said years later, "I don't recall her ever being with somebody, sitting with somebody. I can't think of one friend she had."

Shirley Wolf was an outcast, and she knew it.

Nine

In March of 1981, when Shirley was in her last quarter of the sixth grade at the Gold Trail School just outside of Placerville, Tina Beaulieu came into her life. Tina was in high school, a tall, thin, somewhat inward girl with hair the color of late-summer wheat that framed her angular face. Despite her reserved nature, Tina genuinely liked people—especially kids. So when she heard about the Cross-Age program that New Morning Youth and Family Services was running, she decided to take the training.

The Cross-Age program was built on the Big Brother-Big Sister model, except that it was designed to match up older kids—kids in high school or junior college, usually—with younger, elementary or junior high kids who were having trouble at school or at home. The older student would act as a special friend to his or her younger "match," doing things with them, helping with schoolwork if that was what they needed, just being there to talk with. Kids needing help could be referred into the program by either their school or their parents, or both.

No one remembers how Shirley Wolf ended up

there. More than likely it was one of her teachers at school who, like Dennis Price, saw and heard Shirley's unspoken pleas for help and decided to do something about them. Not that anyone expected Cross-Age to be able to work miracles in Shirley's life, but it had seemed worth a try. At least it would be something positive in the kid's life.

When Tina Beaulieu got the news that she was going to be matched up with Shirley Wolf, she didn't think much of it. She didn't know anything about Shirley except for what the younger girl wrote on her application for the program: that her main interests were "fishing, baseball, boys, swimming, new things, studying, and being outgoing." It all seemed pretty normal for a kid that was almost twelve years old.

From the beginning, Tina liked Shirley. In the twice-weekly group meetings where the counselors in the Cross-Age program talked about how things were going between themselves and their "matches," Tina told the others that Shirley was considerate and friendly, and that she seemed to have a lot going for her. Lots of dreams, goals, ambitions, lots of plans for what she wanted (and didn't want) for her future. She did seem awfully mature for her age, Tina commented, but with a funny kind of dependency at the same time. Like she always wanted—needed—to be *with* you, to be a part of whatever you were doing, all the time.

And then there was Shirley's father. The first time Tina saw him was also the last time. The weather was unseasonably warm for springtime, and she'd asked Shirley if she wanted to go swimming. As usual, Shirley seemed almost desperately enthusiastic about the outing, as if she simply couldn't wait to get out of the house and be with her special friend.

When Tina arrived that afternoon to pick Shirley up, the younger girl demanded she come into the house and meet her parents. Tina had spoken with Mr. Wolf on the telephone when she was first matched with Shirley, and recalled with some discomfort how she felt like she was being given the third degree about who she was, where she came from, what kinds of things was she going to be doing with Shirley, where they would go, and on and on. She also remembered him cautioning her about his daughter: don't forget, he said, that Shirley has an extremely overactive imagination. It seemed an odd thing for a father to say.

Tina walked in the house, dimly aware of an odor of animals and untended litter-boxes. Katherine Wolf stood near the doorway, a small, dark-haired figure in slightly threadbare denim jeans, nervously smoking a cigarette. After nodding a brief and perfunctory hello, she disappeared down the hallway. Shirley clasped Tina's hand and pulled her into the living room, where a bulky, dark-haired man sat in a wheelchair, also smoking.

"Tina, this is my dad. Dad, this is Tina." Shirley smiled expectantly at her father.

"Good. Okay, Shirl—I want you to go outside now so's I can talk with Tina."

"But Da . . ."

"NOW!" His voice thundered in the little room. Tina saw Shirley cower slightly—she herself had jumped what felt like halfway to the ceiling when Mr. Wolf shouted. Shirley slunk out the front door without another word.

"Sit down, Tina." It was an order, not a request.

Obediently Tina perched on the edge of the chair across from where Louis Wolf sat, his bulk nearly filling the wheelchair. He lit another cigarette and began asking the teenager questions. Some of them were the same questions she'd already answered that day on the phone. At one point Tina heard the front door open and turned to see Shirley's head poking in.

"Get out of here!" Again, the sudden intensity of his voice made Tina jump. When she turned again to look, the door was closed and Shirley was nowhere to be seen.

"You know, Tina, I really hope this program can help my little girl. See, she has some problems, and we really hope this thing's gonna be just what she needs to straighten herself out."

"She seems like a really good kid, from what I can tell, Mr. Wolf. I like her a lot. . . ."

Aware of the man's jet-black eyes boring into her, she was beginning to feel distinctly uncomfortable. Tina felt his gaze begin a slow, languid sweep down her body and back upward again. She felt naked, exposed, vulnerable.

"You're probably wondering why I'm in this chair," he said, exhaling softly and crushing out his cigarette in the near-overflowing ashtray. Silver

151

sprinkles of ash littered the tabletop; a cigarette butt lay on the carpet near the table leg.

He wheeled himself a little closer to Tina and began to tell her the story of his accident and the aftermath. How he was always in pain, how he wasn't the man he used to be, how tough things had been for him and all of them.

Tina was getting more and more uncomfortable.

Then suddenly the room was silent, and Tina realized the man had finished his story. Seizing the opportunity, she took a deep breath and stood up.

"Well, it's been nice to meet you, Mr. Wolf." Tina bobbed her head and gave a little smile. His eyes wandered down her body again. "I guess me and Shirley'd better get going or it'll be too late to swim." She felt like making a fifty-yard dash to the front door, but restrained herself.

She waited for him to say something—good-bye, or have a good time, or nice to meet you, or something—but all he did was reach for another cigarette.

" 'Bye." Tina turned and scurried out the door, overcome with relief.

The next day when Tina went to New Morning for the group meeting, one of the staff members called her aside.

"Tina, you spent yesterday afternoon with Shirley, right?"

Tina nodded.

"Well, Mr. Wolf called us right after you left the house to talk about you."

Tina felt her heart freeze for an instant. "About

152

me? What did he want to talk about me for?" She had a bad feeling about this.

The staff counselor looked a little uncomfortable. "Well, he said that you . . . well, that you were dressed very provocatively. He said you had on very short shorts, and that you were being seductive with him, letting him see things he shouldn't see and that he got a hard-on because of it."

Tina felt like someone had knocked all the air out of her. Her pale face began to flush with embarrassment and anger.

Fortunately, she didn't have to explain that none of it was the truth, that her shorts hadn't been that short or that she hadn't done anything at all to lead Louis Wolf on or give him ideas. No one at New Morning believed what Shirley's father had said about Tina, but they felt it was only fair to let her know—if only so she'd know to give the man a wide berth in the future.

Ultimately, Tina Beaulieu only stayed matched with Shirley for three months. Summer arrived and things slowed down, and then Shirley just dropped out of the program. But during those months, Tina found herself becoming increasingly fond of the younger girl. She seemed so frail in some ways, so needy for attention and affection, that it really tugged at Tina's heart.

Tina recalled one day when she and Shirley were sitting under a big oak tree, just talking and having a Pepsi together. The conversation turned to friendship, and Shirley's face seemed to darken. After a few seconds, she spoke softly, a hurt and wondering tone in her voice.

"I guess I don't really have any friends. I try and be nice, I try and make them like me, but it never seems to work. Nobody really wants to be my friend."

Tina's sister Harriet was married to Don Schaeffer, a seventh-grade math teacher at the tiny, rural Gold Trail School. That next year, as Don surveyed the roll call list of students assigned to his class, his eyes paused at the name, "Shirley Katherine Wolf."

Don knew more than a little about the Wolf family—partly because it was a small school and the teaching staff invariably talked among themselves about the kids, and partly because in the past he had occasionally stepped in as acting school principal when the regular principal was out of town. More than once he'd gone face-to-face with Louis Wolf after Shirley was involved in a fight or disruption. The previous year the man even managed to interrupt a class, looking for the girl who had been in an argument with Shirley the day before. He was going to settle the issue with the girl himself, he had said.

Finally, the order went out from the administration that anytime one of the teachers or staff saw Louis Wolf on campus, they were to call the principal's office right away. Wolf was known to carry a gun—in fact, he made that point quite clear during those angry conferences with school administrators—and it was only common sense to err on the side of caution.

154

The teacher remembered once when Shirley's father was on campus, in the office with his daughter over some minor altercation; after the events were described, he glared at the girl and said, "When we get home I'm gonna pull your pants down and give you a real whipping." Don recalled saying something about Shirley being a little old for that; after all, she was twelve years old. Wolf threw him a murderous look, then simply ignored him.

By this time, Shirley had become even more alienated from her classmates. Fights, both physical and verbal, were even more common, although they weren't usually bad enough to suspend her or anyone else from school or cause any lasting problems. The pattern was almost always the same: Shirley tried to make friends with someone, tried to fit into a group of kids, only to be rejected; in response, she became aggressive and angry, turning what must have been immense pain into bitter hostility toward her tormenters. Which, of course, only served to further fan the flames of their distaste.

Don remembered the day one of his fellow teachers told him about intercepting a note from Shirley in class. It read: *Will you be my friend? Check the box, yes or no.* The "no" box had an ugly, black check mark in it.

Maybe if Shirley had been in a larger school district, perhaps in a city, she'd have been able to get lost, to find one or two friends and just survive. But at Gold Trail there were only 122 students in the entire school; in that kind of environment, if you're not accepted, you stick out like a sore thumb. And Shirley Wolf was clearly not accepted.

Adding fuel to the already roaring fire was the fact that by this time, Shirley was showing a marked interest in boys. This was more than just the normal boy-girl fascination that accompanies puberty. With Shirley, it was more like a fanatical obsession. Time after time she would spot a boy she felt attracted to, try to make overtures in her own awkward, excessive way, and then attach herself to him "like a leech you couldn't shake off," one boy recalled. It frequently took weeks of unreturned phone calls, unopened letters, and blatant verbal rejections before Shirley gave up or got angry and began obsessing about someone else.

Even acts of outright cruelty didn't affect her pursuit; she seemed just as oblivious to the scorn and derision of the boys she tried to entice, as she was to the rebuffs of the girls with whom she tried to establish friendships. Of course, that was just how it looked to the outside world. Shirley knew well how to hide her real feelings, how to cover up the soft and wounded places with a thick crust of numbness and anger just so she could survive.

It was a vicious and seemingly never-ending cycle. In her desperate search for recognition, for some level of validation of herself as a person, Shirley engendered only antagonism from her peers. By engulfing them with her overpowering need for closeness and love, she found only estrangement. She was an alien in her own land, a mutant foundling who was slowly losing all hope of ever finding her place in the world.

More and more people in the community were becoming aware of just how bad things were in the Wolf household, but there was nothing concrete enough to take any action on. Or perhaps most townspeople were simply too terrified of Louis Wolf to come forward and tell the authorities what they knew or suspected. This was, after all, in the years when child abuse — particularly incest and sexual abuse — was kept under a dark shroud of shame and secrecy, away from public discussion or even awareness. It was also just before the state law took effect requiring people like teachers and counselors to report their suspicions of abuse to the authorities.

Besides, many people in small towns like Placerville pretty much believed that whatever happened in a person's family was their own business — even if most folks in town knew the most minute details of that business.

At the heart of the matter was that no one in the Wolf family would talk about what might have been going on. Even if Shirley or L.J. or William or little Brian talked to other kids . . . and even if those kids happened to talk to someone like a parent or a teacher . . . the fact remained there was no proof. No testimony from anyone in the family, no incontrovertible evidence that any laws had been broken or anyone was in danger.

But there was talk from others in town. . . .

Like how strange it was, this paralysis of Louis Wolf's. It seemed to come and go almost at will. When he visited the Social Security and Welfare departments to get assistance, he was wheelchair-bound. He also wheeled himself into the offices of a local doctor—a man with a somewhat shady reputation for, among other things, freely handing out medications to his patients—and asked him to write a letter to the state Department of Rehabilitation, saying he needed a special van with a wheelchair lift. And yet two or three days later, he would be spotted at a local skating rink with his children, somehow making those helpless legs move him around the rink on skates. By the next week, he might be wearing braces and using metal crutches to maneuver through the streets of town.

Then there was speculation about his drug usage, and whether it extended outside the bounds of his prescription medication. On more than one occasion he passed along information about illegal drug activities to Placerville and El Dorado County law enforcement—but strangely, even though once in a while the information was good, more often than not officers would arrive to find the buy had been called off or the stash had been flushed down the toilet or something else had gone askew to kill the bust. After a few times it became clear that nearly every time Lou Wolf came in with a hot tip on some drug deal, the department ended up with empty hands and no case. Privately, some officers figured Wolf was playing both ends against the middle: informing on the drug dealer to the cops, but before the deal or buy could go down, running to the dealer to say he'd gotten word the cops were on their way to make a bust. As long as the system worked, he could ingratiate himself with both the police and the dealers, staying one step ahead of both. Add to that Wolf's long-standing friendship with known drug offender Tom Biggs—not an indictment in and of itself, but taken with everything else, it raised some huge question marks. Naturally, Shirley never breathed a word of what she knew to be her father's considerable involvement in the town's drug scene.

Even the school children talked about the Wolfs, sharing stories, observations and occasional shudders but seldom with any adults. Like David Carver, who witnessed Shirley and L.J. being beaten in Louis Wolf's homemade pillory, other children remembered hearing and seeing other things.

One hot summer day a young boy named Billy and his friend Shane recall building a fort in an empty lot outside of town, when Lou Wolf drove up to the house next door. This time it was L.J. in the van with his father, not Shirley. After Louis disappeared inside the house, L.J. got out of the car and wandered over to where the two boys were playing; looking up, Shane saw that L.J.'s head was covered with nothing but brown stubble. He cocked his head in puzzlement and asked the boy what had happened.

Defiantly at first, L.J. responded with the story

of how his father frequently punished him and his brother by shaving their heads. "My dad, he gets pretty mad sometimes," he'd said. "He does all kinds a' stuff . . . like with our hair . . . and other stuff, too. When my sister gets in trouble, he does other stuff."

The two boys waited for him to continue.

"When my sister does something bad, my dad does . . . well, he does sex stuff with her."

They remember that he was about to elaborate, when loud voices from the house next door and the sudden appearance of Louis Wolf in the doorway interrupted the conversation. L.J. quickly scurried back to the van and clambered inside; moments later, his father gunned the engine and roared off down the street.

The two boys went back to building their fort until it was time to head home for dinner. They said nothing more to each other, nor to their parents, about the strange conversation they'd had that day with Shirley Wolf's younger brother.

By the third quarter of her seventh-grade year, Shirley's family moved again, and once more she was faced with changing schools. Placerville's Markham Intermediate School was the third school she'd been to since leaving New York four years before — and for someone like Shirley Wolf, someone who found it nearly impossible to make a place for herself among her peers even after she'd been around for a while, starting over at a new school was excruciating. The feeling of being a despised outsider was stronger than ever.

But for what may have been the first time in her life, something good happened at this new school.

Early in the year, Shirley unknowingly secured an ally at Markham in the person of David Baker, the school principal. Baker, a slim, wiry man in his early forties with a ready smile and piercingly clear blue eyes that somehow conveyed immense warmth despite their icy hue, came to know Shirley exceptionally well over the months she was at Markham. Almost from her first day at school, he spotted the cleft between his newest student and her classmates, and watched as she reacted to their boycott with belligerent hostility. He watched as, time after time, she attached herself to someone in a desperate bid for friendship, but lacking the skills for cultivating and maintaining a relationship, would soon alienate herself from them. And he watched as she continued the slow, inexorable decline that had dominated most of her young life.

But unlike many others in Shirley Wolf's world, David Baker did more than stand on the sidelines and watch. He decided to try shaking her loose from the patterns and habits that were poisoning her. In the beginning he made it a point to meet her on her way to class in the morning, just to check in and say hello. Gradually, he began to expand his talks with her.

He would talk to her about how the best way to deal with difficult situations with her classmates was to simply do nothing — say nothing, do nothing, just walk away.

He recalled how Shirley would nod and smile that vacant smile, and later that afternoon he would hear about how she'd gotten into it with some other kid over some stupid insult thrown her way. But he didn't give up trying to reach her. As time went on, Baker met with Shirley more and more often throughout the school day, eventually getting to the point of doing some minor role-playing with her about situations she might encounter. Very little of it, however, did any good.

Mr. Baker realized that Shirley's fame as an easy mark—she was constantly putting herself in situations where she could be used and abused—was the reflection of a much more deep-rooted problem. Shirley Wolf was a victim. A very good victim. Even all her sound and fury—all the mouthy retorts and threats she constantly threw back at her adolescent tormenters—was a part of that role.

In mid-February of 1982, soon after the beginning of Shirley's third quarter of seventh grade, the young girl's acid temper finally exploded in a bitter fistfight with another girl, resulting in a two-day suspension from school. Less than two weeks later, Shirley started her day by shoving another student down at recess, then pushed a boy around during shop, and was finally caught trying to forge her lunch ticket; those actions cost her a seven-day suspension. The next month she erupted for no apparent reason and began striking at an unsuspecting boy in class, to the point where he

162

had to hold her arms to keep her from smashing his face — and once more she was suspended from school. Within ten days she was at it again, this time stealing a handful of candy bars from the school snack bar.

Every time she got caught and hauled into the principal's office to explain herself, her pattern was the same: whether the offense was slugging a classmate in the nose or cheating on a test or snitching something from the cafeteria, Shirley reacted by denying she had anything to do with the incident. It usually took several minutes of slow, methodical chipping away at the edges of the lie before it crumbled enough for her to be forced to admit it; and invariably, once the truth was out she ardently pledged that she would never, *ever* again do anything like she had done, and that in the future she would try even harder to do better.

But regardless of how many times Baker had to levy some form of punishment against the girl, the young principal refused to give up on Shirley. Along with her teachers, he was impressed with the young girl's creative abilities with art, her powers of imagination, her ability to express her thoughts on paper when she was in the mood. She had a remarkable vocabulary, especially in light of her inability or unwillingness to apply herself in class. And by and large, she was a fairly quick learner, if you could once get her attention and keep her focused for more than a few minutes. Shirley Wolf, he was sure, had the potential of being a better-than-average student.

So day after day the young principal continued

to meet with Shirley, trying to build her self-confidence, trying to help her learn new ways of coping, of dealing with rejection and loneliness, of handling the craziness of her personal life. Part of that craziness, Baker knew, was Shirley's family. More specifically, her father.

Baker recalled one of their first encounters, when Wolf brought his eldest son from his first marriage into the principal's office the first day of school. The boy had been living in a large city in Ohio with his mother, and for some reason she'd sent the kid out to California to live with his father. So there they sat, father and son, one dark and one fair, but otherwise carbon copies of each other even down to the vocal inflections, talking about how the boy had been expelled from school for breaking his teacher's fingers. Both of them smiled as they told the story. Baker wasn't the least bit disappointed when, after a few weeks and some sort of blowup with his father, the boy went back to his home in Ohio.

As Shirley's behavior at school grew worse, Louis Wolf was reentering David Baker's life. Baker became involved in more and more frequent convulsive telephone conversations with Wolf over Shirley, during which he would explode without warning from calm discussion into raging fury, hurling threats and insults and accusations of malfeasance against the principal until Baker had no option but to hang up just to halt the fusillade. Usually, all he had to do was give it five or ten minutes, then call Mr. Wolf back; in that time, the man had cooled down and regained enough composure to listen to what Mr. Baker had to say, and discuss what should be done about his daughter.

It was different when Baker could talk with Mrs. Wolf, alone or just with her and Shirley. Katherine always seemed to have a better understanding that Shirley had some real problems, and she seemed much better equipped to deal with helping her daughter understand the effects of her actions. The problem was, it was extremely rare that he would even get to talk with Shirley's mother, much less meet with her, without her husband present. It was as if Wolf didn't want his wife to have the opportunity to say anything without him being present to censor it or rationalize it or reinterpret it. His control of her, and of the entire family, seemed absolute.

That control was maintained, Baker soon realized, by Louis Wolf's intricate, systematic emotional and physical persecution of those who were in his domain. More often than not, his primary targets were his children. Like the neighborhood bully, Wolf's terrorist tactics worked best on those weaker and smaller than himself whom he had already intimidated into submission. And like the neighborhood bully, Wolf often boasted about his conquests. More than once he told Baker about his belief in the effectiveness of tough physical punishment, and how he acted on that belief with his own children, asserting his rights as a father to back up his position.

Even the frequent intervention of Children's Protective Services didn't make any difference. Nor did the presence of the city police's Juvenile Diversion Officer, Bob Ewing, who often came onto campus or drove out to the Wolf house in response to Shirley's growing lack of control, and in the hopes of establishing some measure of trust with the girl. No matter who it was, every time someone went to talk with Shirley or L.J. or William or Brian about a report or suspicion of abuse, they came back with an empty notebook. No one would talk at all, admit that anything at all out of the ordinary was going on. They were like a family of sphinxes: mute, immovable, unfathomable.

David Baker's concerns about Shirley grew as she became a fixture around Markham. The young principal was one of the founding members of the county's first Child Abuse Council and had more than a passing familiarity with the signs and signals of abuse. As time went on, Shirley was exhibiting more and more of them—and yet without an eyewitness or victim's accusation, without some sort of proof, virtually nothing could be done. No matter how much Baker questioned Shirley's frequent absences from school, especially when he knew her mother was out of town, it wasn't enough. It wasn't enough that after these absences Shirley often came back onto campus heavily made up and dressed to kill in some new and usually very sexy outfit. It wasn't enough that Lou Wolf strutted into the principal's office one day to brag about how his daughter started her period and was beginning to develop into a woman. And it wasn't even enough when, during the last month of her seventh-grade school year, he came in again to say that he—not he and Katherine, but he alone—was putting Shirley on birth control pills because he thought she was sexually active.

David Baker knew full well you can't snatch a kid out of her home just because you *think* something rotten is going on. The best you can do is try and build up her trust in you, make yourself a "safe space" in her life, and hope that maybe one day she'll tell you at least some little piece of the truth.

Just after the first day of eighth-grade classes, a small group of girls asked Shirley to come and sit with them at lunch. Most of them—like Christi and Christine and Jill—Shirley had known for years, ever since she had first come to Placerville. She knew them, but she'd never had much to do with them, or they with her, except to say an occasional "hi" in the halls or around town. She never could figure out why they sought her out this time, but she wasn't about to question her luck.

Some in the group, sensitized by their own experiences to the pain of others, saw Shirley's isolation and need for friendship; as they would for a stray and injured animal, they took pity on her and took her in. Some were drawn to her facade of aggressiveness, and the counterfeit stories she told of life on the mean streets of Brooklyn. Almost all of them sensed that, despite her status as social pariah, Shirley Wolf could be an asset to the group in terms of power. They knew that if it came time for a fight, Shirley was tough enough to slug it out with the best of them. And at some unspoken level, they understood that in offering her their friendship, they were buying Shirley's unquestioned loyalty. She would stand up against anyone for them if they asked her to.

There was no question that Shirley Wolf was still an outcast, but in many ways she had found a small band of kindred spirits. Most of the girls in this group were also outsiders: products of broken if not mangled homes and borderline poverty, they were marginal students, in voluntary isolation from most of their peers, with tough-guy, streetwise exteriors that for the most part masked profoundly wounded souls. One or two were fairly steady users of drugs like marijuana and alcohol, but they were in a different and much more minor league than the crowd known as "stoners" who came to school loaded and were always on the verge of being expelled.

Although none were older than thirteen, with one or two as young as eleven, many of these girls who offered sanctuary to Shirley were, like her, already well on their way to becoming sexual veterans. This link which bound so many of them together was forged by common fires: childhoods ravaged by sexual abuse. For these child-women, the "love" they had been shown by their molesters all through their childhoods—no matter how perverted that love may have been—was in most cases the only source of affection and attention they knew. In time, it became their only means of experiencing closeness or intimacy with others. They had simply learned what they lived—and a childhood lived under the shadow of sexual abuse, where sex is equated with love and acceptance, is a powerful teacher.

Christi Crosby—her real name was Christina, but everyone called her either Christi or Chrissey—had made a new friend at school, and for some weeks they'd been palling around together with the two or three other girls that Christi was close friends with. Christi Crosby was Gladys Thompson's great-granddaughter, and had lived with her ever since she was a small child. The girl had had a rough time of it: she was one of twins, but her sister had died of crib death several weeks after they were born. Then her mother simply decided she didn't want a child after all, and took off for San Francisco's hippie Haight-Ashbury district, never to be heard from again. Soon after, Christi's father Don moved them in with his grandmother Gladys, until the day when Christi was seven and found her father's blood-soaked body minutes after he had put a bullet in his head. Christi had lived with her great-grandmother ever since.

Christi's new friend was named Shirley Wolf, a name that didn't mean a thing to either Gladys or Warren, her husband. When Shirley called to ask if Christi could spend the night with her, Gladys answered the way she always did: no, she had said, I don't allow Christina to stay overnight at people's homes I don't know—but if you would like to come over here for the weekend, you'd be welcome.

That evening, Shirley's father drove her over to the tiny, one-bedroom house that perched on a hill just above the railroad tracks. Gladys invited the two of them in, the big, dark-haired man with a cane and a slight limp to his left leg and his grinning daughter. Louis Wolf launched immediately into a discourse about his injuries, and about how no one in the community had ever lifted a hand to help him. He even took a snipe at a man he thought was the minister of Gladys's church, until the angry great-grandmother set him straight about what church she attended, furious that he would insinuate that her pastor was anything but a kind, decent, and loving man.

After a few minutes' more conversation, Gladys excused herself to go make a sandwich for Shirley, who said she hadn't eaten dinner yet. She seemed like a sweet child, Gladys recalled thinking as she spread peanut butter on a thick slice of bread.

She could hear voices from the living room— Warren and Mr. Wolf—but couldn't tell what was being said. Then she heard Mr. Wolf call for Shirley, who had gone into Christi's room with her to unpack her things. As Gladys walked across the kitchen floor toward the open doorway, she heard the man say, "Are you gonna miss your daddy?" and Shirley's reply of, "Yes, I really am." Gladys just began to step onto the living room carpet when she saw them together.

Louis Wolf had his daughter in what could only

170

be described as a lover's embrace. Both arms were around her, holding her tightly against him; his head was tilted to one side and bowed down to reach Shirley, who stood nearly a foot shorter than he. His eyes were closed, and Gladys could see that his lips were parted as he kissed his daughter's mouth. The kiss lasted several seconds.

Later that night, after the girls went off to their room and Gladys and Warren were alone, Warren told her that when he and Shirley's father were together in the living room, Wolf asked whether Christi wore a nightgown in bed at night. Shocked at the question, and more than a little disturbed, Warren blurted out, "Of course she does!" and then shifted the talk to another subject. After he and Gladys talked over the passionate good-bye kiss they'd witnessed, he thought it was *more* than a strange thing for a teenager's father to ask.

Months later, Shirley talked her girlfriend Cheryl Sterling—whom everyone called "Tina"—into staying overnight. When "Tina" arrived at the Wolf house, Shirley and her brother L.J. and a neighbor named Eddie were there, along with Mr. Wolf. Shirley's mother and two other brothers were nowhere to be seen. As the night wore on, the four youngsters became more and more playful and energetic, while Louis Wolf sat off to one side in his wheelchair, smoking cigarettes and watching their antics. From time to time he would get up out of his chair and move into their foursome, teasing and laughing and egging them on.

One of those times, L.J. grabbed his father's

171

wheelchair and offered to take someone for a ride. Tina, always ready for new adventures, hopped in and L.J. began rolling her through the living room and kitchen while Shirley and Eddie laughed and coaxed the boy to go faster.

Suddenly, Louis Wolf took command of the chair, laughing to Tina that he would show her a *real* ride. The chair began to move faster and faster through the rooms, weaving in and out between chairs and tables and the shabby couch, then whirling and turning in ever-tightening circles.

An instant later the walls began to tip, and with a dull plop Tina found herself spread-eagled on the floor. Then strong, rough hands grabbed her by the ankles and lifted her off the ground, shaking and bouncing her like a rag doll. As her elasticized tube top slipped up, exposing her bare breasts, the embarrassed teenager cried out in alarm, but still Louis Wolf didn't stop.

Finally he let her go, and once again she was lying on the living room carpet, this time with Wolf standing over her, still laughing and enjoying the teenager's mortification. Before he could grab her again, she darted off into the nearest bedroom like a frightened jackrabbit and closed the door, trembling and gasping for breath.

Later that night, as she stood in the kitchen drinking a glass of water, she heard Shirley's father come into the room behind her. She barely had time to react to his presence before he reached out and grabbed her breast.

Tina later told Shirley what her father had

done, and watched as a bitterly dark look passed over her friend's face.

It was close to midnight when she and L.J. and Eddie were standing in the living room just talking, and Wolf slipped up behind her and surreptitiously squeezed her buttock. She gave out a startled gasp, but said nothing. With mounting fear, Tina hurried outside to spread her sleeping bag out on the lawn with the others—and suddenly he was there again. In slow motion, his arm snaked out toward her, his fingers reaching, probing, grasping for the girlish mound between her legs. He laughed once and then was gone.

Tina decided not to tell Shirley about these last two attacks, for fear her friend might think she'd been leading Mr. Wolf on somehow. In fact, it would be almost two years later before she told anyone except Christi and Christine, and then it was to a courtroom full of strangers.

It wasn't long before Shirley started to confide in her new friends. She had been so long, so many years, without the support and understanding that friendship can bring, that once it was there she hungrily devoured it like a person who had been starving. It wasn't enough to see Christi, Tina, Christine and Jill before school, and maybe talk to one or two of them on the phone at night—Shirley wanted to be with them every second of the day. Between classes, during class, at lunch, after school, at night, on weekends: she was like a kid in love for the first time. It felt so

173

wonderful to know that somebody liked you.

Christi was the first one she told. It had been building for weeks, this need to finally tell the truth about what was going on in her life; finally one weekend when the two girls were out riding on Christi's beautiful bay quarter horse, Shirley blurted it out. About the turmoil, the violence, and ultimately, about the sex. No one had ever told Christi anything like this before, even though she knew girls who'd been molested by their fathers or brothers or other people in their family. But somehow with Shirley it was different—maybe because she seemed to have this need to tell everything once she started to talk. It was like opening up the floodgates and just watching in awe as tons of water exploded out. There was no detail too small for Shirley to omit.

A few nights later, Shirley called Christi in tears. Her father was after her again, this time more violently than usual, and the girl seemed terrified. Sobbing, she told Christi this had been going on for what seemed like forever, ever since she was a very little girl. She didn't know what to do to make it stop, to make *him* stop. It wasn't like she could just tell him "no" and that would be the end of it—you just didn't do that with Louis Wolf and expect to come out unscathed. Shirley knew all too well the price of resistance, and it wasn't one she was willing to pay.

After that, Shirley talked to Christi pretty freely about the incest, although never with the same degree of sorrow and grief that she'd expressed on the phone that night. Most of the time, what came out was anger—sometimes eruptions of it, full of vituperation and hatred for her father, and sometimes just a low sullenness simmering beneath the surface. Except for the anger, Shirley didn't do well at showing her feelings, especially feelings like sadness and loneliness—in fact, over the years she'd worked so hard to cover up those softer emotions that she was completely out of touch with them most of the time. It was as if she didn't feel them at all. As if they simply didn't touch her. She hated it when the tears came without warning, because they made her feel vulnerable and weak. Tears signaled to the whole world that Shirley Wolf was capable of being hurt. And if people knew you could be hurt, that gave them power over you. The power to hurt you even more.

It wasn't long before she confided her story to the other girls in their group, too. In that you-and-me-against-the-world kind of thinking that seems to invade the minds of most teenagers, no one in the group ever dreamed of telling anyone else what was going on with Shirley. Shirley had told them in confidence, and that was the way it would stay. Confidential. Secret. Secrets, after all, were something most of these girls knew instinctively how to keep.

Ten

Pressure had been building for a long time at the Wolf house, and there was an overriding sense that some sort of lethal explosion was just around the corner. Louis still wasn't working, and the money they got from welfare and state disability just didn't go far enough. L.J. was starting to be a problem at school now, too. Like his father, he suffered from dyslexia, only adding to his frustration and anger.

At the same time, Shirley's increasingly frequent absences from school were causing an equally frequent barrage of inquisitive and unwelcome telephone calls to the Wolf household from teachers and Principal Baker and even Officer Ewing. She started the new year off with a bang by getting caught stealing money out of another girl's purse, then less than a month later she shoved a door closed on a boy's nose causing him to be sent home in pain, and knocked another student down as she was running away from the scene. As pleased as David Baker was to see that Shirley had found herself a little cadre of friends, his worries about what was going on in her personal life were only intensifying; as the days wore on, he became more and more convinced in his own mind that she was being victimized, certainly sexually and probably physically as well, by her father. But again, absent any direct evidence, all he could do was wait and keep his ear to the ground for any rumblings.

Louis was acting stranger than usual that fall of 1983: wandering down the hill from their house on Placerville Drive to the Raley's Supermarket, brandishing his .357 Magnum inside the store and in the parking lot; threatening to run people down with his van; spinning off more and more often into savage and ugly fits of temper at home; less and less able to satisfy Katherine's sexual needs because of his frequent impotency with her; and becoming increasingly possessive of Shirley, infuriated that she'd been having sex with boys and didn't seem to care that he knew. Katherine felt totally helpless to change anything, just like the year before when Lou told her he wanted his twelve-year-old daughter to start taking the Pill.

She felt that same sense of powerlessness that fall. She was tired of the constant verbal battles, tired of never getting her needs met, tired of always having to be the bad guy whenever the kids needed sensible discipline about household chores or manners. She was tired of being threatened by her husband, tired of the slaps and painful blows that targeted her too often these days, tired of wondering when and if things would get even worse. More than anything else, though,

177

Katherine Wolf was tired of being scared.

It all came to a head on October 27. The blast they'd all felt was coming finally came, but in a way none of them expected it to.

Late that afternoon Louis exploded like a rocket about something Katherine had done, screaming and hurling threats and insults at her for twenty minutes or more. It felt like a bombing raid, with each concussion stronger than the last until Katherine thought she would go insane. Unable to withstand the attack any longer, she dashed down the hall for her bedroom, slamming and locking the door behind her before her husband could follow. She waited for the hollow sound of his boots, for his huge fist to come crashing through the bedroom wall, but instead all she heard was the front door thundering closed and the cough of his van's engine coming to life.

Trembling violently, Katherine lay back against the pillows and began to sob. Suddenly she heard a hesitant tap-tap-tap on the bedroom door.

"Mom? Mom, are you okay?" It was Shirley's voice, full of fear and concern.

Katherine got up and unlocked the door, then staggered weakly back to the bed and sat down. "Yeah, I'm okay." She smiled a thin, humorless smile.

"Did he hit you? Did he hurt you?"

"No, Shirl—it's okay. Really it is. I'll be fine."

But Shirley knew she wouldn't be fine. Shirley knew something had to be done, and done now, before her father ended up killing someone. She didn't even think before she started to talk.

"Mom," she said softly, "if Dad did something wrong, would they take him away?"

"Well, I suppose if it was really bad, they would."

"Uhh . . . well, I have something to tell you. I think it'll get Daddy out of our lives."

At around five o'clock that afternoon, the telephone intercom in Bob Ewing's office buzzed.

"Bob, Katherine Wolf's on line two."

Officer Ewing punched the blinking light and picked up the receiver. "Katherine, hello! What can I do for you?" His Brooklyn accent was nearly as thick as Lou Wolf's.

"Bob, I—uh, we—need help. Shirley just told me that Lou's been having sex with her."

The telephone receiver almost fell from Ewing's hand. Katherine sounded so businesslike, so untouched. It was weird. For an instant his mind conjured up a picture of Louis Wolf in bed with his daughter, then he shook his head quickly, turning his attention back to Katherine Wolf asking him if she could come in to speak with him.

Ewing glanced at his watch, and told Katherine he could be there within ten minutes. On his way out of the building, he poked his head in the door of Sergeant Robert Harmon's office. "Hope you weren't planning on getting out of here early tonight," Ewing said. "We got ourselves a child molest case."

Harmon looked up from his paperwork, a dark look crossing his face. "Who's the perp?"

"Louis Wolf."

"Whew," whistled the sergeant. "Who made the call?"

"His wife. I'm gonna drive over there now and pick her and Shirley up and bring them in to get their statements. Hang around, okay?"

"Right." Harmon said. It was going to be a long night.

Katherine Wolf, looking fragile and shabby in a pair of faded jeans and black knit top, sat across the desk from the two Placerville police officers, smoking a cigarette and fidgeting nervously. Shirley sat next to her, her face impassive. Off to one side, quietly taking notes on a yellow legal tablet, was Adelle Nelson, a social worker from El Dorado County Children's Protective Services, who'd been called in by Ewing. Mrs. Nelson had worked with the Wolf family on and off for the last year and had heard her share of uncorroborated stories about what might be going on in that house. Now she was about to find out the truth.

"Well, Shirley, maybe you'd better just tell us what happened." Officer Ewing smiled at the young girl, and hoped she felt safe enough to finally tell the truth.

Shirley looked at Ewing and felt a little more comfortable. At least he wasn't a stranger; besides, even with all the trouble she'd caused him, all the times he'd had to come to the school or the house to talk to her about some stupid thing or other, he was always kind to her. He seemed to understand somehow what she was going through, and despite it all, he didn't hate her. She only hoped he wouldn't develop that hatred once he'd heard what she had to say.

"Well, uhh, it was about two weeks ago, around seven or seven-fifteen at night, and me and my dad took off in his van to meet some guy about something or other.

"He drove on out Forni Road for quite a ways, you know, past that big lumber place, and then he pulled over into a big wide spot on the side of the road. It was just before you get to Gold Nugget Way. There was no cars out there, nobody around.

"I asked him what he was doing, and why were we stopping here; and then he reached over and put his hand under my shirt. I knew what was coming, and I didn't want to do it, but I know my dad. . . .

"Anyways, he got his hand under my bra and kind of pushed it up and started rubbing me; I said somethin' like, 'Please, Daddy, I don't want to,' but he didn't even listen. He never does. Then he tells me to get in the back of the van, and then he climbs over the seat right behind me and gets back there with me. He handed me a towel — it was white, with these pink and blue stripes going up and down — and I laid down on it in the back, and he unzipped my jeans and pulled them down to about my ankles. All the time he was kissin' me on my neck, my ears, you know, and not saying much. Then he pulled his pants off and — well — he got on top of me and stuck himself inside me. He came pretty fast, like always." By now Shirley was looking down at the desk in front of her. Throughout the entire soliloquy, her voice showed almost no emotion at all, as if she were numb; she sat stiffly in the chair, barely moving at all, her hands folded in her lap.

"What happened next, Shirley?" Harmon was taking notes furiously.

"He put his pants back on, then told me to clean myself off with the towel. Then he threw the towel out the window, and we went back home."

Ewing sighed softly. "Okay, Shirley—can you tell me, was this the first time this has ever happened?" He knew full well it wasn't, but he needed to hear the girl say it herself.

Shirley gave an odd little smile and shook her head forcefully. She glanced at her mother, who had been sitting quietly all during the confession, her face an unexpressive mask.

"It's been going on for a long, long time. Maybe as long as I can remember."

At that point, Ewing and Harmon asked her to detail as many incidents as she could recall and try to remember when the first time was that her father had had actual intercourse with her. That wasn't a tough one: Shirley almost eagerly told the story of being alone with her father in the bathroom that cold October day when she was nine and how it had hurt so much and even made her bleed a little. But even before that time, she said, he had done things with her, lots of things. After that day in the bathroom, though, they had sex a lot—sometimes two or three times a day, four or five days a week — and lots of times he would make her go down on him, and he would do the same to her.

It's like she's describing a movie, Ewing remembers thinking to himself. *Like it isn't really real. No sadness, no grief, not even any fear. It's been going on for so many years that she's just kind of accepted it as the way things are.*

Suddenly Katherine spoke up. "For a lot of years I been worried that somethin' funny was goin' on between Lou and Shirley — I just had this funny feeling — but Shirley wouldn't ever admit it. A couple months ago I even asked her right out: 'Shirley,' I says, 'Is your dad tryin' to get familiar with you?' but she said no."

Katherine went on to relate the story of Lou waking her up in the middle of the night back when they lived in New York, to tell her Shirley had been orally copulating him and she should go in and clean the little girl up. Yes, she said, she found what looked and felt like semen all over Shirley's crotch — but as much as the whole thing seemed crazy, she said, and as many times as she'd thought about it over the years, she had to believe what her husband told her about the way it had happened. Until now.

A few minutes later Shirley told the officers about her father putting her on birth control pills earlier this year — to "avoid accidents," he'd said — and how one time before when she was afraid she was pregnant, her father called Bob Ewing and told him Shirley had been raped at some party that weekend, just to cover his tracks. When she

183

finally got her period, her father called the cops back and said he might have been wrong about the rape, and would deal with it himself.

Then in what turned out to be the most bizarre part of the whole interview, Shirley and her mother began talking together, "comparing notes," as it were. They talked about the size of Louis's penis, how hard it would get and how long it would stay that way, what things he liked to do in bed, and what he liked to have done to him. The two officers and Mrs. Nelson listened in shock and disbelief to the mother and daughter, gossiping almost giddily about the sexual habits of the man who was husband to one and father to the other. Ewing felt sick to his stomach. They all did.

"Shirley," Harmon interjected when he felt like he couldn't stand it another second, "I need to ask you why you waited all this time to tell someone about your dad."

Shirley paused and looked again at her mother. "I was afraid he was going to hurt my mom," she said earnestly. "They'd had this huge, big fight—worse than the others—and I was afraid he would do something really bad to her. I figured if I told her what he'd been doin' with me, she would leave him. Or she'd tell the cops and they'd make Daddy get out of the house. Then we'd all be okay again."

Ewing asked Katherine if there was anything else she wanted to say.

"I really don't wanna go back home," she said, showing some fear for the first time that day. "I'm afraid of what Lou'll do to me—to us—once he finds out what Shirley's said. And I want the boys outa there, too."

Between Harmon and Police Investigator Howard "Tom" Carroll, they arranged to pick up the boys and get the family a voucher to stay at the Broadway Motel in Placerville that first night. Knowing it was only a matter of time before Wolf found out where his family was, Carroll contacted the Women's Center, which arranged to have Katherine, Shirley, and the boys transferred the next day to a "safe house" in the tiny town of Swansborough, some miles away.

That next morning Tom Carroll called Louis Wolf and told him to come into the police department. When Wolf arrived, Carroll pulled out the Miranda card from his wallet and began to read him his rights.

"What the hell is this all about?" Wolf stood up and leaned toward the officer menacingly.

"Sit down and shut up, Lou," commanded Carroll, rising to his own six-foot-two-inch height. He wasn't about to let Louis Wolf intimidate him. He finished reading Wolf his rights, then told him why he was there and asked if he'd be willing to talk.

"Sure," said Wolf. "I got nothin' to hide. And I ain't done nothin'."

The investigator recounted the story Shirley had told the previous evening about how her father had sexually molested her in the van on October the sixth, and about the numerous other times over the years he'd forced her to have sex with

185

him. Not surprisingly, Louis Wolf denied it all.

He sat back in the chair, relaxed and sure of himself. Smoke from his cigarette curled lazily up toward the ceiling; taking a deep drag, he smiled tightly. "I'll tell you one thing, though: Shirley was always a sex maniac. Once when she was only two or three years old, she came into my room one night and gave me one hell of a blow job." His smile widened. "I couldn't believe it—I mean, she actually made me come! And she was only a kid!"

Then he told Carroll about finding Shirley orally copulating his stepbrother Artie on the living room couch back East. "I damn near killed the fucking bastard," Wolf said. "I mean, this was my daughter. My child. And she wasn't much more than two years old!

Anxious to discredit his daughter in any way he could, Wolf talked about her overactive imagination, saying she always made up stories about one thing and another that were nothing but lies, then pretended to be the innocent. He'd known for a long time, he said sagely, that she was sleeping with boys in town—that was why he wanted her on the Pill—but to hear her tell it, she was the Virgin Mary. A look of consternation passed over his face as he admitted his daughter even tried to seduce him—proving his point that if someone was trying to be sexual, it was Shirley and not him.

"Well, Lou, as you can tell, your story doesn't exactly match with Shirley's. For now, we're going to have to proceed with our investigation, and turn the case over to the D.A. They'll be the ones to file a criminal complaint against you if it's war-

Shirley Wolf at three years old.

Four-year-old Shirley on the sidewalk outside the apartment building where she lived with her family in Brooklyn, New York.

Shirley in her fifth grade class picture at Public School 65 in Brooklyn. She is the fifth child from the left in the second row.

Shirley, eleven, at home at Placerville, California.

Shirley's eighth-grade school picture.

Cindy Collier, thirteen,
in her eighth-grade
school picture from
the E.V. Cain School
yearbook.

Cindy, fourteen, in her Placer Union High School yearbook. (*Courtesy of Placer Union High School*)

David Lee Collier, Cindy's father. (*Courtesy of Cheryl McCall*)

Anna E. Brackett and Jim Wedgeworth, less than one year before Anna's brutal murder. (*Courtesy of Audra Wilson*)

Carl Brackett, Anna's son. (*Courtesy of David Strick*)

The modest four-plex on Quartz Drive where Anna Brackett lived.

Pool Number One at the Auburn Greens complex where Shirley and Cindy swam and planned the murder.

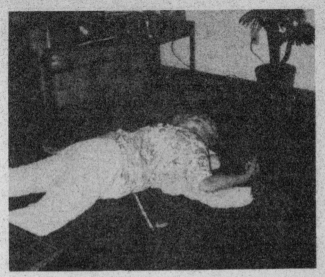

Anna Brackett as she was found by her son Carl after her murder. (*Courtesy of Placer County Sheriff's Office*)

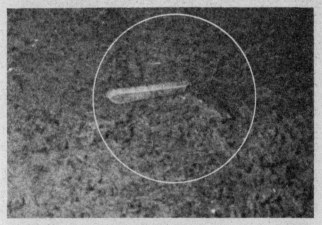

The paring knife Shirley first used to stab Anna. Its blade was bent from the savagery of the attack. (*Courtesy of Placer County Sheriff's Office*)

The actual murder weapon: an eight-inch butcher knife, shown here as it was found on the floor of the car in Anna Brackett's garage. (*Courtesy of Placer County Sheriff's Office*)

Anna Brackett's ransacked bedroom dresser as police found it. (*Courtesy of Placer County Sheriff's Office*)

Cindy Collier's home in Auburn where she and Shirley were arrested the day after their murder of Anna Brackett.

Shirley Wolf, *left*, and Cindy Collier on the first day of their formal hearing. (*Courtesy of David Strick*)

Cindy Collier, *left,* and Shirley Wolf being led into court by Bailiff Fred Pitz on the first day of their formal hearing. (*Courtesy of David Strick*)

Deputy District Attorney Larry Gaddis. (*Courtesy of* Auburn Journal)

Left to right: Thomas Condit, Shirley Wolf's attorney, April Maynard, Cindy Collier's attorney, and Cindy Collier. (*Courtesy of* Auburn Journal)

The Alborada unit (note the incorrect spelling "Alborado" on sign) at the California Youth Authority, Ventura, for girls with severe emotional disturbances. Both Shirley and Cindy spent time there. (*Courtesy of Ron Howard*)

The California Institute for Women at Frontera from which Shirley tried to escape on December 4, 1989. As a result, she spent eighteen months in "Greystone," the facility's maximum security cellblock.

Shirley, twenty-two, as an inmate at the Central California Women's Facility near Chowchilla, the largest women's correctional institution in the world.

ranted."

At this point Wolf exploded, stabbing out the last of his cigarette in the ashtray and lashing angrily against the investigator and flooding him with denials, threats and accusations, ending with how he'd make Shirley tell the truth.

"Well, I hate to disappoint you, Lou," responded Carroll when Wolf finished, "but Shirley and her brothers and Katherine have left town for a while until you cool down. We've made sure they're some place safe."

"They're safe with me!"

"I sincerely doubt that." Carroll was fascinated with the man's hair-trigger temper. His heart was pounding wildly, but he was an experienced enough cop that whatever degree of anxiety he may have felt didn't show. "At any rate," he continued, forcing his voice to remain calm, "you don't have a choice in this. They're not coming home for a while, and you'd better get used to it."

Wolf tried a different tack, demanding that Carroll find a way he could prove he wasn't guilty.

Carroll suggested a lie detector test and Lou agreed.

Before the test date, however, there were a few other dramatic developments. The first thing to happen was that L.J. Wolf, Lou's oldest son, snuck out a bedroom window of the house in Swansborough and ran to a telephone to call his father. Before the elder Wolf could arrive and grill his son about where the rest of the family was, however, the people guarding Katherine and the other children realized L.J. was missing. Because the boy had been so ferociously adamant about his father's innocence, and so furious at having to be on the run with his mother and siblings, everyone knew the first thing he would do would be to call his father and tell him where he could find the others. Before that could happen, the family was moved to another safe house, this one in Marysville, some ninety miles to the northwest in the central Sacramento Valley.

During the week the Wolfs were in Marysville, the Placerville police continued working on the case. Louis Wolf's polygraph exam was set for November 3 in the District Attorney's office; meanwhile, bits and pieces of additional information were coming in from Katherine and Shirley. Shirley told Carroll about other incidents she remembered, other times her father had forced her to have sex. She also talked about the violence at home, and how her father took his fury out on her and the boys. Then she told him about confessing the incest to Christi Crosby, and telling Chris that she was afraid she was pregnant.

Louis Wolf failed to show up for his lie detector test, and the day after Bob Ewing and Tom Carroll went to Markham Intermediate School to interview Christi about what Shirley told them. The girl was hesitant at first, but after Ewing convinced her they already knew the whole story and just needed her to corroborate what Shirley said, she relaxed and told him everything.

It all fit. Like huge pieces of a sick jigsaw puzzle designed by a madman. It all fit.

That same day Tom Carroll received a call from

a man named Vic McCarthy, who had been living at the Wolf house and had just heard about what happened. "I want nothing to do with this," McCarthy told Carroll. "I just thought you should know that this morning Lou packed up his shit and took off in the van." McCarthy had no idea where Wolf was headed.

By the next morning, Katherine, Shirley, William, and Brian were on a plane, bound for New York and Katherine's mother.

On November 8, the El Dorado County District Attorney issued a felony arrest warrant for Louis Wolf, charging him with committing "lewd or lascivious acts upon a child under fourteen, in violation of Section 288 of the California Penal Code." It was signed by Lloyd P. Hamilton, El Dorado County Superior Court Judge. That same day Tom Carroll heard from Vic McCarthy that Wolf called him from New York to say he was trying to locate Katherine.

Carroll called Muriel Kettering's number in New York and warned Katherine that they had an arrest warrant for Louis. "If he shows up or tries to contact you," he told her, "just notify us and we'll take care of it." Next he contacted N.Y.P.D. and talked to the detail that worked Howard Beach, where Katherine's mother lived, to alert them. "I'll be sending out an APB within the next hour," Carroll said.

The teletype described Wolf—dark-haired, male Caucasian; thirty-nine years old; six feet one-and-one-half inches tall, weighing approximately two hundred thirty pounds; frequently wears metal brace on left leg; tattoo of eagle on upper left arm, Jesus head with cross behind the head on upper right arm, two hearts with "Love" and "Kathi" on lower right arm—and described the van in which he was driving with his son Louis Jr. as a 1976 Dodge, off-white with brown-striped top, California license plate number 1DPE958, equipped with a hydraulic handicapped lift at the rear door. The teletype also read: "CAUTION—CAUTION—CAUTION. Suspect armed with numerous weapons and has stated he will not be taken into custody."

Unfortunately, Louis Wolf eventually tripped up Katherine's mother in a phone conversation and discovered his wife and children were with her at the house in Howard Beach, in Queens County. Rather than continue running—after all, there really was nowhere else to run—Katherine simply waited for her husband to show up.

He jammed them all into the van, and they started out across the country, through the winter cold and snow.

Vic McCarthy telephoned Tom Carroll shortly after to report that Wolf and his family were headed for the Pacific Northwest, and were talking about fleeing to Alaska; soon, Wolf himself was on the phone to Carroll, saying he was going to Washington or Oregon, and to forget about ever finding him. Undaunted, Carroll teletyped authorities in both states, and just for good measure the Alaska state troopers in case Wolf tried to cross the border on the Al-Can Highway. Then he just waited.

Around the second week of November, Mc-Carthy called Tom Carroll once again. Lou's on his way back with his wife and kids, he said, to turn himself in. He wants me out — which is fine by me — but I don't know what to do with all his stuff here. Carroll told the man to just leave it at the house, that the state Department of Rehabilitation would probably eventually take it all back. Wolf had been getting regular help from Rehabilitation for some time — and over the years, between Rehab and Social Security Disability, the man had acquired thousands of dollars worth of engineering equipment and drafting supplies, office furniture, tools, wheelchairs, crutches, braces, and drugs, plus his van and all its specialized handicapped accoutrements. Chances were, Carroll figured, that a lot of that stuff would be going back to where it came from, once Louis Wolf was convicted.

On November 22, Wolf called Tom Carroll to say he wanted to "clear things up." That afternoon he was taken into custody and booked into the El Dorado County Jail; the van was confiscated and towed to the G & O Body Shop, where investigators searched it for evidence.

One of the things Katherine told police after she left her husband was that papers and documents, including his own diary, existed to prove that he was not impotent at all. His impotency was one of Louis Wolf's major alibis which he said pointed to his innocence of the incest charges. For

191

at least two years, he said, he had been totally unable to get an erection — *and* he had doctors' certificates and affidavits to prove it, which he proudly showed off to anyone who was interested.

In separate interviews, Vic McCarthy backed up Katherine's assertion that there were other medical documents refuting Wolf's claims of impotency — the man frequently boasted to McCarthy about his sexual prowess, and how he'd conned everyone into thinking otherwise. McCarthy also confirmed the existence of Wolf's diary. Along with their hunt for the papers and Wolf's diary, investigators also searched the vehicle with a blacklight for evidence of semen, even though the incident Shirley had described was nearly two months old. No one was terribly surprised when a thorough exploration of the van revealed nothing.

A search of the house, however, turned up some interesting items, and even more damning stories. Katherine, looking even thinner and more haggard than before, seemed eager to pin just about anything short of the Pearl Harbor attack on her husband, and wasn't the least bit hesitant about showing the detectives provocative evidence of their more-than-kinky sex life. To begin with, there were the magazines. Not just *Playboy* and *Penthouse* and *Hustler* — those were practically nursery-school fare compared to some of the other publications Katherine dragged out of the bedroom. There were magazines, some of them with covers ripped and pages stuck together, like *Game, Genesis* (with sadistic photos of power drills entering women's vaginas), *Split Lips, Velvet,* (sporting full-page pictures of women in shackles and chains), *Screw, Swingers, High Society* (featuring a half-page photo of a penis inside a meat grinder, and an article entitled "Incest: The Family That Lays Together Stays Together"), and dozens more. Many of the magazines were hard-core child pornography, showing graphic photographs of prepubescent children in every imaginable sex act with one another and adults of both sexes.

As police officers gathered up the pile of magazines to take as evidence, Katherine began talking about her and Lou's personal sex life. How they were into swinging and wife-swapping — she even showed them one of the ads they'd placed in a swingers magazine — and how Lou often tried to get some of the women around town to do a "threesome" with them. How sometimes Lou wanted so much sex she couldn't handle it, so she asked this friend of hers to have sex with him just so she didn't have to. And how sometimes when Lou was having the opposite problems and couldn't get it up, she would go down to Sacramento and find men for one-night stands. How one time she was so mad at Lou about something that she told him about having sex with this guy she didn't even know in the back seat of his car. And again, how she'd "had a feeling" for a long time that Lou was fooling around with Shirley, but how she never could prove it.

Tom Carroll and Bob Ewing spent a large portion of the next day interviewing Louis Wolf. He was just as unyielding as before regarding his innocence, but this time he talked a lot more about what had gone on in the family. According to Wolf, his wife was completely to blame for Shirley's sexual promiscuity: she had, he said, provided Shirley with any number of sexual toys and devices to help her achieve orgasm and as a result Shirley was now a nymphomaniac. He also accused Shirley of trying to seduce her brothers, saying the boys had told him of Shirley slinking into their room completely naked and inviting them to have sex with her.

As far as the wife-swapping was concerned, again he placed the blame squarely on Katherine's shoulders. "It was something *she* was into," he said defensively. "She tried to get me to have sex with her hairdresser, but I told her I couldn't because of my impotency problem. She even wrote this letter to a couple and asked them to have sex with the two of us—then she took some nude pictures of herself, and put them in the letter. For some reason it never got mailed, though; I still have it in with my personal letters and stuff at home." Later, when the officers went through the material Katherine gave them, the letter, complete with photos, was there.

When Sergeant Carroll pressed Wolf about his lack of sexual ability, the man continued to insist that he "positively" could not get an erection at all. Later in the conversation, however, the tune to that particular song changed just a little. It was the story of a family outing on the north fork of the Consumnes River near Capps Crossing, a few miles below Placerville. They had driven to a very remote area of the river, and the entire family took off their clothes to go skinny dipping. "It was all completely innocent," Wolf insisted. "The boys were playin' in the water, and Katherine and Shirley and me was just layin' there on the beach. Shirley was layin' with her legs toward me, kind of open, and I looked at her and thought to myself, 'She must be really sexually active, because a young girl just doesn't have a vagina opening that big.' "

Carroll and Ewing exploded. "What the hell were you doing out there in the nude like that? And why were you looking at your own daughter like that?" Their words tumbled across one another.

"I couldn't help seeing her," Wolf said. "She was just lyin' there with her crotch pointed toward me, and I couldn't help but look."

Then Wolf went on to describe how Katherine rolled over on top of him, fondling and kissing his penis until he finally got an erection and climaxed.

The interview ended with Wolf loudly insisting that the incest charges were false, and that the whole story was a concoction to get him out of the house. Then as if to reinforce his innocence, he repeated the story of his stepbrother Artie's seduction by two-and-a-half-year-old Shirley.

"That proves somethin', doesn't it?" he said as he walked out the door.

"Sure does, Lou," replied Ewing, closing the door behind the now-handcuffed Louis Wolf.

* * *

It seemed to Tom Carroll like the D.A. was dragging his feet. They had a strong case: testimony of the victim, partial corroboration by the mother, and a mountain of circumstantial evidence—so why the delay in prosecuting Wolf? The only thing that had been done was that the judge issued a "no contact" order, forcing Lou to stay away from Shirley until the trial; and because Katherine wanted her husband home—apparently more than she wanted her daughter there—she shipped Shirley off to a foster home until things got settled. Other than that, nothing was happening. Louis Wolf had been out of jail on his own recognizance for almost a month.

But the case wasn't as strong as Carroll thought. A few days after Wolf's arrest (and subsequent O.R. release), Katherine Wolf called Ron Tepper at the D.A.'s office to say it had all been a mistake. Shirley lied about the incest, Katherine said, just to get her father out of the house. The girl was scared, and she had lied. It was as simple as that.

She also called Adelle Nelson at Children's Protective Services and tried to tell her that Shirley made the whole story up—but Mrs. Nelson refused to buy the new explanation, and wasn't the least bit shy about telling Katherine just that. It wasn't long before the D.A. and C.P.S. got together to share notes, and realized they were in big trouble with the case. If Shirley recanted her story, then there was no witness—and even with the kind of evidence they had, which by itself was pretty scathing, it would be tough to make a felony charge stick without corroborating testimony. As much as he hated to do it, Tepper realized he had no option other than to cut a deal with Wolf's public defender.

Shirley was enormously confused by everything that had happened since that afternoon in late October when she finally blurted out the truth about her father. Christi had told her to tell her mom about the molestation, because her mom would do something to make it stop. At the same time she remembered Mr. Baker, and lots of other people, saying that telling the truth about things was good, and that telling lies would get you in trouble. But somehow, everything had gotten all twisted up. She'd told her mother, but now her mother was angry at her for what she had said; and she'd told the truth, but had gotten in trouble for it and been taken away from her home and family — *and* she'd gotten her father in terrible trouble, too, much worse than she ever dreamed would happen. So she decided to fix it by saying she lied.

The problem was, it didn't fix anything. It only made things worse.

The social worker got mad at her and said she didn't believe her; the D.A. wouldn't even talk to her; and even though her mother seemed to believe her new story that nothing ever happened, she kept telling her daughter frightening stories about how they were threatening to take the boys away and put Shirley in jail for perjury if she didn't stick to her original story. Just before Christmas, Shirley's fear got the better of her, and she went back to that original story. But by now the case was so shaky because of her vacillation and Katherine's new insistence that her husband was innocent that Ron Tepper agreed to reduce the felony charges.

On December 23, Louis Wolf pled no contest to misdemeanor child molestation. The only reason he hadn't insisted on pleading not guilty, he said later to anyone who would listen, was because the authorities threatened that if he made them go to all the trouble of a jury trial, they would see he spent up to fifty years behind bars.

On January 4, 1983, Louis Wolf was sentenced to 180 days in the El Dorado County Jail, with 30 days suspended. He walked into the big concrete building that squats on the hill overlooking Highway 50 on January 18, and walked out 100 days later—time off for good behavior—on April 28.

Eleven

In the interim, Shirley had plunged off the deep end.

After Louis was charged in late November, Katherine sent her daughter to a foster home on the outskirts of town. Katherine figured it made sense to get Shirley out of the house and away from everything for a while, particularly since the Court said that she couldn't live under the same roof with her father while he was awaiting sentencing. Of course she could have insisted that Lou live somewhere else for those weeks — get a motel room or stay with one of his friends — but it never really even entered her thoughts. After all, he was her husband, and in Katherine's mind a husband belonged with his wife and children.

That same kind of reasoning insisted that it wasn't right that a man should get thrown out of his own home, just because the law couldn't tell when a kid was telling the truth and when she was lying. And it only stood to reason that Shirley should be the one to leave; even the C.P.S. social worker said the girl might be better off away from all the family pressure and upset. Besides, Katherine really didn't want to be alone anymore.

The trouble was, no one thought much about the emotional impact on Shirley of such a forced move from her home. The message she heard was loud and clear, whether or not it was the message anyone intended: IT'S ALL YOUR FAULT.

And so Shirley Wolf's disintegration escalated with each passing month. Her first foster home situation was a three-month disaster: she was sullen and unreachable, angry much of the time and almost totally unresponsive to discipline. The older woman with whom she'd been placed in the hopes she could give Shirley the love and nurturing she so desperately needed was simply unprepared for such a drastic degree of upheaval in her life. She hadn't bargained for a kid with so many problems. The next foster placement was in the home of a couple on the other end of town who C.P.S. officials felt would be able to provide a little more of the structure and discipline Shirley needed as well as the love she wanted. Unfortunately, this placement didn't work out any better than the first, and it wasn't very many weeks before Shirley began coming apart at the seams there, too.

Meanwhile, school had turned into a nightmare again. Before she headed for New York with her mother to escape her father's rage, going to school was something Shirley looked forward to instead of dreading. There was sanctuary there: friends who accepted her as she was, a kind-hearted principal who really seemed to care, and even a few teachers who tried hard to help her along. But by the time she got back from Brooklyn just after Halloween, nearly everyone in school knew the whole story of

200

why she'd gone and what had happened between her and her father for all those years. That knowledge did nothing to enhance Shirley's standing among her peers; in fact, in that peculiar streak of cruelty which children and adolescents can show to one another sometimes, this latest morsel of lurid information only provided the other students at Markham with a new reason to blackball Shirley Wolf.

Despite the noble efforts of Mr. Baker and several teachers, Shirley found herself set apart even more after she came back to Markham. The whispers were louder, the words of derision were stronger and more frequent, and the mild distaste many had felt toward her turned to revulsion. Part of it was simply the stigma of being an incest victim, and of being what the other students saw as a participant in something that was so obscene, so aberrant, that it defied description. But part of it related to Shirley herself, and how she was when she came back.

Something undefinable had happened to Shirley Wolf during those weeks she and her family were on the run, and when she returned to Placerville it was as if some repellent and painful metamorphosis had occurred. Everyone noticed it, or at least sensed it: teachers, students, David Baker, even her social worker and Officer Bob. Physically, the change was readily apparent — she was even more unkempt than before, her hair even dirtier, her outfits even more eccentric and more frequently erotic. At the same time, her behavior had deteriorated even further. She seemed more withdrawn than ever, and totally unable to concentrate on mundane tasks such as homework and tests. She even developed a problem reading, as if there had been a kind of short circuit in the synapses of her brain. Add to that her quirky bursts of giddiness and flightiness, interspersed with periods of wrenching fury, and even her most devoted supporters at Markham were beginning to question whether she would ever be able to escape the oppressive darkness in which she had become enmeshed.

She began to talk, openly and almost proudly, about the incest. At first it was just to her friends, to whom she confessed everything and more with a curious mixture of self-hatred and ecstasy at the recollection. Even the most hardened among them were sometimes taken aback by her immodest boasting—like the day she confided that it felt "absolutely terrific to have eight splendid inches going straight into you!" Then she would follow up with a comment about how much she hated her father for doing what he did to her, and how it made her feel like a piece of meat.

As she talked more to others, the students were curious, despite the repellant nature of her tales. It didn't take long, however, for their curiosity to turn to disgust as her retelling became more and more frequent and her descriptions more and more graphic. One day during gym, the young gym teacher spotted Shirley sitting on her tumbling mat in the center of a tight little bundle of girls, all eyes focused on her. One girl in particular had turned ashen, and looked like she was either going to throw up or pass out.

The teacher called to Christine Falkenstein—who

was standing on the edge of the group, to come over and explain what was happening.

A little embarrassed, Chris looked down at the floor and mumbled her reply. "Uhh . . . she's, uhh, telling them about . . . you know, the stuff with her father."

The teacher stood for a moment, trying to figure the best way to handle the situation. Opting for the direct approach, she simply blew her whistle and called for Shirley to come over. After a few minutes spent trying to explain that talking about those kinds of things was completely inappropriate, the vacant look on the girl's face told her that nothing much was getting through. With a sigh of resignation, she told Shirley to go on back to her mat and do some stretches. She would have to watch her much more closely from now on, that was for sure.

Soon, even the friendships which had meant so much to Shirley began to disintegrate—not because the other girls abandoned her, but because of her own campaign of sabotage. The first thing she did was try to play one girl against the other. Successively, she went to each girl in the group and told her that the other girls were mad at her. Tina, she would say, Christi told me she doesn't like you anymore; then she would go to Christi and tell her that Jill said she didn't want to be friends with Christine anymore; and on and on until everyone in the group was alienated from everyone else. Everyone except Shirley, of course, who remained the one constant.

It took some weeks before a minor incident brought two of the girls together in a face-off; after a few minutes of heated conversation they realized what had been going on, and that Shirley had engineered the rift. For some reason she had ceased being satisfied to be just a part of the group — she needed to be its focus, to have everyone be friends *only* with her and no one else. They also surmised that Shirley was the culprit in the earlier theft of a porcelain horse given as a birthday gift to Christine a few days before. That night Christi and Christine called the others in the group, plus Bill, the current object of Shirley's considerable affections, and a plan was laid. Shirley would pay, and pay dearly, for her acts of treason.

That night they all angrily confronted Shirley at her foster home. It wasn't long before the battle of words escalated into a battle of fists. Although nearly everyone managed to get in a few swings, Christine was the principal contender in the brawl that ranged from the front lawn, into the house, then back outside again. They all were angry and hurt, but Christine was the most infuriated. She was a tough, savvy, and streetwise kid, far older than her years, with her own deep reservoir of anger over the injustices she had suffered in her life. She'd always felt a strange kind of affinity for Shirley, who like her carried her scars and wounds close to the surface. But what Shirley had done was unforgivable. She had not only lied to her, had not only manipulated her, but she had stolen from her.

No one was really hurt in the fracas, not even Shirley. For the most part, the battle strategy of open trench warfare deteriorated into a shouting match, with a few wild punches thrown here and there for effect. Yet the whole scene had been a little bloodcurdling, especially to the elderly foster mother. This was the final straw for her. She called C.P.S. the next day to come and take Shirley somewhere else.

It was also the final straw for her friendship with Christi, Christine, Tina, Jill, and the others. When the penitent warriors went back the next day to apologize to the kindly foster mother for the fight they'd provoked and the damage they'd done, she told them Shirley was gone. And because the home she'd been sent to was out of town, she also never returned to Markham. It would be midsummer before any of her former friends saw Shirley again, under circumstances that were very different and much more tragic.

Those three months of February, March, and April that Shirley spent with her new foster family proved to be just as rife with difficulties and demoralizing failures as the previous three. There was one difference, however: on February 2, she began keeping a diary, the first she'd ever had. It was written in one of those $3.95 hardbound empty-page books that can be found on the shelves of almost any Hallmark store or card shop, somewhere near the white leather-bound guest registries and the "Baby's First Year" memory albums. The one she chose, adorned with a profusion of soft-colored tulips and daisies, was entitled "A Woman's Notebook—Being a Blank Book with Quotes by Women." Each blank page featured a short, inspiring quote from a famous woman; many were bordered with the muted outline of flowers. It seemed perfect for what she needed.

"I wish to be," she wrote as an introduction, "a writer, singer, actor, model, and a stunt woman. With all this I have lots to live for."

She signed it with her name, just as she did each day's entry — sometimes twice, sometimes with her first, middle, and last name, and sometimes with the word "love" added, so the signature read "Love, Shirley."

The journal reveals a deeply wounded, troubled, and often angry young woman struggling valiantly to keep her head above the cesspool of her life. The entire book is filled with the kind of inconsistencies that marked Shirley's life and puzzled those who tried to understand her. It is replete with peculiar observations and turns of phrase, ranging from the deeply philosophical to the incongruously childish; and while the grammar and spelling evidence her poor scholastic achievements, from time to time there are words or statements that point to that much deeper level of sophistication and literary awareness which Mr. Baker and some of her teachers saw in the young girl. Her handwriting, even within a single entry, varies just as wildly: one part of a sentence may be neatly printed, or in a very legible and even script, and then suddenly it becomes little better than a primitive scrawl angling off the page. In reading the journal, it becomes clear that Shirley Wolf's life was one of crippling confusion and chaos.

That first day she made this entry, dated February 2, 1983: Age 13. "I've done bad things in my time but I plan to do my best so I will make others happy. I will be honest with my self and others I will not lie in this book. . . . I will tell every thing about my life. I wish my self luck." Then on the inside back cover of the book, also dated February 2, she wrote: "If this book is ever found and I am famous alive or dead please keep good care. If you sell it, please rember this book holds my memorise, feelings and thoughts & troubles & needs. Thanks."

A few days later, she wrote: "Guys are getting to see me different Lately. Being popular is hard but I enjoy it."

The very next day brings this entry: "I really hope my popularity plan works because I'm trying. Some Guys are getting back to the way they were but some of them are still changing in time I will be popular."

But time made no difference at all, except to make things that were already bad, worse. Cut off from her previous circle of friends, Shirley reverted to her old behaviors of grasping at people and making them her "best friend;" then when the relationship disintegrated in a few days or a week, she would begin the desperate search for someone new. The pattern extended to her search for a boyfriend: she would go out with a boy once or twice and have sex, promptly declare she had fallen in love with him, and then just as promptly either get dumped or find some new boy that she thought she was falling in love with.

In late February Shirley slept with the brother of one of the girls she knew from school, even though she was "in love" with another boy whom she'd been dating for about ten days. She began obsessing about being pregnant, and for the next month her diary reveals even more about her feverish desire to find both an object to love and a source of love for herself.

February 21: Yesterday I messed around with [E]. I think I'm pregnate I do not love him but I think I'd better lern before anything happens. I'm dead against an abortion I don't know if I should have the baby or not. I don't know how to explain it to my boyfriend.

March 4: My boyfriend said he wants to break up I think he hates me because he denied every thing he said to me. oh well. I'll have to Lern to live with it.

March 9: Today [T] asked me to go with him. I said yes. [K] and [A] have a crush on me.

March 10: [T] & I are fine.

March 11: [T] and I broke up. [S] asked me, I said maybe.

March 12: I've decided to have the baby. A lady, my Mom's friend, can't have children and I can't raise the child & I'm dead against abortion. At school they found out about me & [E] so now I have to start from the bottom & try to be popular. For now I like [G] but I want to go out with [C].

March 13: I will nurse the baby after it's born. if I have it 9 months after it will be born Nov. 20, 1983. I'm really excited my real mother said you can feel the baby kick inside you 3 months after you are pregnate and I could breast feed the baby. I all ready Love it & I'm not even sure if I'm pregnate. I love [B].

The third week in March — almost 28 days exactly after her last menstrual period — her period began again, and she wrote these words: "I'm really glad I'm not pregnate."

During these months in the second foster home, Shirley was tormented about what had happened to her father and the rest of her family since she revealed the incest. As much as she had come to care for her foster family — at one point she not only assumed their last name, but told Katherine she wanted them to legally adopt her — she struggled fiercely to be returned to her real home and family, and make peace with all of them and herself at the same time. Yet her contacts with Katherine were fraught with conflicting emotions of anger, disappointment, and titanic need, leaving the teenager feeling even more alone and hopeless.

In mid-March she resurrected her plan to make everything all right again. She wrote: "Today, I plan to go home by saying I Lied about my father molesting me."

Again, she talked to Katherine first, testing out the story on her to see if it worked. Katherine, whose own life had been turned upside-down by Shirley's revelations about the incest and the subsequent events, wanted desperately to continue believing that it had all been some sort of grotesque plot hatched by a daughter desperate to protect her mother against her father's violent anger. In addition, the last five months of turmoil and guilt at seeing Louis behind bars had worn away what little ego strength the woman had, leaving her even more willing to accept that the whole incest story was nothing but lies.

Of course, Shirley's protestations, accompanied by those of her mother, made little difference to the authorities. No matter how circumstantial it might be, the evidence was simply too overwhelming to give any credence to Shirley's second renunciation of that initial accusation.

On March 22, Shirley began to see that her plan would fail. She wrote: "I'm trying to get my Dad out of jail," she scrawled, "but Looks like It might not work!"

The next six weeks created an even deeper rupture in Shirley's already abysmal sense of self-worth. Because of her chronic behavior problems and resistance to discipline, she was transferred to another foster home, and then another. No one really wanted her, even though they all felt deep pangs of sympathy for the girl and what she'd been through. But the bottom line was that Shirley had to make at least some attempt to get along with the people around her, and to control her explosive temper—neither of which she seemed capable of doing. Everyone hoped it would help when Louis was released in late April, but things just kept on sliding downhill.

Shirley felt even more guilt at having put him through all those months in jail—and he made certain she knew just how horrible it had been for him, how much it had cost him. All he ever did, he said, was to love her, and look what she'd done to him. The final insult, and just one more burden of guilt for Shirley, was that he was forced to register as a sex offender when he got out. Even after all that, they wouldn't let him have his daughter back home where she belonged. Finally, on May 10, Shirley's anger detonated again and she violently kneed a boy in the groin. She was suspended from school, and the next day the frustrated C.P.S. authorities sent her off to the Lieben Group Home in the Sacramento area, where they were better equipped to handle tough cases like Shirley Wolf.

One week later, Shirley wrote this statement on the inside back cover of her diary, and dated it May 18: "Ages 3–13 I was molested by my father. I resent it and I may be 13 now but my dreams are to sing, write, act, art, model, do stunts and make others happy."

The Lieben Group Home in Fair Oaks, a suburb of Sacramento, was too much like a prison to Shirley. There were no bars on the windows, and it looked like a regular house in a regular neighborhood, but there were all kinds of rules and regulations you had to follow, and the people there were much tougher and less understanding than any of her foster parents had been. Besides, she was far away from her mother and brothers and her boyfriend Bill—the same one who had witnessed the battle between Shirley and her former girlfriends so

211

many months before—and she felt even more isolated than before.

All of the girls in the home came from families fractured by sexual or physical violence or some other kind of serious dysfunction. Two of them were simply thrown out of their homes because their parents couldn't handle them, one had gotten herself pregnant, and the other three had been raped and molested. At first, they hung back from approaching Shirley while debating who and what she was. After a week or so, and after Shirley had run away from the home three different times, one or two tentatively accepted the new girl as one of their own.

That wasn't the case at the school she was attending. As she had at every school she'd ever gone to, Shirley found herself ostracized from the other students at Will Rogers Intermediate School. And as before, she quickly made a name for herself on campus with both the students and faculty—mostly for her outbursts of temper and physical violence and her inability to settle down in the classroom. Pat Vogel, the tall, strawberry-blond teacher in the school's specialized on-site detention program for kids with disciplinary problems, came to know Shirley fairly well over the weeks she was at Will Rogers—and yet, there was something about the girl she just couldn't figure out. She was troubled, that much was obvious; but there was something more. Even most of the other kids in the detention program avoided her like the plague, and that just didn't happen. Usually those kids stuck together pretty well, because they were all so much alike and

212

had the same kinds of problems. But Shirley Wolf was different, too different. She just never fit in.

There were fights at school, fights at the home, midnight escapes that backfired and left her in worse trouble than before, a four-day stint in Juvenile Hall after a particularly vicious brawl with one of the girls in the home, and long telephone talks with her mother and father that left her feeling shamed and despondent for days afterward. Then one of the two girls at the Lieben Home that Shirley had connected with was moved to another foster home, prompting this series of journal entries:

> May 20: Cheryl is leaving. I'm so sad.
>
> May 21, 9:08AM: Cheryl's leaving today. I'll miss her she's the only one except Carrie that I feel I love.
>
> May 21, 9:19AM: Cheryl's out of sight, gone forgoten. I'm hurt & crying.
>
> May 31: I woke up screaming.

The next morning she ran away from the home, and ended up hitching a ride to nearby Folsom, an historic town at the base of the Sierra Nevada foothills, just off Highway 50 and about ten miles northeast of Sacramento. Another fifteen miles or so would have taken Shirley back home to Placerville, where she wanted to go, but the boy she was riding with was only going as far as Folsom. Hitching another ride, she got as far as Folsom Lake, less than a mile outside the town, where she spent the next three days camping on the beach, bumming food and cigarettes and an occasional beer or joint from

213

other campers, and fantasizing about going home and being with Bill.

One night Shirley awoke to the soft clicking of a rattlesnake. Terrified, she snatched up her few belongings and ran for the nearest house, where she pounded on the door until a middle-aged woman let her inside. At first she called the Sacramento police and confessed to being a runaway, but they said she was outside their jurisdiction because she was in Folsom. Next she called the Folsom police, who told her because she wasn't a resident of the city, she was outside their jurisdiction as well. Her third call was to the police in Placerville, who said because she had been transferred to the group home in Sacramento, she was Sacramento's responsibility. In desperation, she called Sacramento again. They agreed to have an officer come by to pick her up, so she went out to the road to wait.

Exhausted after hours of waiting, she finally fell asleep; when she awoke, the sun was just beginning to peek over the horizon. Once again, she told herself, she'd survived something she thought she could never survive. It was time to move on. Once again she gathered her clothes and began trudging up a nearby hill. When she reached the crest, the sparkling lake stretched out before her in all directions like an awesome beauty mark in the midst of all the ugliness surrounding her life. Then and there, Shirley Wolf set down her own golden rule: she would never again be afraid of another person, and she would never again allow herself to be a victim.

On June 4, the police finally caught up with her and returned her to the Lieben Home.

During the last week of school, just before eighth-grade graduation, Shirley ended up in Pat Vogel's detention program again. During lunch break all the students huddled around one another at the tables, laughing and signing their school yearbooks for one another. All the students, that is, except Shirley. For one thing, she had come to the school too late to get a yearbook. For another, she was simply not a part of their world, and never would be. Pat recalls watching as Shirley got some pieces of scratch paper and stapled them together, then created a makeshift cover in a crude imitation of the book she saw the others had.

"Mrs. Vogel," Shirley said with a grin, "would you sign this for me?"

Pat's heart nearly broke at the girl's wistful expression and her wretched attempts to be included. "Of course I will, Shirley." She wrote something about wishing Shirley all the best in the future, and signed her name.

"I'm gonna go ask the rest of them if they'll sign my book, too!" Shirley was like a child who had been told she could go to the candy store and have anything she wanted. Her face shone with gleeful anticipation.

"That's a good idea, Shirley—I'm sure they'll be happy to."

Although none of them sought her out like they did their other friends in the room, they all signed her homemade yearbook. For once, the day ended on a happy note for Shirley.

Yet within a week she'd gotten into another fight,

this time with her new roommate Jana Jarvis. The next day was the last day of school, and graduation day for Shirley. She was leaving the cocoon of grammar school and moving into the big leagues of high school, where who-knows-what awaited her. She was excited and terrified at the same time.

The night of the graduation ceremonies, Shirley wrote this in her diary: "Today was graduation. Got lots of hugs & kisses and a rose."

Four days later, around eleven o'clock in the morning, someone knocked quietly on the door to Shirley and Jana's room.

Jana opened the door and saw a tall, big-boned girl with hard features and heavy makeup standing there.

"Jesus Christ! Cindy!" She grabbed the girl by the arm and hauled her inside the room, peering down the hallway in both directions to make sure no one had seen them. "What are you doing here?"

"I split from my Work Project up in Auburn and hitched a ride down here. I thought we could take off together, you know, get away from all this shit. Whaddya' say?"

Jana thought for a minute, intrigued with the idea of getting away from Lieben and being on her own.

"I don't know, Cindy," Jana whispered. "Things have been goin' real good for me lately, and if I took off it'd just blow it all to hell." She hesitated, then shook her head resolutely. "Naw, I don't want to go. Sorry."

"Your loss," grumbled Cindy, and started for the door.

216

"Wait," hissed Jana. She turned and looked at Shirley. "This is my roommate, Shirley Wolf. She might want to go with you."

Shirley grinned an eager smile, and sealed her fate.

Part Three:

Retribution

Twelve

Standing on the shoulder of Highway 49, puffing from their dash away from the condominiums, Cindy and Shirley began to smile at each other, then laugh—tentatively at first, and finally with more and more abandon. It had been an incredible adventure, something neither one of them had ever done before but that now they shared as a common, unifying experience. It made them feel special and unique, set apart from the rest of the world that was too timid to go where they had gone, too lifeless to feel the throat-tightening, exhilarating mix of fear and absolute power they had felt. It was like a drug, that feeling: a powerful, addictive narcotic that only left them both craving more.

A mustard-colored Datsun B-210 slowed down as it passed the two hitchhikers, then screeched to a stop a few yards ahead. Cindy and Shirley ran to the side of the car and looked in at the driver, a young man of about twenty-five. "You guys need a ride?" he asked.

"Yeah! We're, uh, headed down 80, to Fresno. But we need to get to Roseville first."

"Well, I'm only going to 80 and 49. I can take you that far."

Thinking that something—even four or five

miles — was better than nothing, Cindy agreed.

"But you'll both have to sit in the front seat," he said, gesturing to the pile of cardboard boxes in the back. "There's no room back there."

Giggling, the two girls clambered into the car, Shirley perched atop Cindy's lap. During the five-minute ride to the intersection of Highway 49 and Interstate 80, they continued to laugh and talk between themselves, telling the driver they'd been in a fight with one of their boyfriends, and that he'd tried to beat them up.

It wasn't long after the first car dropped them off that another one came along and rescued the two slightly ragged-looking teenagers. This one was going all the way to Roseville, and the driver said he'd be happy to take them wherever they wanted to go there. A few minutes later the sedan was speeding easily down the highway through the placid early evening traffic, its two passengers subdued and silent. The flowered diary lay next to Shirley's bright pink jacket on the seat, its pages ruffling in the wind that rushed through the car's open window. Shirley whispered something to her companion, but Cindy just stared blankly off into space, lost in thought.

Stealing an occasional glance in the rearview mirror at the two hitchhikers, the middle-aged driver wondered what the hell these young kids today were thinking, wandering around like Gypsies and jumping into anybody's car without a second thought. *Good God,* he thought, shaking his head, *don't they realize how dangerous the world is these days? After all, how could they know I'm not some weirdo with a knife or gun or whatever? Don't they understand how crazy it is to trust some people? Not only crazy, but deadly?*

Shirley picked up her journal and riffled to the last page she'd filled with her scrawling, childlike hand. Four days ago. *More like a lifetime,* she thought to herself. Digging in her tattered purse for a pen, she began to write: jumbled, jerky letters that danced to the motion of the car. She smiled as she wrote what was to be the final entry in this chronicle of a fourteen-year-old girl's life passages; then looking at what she'd written, she smiled again.

Re-reading the words she'd just scrawled, she realized they were true. It *had* been fun.

Then she paused for a moment, and added a final sentence.

I'm becoming meaner.

"Umm, could you drive through the park?"

"You mean, Royer Park?"

"Yeah, that's the one." Cindy had something she needed to get rid of, and the park seemed like the perfect place. There was always a vagrant or wino or two hanging around, especially at night, and they'd pick up anything that anybody left there.

"Sure, okay; but then I'm going to have to let you two out and head home." They had refused to tell him exactly where they were going, even though he'd asked a couple of times. Just Roseville, was all either one would say. *Oh, well,* he thought. *I guess they'll be okay by themselves.* He looked in the rearview mirror again and gave a quiet chuckle. *They're not exactly delicate little flowers, either one. Guess they could pretty well handle themselves in most situations.*

The car turned down Park Drive, and Cindy carefully leaned over and untied her brown deck shoes, tugging at the Garfield laces. Keeping one eye on the driver to make sure he couldn't see what she was doing, she dropped first one and then the other out the open passenger window. *That should get rid of them.* True to form, Cindy was always thinking ahead. She was afraid she'd gotten some of Anna's blood on the shoes, and didn't want them around as evidence in case she got picked up. And being barefoot didn't bother her — especially when it was a nice warm night like this one.

Shirley and Cindy walked around Roseville for a while after their ride dropped them off, but after less than half an hour they both agreed it was "deader than Auburn." They talked about what to do next, reevaluating their earlier plan about heading to Fresno. That San Joaquin Valley town was a long way off, and it would take at least a couple of hours to get there — assuming they found a ride right away that was going that far. Then there was the question of what they'd do if Cindy couldn't find her girlfriend. Finally, Cindy suggested they hitch back up to Auburn and spend the night at her house, then decide how to get away the next morning. That sounded just fine to Shirley, who was a little tired of hitchhiking all over the country and never ending up anywhere. Something to eat and a good night's sleep sounded perfect. Cindy, too, was getting tired — and her cramps were back again. Plus if they got a ride back up the hill right away, she figured she could still make it home before her nine o'clock curfew so her mom wouldn't have a shit fit.

It didn't take long for the pair to find another willing motorist to take them the fifteen miles east to Auburn. Most people weren't too fearful of picking up a couple of young girls, not unless they were wearing black leather boots and jackets and motorcycle chains around their waists. And while Cindy and Shirley had been on the run now for almost ten hours and were beginning to look a little the worse for wear, they still didn't appear all that much different from any other teenager you might see on the street on any other summer evening. Even the few spots of blood on Shirley's pants weren't all that noticeable — by now they had dried to a dusky brown, and could have been taken as mud stains or just about anything else.

Once again, the girls ended up in downtown Auburn. It was a little before eight o'clock, and they were dying of thirst. "There's a Foster's Freeze just around the corner," Cindy said. "We can get something to drink and then figure a way to get to my house."

The cashier looked up from counting her till to see Cindy standing there. "Oh, hi, Cindy," she said. "How you been?" She and Cindy were good friends at one time, but over the last year or so their friendship had died to almost nothing. She hadn't seen Cindy in weeks, if not months.

"Hey, Stacy! I been great — we just got back from hitchin' to Roseville and back; this mornin' we were out at the Greens, and we even stopped by your place, but nobody was home; then we spent the day just, you know, foolin' around and stuff. . . ."

"Haven't seen you in a while."

"Nah, I been in Juvie" — Juvie was short for Juvenile Hall — "and then before that, I was at this place in Shingle Springs, and before *that* I was up in a group home kinda by Reno or Tahoe. Any chance we can get a couple cups of ice water?"

"Uh, sure."

"Thanks." Cindy took a huge gulp of the water. "We're gonna go make some phone calls — see ya later."

"Yeah, see ya."

They rounded the corner of the building to the telephone booth. "I got an idea," said Cindy. "Why don't you call my mom and ask if I'm home; then a few minutes later I'll call her and say I ran into you, and that I'm on my way home." Cindy figured that if her mom knew about her skipping out of Work Project, she would say something to Shirley about it. She also figured Linda might be suspicious if she just showed up with a strange girl she'd never seen before, so she wanted to set the stage a little bit.

"Can I say my name's Melissa?"

"Sure. You can call yourself anything you want."

After they called Linda — who didn't know about her daughter's disappearance from the work site, and simply reminded her of the nine o'clock curfew — Cindy made another call. She told Shirley there was this boy she used to go with who she knew she could trust — and, she said, she felt like if she couldn't tell somebody about what they'd done that afternoon she would absolutely burst apart in a zillion pieces. The problem was, after she got him on the phone and told him the story, she could tell he didn't believe her. She tried to convince him by giving him details — how they'd stabbed the lady so many times, how the one knife got bent — but he just mumbled something about needing to take a shower and get dressed for work, and that he had to go. Cindy was furious: all she'd wanted to do was share her triumph, relive the

226

high of it all, and that stupid asshole thought she was lying. She slammed down the receiver so hard the entire booth rattled, and they began walking through the downtown area on their way toward the little canyon street where Cindy lived, about two miles away. As they were crossing the street near Pryor's Exxon station, Cindy spotted Stacy gassing up her Camero. "Stacy!" Cindy called. "Hey, could you give us a ride over to my house? I'll give you a dollar for gas."

Stacy looked at her watch, and saw that she had enough time to make a slight detour before she herself was due home. "Sure, okay. Hop in."

On the way, Cindy asked Stacy if she'd heard about a murder that day at Auburn Greens. No, she hadn't, Stacy replied. She'd been too busy all day to listen to the news.

After Stacy dropped them off the two girls walked into the dimly lit house and Cindy introduced Shirley as Melissa Brown, one of the girls who'd been with her on the Work Project. Melissa's mother, she said, had to go up to Reno and Melissa was afraid to stay home alone. Could she stay the night at their house?

Linda didn't usually allow kids to spend the night, but figured it was better than having the poor thing spend it on the streets. The girls sat down in the living room and chatted for a while, sipping out of their Foster's Freeze cups.

"Uh, did you hear about the murder today at Auburn Greens?" Shirley posed the question to Linda, and Cindy felt her stomach tighten.

"Murder? At the Greens? When? Who?" There was an edge of fear to Linda's voice. She knew a fair number of people at the Greens.

"Well, we went swimmin' out there right after Work Project," Cindy explained, "and that's when we heard about it. Some old lady got knifed to death. It was somebody we didn't know."

"The lady—the lady that got murdered—she was my best friend's grandmother," Shirley chimed in. "I didn't know her too good, but she seemed like a really nice lady from what I knew."

Linda felt relieved, but at the same time remained distinctly uneasy at the idea of a violent murder happening so close to home, even if it wasn't somebody she knew. They talked for a few minutes longer about the killing, and then Cindy announced she was going to bed. She usually was asleep by nine or nine-thirty, and it was later than that already—besides, she said, her stomach had been hurting her all day from the cramps, and she thought that lying down might help. A few minutes later, though, she came back upstairs and told her mother she was going to fix a sandwich for herself and Melissa, because they hadn't eaten since lunch. After Cindy wandered back downstairs, Linda turned on the television to watch *Hart to Hart,* one of her favorite shows. Within minutes she was asleep on the couch.

In the basement recreation room Cindy and Shirley switched on the radio and spent the next hour singing and laughing and talking together, and giving one another tattoos with felt-tip pens. Giddy with anticipation, at eleven o'clock they clicked on the television to see if anything about the murder was on the news. Toward the top of the hour the perky Channel 3 anchorwoman reported that an elderly Placer County woman was stabbed to death in Auburn that afternoon, and the authorities were looking for two

228

teenaged girls in connection with the killing. Half in genuine shock and half for effect, Cindy fell sideways on the couch and lay there with her hands covering her eyes while Shirley jumped up and began asking what they should do.

The first thing she thought of was to get out of there. This minute.

It made sense that they couldn't stay there—but at the same time, it would be pretty stupid to take off in the middle of the night with no car, no food, and no money. The whole thing was going as sour as old milk.

"Maybe . . ." Cindy started, then stopped herself. "What about . . . uh, what about turning ourselves in?"

"Well . . . I dunno . . ."

The pair looked at each other for a moment, then in unison both chorused, "No way!"

"But what *do* we do?" asked Shirley.

"I dunno. Let's think about it some."

Back upstairs, Linda was awakened by a key turning in the front door lock. "Keith? That you?"

"Yeah."

The two talked together for quite some time, then Keith said good night and headed for the basement.

Both girls heard the creak of the stairs.

"Shit, lay down!" Cindy said, figuring it was her mother. "Pretend you're asleep!"

Keith rounded the corner and saw his sister and another girl asleep on the couch. He really didn't want to get into it with Cindy, so he went back up to the living room and told his mother where the two girls had crashed. Walking downstairs, Linda ordered Cindy and Shirley to go on in to bed, which they did.

According to the two girls, as soon as Linda left the room they called out to Keith and told him about the killing. At first he was just as dubious as Cindy's friend on the phone had been, but after they provided him with some of the specific details — and after Shirley said, "It's not every day I go around saying I murdered somebody if I didn't" — he became a believer.

"So what're you guys gonna do?"

Cindy shook her head and said she didn't know. All she knew was that she was absolutely, totally exhausted, and that if she didn't get some sleep she would fall down right in the middle of the floor. Shirley made no move to join her, so Cindy simply walked into her bedroom and closed the door.

Shirley didn't really know what she wanted to do. She was tired, too, but parts of her didn't feel like sleeping at all. Parts of her felt like she was on some ferris wheel gone crazily out of control, or inside a washing machine on perpetual spin dry. Then there were the parts that felt a darkness like she'd never known before, something raw and congealed and blacker than sludge that smelled like a rotting road-killed animal and that seemed to be blotting out everything in its path. She kept looking for the light, but it was gone. Just the ebony void of nothingness.

Later, Shirley says, she and Keith snorted a line of cocaine, took a few hits off a pipe full of dope, then had sex. It was getting harder to keep it all separated: the murder, the sex, her father . . . they were like kaleidoscopic images that just kept blending into one another over and over and over. Death . . . life . . . pleasure . . . need . . . pain: they were all the same thing now. Shortly afterward, Cindy's brother left the room.

The only light upstairs was the yellow glow of the television set. Linda was lying on the living room couch trying to get some relief from her chronic back pain, when she was startled by a presence standing near her. Shirley had simply appeared in the doorway like an apparition, absolutely soundlessly despite the creaky floors of the old house.

"What—what are you doing?" The girl had frightened the hell out of her.

"Did you see it?"

"See what? What are you talking about?"

"The news. About the murder." She had both hands behind her back, and moved a few feet closer.

"Uh, no—I fell asleep during *Hart to Hart,* and slept through the news." Shirley took a few more steps toward Linda, who finally hoisted herself into a sitting position. The girl still had her hands clasped behind her. "Um, you really better go back downstairs, 'cause Robert will be home soon and he won't like it that you're here in the house. So please just go on back downstairs to bed." Linda was beginning to feel extremely nervous. There was just something about this girl that made her skin crawl. Again, Shirley moved toward the woman—by now she was no more than a foot or two away. Suddenly, there was a noise from the stairwell, and Shirley turned to see Keith mounting the last step. She looked from him to his mother, then backed away into the doorway; when she reached the kitchen counter, she turned and walked downstairs without a word.

Early the next morning Linda was cleaning up the kitchen when she discovered her large butcher knife lying on the back of the stove. Puzzled, she picked it up and looked at it as if she wasn't sure exactly what

231

to do with it. She remembered putting it on the counter after having made a grilled cheese sandwich the night before. It would be some time before the significance of her unusual discovery finally hit, as she thought about the events of the night and suddenly remembered Shirley standing in the doorway, looking like she was holding something behind her back. No one ever found out what—if anything—the young girl had in her hands.

Shortly after Shirley thumped back down the stairs and Keith headed for bed, Linda's live-in lover Robert came home and went off into their upstairs bedroom. Before she knew it, the frail-looking blond woman once again fell into a light sleep on the couch in front of the flickering television screen.

In her dream, someone was hammering something into the wall. No, it was into a door. The front door. They were pounding something into the front door. Struggling out of her twilight sleep, Linda realized someone *was* pounding on the door. She looked at the clock, surprised to see it was two-thirty in the morning. *Who the hell would be knocking at the door at this hour of the night?*

Blinking in the bright porch light, Linda saw that it was the police. No matter how many times over the years the cops had shown up on her doorstep to roust one of the kids or one of her boyfriends or someone else, she never got over the fear and never stopped feeling the sick knot in her stomach. She was always terrified that one of these times they would be there to bring her some horrible nightmare news about someone she loved.

This would be one time when she was right.

Thirteen

When Sergeant Mahlberg told the woman they were looking for Cindy, and that they were investigating a homicide, Linda Osborne staggered backward a little and cried out in shock.

"I'm sorry, ma'am," Mahlberg said. "May we come in?"

"Yes, of course, officers." They stepped into the semidarkened room.

"Is your daughter at home, ma'am?"

"Yes, she is—her and her friend Melissa are asleep downstairs. Could you tell me what this is all about?"

"There was a homicide earlier today—uh, early yesterday evening—out at Auburn Greens, ma'am, and your daughter was identified as being in the vicinity by several witnesses. At this point we are investigating all possible leads." Sergeant Mahlberg always lapsed into a stilted, Joe Friday kind of prose whenever he was in his official role, which he was now. "You indicated your daughter was downstairs now with a friend; do you have any indication of what time they arrived home this evening?"

The blond-haired woman thought for a moment and then said she thought it was around nine o'clock. "Umm, they said they'd been out at the Greens, that there'd been a murder out there and there were cops crawling all over the place." She was shaking badly.

"Mrs. Osborne, the sergeant and I would like to go downstairs and speak with the girls. There are three other officers outside, and they'll be coming in, too. Can you please direct me to the basement bedroom?"

Linda Osborne led the two sergeants down a set of uncarpeted, dark wooden steps toward the basement; whitewashed slumpstone bricks lined the exterior walls. At the bottom of the steps was a small shingled room with a brown and white shag carpet, a gold brocade couch and matching chair, and a wooden coffee and end table set. A portable television perched on the top shelf of a set of built-in bookcases.

They continued through this outer room into the bedroom, where the two girls continued to sleep undisturbed. The floor of this room was covered with a thin brown carpet, and the walls were paneled with blond pine. The rough-hewn, knotty pine bunk beds where the girls slept were fastened together with huge silver bolts, giving them a rustic, country look. At their feet was a TV stand stacked with boxes of games like *Monopoly, Hangman, Battleship,* and *Clue.* One section of the room was littered with piles of cardboard boxes and scattered personal effects. A large box labeled Carlton Air-Stream Filter Cigarettes was stuffed with items of clothing; others overflowed with an assortment of books, shoes, blankets, cosmetics, a vanity mirror, and a multicolored afghan.

Sergeant Mahlberg signaled for Coelho and Thompson to come inside; as soon as the two deputies arrived downstairs, they tried to awaken Cindy, who kept pulling the covers up over her eyes so as not to be disturbed. Finally she roused enough for the officers to tell her why they were there, and what they wanted.

234

"Miss Collier," said Mahlberg, "can you understand what it is we have just told you? Are you awake enough to understand?"

"Yeah, yeah, yeah," the girl mumbled sourly, rubbing her eyes.

After the officers woke Shirley, they asked her the same questions.

"I'm awake," she said, sounding more than a little groggy. She struggled to sit up, shook her head as if to clear it, and smiled. By now Cindy was also sitting up in bed.

They were there, Mahlberg explained, because they were investigating a murder at Auburn Greens, because Cindy had been spotted in the area around the time of the killing, and because the conditions of her probation allowed the authorities to come in and search her room and personal belongings.

Cindy just shrugged her shoulders and said, "Go for it."

While Mahlberg began his search, Deputy Coelho read Cindy her rights. "Do you understand these rights as they have been explained to you?" he concluded.

"Sure."

"Are you willing to talk with us about what happened?"

"Sure."

"Okay, Cindy, I'm going to leave you with Sergeants Mahlberg and Nelson. They'll be the ones questioning you."

Cindy grunted an acknowledgment and Coelho left the room, taking Shirley with him.

She and her friend had been at the Greens the previous day, Cindy acknowledged. Yes, they swam at the pool, and they went to the apartment of an older lady and her husband to ask for water and the phone. She tried to call her mother, but the call wouldn't go through, so they gave up and left. After that, they just wandered around the complex and finally hitched a ride to Roseville.

"Did you observe anything unusual while you were at Auburn Greens?" asked Mahlberg.

"Uh-uh."

"Didn't you inform your mother when you arrived home that a homicide had occurred there that evening, and that 'there were cops crawling all over the place'?"

"Oh, yeah."

While he and Nelson were searching the room, Mahlberg asked Cindy what she'd been wearing that afternoon. She pointed to the floor, where an orange football jersey and a pair of Levi 501 jeans had been tossed. Her shoes, she said, were an old worn-out pair of brown oxfords, and she threw them away somewhere in Royer Park after their ride dropped them off at Roseville.

"Could you show me what Melissa was wearing?"

"Who?" Cindy sounded genuinely puzzled.

"Melissa. Your friend."

"Oh, you mean Shirley. Shirley's her real name."

Cindy told Mahlberg that Shirley was wearing some light blue Jordache cords, which were lying on the floor in another area of the room. Mahlberg picked them up and something clanked to the floor. It was a key ring, with three keys and a large plastic number one that read *You're Number One With Us!* A yellow tag with the inscription Auburn Greens Pool was attached to one of the keys.

"Where did these come from?"

"How the hell should I know?" snorted Cindy. "They don't belong to me."

By now Coelho and Thompson had escorted Shirley into the adjoining room, read her her rights, and begun questioning her. What they were getting was much, much different from what Mahlberg was hearing in the next room.

George Coelho took the lead. He'd worked with kids all his life, he understood them, and he liked them. Most of the time, he also found they liked him. George didn't really seem like a cop—at least, not in that stereotypical, rigid, yes-ma'am-no-ma'am kind of way. He couldn't have stood much taller than five-foot-seven or -eight, and even though he was only in his early forties, his black hair had receded so far that the top of his head was completely bald. A true olive-skinned Italian, his generous and frequently smiling mouth was framed with a huge, bushy black moustache, and his deep brown eyes sparkled mischievously, as if he were in on some wondrous joke no one else could understand. George Coelho was an easy man to talk to.

The first thing they learned was that her name wasn't Melissa, but Shirley. Shirley Katherine Wolf. Leaning toward the girl, he quietly explained again why they were there, and that the authorities knew she and Cindy had been out at Auburn Greens near the murder scene. "You know, Shirley, murder is a very serious thing. Would you be willing to give us a hand here, help us clear the matter up?" He honestly didn't think she knew a thing they could use, but he had to ask. It was part of the drill.

Shirley smiled broadly and nodded. "Sure, I'll help you. I really would like to clear it all up, too."

"Good. Now maybe you could start by telling us what happened."

Shirley hesitated, then looked from Coelho to Thompson and back again. "Well, uhh—we talked

237

about turning ourselves in. Would that have helped?"

George Coelho felt his heart stop for an instant. "Just tell me what happened, Shirley." His mind was hurtling a million miles a minute in at least three different directions at once.

"We did it," Shirley said flatly. "We killed her."

Coelho swallowed hard, and asked the girl to start at the beginning. He was still having trouble believing that these two kids had slaughtered Mrs. Brackett the way they had. Step by step, Shirley led them through the day's events. Her meeting with Cindy, lounging around the pool at the Greens, their decision to steal a car and kill the owner followed by their apartment-to-apartment search for a suitable car and victim, and their eventual discovery of Mrs. Brackett. She then told the deputies how they talked with the old woman for a long time and after the phone call from Mrs. Brackett's son realized it was time to kill her.

With very little prompting from either of the two officers, Shirley described the murder. She was, Coelho reflected to himself, just like a little police cadet. Eager to help, to make the whole thing go easily and smoothly, to answer all of their questions like a perfect honor student. It was creepy. Yet she was so — well — *likeable*. That was the really weird part: he had to keep reminding himself over and over that this sweet little kid sitting there smiling at him was a vicious murderer.

Then it was quiet. He could hear voices coming from the other room, and someone moving around upstairs, but among the three of them in the little den no one said a word for several seconds.

"Uh, Shirley," Coelho asked, "could you tell me what you were wearing today?"

"Sure. I had my bathing suit on, and then over that

I had on some old blue Jordache pants, and my pink satin Roller Disco jacket."

Ah, that was it, thought Coelho. *Not Rock and Roll or Rockettes: Roller Disco!*

"Where are those clothes now, Shirley?"

"In the bedroom."

"Okay. Well, we're going to go . . ."

"Umm, there's somethin' else in there, too. In the bedroom, next to the bed on the nightstand, on top of this big pink can. It's my journal. I been keeping it since February. It's okay if you read it. Uh, look at the last page. I wrote it in the car, the one we hitched a ride to Roseville in this afternoon after we killed the lady."

Every time she said that, Deputy Coelho had to work to keep himself from reacting with a shudder of disbelief.

He went back toward the bedroom, leaving Deputy Thompson to guard Shirley. Standing in the doorway, he gestured for Mahlberg and told him Shirley had confessed. Even the normally unflappable Ray Mahlberg looked shocked for an instant.

"She told me what she was wearing—the blue pants, and the pink satin jacket—and said they would be in here. She also told me I should look on the last page of her journal."

Mahlberg nodded and jerked his head toward the room. "Go ahead. We've pretty much finished in here."

The deputy looked around for a minute or two, then spotted the jacket and pants and a blue pair of Nike running shoes that Shirley also said were hers. He gathered them up and handed them to Sergeant Nelson as evidence. Wandering over toward the beds, he saw a small flowered notebook lying on top of the nightstand.

He flipped it open to the first page, and saw Shirley's signature.

Thumbing through the pages, he finally reached a spot where there was no more writing, and he turned back to the final entry Shirley had made. As he reached the last two sentences on the page, penned in an awkward, childlike scrawl, some of the color drained out of his olive complexion. Even years later he would remember his feelings when he read what the fourteen-year-old girl had written.

Today Cindy and I ran away and killed an old lady. It was lots of fun.

Deputy George Coelho could hardly believe the words that danced obscenely on the page in front of his eyes. They were in plain, simple English, but nevertheless they just didn't make sense. Not in a fourteen-year-old girl's diary. Frankly, not in anybody's diary.

He read the words over and over again, trying to convince himself he was seeing things.

"What've you got, George?" The voice of Sergeant Mahlberg snapped him out of his trance.

"Well, Ray, what I've got is what you won't believe. Read this." He handed the journal to Mahlberg, who looked at the page and then slowly raised his head toward his deputy.

"Good God," Mahlberg said softly. There wasn't much else *to* say. After several seconds he closed the cover of the book and handed it back to Coelho. "We'll need that as evidence, of course. And the clothes, too." His voice was quiet and restrained.

"Right. I'll see to it." With no small effort, both officers began to detach from the emotional aspects of what they had just seen and heard, and resumed doing what they had to do to get the job done. That kind of separating from feelings didn't necessarily come naturally to either man—particularly not to George—but years of law enforcement training and experience had taught them both the absolute necessity of being able to do it, if only to preserve your sanity. If you let it all get to you, if you took it all inside yourself every day, sooner or later you'd end up drowning in it or turning into a blithering zombie. Either way you'd be no good to anyone, much less to yourself. So in response you learned how to hold all the pain, all the horror and violence and putrefaction away from you, so far away that most of the time it didn't even touch you. It was the only way to survive.

Ray Mahlberg took a deep breath and turned to Cindy, who was still seated on the side of the bed. "Cindy, I'm going to have to put you under arrest for the murder of Anna Brackett." He snapped on the handcuffs, then went into the other room and repeated the procedure with Shirley. Neither girl made any moves to resist him, and even Cindy didn't bother to throw the kind of fit she usually did when she was caught at something. "I didn't do nothin'," was about all she would say.

By now it was well after four o'clock in the morning. Two officers from the Auburn Police Department who'd been posted outside the Osborne residence as backup had already left after receiving a call from their dispatcher; the remaining man now returned to his station house. Someone called for another Sheriff's patrol unit so the two suspects could be transported separately to the Sheriff's Department for booking and further interrogation; even after the extra car arrived at the scene, it was nearly thirty minutes before the investigators completed gathering evidence and were

241

ready to leave. In the meantime an officer placed the girls into the back seats of the two cruisers, where they appeared to fall asleep.

Coelho, Mahlberg, and Thompson escorted the teenage suspects through the deserted streets of the city, where downtown late-night stoplights merely blinked red and yellow in deference to the nearly non-existent traffic. Once inside the Sheriff's Department building, they mounted a steep flight of stairs and settled the girls into separate rooms: Shirley in a small clerk-typist's office, and Cindy in the Crimes Against Persons office next door which Mahlberg and Coelho shared. In a whimsical comedy of errors that lasted nearly forty-five minutes, Ray Mahlberg—later joined by others in the office—mounted a frantic search for the tape-recording equipment, which they finally realized was locked in Lieutenant Eric Engellenner's desk drawer. Frustrated, Mahlberg telephoned the off-duty officer, who lived in a small farming community some fifteen miles away, and asked him to come in and unlock the recorders. Once he was there and the equipment was in place, Engellenner agreed to stay and witness Mahlberg's interrogation of Cindy. Coelho and Thompson, meanwhile, had begun their taped interview with Shirley.

Thus far, all Cindy knew was that she was under arrest—she had no idea of what Shirley had confessed to Coelho in the basement of her house. For the forty-five minutes Sergeant Mahlberg questioned her about the events of the day Cindy maintained an irrevocable posture of innocence. She admitted they'd been at Auburn Greens, that they'd swum in the pool and walked around, even that they'd been to two or three of the condominium units in the complex—but she insisted they really *had* been looking for a friend, and to borrow a telephone to call her mother. That was all.

"Cindy, the more you talk the deeper you get," Mahlberg sighed. "Why don't you just level with me? Tell me what you and Shirley did in that apartment."

"We didn't go to anyone's apartment, except the ones I told you."

"Can you tell me why you have bloodstains on your pants that I took out of your bedroom?"

Cindy smiled. "There's no bloodstains on any one of my clothes."

"Oh, yes there are."

"I'm not worried about anything."

"You ought to be."

"Well, I'm not," Cindy retorted hotly. "Because I didn't do anything whatsoever to be worried about. Because if I would have done something, I wouldn't have stayed home at all. The first thing I do when I do something is run. And I *didn't* run. Because I had nothing to run for."

"Did you see what Shirley wrote in her diary today?" Mahlberg decided to try a different tack.

"As far as I know she didn't write in no diary. She kept asking me for a pen. I didn't have one."

"Well, she *did* write in the diary today."

A tiny spark of tension was ignited in the room.

"And you know what she wrote?" Mahlberg asked. "She wrote, 'Me and Cindy killed an old lady. It was fun.' Now, why don't you just tell me about it. . . ."

"There's nothing to tell." Her face was getting hot.

"Cindy . . ."

"Nothin'. Nothin'." She wasn't about to get caught in his trap.

"Cindy, I've got a pair of pants that have bloodstains on them. I've got witnesses that put you and Shirley by the condominium where the murder occurred — witnesses that named you by name because they knew you. I've got a diary written by Shirley that says you killed the old lady and that it was fun. And I'm going to have your fingerprints from inside a tan Dodge that was in the carport. Finally, I have a set of keys that was in your and Shirley's possession that's going to unlock the door to the apartment where the murder was committed. Tell me the truth."

"I am."

"Then how can you explain all of this?"

"I don't know. I . . . uh, there's a million people in this world that look like me. And I could name a hundred of them."

"How is it that the man and woman who let you use their telephone saw you and Shirley get into the tan Dodge later?"

"I don't know. . . . I already told you. . . . You — you're getting me all frustrated here." She couldn't keep anything straight all of a sudden.

"Cindy, they had seen you before."

Cindy stuck her chin out in defiance. "Well, what they saw and what they know are two different things. Because I didn't do a thing. As far as you go, you can believe what you want to believe."

In the tiny office where Deputies Coelho and Thompson were talking with Shirley, things were going much more smoothly. Again, Shirley obediently repeated the story so her confession could be taped. About halfway through the interview, Coelho asked Shirley why she was being so open with them.

"I'm just telling you facts. So you can see I'm not holding nothing back."

"Why?"

" 'Cause I don't want to get in no more trouble than

I'm in."

Even though he had no doubt the girl was competent, George needed to make sure—for the record—that she understood the difference between the truth and a lie. "You're telling us the truth, Shirley—is that correct?"

"Mmm-hmm."

"What's the difference between the truth and a lie?"

"Well," Shirley explained, "you have to keep adding on to a lie. To, you know, to keep making up more stories to make it fit. And then you get caught. I was telling you the truth, the facts: what we wanted, and how we did it, and why we did it. Just so that you know."

Later on, Coelho asked Shirley whether she thought she and Cindy were equally guilty.

"Uh, seeing as how we both . . . well, she insisted on . . . Umm, at first I wanted to leave, and said I didn't want to do it. I go, 'Let's just leave.' And she goes, 'No, we're gonna do it.' I was scared, so I says, 'You grab her,' but she tells me to do it instead. So then I grabbed her, and then Cindy hit her a couple of times. . . ." Shirley was beginning to feel really awful about talking to the cops like this about Cindy. "I don't know. I don't want to say anything, because she's my friend. But I—I think we both share the guilt in a way because, you know, we both went there, knowing we were going to kill her and get a car. And she handed me the knife, and I killed her. She took care of the phone and other things. Those were our jobs. She knew what was going on as much as I did. I mean, if she—if she hadn't of . . . well, I wouldn't have stayed. I'd have jammed."

"And you said when you got there that Cindy knew you were going to kill the lady? You had talked about

245

it before?"

"Yeah." She looked thoughtful, and then added, "It was just a crazy game. I wonder how it happened."

Yeah, little girl, thought George sadly. *I wonder how it happened, too.*

After finishing with Shirley, he and Sergeant Mahlberg met in the hallway to discuss the results of each other's interrogation.

"Maybe," George suggested, "Jerry and I could give it a try with Cindy. Jerry knows her from before, and that may make a difference."

"Sounds like a good idea to me." All Ray Mahlberg wanted were two nice, clean, legal confessions. He didn't really care who got them.

By this time George had already been on duty for nearly twenty hours, and he was beginning to feel it. But this case was just as important to him as it was to his sergeant—he'd been in on it since the beginning, had been involved in the major breakthroughs, and he wanted to see it to the finish line. He also had a nagging feeling that Cindy would talk to him and Jerry, where for some reason she had locked up like a clam with Ray.

Cindy was staring out the window when the two deputies walked in.

"Cindy? I'm Deputy Coelho, and you know Deputy Thompson from earlier this evening." Thompson had stayed with Cindy in the little office while the others were on the great tape-recorder hunt.

"Yeah. Hi." She managed a weak smile.

"Okay, Cindy. I know you've been talking with Sergeant Mahlberg, and that you've told him you weren't involved in the murder out at Auburn Greens yesterday afternoon."

"That's right. I—we—didn't do nothin'."

246

"Well, that's not exactly what Shirley told us in the other room. In fact, she confessed to the whole thing: how the two of you planned the murder to get a car; how you went from door to door looking for the right victim; how you met Mrs. Brackett and sat with her for maybe as much as an hour, just talking; then how you killed her and what happened afterwards. All the way up to the two of you finally going to sleep tonight. So we know everything, Cindy."

She looked from one officer to the other, then let out a brazen, nervous laugh. "Damn her! I told her we shoulda turned ourselves in. . . ." Then she shook her head and sighed. "Oh, well. Okay: I'll tell you what you want to know. Let's go for it."

Coelho had the girl read and sign a *Miranda* waiver and then turned on the tape recorder, noting the time was 7:34 A.M. The entire session lasted slightly more than half an hour; in that time Cindy confirmed most of the details of what Shirley had said, added a few of her own, and filled in a couple of blank spots. It was all coming together—all except the reason. Yes, there'd been a *motive:* to steal the car. But identifying a motive didn't automatically make the crime comprehensible. Needing a car wasn't reason enough to kill someone—at least, not the way they had killed Mrs. Brackett. The more he questioned Cindy, the more crystal clear it became to Deputy Coelho that something much bigger, much more powerful, had to lie behind the brutality of this kind of act.

"What did you feel like after you killed her?" George was trying to get a handle on this thing, and it just kept eluding him.

"To honestly tell you the truth—this goes for me and Shirley both—we didn't feel any badness. We felt good inside. We wanted to go out and celebrate. We were full of laughter, and we were just . . . like, it was fun. We enjoyed it."

"Can you explain why?"

"I don't know. It was like . . . well, it was like afterward, we wanted to do another one. We just wanted to kill someone. Just for fun. I felt like just going out and celebrating, laughing, and telling everyone what I did."

"Uh . . . Oh." He felt speechless. "How old did you say you were?"

"Fifteen. I just turned fifteen two months ago."

"Fifteen years old." *Mother of God . . . what makes a kid turn into something like this at only fifteen years old?*

"When you got to the pool and you dyed your hair and that kind of stuff, when did you start talking about getting a car?" Coelho wanted to understand how the two girls had made the decision to commit the crime.

"We talked about it as we were walking away from the pool. I said, 'I want a car,' and she goes, 'So do I.' I was going to show her how we could do it, and then I turned around and said to her, 'We'll just go to some old lady — and then if we have to, we'll kill her.' Shirley goes, 'What do you mean, commit murder?' And I said, 'That's right.' "

"Because why?"

"Because I wasn't about to have her open up her mouth. See: we wanted her car, and we knew she wouldn't give it to us. And we couldn't just tie her up because then she could identify us."

"You've never really hurt anybody before yesterday, have you?" asked Deputy Thompson.

"Oh, yeah," Cindy replied casually. "I've hurt lots of people. I've stabbed people, I've shot people, I've tried to run people down, I've beaten people. . . ."

"Ever kill anybody before?"

"No. And I've tried so many times."

"Yet here's a girl you met for the first time a few short hours ago — and you got it together enough to do it. How?"

Cindy barely hesitated before answering. "She . . . you see, she's exactly like me. She has the same childhood. We're like . . . well, we're one."

"Who do you think is more guilty, if I can use that word? You or Shirley?" Thompson, like Coelho, was also searching for answers to the whole insane puzzle.

"I don't think either of us is guiltier. We did it together. We did everything. I did it — she did it. It was like there was just one of us doing it all."

"What do you think are going to be the consequences of what you and Shirley did?"

"Oh, I know for a fact that I will be put in Juvie, and then go to prison."

"How do you feel about that?"

"I won't live that long to go."

"What do you mean, Cindy?"

"I would kill myself before going to prison. I can't see myself going there — can't handle the fact of being locked up."

"Can you handle the fact of seeing yourself running around loose with the idea that it's fun to kill people?" Coelho asked.

"I've tried to kill myself before. . . ."

"We're talking about other people here."

"I know. But all I have is frustrations, so I take it out on other people. I don't like them because they're probably better than I am. Because my childhood has been so rotten . . . and they lived a good one . . . and I don't want them around. I want them to pay." Her face had become clouded and angry.

"What's rotten about your childhood, Cindy?" asked Coelho. He really did want to know. Maybe it would help him understand somehow.

"Lots of stuff." She was quiet for several seconds, and the hardness in her eyes became veiled by a thin film of what looked like sadness. Or hopelessness. "For one, having been beaten since I was born. And been raped a few times."

"By whom?"

"My brother Keith for one. Been raped last time I got out. Then there were others—I got raped when I was living at the group home. I tried to kill myself after it, but Jana stopped me."

"Do you feel you have anything to live for right now?" Despite the girl's crusty veneer of hardness, George Coelho could sense a soft and terribly vulnerable core inside of her.

"No. Nothing whatsoever."

"Anything to die for?"

She hesitated only briefly, and then looked out the window again at the clear, bright morning sky. "Hell," was all she said.

Fourteen

By eight o'clock on the morning of the fifteenth, Placer County's DeWitt Center — home to most of the county governmental departments — was buzzing with activity, more so than usual for a typical Wednesday in mid-June. Rumors about the two teenage girls who'd been brought into the Sheriff's Department earlier that morning, one of whom was still in the building being interrogated, were spreading like a late-summer forest fire throughout the huge county complex; at the same time, news media from all over northern California had begun to bombard the Sheriff's and District Attorney's offices with demands for updated information on the killing and the suspects.

All morning, departmental employees gathered in tight little knots over office coffeepots and in the neon-bright hallways to share what they knew about the murder of the elderly woman at nearby Auburn Greens, while at the homey C Street Café, the county center's only coffee shop, alternating waves of disbelief and horror over the revelations and rumors filtering out from the Sheriff's office spread through the early-morning crowd.

The *Auburn Journal* newspaper ran a front-page story about the murder in that morning's edition, but since the paper's deadline had come and gone before the two girls confessed, the only details the paper could report were that two teenage girls were wanted for questioning in connection with the killing. Of course, by now the paper, as well as every other newspaper and radio and television station in the region, had received Sheriff Nunes's press release outlining the capture and subsequent confession of the girls, whom he declined to name because of their ages. In the final paragraph of his press release, the sheriff noted that "an autopsy is scheduled for later this morning to determine the exact cause of Mrs. Brackett's death."

The Placer County Morgue is sequestered on a short side street within DeWitt Center, very near the Sheriff's Department patrol car parking lot. The narrow, low-slung structure was originally faced with appealing, ruddy red brick — but like nearly all of its companion brick buildings in the sprawling center, in recent years this one, too, was forced to suffer the supreme indignity of being painted a sickly, mucous yellow. The 225-acre complex was built in early 1944 as a part of the DeWitt Military Hospital and then abandoned two years later when the war ended; yet in less than six months, it was once again open for business — this time as DeWitt State Mental Hospital. It continued to operate until the late 1960s when then-Governor Ronald Reagan closed it and most of its sister state hospitals down. By the early part of the 1970s, the legislature authorized the sale of DeWitt to Placer County for the staggering sum of one dollar — setting the stage for the ultimate migration of many county departments to the center.

More than a few local cynics and old-timers still chuckle over the fact that today, Placer County's government is run out of a former mental institution.

Dr. Tony Cunha finished washing his hands and tied the black plastic-coated apron around his back. He glanced up at the large clock on the gray concrete block

252

vall, noting that it was 8:30 A.M. Standing off to one side
n the chilly room were Sheriff's Captain Marvin Jacinto,
photo I.D. technician Bonnie Norman, and Ray
Mahlberg. Dr. Cunha's assistant strode over to the huge
double steel doors and pulled them open, and a blast of
even colder air swept through the windowless, cement-
floored chamber. In a moment he wheeled out a narrow
gurney, on top of which lay a white plastic zippered body
bag with a tag at one end labeled "Case No. 3915-83."

"Time to get started, gentlemen," the doctor said. "Oh,
excuse me: and Ms. Norman."

Dr. Cunha was a forensic pathologist, on contract with
the county of Placer to perform autopsies for the Coroner's Office. This day, he would spend the better part of
the morning examining the body of Anna Eugena Brackett, murder victim. During the course of the lengthy autopsy, recorded in the nineteen-page coroner's report, Dr.
Cunha discovered the real extent of Mrs. Brackett's injuries.

He unzipped the plastic shroud and began to tape his
comments. After he chronicled in the most minute detail
every aspect of Anna's clothing and the blood spatters
staining her blouse, pants, and undergarments, he began
the tedious job of measuring and describing each and
every mark on her waxen body, even the faded scar that
sliced across her chest from the mastectomy she suffered
so many years ago. All in all, Cunha counted at least
twenty-eight stab wounds to Anna's back, neck and chest,
plus a number of smaller scratches and abrasions. On
some areas of her back, it was nearly impossible to delin-
eate one gash from another, there were so many so close
together. Bonnie Norman snapped away with her camera, recording for posterity the legacy of the madness of
June 14.

As he probed and studied, the pathologist discovered
the cause of Anna Brackett's death: the massive knife in-

253

jury to her back which perforated her aorta, the major artery which carries blood from the heart to the rest of the body. Two other catastrophic and potentially fatal wounds had punctured her left lung and spleen, and right neck. Either one would have been capable of causing death, the pathologist said, except for that brutal thrust which severed Anna's thoracic artery. At that moment, blood would have poured into her chest cavity like churning flood waters through a rupture in a dam, resulting in a sudden and lethal drop in her blood pressure which she could not have survived. More than likely, Anna Brackett was already unconscious and near death by the time these other deep and angry stab wounds were made.

Dr. Cunha also discovered a small, nearly insignificant bruise on Anna's forehead just at the hairline, which suggested she had been struck with some type of blunt object. In her robin's egg blue eyes, now glazed with death, the pathologist also found a dozen or more tiny hemorrhages, mute testimony to the fact that the woman had been viciously throttled at some time during the struggle, although no marks from the strangulation were evident.

There were other bloody gashes as well, scattered over her rear torso and neck—these lacerations ranged in length from a quarter inch to almost two inches, and in depth from scant millimeters to over four inches. That meant that in some areas, Anna's body had been pierced halfway through by the huge, ugly butcher knife. No one in the room that day could help but feel astonishment mixed with revulsion as they envisioned the blood-crazed Shirley Wolf, a young woman barely past childhood who was by all appearances sweet and polite and considerate, with all the light and life gone from her eyes as she impaled Mrs. Brackett over and over and over again in a fury born of God only knew what.

Some time later, Ray Mahlberg stepped out into the warming air and took a deep breath. Even the cloud of noxious exhaust belched from a passing truck was better than the pungent, choking odor of antiseptic mingled with stale blood that permeated the frigid morgue. No one could be blamed for being grateful to leave that scene, to try and push from their mind the image of the woman whose lifeless body lay inside the stone building. No one, of course, needed an autopsy to know what killed her—but at least now they all understood a little better how she died. The carnage that was evident from Anna Brackett's mutilated body was almost overwhelming, even for those who were fairly seasoned and hardened. Especially considering that two kids—two *girls*—had done it. It was almost incomprehensible.

"Umm, we're going to want both girls' suits for the lab." The Sheriff's deputy who had brought Cindy to the Juvenile Hall that morning was talking to Liz Maher, the soft-spoken counselor who earlier booked the girls into the Hall. "You know, for blood analysis and so forth."

"Okay," Liz said. "We need to get them showered anyway, so as soon as they're out of their clothes you can have them." Both girls were still wearing the bathing suits they'd had on during the murder.

Since the time they first had been separated in the basement of the Osborne house several hours before, the only time the two teenagers had seen each other was through the windows of separate patrol cars as they waited to be taken to the Sheriff's office. Now they were being isolated from one another again, this time to be locked into individual cells in the girls' wing. Because Shirley had arrived first at the Hall, she showered first. A few minutes later, Liz and another counselor took Cindy in to get cleaned up; as the girl stood under the pounding spray, Liz noticed some homemade tattoos on her back that looked as if they'd been made with a felt-tip pen. Some of the design had been washed away by the water, but a fair amount of ink still clung to Cindy's skin. Liz reached in with a washcloth to wipe her back, and at the touch of the counselor's hand Cindy began to weep—huge, racking sobs that shook her entire body.

"I . . . I ca . . . I can't believe . . . can't believe th . . . this is . . . this is happening," she whimpered unevenly through a sudden fit of violent hiccups. "I don't . . . I can't . . . it isn't real, isn't true." The rest of her words were drowned in a flood of tears, as if all the pain and torment of her fifteen anguished years had been unloosed in response to that one brief moment of honest human contact. When they took her back into her tiny room and locked the door, Cindy simply lay there in a fetal position, eyes wide and staring, for the next four hours.

Shirley, on the other hand, was her usual loquacious self, emotionally anesthetized to the life-shattering implications of the past day. Her principal concern seemed to be for her friend Cindy. Is she okay? she asked over and over again. How's she doing? Is she crying? When can I see her? But by the time the staff checked on her a few minutes after she'd crawled into bed, she was fast asleep, snoring loudly.

By the next day the entire city of Auburn was aflame with shock and indignation over the killing, which by now was being widely reported in not just the local media, but on the front page of both major Sacramento newspapers, by all three network-affiliate and the two independent television stations in the capital city, and every radio station between San Francisco and the Oregon border. By mid-afternoon, major metropolitan newspapers from as far away as Los Angeles picked up the story as word of the savage murder began to spread over the Associated Press and United Press International wires.

People everywhere were having a difficult time coming to grips with the reality that such a vicious crime had occurred in a town like Auburn, a place light-years away from the inhuman brutality of the inner city where such bloodthirsty events were, if not more tolerated, then at least more grudgingly accepted as inescapable elements of the urban landscape. What made it all the more disconcerting was that both killers were more-or-less local kids, products of local schools and local communities, and that neither one had a record of serious violence which would set them apart from the horde of other borderline juvenile delinquents and troubled teenagers who drifted through the system.

But most staggering of all was that these two remorseless young murderers were girls.

Girls who had celebrated their fourteenth and fifteenth birthdays just two months before.

By one o'clock on Thursday afternoon, state Department of Justice criminalist Torrey Johnson and latent print specialist Cornace Sanders had completed their search of Mrs. Brackett's impounded automobile. On the dusty hood were three perfect footprints, as well as a faint fabric impression where someone had leaned against the edge of the car. When the two men opened the car door, something white under the passenger seat caught one of the investigator's eyes; he carefully reached in and pulled out a rag, smeared with crimson. Next to the rag lay an eight-inch-long butcher knife, its steel blade encrusted with clots of dried blood. These critical pieces of evidence were added to the long list of items already in the department's Bureau of Forensic Services lab, including three medium-long brown hairs removed from Mrs. Brackett's right hand, and her still-running Timex wristwatch with a similar hair caught in the metal band.

Placer County Deputy District Attorney Larry Gaddis, meanwhile, had been assigned to the case. Gaddis, a four-year veteran of the D.A.'s office who would celebrate his thirty-fourth birthday that following month, was looking forward to being involved in a case of the magnitude this one was turning into. It would be a personal challenge for him — something he always enjoyed — and could be a real boon to his career if all went well. Tall, blond, and with a muscular physique that gave no hint of the unwelcome middle-aged spread that frequently accompanies a sedentary job such as his, Gaddis was one of the D.A.'s top prosecutors. Although he wasn't the type to leave a host of bodies in his wake as he marched up the public-service ladder, at the same time this extremely personable and well-liked attorney understood all too well that doing a creditable job on a major case could be a significant stepping stone to bigger and better things.

By late afternoon he had already completed most of the paperwork for the next day's preliminary hearing, where he would argue for keeping both suspects in custody until the detention hearing, and where the judge would explain the proceedings to both girls and formally appoint attorneys to represent them. He also started the ball rolling on his motions to obtain certain items of physical evidence, including hair and blood samples from both Shirley and Cindy and hand, palm, and fingerprints from both girls. Heading home to his wife and children that night, Larry suspected that over the next several weeks he might not be seeing quite as much of his family as before. Denise would understand, he knew that — but still, it might be a little tough on all of them, what with summer just beginning and the kids itching for a vacation. He glanced at his watch. A little over twelve hours from now he'd be standing in court, and the whole crazy roller coaster ride will have begun.

Across town, at Harry Sands's Chapel of the Hills mortuary, the body of Anna Brackett lay in a large, gleaming casket inside the darkened funeral home. Another coffin rested on the floor beside her — in it was the body of Anna's long-time friend and lover, James Wedgeworth. Jim, whom Anna had hoped to visit on the early evening of June 14, died of cancer less than twenty-four hours after Anna was killed. Both of them would soon be flown to Meridian, Mississippi, a city some twenty miles from the Mississippi-Alabama state line and the seat of Lauderdale County, for burial together on Monday. Jim was going home for the last time, and his beloved Anna would be at his side.

The Placer County Juvenile Hall hunkers into the banks of a barren Auburn hillside, on top of which whizzes the incessant traffic of Interstate Highway 80. Less than two hundred yards away across a narrow asphalt road is a large department store, the hub of the bustling Auburn Town Shopping Center where the old Placer County Hospital — birthplace of Cindy Collier — once stood. A twelve-foot-high chain-link fence surrounds the mustard gas yellow Juvenile Hall building and the small exercise yard to the rear, shielding the adjacent world from the youthful transgressors inside — at the same time shielding those youngsters from the sweet freedom their actions had forced them to relinquish. The boxy concrete-block structure, built during the early 1950s, has somehow managed to withstand the test of time and thousands of angry young inmates, although the cheerless facility is inarguably inadequate, outdated, and badly in need of repairs.

Visitors and inmates alike enter through a tiny lobby, to the right of which is a glass-walled guard's station with its massive communications console. Beyond the station is a large, windowless day room, where wards mingle with one another and visit with friends and relatives from the outside world; flanking the day room are two hallways leading in opposite directions toward the girls' and boys' wings.

Both Cindy and Shirley were placed in isolated, one-person cells in the girls' wing, partly in response to the seriousness of their crime and the need to keep them separated from one another until after the detention hearing, and partly to allow staff to keep a constant vigil over them. Because of the statements they made during their interrogation, and later to counselors at the Hall, the girls were placed on suicide watch: every five minutes a staff member made a physical check to insure neither suspect had attempted to take her own life. No one knew how real a possibility suicide might be, but at the same time, no one wanted to take any chances.

As a security precaution, both teenagers wore metal shackles around their ankles most of the time, creating a pinched, old-woman kind of shuffling gait in the two normally effervescent teenagers. By now, Cindy was her old self once again: cocky, despotic, and openly hostile when pushed beyond her self-imposed limits. The only crack in that veneer of arrogant self-confidence came when Linda arrived at the Hall to see her daughter for the first time since the night she was taken away by Placer County Sheriff's officers. The minute Cindy saw her mother standing in the day room, she ran into her arms, sobbing profoundly. Shirley, on the other hand, continued in a state of near-obliviousness: the appearance of her own mother seemed to affect her very little, except to intensify her childlike giddiness at this new and unique adventure. There in the day room together, mother and daughter sat playing with one another's hair like two adolescent girlfriends, smiling and giggling at their own private jokes.

as if they were at home in Katherine's bedroom. When Katherine left, Shirley asked only one thing: "When am I going to be able to see my daddy?"

The morning of June 17 dawned bright and clear. The temperature, which for days had been hovering in the balmy low-to-mid eighties, was supposed to shoot up to near ninety-five by the middle of the afternoon—a little warmer than average for June, but by no means unprecedented. By eight o'clock Shirley and Cindy were showered, dressed, and ready for the ride out to the Superior Court for their initial hearing. Juvenile Hall Group Supervisor Mike Rains and counselor Liz Maher were assigned to transport the two girls in the green-and-white Sheriff's patrol car, and to keep them in line and away from each other. The minute they saw each other, both girls broke into laughter and started to talk.

Mike broke in immediately. "Hey, you two—no talking."

Cindy spat out an angry curse.

Mike, who had known Cindy before, was a little shocked at her tone of voice. He'd known her to be hostile and aggressive with the other wards at the Hall, but never with the staff. He threw her a quizzical look and then shook his head.

The six-mile ride out to the Superior Courts, temporarily housed in a series of buildings between B and C Streets in the administrative center until the renovation of the historic Placer County Courthouse could be completed, was quiet and uneventful—although the tension in the car rose precipitously the nearer they got to their destination. Turning the corner onto C Street, Mike noticed the newspaper photographers.

"Oh, boy, we've got company," he groaned.

"Is the TV here? Where's the cameras? I think I see Stan Atkinson!" The two girls' excited voices toppled over one another like struck bowling pins. They both peered out the window toward the small group of people assembled near the front of the courtroom.

"Never mind the cameras and the TV," said Liz, suddenly conscious in spite of herself of her own appearance.

Thus far, officials hadn't released the girls' names, a prohibition built into the state law to protect the identities of juveniles involved in crimes. Under the original form of this law, juvenile court proceedings were also closed, the rationale being that individuals should not be branded with the public stigma of criminality because of mistakes made in their youth. However, recently that law was modified to exclude certain cases of violent crime from the dictum, allowing these types of proceedings to be fully open to the public. That would ultimately be the ruling with the Cindy Collier-Shirley Wolf case — but until the judge formally announced the proceedings to be public, no one in authority could reveal the girls' identities.

As they drove up to the side entrance to the courtroom, several officers were shouting, "No pictures, please!" and "Please wait until after the hearing to take your photographs!" As far as Mike could tell, most of the reporters were complying.

The two teenagers crawled out of the car, hands and legs shackled, and shuffled up the concrete steps. Once inside, the court bailiff took them to a holding room where again Mike attempted to keep them from talking to one another. This time, Cindy's verbal attack was even more direct.

"Listen," she growled, "I could whip your butt any day. Just gimme a chance."

Mike was well over six feet tall, but even at that he didn't doubt that Cindy could give him one heck of a run for his money. He had never particularly liked the girl, and he liked her even less now. He admonished her once again to be quiet. She simply snorted with derision in reply, smiling tightly.

"Okay, the Court is ready. Miss Collier, you first." The bailiff gestured for the stony-faced teen to come with him, and the duo disappeared through a side door into the sanctum.

It was several minutes before the presiding judge emerged from his chambers; during that time Cindy and her attorney engaged in intense and sometimes animated conversation. Among other things, the lawyer was warning her client about appropriate courtroom behavior and the need for a certain degree of sobriety during the proceedings.

"All rise!" commanded the unsmiling deputy. "Department Two of the Superior Court of the State of California, in and for the County of Placer, is now in session—the Honorable Wayne Wylie presiding." Judge Wylie was sitting in for Juvenile Court Judge J. Richard Couzens, who was out of town on vacation.

"Matter Number 3912, in the matter of Cindy Lee Collier, also known as Osborne," the judge intoned. "Let the record show that the minor is in court with her attorney, Miss April Maynard, Deputy Public Defender." After ascertaining that Cindy's mother would not be present for the proceedings, Judge Wylie continued. "Let the record also reflect that pursuant to Welfare and Institutions Code Section 676 requiring that in those cases in which the charge is one of several enumerated charges in the case of a juvenile, that the members of the public shall be admitted on the same basis as they may be admitted to trials in a court of criminal jurisdiction.

"Pursuant to that section, the public has been admitted to the courtroom."

A quiet murmur spread through the packed room, and Cindy turned her head to assess the crowd. Her attention returned to the black-robed judge as he asked if she was able to afford an attorney.

"No." Her mumbled reply was barely audible.

263

"The Court will appoint a public defender to represent you. Is that your desire?"

"Yes."

He then outlined the charges against her. Count One: murder, a felony. Count Two: special circumstances involving the use of a deadly weapon in the commission of murder. Count Three: burglary, including special circumstances involving the use of a deadly weapon in the commission of that crime.

After Judge Wylie explained that the Probation Department had recommended Cindy be detained in Juvenile Hall pending the remainder of the proceedings, her attorney spoke up.

"Your Honor, I would like to set the matter for a *Dennis H.* hearing—I believe that the date of the twenty-eighth was agreed upon in chambers."

A *Dennis H.* proceeding is a special hearing to determine whether or not there is probable cause to continue holding a juvenile in custody on the specific charges.

"I might also add for the record," said Maynard, "that in the event the coparticipant Shirley Wolf sets a similar hearing on the same date, Cindy would not object to having that hearing held at the same time."

"Fine," said Judge Wylie.

Earlier that morning in the judge's chambers, April Maynard had requested that Cindy be given a psychiatric evaluation, which the judge now ordered. As a final step, Maynard also asked that, pending the outcome of the evaluation, Cindy be allowed to postpone entering a plea until the *Dennis H.* hearing in eleven days.

"Anything further to come before the Court this morning? All right," he said, looking up from the stack of papers in front of him, "the Court finds that detention is a matter of immediate and urgent necessity for the protection of the person or property of others. The Court also finds that the minor, because of the serious nature of the

264

offense, and because she is on probation now from this Court, that she is likely to flee to avoid prosecution. Therefore, I order the minor to be remanded to the probation officer for detention in the Placer County Juvenile Hall."

Judge Wylie then went through the same procedure for Shirley, appointing a private attorney, Thomas Condit, to represent her. Unlike her more sophisticated cohort, however, Shirley appeared confused and unsettled during the ten-minute hearing, at one point wiggling her left wrist out of the steel cuff until the bailiff sternly reprimanded her. Meekly, she slipped her hand back inside the handcuff before anyone else noticed. During the judge's explanation of the *Dennis H.* hearing and the evidence which would be presented at that time to justify continuing to hold her in custody, Shirley interrupted.

"What evidence?" she blurted out. "Do you have any?"

"Well," Judge Wylie replied, "*I* don't have any—but it's the District Attorney, not me, who will be attempting to prove the case against you."

"Umm—can they prove it right now?"

The judge seemed momentarily at a loss for words, struck by the brash guilelessness of the youngster sitting before him. "Well, Shirley, that's what the *Dennis H.* hearing is for. That's when the District Attorney presents whatever evidence he has to the Court, so the Court can rule on that evidence. But we need to give him enough time to do that, so we are asking that you agree to postpone the hearing until the twenty-eighth. Do you understand?"

Shirley looked from the judge to her attorney, who bent over and talked quietly to his client for several seconds. At first she just shook her head; but then after Condit said a few more words, she nodded quietly. "Okay. I'll wait until the twenty-eighth."

Judge Wylie sighed audibly, foreseeing the next obstacle. "Shirley, the Probation Department has recommended that you be detained in the Juvenile Hall pending any further proceedings. Do you have any questions of the probation officer concerning his recommendation that you be detained?"

"I want to go home." Shirley swiveled around in her seat toward her parents, who were sitting in the first row of the courtroom. "All I want to do is go home with you."

Katherine looked down at her hands, a pained expression on her face. Louis smiled at his daughter and mouthed, *I love you, princess.*

Flustered, Tom Condit asked the judge's indulgence while he spoke with his young client. Again, Shirley's violent head-shaking, punctuated by frequent whispers of "No!" communicated her displeasure at the recommendation.

"Your Honor," said Condit, clearing his throat, "my client has requested that rather than being detained in the Juvenile Hall, she be released to her parents until the *Dennis H.* hearing." He knew full well the judge wouldn't even consider such a request, but as Shirley's attorney he felt obligated to at least ask.

"I understand your client's desire, Counselor, but the Court simply cannot allow the minor to be released from detention at this time. In consideration of the seriousness of the offense, and because the minor is currently a runaway from her court-ordered placement, the Court finds that she is at great risk of fleeing to avoid the jurisdiction of this Court. Therefore, the Court hereby orders the minor, Shirley Katherine Wolf, to be detained in the Placer County Juvenile Hall."

Shirley's face fell, and for a moment it looked as if she would break into tears. Then, as she had done a thousand times before in her life, she sat up straight and threw her head back a little, giving a slight shrug as if to shake off some unpleasant insect which had fallen onto her. She

266

wouldn't let any of this get to her. She wouldn't allow herself to be touched — to be hurt — by any one of them. Turning back to her parents, she smiled widely, as if to say, *It's no big deal*. For an instant she was just another average teenager called up to the teacher's desk for fooling around in class, and told she would have to spend an extra hour in study hall after school that day. She'd gotten through a lot worse in her life, and she could get through this too. Just like whistling "Dixie."

Outside the courtroom, the band of reporters was waiting. April Maynard, never very comfortable in the glare of the spotlight, politely refused to comment, and quickly walked away from the impromptu press conference.

"Mr. Condit," asked one of the reporters, "what's your tactic for the trial? After all, Shirley did confess to the murder."

"Well, I'd rather not show my entire hand at this stage of the game," he smiled, "but I will say that I plan to argue against the introduction of any statement that Shirley may have made after the arrest. According to what I've been able to learn, a statement may have been taken at the time Shirley had had virtually no sleep, after she had ingested drugs, and after she had asserted her right to see an attorney."

"Why do you think she killed Mrs. Brackett?"

Condit hesitated, and then replied softly. "There are a lot of things that have made Shirley Wolf the way she is. A lot of things that are pretty unpleasant to look at, and even more unpleasant to talk about. The bottom line is this: Shirley Wolf is the end product of fourteen years of rejection, violence, and physical and sexual abuse." It was the first time there had been any implication in court that all might not be rosy with the Wolf family; almost a month went by before the subject was raised again.

A few feet away, Larry Gaddis reflected on his vision of the events to come. "We have a very strong case," he said

267

with confidence. "I'm looking for a straight plea to first-degree murder from both suspects—in fact, I won't accept anything less." It might not be a completely open-and-shut case, but it was the next best thing. The young Deputy D.A. had very little doubt that after the dust settled both girls would be found guilty.

For the next several days Shirley and Cindy continued to be prohibited from mixing with the general Hall population—again out of concern for the potential of violence, mixed with the unsettling fact that, as yet, neither girl seemed to have connected with the terrible reality of what they had done in taking a human life. With few exceptions, their attitudes continued to be carefree, remorseless and, in Cindy's case, insolent. In their now-unforbidden encounters with one another they were much as they had been that day after the murder: two teenagers caught up in the frenzy of an extraordinary experience, bantering flippantly in an attempt to recreate its heart-pounding intensity and at the same time shore up their own sense of control and potency in the face of imminent failure.

Their initial isolation within the facility didn't impinge on their celebrity status with the other wards, however. Many of the kids in the Hall had known Cindy before this—they had gone to school with her, partied with her, fought with her, perhaps even were involved in some of her earlier criminal activities. They were, in many respects, part of a large extended family. The fact that someone they knew that well—or *thought* they knew—could do something like Cindy had done was alternately intriguing and terrifying. There was hardly a person there who didn't want to know more, who wasn't curious to hear about what had gone on in her mind and soul to make her cross that invisible line. Everyone, it seemed, wanted to know what these two killers were *really* like. The counselors remained mum.

The wards at the Hall weren't the only ones whose curiosity had been piqued. Within days, journalists from across the nation were clamoring for information and interviews with the "Thrill Killer Teens," as they had been dubbed. Every media representative worth his or her salt could smell a monumental story brewing, and the fact that no one but family, law enforcement officials, and the girls' attorneys were allowed to see the suspects didn't divert them so much as an inch from their goal.

Switchboards at the Sheriff's and District Attorney's offices were overloaded with calls from city editors and news directors, staff reporters and stringers, and even television anchors, begging for any scrap of available information. Meanwhile, the *Sacramento Bee* newspaper ignited a controversy by publishing the names of the two suspects shortly after their reporter learned them from one of her sources. Letters and telephone calls inundated the *Bee*'s editorial offices, some readers applauding the newspaper's stance and others horrified at the implications of publicizing the identities of juveniles.

A response came in the paper's "Ombudsman" column on Sunday the 19th: "I sense a growing feeling among many newspapers, including the *Bee*, that juveniles accused of serious crimes ought to be named in print, regardless of the government's ban on releasing names. (Remember, the law enjoins governmental officials, not the press.) [The *Bee* believes that] the public is entitled to know which individuals in its midst, young or old, are accused of this kind of enormous aberrant behavior." The genie had been let out of the bottle, and the names of Shirley Wolf and Cindy Collier would soon become part of the nation's collective consciousness.

At the same time, the city of Auburn was gaining its own notoriety. The local Chamber of Commerce and assorted city officials scrambled to find anything that might mitigate the effects of the unwelcome publicity about the town as the site of a gruesome and vicious crime. They wanted people to remember the name of Auburn, California—but not for something like this. Unfortunately, the effects of the murder and subsequent events were as immutable as the blistering summer heat that would all too soon oppress the foothill town. There wasn't a thing you could do about it, except live with it until it was over. Even the staffers at the Juvenile Hall began to feel as if they were in a fishbowl, reluctant to even so much as blow their noses for fear of having the act captured on celluloid for the entire world to see and critique. Things were starting to get crazy; as the days marched on, they would become even crazier.

"Shirley, wake up! It's okay—it's only a dream!" The young counselor grabbed hold of Shirley's shoulders to shake her out of her nightmare sleep. The sound of the girl's loud moaning, followed by a terrified scream, had brought the staff counselor and a guard racing down the hall to her room.

Looking up from her narrow cot at the two faces hovering above her, Shirley seemed to be in another world. At first she cowered in her bed like a small child, trying to pull the sheet over her head as if the two nocturnal visitors were monsters conjured up from some malevolent fantasy world; then the fear and the life in her eyes faded and she simply lay there, expressionless and mute.

"Shirley? Shirley—can you hear me?" There was no response. "SHIRLEY!"

The shock of hearing her name shouted, coupled with the insistent pressure of the counselor's hand on her arm, finally brought the girl back to reality. She sat up, startled to see she was no longer alone in her barren little room.

Her eyes darted from one corner to another and across the floor and ceiling as if she were searching for something or someone she thought had been there.

"She was here," Shirley said dully.

"Who? Who was here?"

"Mrs. Brackett. She was here, with me . . . inside my head and outside, too . . . and she . . . she . . . wanted to get me . . . like she said when I was killing her . . . 'I'm gonna get you,' she said . . . and she's trying . . ."

"Shirley, it was just a dream. A bad dream—a nightmare. That's all."

"Mmmm." She didn't seem at all convinced.

"When we came in you were asleep, and alone. There was no one in here but you. Do you understand me?"

"I guess so. But she was so . . . so real . . ." She lay back on the bed and turned her head toward the window and the night sky beyond. An eerie pattern of light and dark stripes played over her sallow skin as the phosphorescent glow from a nearby street lamp shone through the black steel bars. The counselor started to reach out to smooth Shirley's hair, and then stopped midway. There was something so odd about the girl—so almost alien—that at times you felt as if you didn't dare touch her. She stood there for several minutes until Shirley fell back to sleep, and then quietly went out and locked the door. It was not the first time, nor would it be the last, that Shirley Wolf would be haunted by her own internal specter of the woman she had helped to murder.

Fifteen

Superior Court Judge J. Richard Couzens returned from vacation to find himself in the middle of a hurricane. It seemed as if the attention of the entire state was focused on his courtroom, and by extension, on himself. But it would take more than media hype and public scrutiny to ruffle the thirty-nine-year-old judge, who had been through his share of hotly contested court proceedings in the three years since his appointment to the Superior Court bench. Couzens was widely regarded both in and outside Placer County as a self-possessed, even-minded jurist with a passionate concern for children's issues and an equally fervent belief that many of society's problems could be more successfully addressed if there were a greater commitment to prevention and early intervention.

It was his assertion that all the attention, the recriminations, the public outcry, simply comes too late. It comes when someone has reached the *end* of the tunnel, where it may already be too late to salvage them, rather than at the *entrance* to that tunnel when little Billy Smith gets caught shoplifting or beating up on his classmate — and when there's still the chance he can be helped and changed. Thirteen years in the legal profession had instilled in Judge Couzens not just an abiding passion for the law, but for its potential as a catalyst for positive social change. The next several weeks would put that passion to the test.

The *Dennis H.* hearing on June 28 was little more than a thirty-minute formality. Both April Maynard and Tom Condit entered pleas of not guilty on behalf of their clients, although reserving the right to enter further pleas at a later time. Both attorneys also objected to the District Attorney's application to obtain hair, blood, and fingerprint samples from the girls, but Judge Couzens overruled their objections. Prosecutor Larry Gaddis called Deputy George Coelho to the stand, questioning him for several minutes about his role in the investigation and arrest of the two teenagers. Yes, he spoke with Cindy and Shirley, he said; and yes, they both willingly admitted the crime to him. No, no one coerced either confession.

After Coelho testified, Tom Condit made a lengthy motion requesting a jury trial, preliminary hearing, and bail for his client. After he finished, Judge Couzens asked April Maynard if she joined Condit in his motion.

"Yes, Your Honor."

"Noted and denied." The judge then suggested joining the proceedings, which meant the cases against both girls would be heard jointly rather than in separate hearings. Both attorneys concurred. From now on it would be known as Case Number 3912. After a short conference, Friday, July 8 was set for the hearing on Condit's and Maynard's requests to suppress certain items of evidence and the girls' confessions. Judge Couzens ordered both suspects detained in custody until that hearing date and adjourned the court.

A week before the suppression hearing, Sheriff's Inspector Johnnie Smith transported Shirley and Cindy to Auburn Faith Hospital for blood and hair samples. He wasn't expecting anything spectacular out of the trip, except the chance to get away from his paperwork for an hour or so. What happened at the hospital was as much a shock to him as the unsuspecting nurse. The R.N. had just finished taking a blood sample from Shirley's arm, and Smith was explaining that he also needed some strands of the girl's hair.

"Umm, you should probably take some from here . . . and from back here . . . and maybe ove . . ."

Shirley interrupted Smith's instructions with a bright smile. "Pull some from the back," she said, placing her right hand near the crown of her head. "That's where the lady pulled my hair."

My God, thought the investigator, *it's like she's describing something that happened at a slumber party!* It was hard to believe that this naively helpful creature with the broad grin was capable of the things she had done . . . and capable of such bloodless dispassion about the whole monstrous episode. *How on earth does someone like this get created?* It was a question that would remain unanswered for some time to come.

June had the reputation of being a quixotic month in the Sierra Nevada foothills. One day resident sun worshippers could be donning shorts and sandals and dusting off their bottles of Coppertone, yet within twenty-four hours the thermometer could drop like a rock to regions that had more in common with late winter than early summer. This year, however, things had been fairly steady all month, with people reveling in daytime temperatures that seldom rose above or fell below eighty or eighty-five degrees. By July everyone was prepared for Mother Nature to drop her other shoe and hit the area with a stretch of unremittingly sweltering days, which almost always coincided with the community's Fourth of July celebrations. But like the month before, July of 1983 would come to be the exception that proved the rule. Not

274

only was it pleasantly balmy for the Independence Day barbecue and fireworks display, by July 8 the temperature plummeted by more than ten degrees to an afternoon high of only seventy-four.

Some of the more scantily clad reporters and photographers waiting outside the Department Two courtroom at eight o'clock that morning were shivering perceptibly in the chilly air. Among the swarm of media were crews from the ABC, NBC, and CBS affiliate television stations in Sacramento, along with evening anchors from two of the city's independent stations, journalists from both major Sacramento newspapers and a score from smaller publications throughout the foothill region, radio reporters from a number of Sacramento and Mother Lode-area stations, and a reporter and photographer from *People* magazine. The Anna Brackett killing had become big news.

When the Sheriff's patrol car turned onto C Street, the assembled reporters swung into action. Cries of, "Is that the girls?" and "Are they in there?" echoed up and down the street while camera crews jostled one another for the most advantageous position. The car slowed as it passed the front ramp into the courtroom and then turned right into a wide, blacktopped driveway which led back twenty or thirty feet to a large, fenced-in area adjacent to the court building. A uniformed officer opened the big steel gate and allowed the vehicle inside the chain-link enclosure. It was several minutes before the driver got out and opened the rear door and Cindy and Shirley clambered out. They started to turn toward the reporters gathered nearby, but the deputy immediately ushered them through the narrow side door and into the building.

Almost as soon as the two suspects disappeared from sight, the expectant throng that had clogged the street and sidewalk only minutes before was also gone, swept inside on the compelling tide of curiosity. Within the small courtroom there was barely room enough for everyone to stand. Spectators overflowed into the jury seating area and clustered near the rear door that separated the main courtroom from the paneled foyer. The whirring and clicking of camera equipment seemed to come from every corner of the room, even though at the moment there wa nothing in particular to shoot. Directly in front of the for ward railing were two long walnut tables, each with sev eral chairs that faced the judicial bench. Square windows lined each of the two side walls; one set overlooked a small lawn and a number of shade trees growing between the court building and the building next door. The court room itself was designed to hold no more than a hundred people at best — and at least half again that many were crowded into it on this cool July morning.

Beyond the door on the left side of the bench, out of sight of the gathered witnesses and reporters and curios ity-seekers, Shirley and Cindy sat waiting to be called into the courtroom. Red-haired Fred the Bailiff — his ac tual name was Fred Pitz, but everyone knew him as sim ply Fred the Bailiff, as if that were his full name — stood beside the suspects, ready to escort them inside as soon a he received word the judge was ready. The two girls gig gled and whispered together virtually nonstop while they waited, each one flushed with excitement at the idea of being the object of so much attention.

Fred looked up as the court clerk signaled him. "Okay ladies, let's go on in."

Cindy, wearing a light blue blouse with ruffles at the neck and elbow-length sleeves, was the first to enter the courtroom. Shirley, in jeans and a sleeveless pink-and purple striped shirt, followed closely behind. As camera whirred and blinked once again and pencils scribbled across dozens of notepads, the two teens shuffled across the room to the tables where their attorneys already sat. The heavy silver chains around each girl's waist that led to shackles at their wrists and ankles jingled softly whenever they moved. Both were barefoot except for white socks.

The door to the right of the bench opened, and Fred called the court into session as Judge Couzens mounted the steps and settled into his large leather-backed chair. At the outset of the hearing, the judge overruled both defense counsels' objections to having the media present in the courtroom during the proceedings; but, he added — much to the consternation of everyone except the radio reporters — after a brief period this morning no additional photographs could be taken while court was in session. Grumbling their disappointment, still photographers and television cameramen hustled to get every possible shot until the judge cleared the courtroom of all camera equipment. He had no intention of allowing any part of this trial to turn into a media circus.

The two defense attorneys spent the next five court days trying to provide grounds for tossing out most of the evidence that linked Shirley and Cindy to the crime. They based their requests on a number of points and presumptions: first, that the evidence taken from the crime scene was obtained without a search warrant; second, that officers entered the Osborne residence illegally and that the search they conducted was more far-reaching than statutorily permissible and was not a reasonable extension of Cindy's probation search-and-seizure order; third, that both Shirley and Cindy asked to speak to an attorney prior to initial questioning and that officers ignored those requests; fourth, that Cindy's confession was the result of coercion by her interrogators and that it violated her Fifth Amendment rights against self-incrimination; and finally, that the evidence found in or on Mrs. Brackett's car was based on a legally inadequate search warrant affidavit.

Probation Department Supervisor Thomas Hoffman was first on the witness stand on the morning of July 8.

Hoffman testified for less than fifteen minutes, after which Deputy George Coelho stepped into the witness box and spent the next four and a half hours being alternately questioned by Deputy D.A. Gaddis and grilled by Condit and Maynard. Under tough cross-examination, Coelho solidly maintained that he had in fact advised Shirley of her *Miranda* rights to counsel, not once but twice — first in the game room of the Osborne basement adjacent to Cindy's bedroom, and second at the Sheriff's Department prior to her tape-recorded statement. There was no doubt in his mind, Coelho testified, that Shirley understood her rights completely and clearly; and no, she never asked for an attorney.

"When you took the second statement from Shirley at the police station later that morning, she indicated to you that she had taken some cocaine, didn't she?" Tom Condit was like a bloodhound, sniffing for any trace of something that shouldn't be there.

"Yes," Coelho replied.

"Did you at any time take blood from her to determine if she had cocaine in her system?" Condit knew the answer before he asked it.

"No, I did not."

"When you went to the Osborne house, did you take any tape recorders with you?"

"No, I did not."

"I take it then that the *Miranda* admonition was not recorded in any way."

"No, I don't believe it was recorded."

"Before taking a statement from Shirley, did you at any time make any effort to contact her parents?"

"No."

"Did you ever advise her that if she wanted her parents present, they could be present?"

"No."

"Did you ever determine from her parents or anyone

278

else how intelligent she was?"

"No."

"Did you ever ask her if she knew what the word 'waive' meant?"

"No."

"When you read her her rights, didn't she indicate she wanted to speak to an attorney?"

"No, she did not." Coelho was remaining remarkably cool and unflustered under Condit's rapid-fire, relentless questioning.

"When you were interviewing her on the second occasion, at some point during the course of the conversation did Shirley indicate to you that she had 'read devil-books about how to kill people'?"

"Yes."

"Didn't that strike you as a bit bizarre?"

"Yes," was all he replied.

"Did you ever ask to see if she could be examined by a psychiatrist, or ever make any attempt to have a psychiatrist look at her after that conversation?"

"No, I did not."

Tom Condit had begun carefully planting the seeds which he hoped to harvest later when he entered an NGI — not guilty by reason of insanity — plea on behalf of his client. And it wasn't just some slick lawyer's tactic: Condit truly believed in his heart that Shirley Wolf *was* insane — or at least, that she had been insane at the time of the murder. Although he hadn't discovered everything yet, what he had learned convinced him that no one could go through what she had gone through and not be a little bit off-center. It was just that in Shirley's case, she had gone further over that line than most.

The following Monday morning court resumed at ten forty-five. Unbeknownst to the judge or the assembled crowd, that weekend had been a momentous one for Cindy. A tall, lanky, scruffy-looking man had come to visit her — a man named David Lee Collier. Cindy hadn't seen or heard from her father in over a decade, and she wasn't entirely sure she wanted him back in her life now. Besides, he wasn't what she'd always imagined him to be: a strong, good-looking truck driver type with a wonderful smile and kind eyes, who had become a solid and responsible citizen in the years since he and Cindy's mother had parted. No, he wasn't at all what she imagined.

David Collier had been in and out of prison in the intervening years, including brief stays in two of the state's toughest and most notorious facilities, Folsom State Prison and San Quentin. For one of those years he was jailed in Mexico on charges he referred to only vaguely as being a "wetback." He listed his occupation as unemployed millworker, but for all intents and purposes David Collier was simply a drifter, a man who spent his days on the back of a motorcycle or hitching rides with fellow nomads and ex-cons, doing whatever he needed to do to stay alive. He heard about his daughter's plight from his mother, who lived in the town of Grass Valley, some twenty miles north of Auburn. No great humanitarian, Collier nevertheless felt it was his duty as a father to spend some time with her while she was going through such a difficult time. Besides, he wanted to find out for himself exactly why she had done what she'd done. Even among his own anarchic, outlaw circle of friends and acquaintances, the kind of brutal crime his daughter had supposedly committed was simply not acceptable.

Over the weekend he visited her several times in the bleak day room of Juvenile Hall. An occasional tendril of long, greasy-looking brown hair fell across his forehead as he hunched over in quiet conversation with his steely-eyed daughter. Underneath his broad sideburns and overgrown moustache, the man's haggard face showed the ravages of years spent in intimate friendship with an assortment of legal and illegal drugs of every description.

Occasionally, counselors at the Hall thought they detected a vague odor of alcohol on his breath as he stood waiting for Cindy to be brought out to the visitor's area. Overall, David Collier was not a particularly savory individual.

Cindy's mother had only been present in the courtroom once, at the first hearing for her daughter. After that, Linda shied away from the proceedings and even from visiting Cindy in the Hall more than occasionally. The emotional impact of seeing her only daughter in shackles and chains, coupled with the relentless presence of news cameras and reporters, was simply more than she could handle. David Collier, on the other hand, walked openly into the courtroom on the Monday after his arrival in town. Several people took note of the slightly menacing, scraggy-looking character in faded bell-bottomed jeans, but at first no one bothered to find out who he was.

It wasn't until after the noon break that someone informed Judge Couzens of the man's attendance at the hearing.

Looking in Collier's direction, the judge asked, "You are Mr. Collier?"

"Yeah," he replied.

"I am required to advise you that as the father of Cindy, you have a right to a separate attorney of your own to protect any interest you may have in what is going on here. Obviously, if you don't have the funds to hire your own lawyer, I am required by law to appoint one, and I will be happy to do so. Do you have any feelings whether you would like to have an attorney during these proceedings?"

"I think I would." There was no telling what kind of protection from the law he might need.

Calling both defense attorneys and David Collier to the bench, Judge Couzens explained that because Collier had indicated his desire for legal representation, he would have to halt the proceedings until a lawyer could be found. After a few moments discussion with the assembled attorneys and some minor concessions on all sides, the judge opened the proceedings again and explained the new schedule. The hearing, he said, would be continued one week, to July 18. Defense briefs on the motion to suppress the evidence would be due in his office by July 19, with the D.A.'s rebuttal brief due six days later, on July 25. Then, the judge continued, he would make his decision on the morning of July 27, the first day of the trial. Thanking everyone for their indulgence, Judge Couzens adjourned the court a few minutes before two o'clock.

By now, metropolitan newspaper articles about the crime, which at first were limited to single-column blurbs in sections variously titled "Metro" or "Community" or "The State," began to appear on the front page, while television network anchors like Dan Rather and Tom Brokaw were including snippets about the killing, the hearings, and the upcoming trial in their six o'clock newscasts. Placer County Chief Probation Officer Ted Smith, on vacation with his wife touring the southern part of the United States, was astonished to see just how widespread the news coverage of the crime was. Whether they were in Virginia, Tennessee, Georgia or Louisiana, in small towns or huge cities, the response was always the same. Attempting to cash a check or register at a hotel, people would notice his address and gasp, "Oh, you're from Auburn, where those two girls stabbed the old lady!" Even the *New York Times* ran a story or two, as did the *National Enquirer.*

Shirley and Cindy reveled in their newfound celebrity. Finally allowed to mix with the other wards at the Hall, Cindy found herself back in her old comfortable role of commander and occasional oppressor whenever she thought she could get away with it. But even she could feel the difference in the other kids' attitudes toward her. Every other time she'd been in the Hall, she was one of them, a part of the gang. They joked and lied and schemed together like old friends, secure for the moment at least in their membership in this social club of dubious distinction. There was a certain degree of comfort in being a part of something larger, and of knowing that everyone around you had walked down pretty much the same roads that you had.

But none of them had walked as far down this particular road as Cindy had on June 14. What she had done was so awesome, so unheard-of, that no one knew quite how to respond to her anymore. A gap now existed between Cindy and her peers in the Hall that nothing would ever be able to bridge.

The Hall staffers were by turns gratified and horrified at the other wards' reactions to Cindy once they were allowed to mix with her. On the one hand, many of the kids were shocked and even repulsed at the cold-blooded brutality of the crime, and had a difficult time coming to grips with the fact that this was indeed the same Cindy Lee Collier they had known before. "How could she do something so terrible?" was a frequently-asked question, which the counselors were frankly at a loss to answer. On the other hand, there were certain wards who seemed totally nonplussed by the whole thing, as if they were saying, "Hey, Cindy's cool, so whatever she did is cool, too." Those were the ones that scared the hell out of the staff.

Cindy's father and Shirley's parents continued to visit their respective daughters during the week before the hearing resumed. By now, Louis Wolf had moved his family to a rented farmhouse hidden among huge Douglas firs and yellow pines on a hundred acres outside of Georgetown, a remote logging community about halfway between Placerville and Auburn. In decades past, the property had operated as a summer camp, testified to by a number of dilapidated outbuildings and sheds and a derelict sign on which the hand-painted words "El Dorado" were only barely legible; but for the last several years it had been rented to a succession of privacy-hungry survivalists, recluses, and "farmers" of questionable credentials, whose only requirements were shelter, running water, and isolation from prying eyes. Louis Wolf fit in perfectly.

Things had become distinctly uncomfortable in Placerville for Wolf since Shirley was arrested for murder. Everywhere he went, it felt as if people were staring at him, judging him, even accusing him — as if he and not his daughter had slaughtered some poor innocent old woman. As if *he* were the guilty party. What few friends he had, he said, had completely abandoned him; he told neighbors that anonymous telephone callers were harassing and threatening him, and that he could hardly sleep at night for fear someone was going to harm him or his family. The world was closing in on him, little by little, and if he didn't get away from it, it would end up driving him crazy. So, like a frightened dictator, Louis Wolf gathered up his tattered, frightened little clan and fled into exile.

Of course, the whole thing had been the system's fault. Everything, from his imprisonment to Shirley's forced removal from her mother's side and even to the murder itself. None of it would have happened, insisted Wolf, if everybody hadn't been out to get him.

"They pretend to be nice," he would say later, never quite explaining who "they" were or why they were so interested in undermining his life, "and all the while they're screwin' me, stickin' a knife in my back. And then they're all blaming me, cursing me, for what happened with my daughter — but it was *them*, not me. I mean, look what they did to her. They abandoned her, rejected her, wouldn't believe her, and made her crazy — then made her believe all kinds of garbage about me and what I was gonna do to her once I got out of jail. She just had this anger all pent-up inside of her because of all this bullshit, and it came out against this woman Mrs. Brackett. I lost a daughter because of *society*, not because of me. Of course," he would add piously, "I forgive her for all she's done — even what she's done to me."

Without batting an eye, Louis Wolf managed to take even something as tragic as his daughter's involvement in murder and skew it to provide a platform from which to proclaim his own suffering, guiltlessness, and rage against society.

Meanwhile, Cindy was growing increasingly uncomfortable with her father and his frequent visits. Staff members as well found the man's presence disquieting, and one or two began to quietly fear for Cindy's state of mind if the man continued in this odd pursuit of his daughter. Yet no matter how concerned or even fearful Cindy might have been feeling, she kept those concerns to herself until the end of the week. That day, even the staff watching over them in the dayroom noticed that David Collier seemed to be in an unusual mood: intense and galvanized, with a curiously dreamy, almost sensual look in his heavy-lidded eyes. During their conversation, his voice was more subdued than usual, sometimes little more than a whisper. Apparently, what he wanted to tell her was meant for her ears alone.

He'd been thinking a lot about their relationship, he told her, and had come to a few conclusions. He said, it's important that she stop thinking of him as her father, and instead think of him as her friend. Her best friend. Someone she could talk to, someone she could confide all her secrets and all her innermost thoughts to, someone she could say anything to. He wanted her to be able to tell him anything, anything at all: things about her feelings, her desires, her sexual thoughts and needs — anything.

The things her father said that day were immensely disturbing. They felt dark and dirty and pernicious, and after a while Cindy simply couldn't keep them inside any longer. There was one counselor there who seemed pretty much okay, so Cindy confided a little bit about what her father had said and how it made her feel. She told the counselor that she didn't want to see him anymore. Ever. The counselor agreed, and said she would pass the word along so the others would know that if David Collier came to visit his daughter, she no longer wished to see him.

Fred the Bailiff called the court into session at eleven o'clock on the morning of July 18. Judge Couzens took note that David Collier was not present in the courtroom, but Collier's attorney indicated that the proceedings could continue regardless of his client's absence. For the next hour, April Maynard and Tom Condit cross-examined Sergeant Ray Mahlberg, who had been the last person to testify on July 11 before the Court became aware of the presence of Cindy's father, and halted the proceedings. After the noon recess, Mahlberg spent another fifteen minutes on the stand before he was excused. The principal concern for both defense attorneys during their questioning of the sergeant revolved around the issue of whether he had coerced and intimidated Cindy during the process of interrogation. Mahlberg consistently denied having done so.

"Mr. Gaddis," asked the judge, "do you have any further evidence to present?"

"Not at this time, Your Honor."

"All right. Miss Maynard, Mr. Condit — do you wish to present any evidence?"

Tom Condit stood up and nodded. "Yes, Your Honor,

we do. I am prepared to proceed at this time." If the truth were known, the attorney had been ready to proceed for some time. He had mapped out his strategy as carefully as if he were a military commander planning the logistics of an artillery bombardment of the enemy's key supply lines. Known for his thoroughness and attention to the most minute details of a case, Condit was not a man to leave much of anything to chance. As a criminal law specialist with sixteen years of criminal trial experience behind him, he knew the intricacies of the legal system as well as anyone. He'd even hired a private investigator to look into Shirley's background and try and dig up anything he could use in defending her. It wasn't a question of whether or not Shirley had murdered Mrs. Brackett— they had her down cold on that one. But in the legal sense, not guilty doesn't always mean what the words imply. In one case, it may mean that the defendant actually asserts his or her innocence of the crime; in another case, it may mean that the accused admits involvement, but that because of circumstances surrounding the crime, he or she might not be considered fully culpable. Such are the vagaries and eccentricities of the law in this land of the free.

For Tom Condit, the driving power behind his defense of Shirley lay in identifying and revealing the forces that may have impelled her toward that bloody 14th day of June. Secondarily, he wanted to prove his contention that Shirley's rights had been seriously violated during the investigative process. Both of these goals were on the attorney's mind as he called his first witness.

Richard Payton settled himself into the witness chair and smiled uneasily at the broad-chested attorney. Mr. Payton, Shirley's seventh-grade English instructor at Markham School, had a remarkably elfin appearance with his round face, well-trimmed silver goatee and moustache and short gray hair, and intense brown eyes that peered out from under wire-rimmed trifocals. A serious and studious man not given to outbursts of either gaiety or anger, his expressed thoughts tended to be somewhat convoluted and rambling, mildly reminiscent of an absentminded professor.

Under Condit's questioning, the teacher revealed that Shirley was not a particularly good student — she had difficulties sticking to assignments and completing them — although she was never belligerent or discourteous toward him in class. Yes, he admitted, she hadn't done well at all on the reading comprehension test, and on the whole she was only borderline passing. If he had been allowed to, he would have also told the Court that most if not all of Shirley's other teachers found the same things in the young girl, despite the fact that everyone could see in her rare flashes of excellence. She was a frequent topic of conversation in the faculty dining room, not because she was a typically "difficult" student, but simply because of her very obvious problems in dealing with her peers and the demands of everyday life. By and large, the teachers at Markham felt sympathy for Shirley and tried to give her as much latitude as possible because they could clearly see the young girl's emotional turmoil and woundedness.

After another teacher's brief testimony, April Maynard took over, calling Placer County Sheriff's Sergeant Richard Nelson and Lieutenant Eric Engellenner, and Auburn Police Department Officers John Strahan and Steven Cash. Maynard, who had also pled her client not guilty based upon her belief that Cindy's rights were violated during the initial search and the subsequent investigation and interrogation, was a very different breed from the slightly flamboyant and media-savvy Tom Condit. Lacking the years of legal experience of her co-counsel, not to mention his expertise in criminal law, the serious young attorney had been thrust into a difficult and enormously challenging situation when she was named to

Cindy Collier's case. Representing teenage murderers was not something the Public Defender's office in Placer County normally faced, nor was it something that April Maynard was accustomed to. Normally, she was happiest dealing with family and juvenile law — matters like adoptions, guardianships, and custody issues — although working for the P.D. didn't really provide the latitude or luxury for much picking and choosing. Her appointment as Cindy's legal counsel was a glaring case in point.

But Maynard was determined not to allow her lack of criminal experience to adversely affect her client. The dark-haired, somber young lawyer had every intention of giving Cindy the best possible defense, a defense which revolved around the procedural issues of the case against her. Like her co-counsel, Maynard understood all too well that Cindy had been involved in the murder. But she also believed deeply in the constitutional premise that all people — even the guilty — were entitled to a fair trial and the best possible legal representation. Whatever it took, she would see that Cindy received no less.

Maynard's tack in calling the four officers to the stand was clear once she started questioning them. Did you actually hear Deputy Coelho advise Cindy of her rights under *Miranda?* Were you present in Cindy's bedroom when anything was searched and recovered? Did she ever ask to speak to anyone? Did she ever ask you whether she would be allowed to speak with her mother? Do you agree that the general tenor of Sergeant Mahlberg's interview was somewhat argumentative? She could only hope that Judge Couzens could read far enough between the lines to see that, even though the girls hadn't been terrorized by law enforcement personnel, there was cause to question some of their tactics and procedures. Whether it would be enough to make any difference in the final cut, she had no idea.

Deferring to her co-counsel to continue, Maynard sat

down and said a few quiet words to Cindy.

"I would like to call Shirley Wolf to the stand at this time," announced Condit. Papers rustled excitedly throughout the courtroom, while spectators in the back shifted in their seats to get a better view of the callow slayer. Shirley, wearing little or no makeup, stood awkwardly and hobbled to the stand in her socks, her ankles still bound in chains. She spoke in a low, even tone, looking directly at her inquisitor.

After a few preliminary questions, Condit broached the subject of the cocaine Shirley said she took that night after arriving at Cindy's house.

"That night, did you take some cocaine or some substance identified as cocaine?"

"Yeah, I did."

"Who gave it to you?"

"Keith, Cindy's brother."

"And how much cocaine did you take?"

"I'm not sure on how much. Uh . . . all I can describe is a lot. Six little piles of it."

Shirley then went on to talk about how it made her feel — "real drowsy, then real active, then tingly" — after which Condit asked if she'd also smoked marijuana that night.

"Yes, I did," Shirley replied.

"And how did you smoke it? Rolled up in a paper cigarette or . . ."

"A pipe."

"Okay. How much marijuana did you smoke?"

"Mmmm — two or three drags."

"Now, at the time Deputies Coelho and Thompson were talking to you, were you still feeling the effects of all the cocaine you had taken?"

"Yes, I was."

Zeroing in for the kill, Condit asked Shirley if she remembered Coelho reading her her rights, and asking if she wanted to speak with him about the crime.

"He asked me, yes, if I would talk to him, and I said I wanted an attorney."

The sound of more papers shuffling.

"When you said you wanted an attorney, did you say that once or more than once?"

"Twice. But he and the other guy were talking, and it was like he didn't hear me. I felt he either ignored me or was deaf." Giggles erupted from one or two corners of the courtroom.

"I see. Shirley, to your knowledge did Deputy Coelho ever ask you if you wanted to waive your rights that he'd read you?"

"Yeah."

"Did you know at that time what the word 'waive' meant?"

"No, I didn't."

During Larry Gaddis's cross-examination he tried to break down Shirley's story about the amount of cocaine she snorted, the fact that she asked for an attorney, and her understanding that she had a right to remain silent. Shirley, however, remained intractable, despite the blatant inconsistencies and discrepancies in her earlier testimony. If, Gaddis reasoned to himself, she really snorted as much cocaine as she said — and *if* it was pure and uncut, or cut only marginally — and *if* she snorted it when she said she had — then chances are she wouldn't have been able to fall asleep as soon afterward as she did. Cocaine, an intense stimulant, produces effects that range from anxiety to sleeplessness to hallucinations; and while these effects may last as little as thirty minutes, when the drug is taken in larger quantities they can last up to two hours. At the same time, the stupor Shirley described after being awakened at two-thirty by the Sheriff's officers simply didn't fit with an ingestion of cocaine less than ninety minutes before. Chances were that if she had taken anything at all, it wasn't coke, or it was coke that had been so diluted that its effects were negligible. Plus her comment to Gaddis under cross-examination that she still felt a "faint buzz" when she arrived at the Juvenile Hall more than six hours later made her testimony even more suspect. But what about the marijuana? That part was a little more believable—but even then, by her own admission she'd taken only two or three drags, hardly enough to render her disoriented two hours later.

April Maynard called her client to the stand and asked her three questions.

"Cindy, did Deputy Coelho advise you of your *Miranda* rights in your home?"

"No."

"And at any time while you were in the bedroom being supervised by Officer Cash, did you ask him if you could see your mother?"

"Yes."

"And what did he respond?"

"He said, 'No, not at this point.' "

"Thank you. I have no further questions."

Both defense attorneys indicated no further witnesses, although Deputy D.A. Gaddis said he had one additional witness on rebuttal. Judge Couzens looked at the clock on the rear wall, noting it was nearly five-thirty.

"In consideration of the time, the Court continues this hearing until ten-thirty tomorrow morning." This part of the process was winding to a close.

The next day, court was in session less than forty-five minutes. The only testimony came from Cindy's oldest stepbrother Keith, who was called to the stand by Larry Gaddis. Before Gaddis could begin, Judge Couzens advised the young man that certain questions might have the effect of incriminating him, and that under the law he had the right not to answer them. He also said Keith had the right to an attorney, and that if he wished to avail him

292

self of that right an attorney was available. Keith said he would, and Roseville attorney Alan Pineschi took up a seat next to the witness.

Gaddis asked his reluctant witness one question. "At any time on the night or evening of June 15, did you give Shirley Wolf any cocaine or marijuana?"

"No, sir."

Under cross-examination, Condit brought out several unsavory aspects of Keith's past, including his current probationary status for burglary and the numerous occasions he had been investigated for narcotics violations. Point-blank, Condit, too, asked him if he gave Shirley cocaine and marijuana and had sex with her that night at Cindy's house. Keith shot the lawyer a surly look before responding that he hadn't. He also denied that his sister and Shirley had told him about the murder.

So ended the suppression portion of the hearing. Judge Couzens stated that he would hold to the agreed-upon schedule of beginning the jurisdictional hearing — the juvenile equivalent of a trial — on the morning of Wednesday, July 27, immediately after he ruled on the admissibility of the evidence under contention.

Outside the courtroom, Larry Gaddis seemed unperturbed by the tight schedule, which allowed him less than a week to submit written arguments to the defense motions to throw out the evidence. "I really don't see a huge problem with the schedule," he smiled, as news cameras clicked away. "Of course, if the judge happens to order some of the evidence suppressed, a few of my scheduled witnesses may not be allowed to testify. In that case, I might have to regroup a little — but if there's a major hang-up, I'm sure the judge will allow me a day or two to get my case together again."

Tom Condit was equally confident that the time schedule wouldn't adversely affect his or April Maynard's ability to prepare for the trial.

"What about the conflicting testimony between Cindy's brother and Shirley about the drugs?" a reporter asked.

"Well," Condit said, "there isn't much to say. I mean, there were only two people there at the time: Shirley Wolf and Cindy's brother Keith. If Shirley says Keith *did* give the drugs to her, and he says he *didn't* — well, I don't know what else we can do to get at the truth. It's just one person's word against another."

Sixteen

On Monday, July 21, Condit appeared before Judge Couzens in a surprise and somewhat hastily called proceeding.

"Your Honor," Condit said after a deep breath, "based upon information which I have received from Dr. Walter Bromberg, the psychiatrist appointed by this Court to determine my client's state of mind — and based upon his belief that she was in fact insane at the time of the crime — on behalf of my client I wish to withdraw our earlier plea of not guilty, and enter a plea of not guilty by reason of insanity."

The judge nodded, then asked Shirley if she agreed with what her attorney just said.

"Yes."

"Do you realize that if you are found guilty of the crime, and found to have been insane at the time of the killing, that you could be committed to a state mental hospital for as few as ninety days, to as long as the rest of your life?"

"Yes."

And did she realize that she would need to be examined again by Dr. Bromberg and also by a second psychiatrist and that based upon their reports she may be found sane?

Shirley replied in a low voice that if she started freaking out, no one would think she was sane.

Judge Couzens chided Shirley, telling her whatever she said to the psychiatrist at this point would be between the two of them. He then announced he would appoint a second psychiatrist, Dr. Alfred French, to examine Shirley and render an opinion as to whether or not she was insane at the time of the murder.

"Since there will not be adequate time for the psychiatrists to examine Shirley and prepare their reports by the anticipated end of the jurisdictional hearing three days from now, I will postpone the sanity phase of the hearing an appropriate length of time to allow for their reports to come in."

"Thank you, Your Honor."

"Court will stand in recess until Wednesday, July 27."

By the time most of the media crews were assembled outside the Department Two courtroom that Wednesday, it was clear something had happened. Armed Sheriff's officers cruised up and down C Street, and there were foot patrols stationed at various points around the complex of jaundice yellow buildings. Rumors, disbelieved at first, began to spread through the waiting crowd that the reason for the intensified security was that David Collier had threatened to kill his daughter before she could be tried. Even the most jaded among the journalists there that day weren't immune to the heightened tension in the air, nor to the gnawing sense of discomfort that, once again, something out of character for this supposedly placid rural community had taken place. After all, this was Auburn, California, not New York City or Chicago.

Scanning spectators and reporters alike with metal detectors before they entered the courtroom that morning, a Sheriff's deputy tried to make the best of an extremely awkward situation by joking lightly with some of the people he knew as they came through the line, while a second officer thoroughly searched every purse and briefcase. Even well-recognized anchormen and women from the evening news found themselves subjected to the indignity of being electronically frisked, although, like most everyone else, they handled it with a fair degree of good humor — humor tempered with the realization that the situation was a potentially deadly serious one.

Once he convened the court, Judge Couzens explained the heightened security to the crowd. "The record should indicate that the security measures taken were not due to any action by the minors on trial today. We had received information regarding a statement made by David Collier, father of Cindy Collier, that he intended to kill his daughter either en route from Juvenile Hall or during the court process. Further, we received information that he attempted to borrow a gun from an acquaintance; it is for that reason that I have ordered all persons entering the courtroom to be searched by a metal detector." Later, reporters discovered that it was Linda Osborne who had called the Sheriff's office late Monday evening, saying she'd received an anonymous telephone call from a man stating that David Collier planned to kill his daughter on Wednesday. Sheriff Nunes took the threat seriously enough to order extra security at both the Juvenile Hall and the courtroom.

For the first several hours of that day's proceedings, everyone's nerves were on edge. Each tiny movement outside the windows resulted in dozens of raised heads and craned necks, and not infrequently the rigid attention of the cautious courtroom sentinel, Fred the Bailiff. At any moment the flash of sunlight off a passing car's chrome bumper could become the glint of a steel revolver; the roar of a nearby lawn mower could become the thunder of a bullet ripping through a wooden door; the harmless scampering of a fluffy-tailed gray squirrel across the lawn could become the crazed onslaught of an assassin lurching toward the courtroom.

Yet not long after the judge made his surprise explanation about the extra security to the packed courtroom, the hearing itself settled down to normal. All three attorneys took the opportunity to argue their case for and against suppression of the evidence, even though each had previously submitted lengthy briefs to the Court detailing their positions. After thanking the lawyers for their efforts, Judge Couzens proceeded to rule against virtually every one of the defense motions. The jurist's decision was not something that came as a surprise either to Condit or Maynard, although as professionals they would probably not have admitted such qualms to anyone other than their own consciences.

After a ten-minute recess, the Court declared forty-seven items of evidence admitted for the purpose of identification. "Mr. Gaddis," said the judge, "please call your first witness." The trial of Shirley Katherine Wolf and Cindy Lee Collier had begun.

Carl Brackett trudged wearily to the witness stand. The strain of his mother's brutal murder and the accompanying publicity was evident on the man's haggard face. Essentially a private person, unaccustomed to calling undue attention to himself, he was extremely discomfited at being on display in front of a room full of strangers. But as much as he hated being there, it was something he needed to do. It was, he thought, probably the last thing he could do for his mother—to help see that her killers were brought to justice. *If,* the cynic's voice inside him added, *justice was possible.*

Carl Brackett's brief testimony was the first in a series of building blocks laid by the prosecutor as he began carefully constructing the foundation of his case against Cindy and Shirley. Brackett confirmed all the known details about his conversation with his mother on the afternoon of her death, his and his wife's arrival and eventual break-in at Anna's apartment, and the appearance of the emergency crews and Sheriff's officers. All in all, he was on the stand for less than ten minutes. During all the remaining days of the trial, he never set foot inside the courtroom again.

The stony-faced Ray Mahlberg was next on the stand, explaining to the Court the details of his arrival at the murder scene and the subsequent events, including his search of Cindy's room early the next morning and the later search of Mrs. Brackett's automobile at Auburn Body Shop. After acknowledging a series of photographs of the murder scene and the victim, Mahlberg was asked to identify a small item Larry Gaddis pulled out of an evidence bag. Most of the audience was too far away to view it well, but there was an immediate and unmistakable impact upon those who were close enough to see the paring knife with the chubby little blade bent grotesquely back upon itself. Yes, Mahlberg said, that appeared to be the same knife he discovered on the floor next to the decedent's body.

Before the sergeant could be cross-examined by the defense attorneys, prosecutor Gaddis asked to take a witness out of order. The witness was Cornace Sanders, the supervising latent print analyst with the state Department of Justice.

Sanders had worked for the Department of Justice for almost twenty-eight years, all of them in the area of fingerprint identification. Over the years, the man had testified in hundreds of cases in more than forty counties throughout the state. It took very little for Larry Gaddis to get him declared an expert witness.

Beginning his testimony, Sanders identified a series of photographs of various locations at the crime scene, certain crime scene items, and latent fingerprint cards which he had developed. Yes, he testified, this one corresponds to the fingerprint of Shirley Katherine Wolf, this one to the print of Cindy Lee Osborne-Collier, this one to the murder victim Anna Eugena Brackett. And yes, this print was lifted off Petitioner's Exhibit 33, a flowered drinking glass, this from Exhibit 37, a telephone receiver, this from the door pictured in Exhibit 21. For at least twenty minutes, the specialist matched up fingerprints to exhibits and exhibits to fingerprints until the crowd was nearly asleep. What was the passion of a lifetime to Cornace Sanders was little more than tedious minutiae to almost everyone else.

Until, that is, Gaddis took Petitioner's Exhibit Number 45-B out of a brown paper bag.

"May the record reflect that I am opening Petitioner's Exhibit 45, and removing the contents — a brown paper bag with something in it. I ask that the bag and its contents to be marked Petitioner's Exhibit Numbers 45-A and 45-B, respectively." After the clerk marked the two items for identification, the prosecutor turned once again to his witness.

"Mr. Sanders," he said evenly, "I am now removing Exhibit 45-B from 45-A, and ask if you can identify it." As Gaddis spoke, he slowly pulled a large, black-handled butcher knife from the paper bag and held it up in front of him. A murmur fluttered through the crowd as they caught their first sight of the long silver blade still encrusted with the brackish red of dried blood. Even those who saw the twisted paring knife minutes before were unprepared for the ghastly vision of this bloodstained cleaver, part of its blade gleaming in the phosphorescent courtroom lights. Somehow, seeing it made everything undeniably, horribly real — even, it seemed, to the two teenagers sitting at the low-slung table in the front of the courtroom. Cindy dropped her head and Shirley turned her face away when Gaddis held the weapon aloft, as if both were struck — even if just for that one instant of time — with the loathsomeness of it all. It was, unfortunately, an emotion which neither exhibited openly again.

Court recessed that afternoon after Sergeant

Mahlberg's cross-examination, and the lengthy testimonies of Sheriff's photo identification technician Bonnie Norman and Department of Justice criminalist Torrey Johnson. Little by little, the prosecutor was engineering the escarpment of a case which he hoped would soon surround the two suspects; and no matter how adept either of the defense attorneys may have been at chipping away a stone here and there, it was clear to everyone that the walls were becoming perceptibly higher and thicker by the hour.

"Hey, shut up! Look—look, everybody! We're on TV!" Shirley was jumping up and down excitedly on the bedraggled couch in the Juvenile Hall dayroom. Images of two shackled teenage girls flickered across the screen, accompanied by the velvet voice of a reporter chronicling that day's events at the trial. The only time she took her eyes off the television image was when she glanced over at an equally riveted Cindy, at which point both of them broke into grins. Thus far, neither girl had tired of her notoriety and daily appearances on the evening news—although of the two, Shirley seemed more obsessed with making sure no one's attention wavered from the news reports whenever they appeared. It mattered little that to the other Juvenile Hall wards, all of whom had grown bored with the two girls' self-importance as well as the media's endless repetition of the murder story, the thrill of basking in Cindy and Shirley's reflected glory was steadily waning.

Linda Osborne, absent from the courtroom since the second day, continued to shun the spotlight and refused to speak to the press; she also steadfastly denied the media access to her daughter, who as a minor was forced to follow the dictates of her mother. What people knew of Cindy Collier's life before June 14 was restricted to rumor and scraps of information from former acquaintances and unnamed official sources.

In contrast no matter how vociferously Shirley's father decried what he saw as society's and the press's blatant attempts to paint him as a villain in his little girl's life, nevertheless was more than willing to allow virtually unrestricted access to her. Shirley had already been interviewed by Cheryl McCall from *People* magazine for what would be a six-page spread in the national publication, and by the *Sacramento Bee*'s feature writer Pat Murkland.

The only exception was television. Despite their incessant clamor for exclusive interviews with Shirley, thus far none of the stations had been successful in securing a parental okay. Wolf's reluctance had nothing to do with a distrust of the medium — rather, he seemed to have an unconscious disdain for the written word, coupled with a deep appreciation for the enormous power of the visual image and the lucrative prospects of that power. In Louis Wolf's world, the rest of the media was pitifully insignificant compared with the omnipotence of television. If TV wanted his daughter's story, they would have to pay for it. After all, he reasoned, *he'd* certainly paid for what she had done — now it was only fair that somebody else should pay. Pay for what society had done to him and his family.

He and Katherine came to visit Shirley several times a week. They were an odd threesome, sitting there in the dingy visitors' room: Shirley and her father side by side, jostling and touching and playing games with one another, and Katherine apart from them, hunched in a separate chair or even standing across the room, a mere observer to her husband and daughter's union. Because of the previous charges against Louis for molesting Shirley, the staff was more alert than usual for signs of inappropriate contact between the two of them — yet even though their seemingly innocent behavior was under the constant scrutiny of watchful counselors, there remained an intangible yet highly charged undercurrent of sexuality which frequently passed between them. Holding her hands in his,

302

he would raise them to his lips and kiss them adoringly, his dark eyes never leaving her face. Sometimes she would lie on the small couch with her head in his lap, his arms curled into a tender cradle, while she coquettishly twisted a lock of his hair in her fingers or playfully tweaked his earlobe.

On the face of it, none of what they did together was prurient or offensive or even particularly suggestive — but almost everyone who saw them together was struck with the almost palpable eroticism of the interaction between the father and his daughter. Confronted with the image, Louis of course would erupt in fury at the "dirty minds" of people who, he said, simply didn't understand that they had always been a family who valued physical contact.

The next morning, Prosecutor Gaddis called another Department of Justice criminalist to the stand. James Streeter was responsible for typing and matching the blood of the two suspects and the victim with blood found on various items found at the murder scene and in Cindy's room. On cross-examination, Tom Condit bore in like a pit bull. There was hardly a single element of Streeter's testimony the attorney didn't challenge, from the number of tests performed on the blood, to the processes used for cross-matching, to the validity of the criminalist's statistical projections.

"Mr. Streeter, how many tests did you do? Six, seven?"

"Well, excluding human blood as a test, I performed five particular tests."

"What are the maximum number of blood markers that have been detected from bloodstains?"

"Probably around fifteen."

"So," Condit smiled, "is it fair to say that of the fifteen marker tests, you performed five?"

Streeter shifted uncomfortably in his chair, realizing where Condit was going. "Yes."

"So there are ten tests you could have performed and didn't?"

"Well, that's not an accurate statement of the facts. We — we didn't have enough blood on the pants, for example, to perform all fifteen."

"All right. But let me ask you this: if you had been able to run those other ten tests, and if they came up with a marker that was different from the Brackett blood — well, that would have excluded Mrs. Brackett as being the donor of the blood that was found on Shirley Wolf's jeans, wouldn't it?"

Streeter sighed. "Yes."

Tom Condit was clearly aware that in some respects he was grasping at straws. But he had a duty to defend his client to the very best of his abilities and to accept nothing at face value without questioning it. If he could plant just one seed of doubt in the judge's mind that the investigative work had been less than thorough, or that the facts didn't totally support the criminalist's conclusions about the blood typology — well, that would be one less piece of evidence they could use against Shirley.

The last person to testify that morning was Dr. Tony Cunha, the pathologist who performed the autopsy. Despite his dispassionate, clinical description of Anna Brackett's wounds, by the time he was finished most of the spectators were several shades paler than they had been before. April Maynard focused her cross-examination on several aspects of the autopsy reports that were inconsistent with what she knew to be Cindy's confession. Cindy said she had beaten the woman — but there was only one contusion on Anna's head, which the pathologist admitted could conceivably have been caused by a fall to the floor as opposed to the blows of an assailant. Cindy also claimed she had stabbed Mrs. Brackett in her head, eyes, and throat — but no, Cunha confirmed, there were no stab wounds to the head, the face, the eyes, or the front of the throat.

No one in the gallery expected what came next, when Tom Condit began his cross-examination. Rather than attempting to limit Cunha's detailing of the autopsy findings, with every query Condit delved deeper and deeper into the grisly details of how Anna had died, and the extent and savagery of her wounds. He had no intention of trying to prove Shirley hadn't stabbed Mrs. Brackett — the evidence was overwhelming, and far more than circumstantial. What he wanted to show — and having Cunha recite every gory detail was the best way he knew to do it — was that Shirley had been completely out of control when she killed the woman, that she had been acting like a lunatic. That she had in fact *been* a lunatic.

"You indicated you found some fourteen incised wounds on the back. There were others as well, isn't that right?"

"Yes. There were actually more superficial wounds that didn't cut through all the layers of the skin."

"Didn't your findings suggest that she was stabbed at least eighteen or nineteen times in the back?" Condit was trying to paint as graphic a picture as possible of his client during those minutes of insanity. In his mind's eye he could see her, hear her voice even, as she madly and mercilessly impaled Anna Brackett over and over with the huge knife.

"Well, my examination of the garment the decedent was wearing showed that there were some sixteen perforating wounds through that garment. . . ."

"Is it possible that there were more stab wounds that could have been from the same perforation? In other words, that she could have stabbed her more than once in the same place?"

"Yes."

"With reference to the wounds that weren't particularly deep, do you feel each of those wounds were caused by a separate attempt to stab the victim?"

305

"Yes."

"And were a lot of those wounds blocked by hitting bone or other parts of the skeletal structure?"

"Yes. All but two of the fourteen on the back."

"With reference to the injuries in the neck, how deep was the cut that went to the voice box?"

"Approximately four inches."

"Is the neck hard to puncture? Is it as hard to puncture, say, as the back area?"

"Well, there shouldn't be much of a difference if the knife blade had traveled between the ribs or entered the neck, because both have soft tissue. Of course, getting through the ribs or the spine would be a whole different matter."

As his audience visibly recoiled, the attorney paused, letting the picture take final form. "Is there any way of determining the kind of force that would be necessary to puncture the back and get into the chest cavity?"

"It would take somebody very strong, somebody wielding quite a bit of energy with a purpose in mind."

A conflict was brewing, centered around the admission of both girls' confessions as evidence. All three attorneys wanted something different, and for different reasons. Larry Gaddis, of course, wanted both confessions brought in exactly as they were taped that night. Tom Condit wanted to bar the statement of Cindy Collier, insisting that it implicated Shirley. April Maynard, on the other hand, wanted to exclude Shirley's entire statement, stating that it was damning to Cindy.

Judge Couzens's dilemma over these divergent opinions was intensified because of a Supreme Court ruling known as the *Aranda* decision, under which a judge is not allowed, in the same proceeding, to hear the confession of one participant in a crime which implicates the other participant. Under *Aranda,* there were three choices which could be made: grant separate trials, exclude both statements, or edit one or both of them so that neither adversely affected the other's rights. To sever the proceedings and grant separate trials at this point, the judge knew, would create a position of legal jeopardy for both suspects which could not be mitigated. To arbitrarily rule that both confessions be thrown out would open the Court to an artillery of appeals that would undoubtedly succeed. All of which left the judge in the position of having to offer to the two defense attorneys that another judge listen to the confessions and "sanitize" them for Couzens's hearing.

That would have been fine, except for one or two complications. First of all, April Maynard didn't want Shirley's statement brought in, because it incriminated Cindy. She had no objections, however, to entering her own client's statement. But Condit objected strenuously to that idea. He had no intention of allowing anything into evidence that implicated Shirley, as long as he had legal recourse. On the other hand, he demanded that his own client's confession be entered exactly as it stood: it was as good a piece of evidence pointing to Shirley's unbalanced state of mind as anything else they had, he reasoned.

All of which left the judge back at square one, considering having the confessions edited before being played in court.

Maynard was well aware that Judge Couzens would deny her request to have Shirley's statement excluded. As a result, she made a tactical decision which in effect, made the jurist's decision a little easier: after making her *Aranda* objection to entering Shirley's statement, she withdrew the objection and agreed that Shirley's confession could be brought in, in its entirety. While that confession did tend to incriminate Cindy to some extent, by and large it showed Shirley as the principal actor and the one responsible for the bulk of the butchery. If anything, April thought, it might help Cindy rather than hurt her.

After the details were ironed out, Couzens asked both defense lawyers to work with the District Attorney and Judge Wylie over an extended noon recess to edit Cindy's statement. Unfortunately, what was supposed to have been a long lunch break turned into an entire afternoon of debate, disagreement, and eventually, compromise. Stomachs as well as voices were growling by the time Judge Wylie asked, "Anything further to come before the Court?" and the three attorneys wearily gathered their briefcases and headed home.

A little after nine-thirty the next morning the public was admitted and Judge Couzens settled himself at the bench. "I think," he announced, "we are now in a position to proceed, at long last."

Today was the day everyone had been waiting for — the day the world would be able to hear for itself the confessions of the two young murderers. Gaddis began by calling George Coelho to the stand and questioning him about his activities on the night of the murder, up to and including his formal interrogation of Shirley at the Sheriff's Department.

"At this time," Gaddis said, "with the Court's permission I would like to play the tape." For nearly an hour the audience sat in strained and sometimes stunned silence, listening to a fourteen-year-old girl talk about murder as if she were talking about a trip to the store to buy a half-gallon of milk. Her voice was, for the most part, flat and expressionless, without so much as a hint of remorse or fear or even nervousness — just a good little girl doing her best to help and do what someone asked her to do. Just a good little girl, telling how she had simply done her job. Sitting at the long table beside her attorney, Shirley barely moved during the playback except to cock her head occasionally as if she hadn't understood something. Every once in a while she leaned toward her attorney to make a comment, but Condit silenced her with a sharp wave of his hand.

For a moment after the tape ended, no one moved or said a word. Then Judge Couzens took a deep breath and called for a short recess. Cindy's taped interrogation would be the next piece of evidence to be heard — and no matter how much they may have edited it, there was no way he could listen to another confession like the one that had just played without a break. From the looks on the faces of most of the people in the courtroom, he wasn't the only one.

Back inside fifteen minutes later, Larry Gaddis continued his examination of George Coelho, this time concentrating on the deputy's interview with Cindy Collier on the morning after the murder.

"At this time I would like to play the tape, Petitioner's Exhibit Number 54, which is the edited copy of the Cindy Osborne-Collier statement."

"Play the tape," ordered Judge Couzens somberly.

Out of what was originally a forty-five-minute interrogation, the Court heard less than twenty-four minutes. Huge sections of the confession were nothing short of unintelligible because of the deletions, although many portions of the statement remained intact. While the tape played on, tension in the courtroom escalated dramatically as the assembled reporters undertook the herculean task of transcribing what they frequently could not understand in light of what they consistently could not hear. As Shirley did before her, Cindy sat immobile for the first several minutes — until she heard her own voice describing how she had tossed Shirley one knife, only to have it bend in half, and then found the butcher knife for her friend to use. Listening, Cindy bent her head forward onto her clasped arms and appeared to weep softly.

"Deputy Coelho," asked Gaddis after the tape concluded, "does that appear to be a fair and accurate representation of your conversation with Cindy Collier on that morning?"

"Uhh — it's very much a part of what was recorded."

"It's not the whole thing?"

"No. It was butchered." The deputy grimaced slightly at his own unfortunate choice of words, but it was too late to take them back.

It was true: the tape *had* been butchered. No one knew that better than George Coelho, who watched that early June morning as the clean summer sun streamed in through his little office window and played across the bitter lines in Cindy Collier's face, and who heard her cough out an acid laugh once she realized she was trapped by the truth. No one knew better than George Coelho how it felt to listen to two girls barely past childhood dispassionately confess to something so horrible it would burn itself like a white-hot branding iron into his consciousness for the rest of his life. As he walked through the packed and silent courtroom after leaving the stand, he thought warmly about his own children, and then let his mind drift past the faces of all the other kids he'd known and been touched by and laughed with and cried for over the years. He thought about the misery and torment he'd seen so many of these children go through, all the needless pain so many of them had suffered, and wondered when and where it would all stop. The large swinging door at the back of the courtroom thunked back and forth quietly behind him as he left, echoing the hollowness he felt inside himself.

A deep and heavy silence as oppressive as a corpulent thunderhead settled in the room. A few moments later, Prosecutor Larry Gaddis looked up at Judge Couzens. "Your Honor," he said quietly, "we rest our case."

After the noon recess, the judge asked if either defense attorney wished to call any witnesses. Neither did. In deference to what he called the "substantial evidence on each and every element of the crimes as charged in the petition," Prosecutor Gaddis declined to make a closing argument, and simply submitted his case to the Court.

April Maynard was the first of the two defense attorneys to make a closing statement to the Court that day. She took a moment to gather her thoughts, then stood and carefully began her arguments in defense of Cindy. Her comments revolved around two major issues: the fact that Cindy had not participated in the actual murder to as great an extent as Shirley, and the inconsistencies in Cindy's statement when compared with the evidence. Explaining her position, Maynard said, "I would ask the Court to make a distinction in the activity of the two girls and find that there is certainly a reasonable doubt as to whether Cindy used any weapon to inflict deadly injury to Anna Brackett. I think the Court has to agree that obviously there were no fingerprints of Cindy Collier on the murder weapon, and no blood found on any of her clothing.

"I think it is also apparent," she went on, "when comparing the statement of Cindy Collier with the physical evidence, there is a great deal of exaggeration on the part of Cindy. She refers to beating the victim, 'beating her bad,' and yet the physical evidence shows no beating or bludgeoning. She also stated she stabbed the victim in the face, the eyes, and the throat, yet none of that was substantiated by the evidence.

"When faced with these kinds of inconsistencies, one question arises: why would anyone claim to do these things, when obviously they weren't done? I think we have to try and understand the dynamics of a situation like this — although unfortunately it does not conform to what most of us would consider 'rational.' Perhaps Shirley acted out of some desire for notoriety, and Cindy sadly was carried along into something over which she had no control and in which she did not directly participate. Perhaps there was some bit of bravado, being caught up in this entire movie that was going on in the minds of all the people involved. It was a drama, after all — one that had been ob-

311

served in books, movies, TV—and perhaps the perverted glamour of it all, the desire for infamy and notoriety, took hold of Cindy and brought forth some claims for activity that never took place.

"I would simply ask the Court to make the distinction between the actions of Shirley and Cindy, to find that my client did not personally inflict any of the injuries involved."

"Thank you, Miss Maynard. Mr. Condit?"

The tall, thickset attorney smoothed his coat and rose with an easy grace that belied his size. He smiled slightly as he began his argument. "Your Honor, I'm approaching this argument with a great deal of restraint. I realize that anything I say at this point may sound like, 'Other than a dead body, fingerprints on a knife, and a confession, what does the prosecution have?' But I would ask you to examine that evidence with some care."

Condit then went on to enunciate what he saw as discrepancies in much of the evidence: the fact that the fingerprint analysis showed only eight or nine common points, whereas many other agencies require a minimum of twelve points for positive identification; that the blood analysis wasn't totally conclusive, as half a percent of the population in the area could have a blood type identical to what was found on Shirley's pants; that none of the ID witnesses were called; and that Shirley described the knife as being double-edged, even though it was single-edged.

"We also," he continued, "have Shirley's statement that she'd read and studied a lot about how to kill people — and yet the way the killing was done suggests a total lack of any kind of sophistication or experience. We have an attempt to murder somebody with a knife that's designed for peeling potatoes — a knife that obviously didn't accomplish the end. We have a whole series of wounds that did no fatal damage, suggesting again that this was the horrible macabre adventure of a couple of inexperienced girls as opposed to sophisticated, trained, or experienced killers.

"I will submit," he went on, shooting a quick glance at Maynard, "that although co-counsel would suggest that Shirley was the prime and perhaps only mover in the scenario, the evidence that you have heard and the evidence that we will ultimately present to you will show instead that Cindy was the catalyst, and Shirley the reaction — that Cindy was the wick or fuse and Shirley the explosion, and that the reasons for that explosion go all the way back into the childhood of a little girl. What the evidence suggests here is one thing only: a compulsive thrill-killing, spawned by madness."

"Thank you. The Court will take a ten-minute recess, after which I will render my decision."

Unlike the scramble for the front door that usually accompanied most breaks in the proceedings, this time very few of the spectators or reporters moved from their seats. No one wanted to take a chance of losing his or her position at such a crucial time. A few minutes after the recess began, the nicotine-scented Louis and Katherine Wolf were ushered into the courtroom by their attorney Richard Steffan, who remained at their side — perhaps protecting his clients from some interview-mad journalist who might seize the opportunity to corner them during the lull.

The seconds and minutes seemed to take hours to pass. Several observers in the audience jerked in startled surprise when the door to the judge's chambers opened suddenly and the jurist strode quickly up the steps to his bench. No one dared to even breathe for fear of missing so much as a syllable of his words.

"The Court finds," Judge Couzens announced after clearing his throat, "that beyond a reasonable doubt the allegation of Count One is true, that it is murder in the first degree. With respect to Count Two, I find that also to be true beyond a reasonable doubt: that it was murder in the first degree, and that the murder was committed during the commission of the crime of burglary. As to the special allegation that each minor personally used a deadly weapon, the Court finds it is true as well. With respect to Count Three — burglary in the first degree, with a personal use of a deadly and dangerous weapon — I find beyond a reasonable doubt that has been proven. These findings are as to both minors."

Neither Cindy nor Shirley showed any emotion at all: they acted as if the judge were talking about someone else, two *other* teenaged girls who were being convicted of this terrible and brutal crime. If any of it was touching them, they weren't about to show it. In the audience, Katherine Wolf sat quietly, her hands clasped tightly in her lap; frequently during the judge's soliloquy she shook her head in what looked like stunned disbelief, and put one hand to her mouth. Beside her Louis was, like his daughter, as impassive as a stone sculpture.

Next, Judge Couzens set the date for Cindy's dispositional hearing for 8:00 A.M. on Friday, August 12, two weeks away. After a brief discussion with Condit, they agreed to begin the sanity phase of Shirley's hearing that same day.

"Is there anything else from either side?" the judge asked.

"No, Your Honor," answered Maynard and Condit.

"Nothing else, Your Honor," said Gaddis.

"Thank you very much. The Court stands in recess until August 12."

Seventeen

Back at Juvenile Hall, the two girls who had been friends — who Cindy once described as being "one" — were drifting apart. Or perhaps, it might be better said that each girl was amputating herself from the other. Cindy's anger and resentment seemed to focus on Shirley's insanity plea. There was a chance, after all, that Shirley might get off with only a few months or a year or two in a cushy nuthouse, while Cindy rotted away for the next decade at some Youth Authority prison. What gave Shirley the right to call herself insane, just to save her own ass?

For her part, Shirley was weary of Cindy's constant badgering and ridiculing, especially around the issue of the insanity plea. Plus, her razor-sharp intuition had been screaming for days that Cindy was becoming disenchanted with their friendship — so to protect herself, Shirley put on her old familiar suit of armor that told the world none of it mattered.

The tension between the two teens only grew as August 12 approached. At this point, Cindy's mother was visiting more and more often, relieved to find that the media had relaxed its vigil at the Hall. The encounters between Linda and Cindy were often punctuated by tears and long minutes of just holding and comforting each other — Cindy frequently taking on the role of parent as she had done so many times in her fifteen years. For someone who has spent the better part of her life protecting and making excuses for and taking care of her parent, there is an undeniable feeling of comfort and security at being in that old familiar role and having that kind of power and control. Clearly, it was something Cindy had searched frantically for in every relationship, every friendship, every angry brawl or battle of words. It was as if the need for control was her life-blood, the thing that kept breath in her lungs and rhythm in her heartbeat. Sometimes it was inconceivable that she could survive without it.

Louis and Katherine visited Shirley several times during those two long weeks as well. Shirley was jubilant that her parents cared enough to make the awful forty-minute drive down and up the treacherous, writhing canyon highway between Georgetown and Auburn, and then the return trip after they'd seen her. There had been times — such as after the last hearing and before they led her away to the police van, when she'd been able to hug and comfort her weeping mother — that she felt a special closeness to Katherine, almost as in her dreams of how things used to be. She was also beginning to feel a little better about her father's attitude, which seemed to soften a little more each time he saw his daughter. A few days before he even told her that he forgave her for what she'd done: not just the murder, but also for accusing him of molestation all those months ago. Of course, he said, she knew how important it was that people learn the truth about that story, about how it was something she'd just made up. He knew, he purred softly, that when it came time to tell her side, she would do the right thing.

The fact that Shirley had rediscovered her father's love — or rather, that he had decided to reconfer it upon her — made the sting of Cindy's ostracism a little less painful. Of course, having your parents' love wasn't like having a friend — but it was better than nothing at all. That nothingness, that total and absolute desolation and aloneness, was the demon in the dark for Shirley, the one thing that terrified her more than anything else. As much as she detested the feelings of vulnerability that accompanied her craving for human closeness and love, her terror of the emptiness that went along with being alone was far more powerful.

August 12, ten-thirty in the morning. The heat wave everyone had dreaded for weeks was finally clamping its jaws around the valley and foothills: by one o'clock that afternoon, the thermometer would register 104 blistering degrees. Once again the cool, brick-walled courtroom was jammed with curious onlookers and anxious press; most of the reporters rustled a photocopied document in their hands that Louis Wolf had passed out before court convened.

Although Wolf usually avoided the media and had little comment to make to them, this morning he was a veritable magpie. In a strategically casual press conference, he handed out copies of a letter that Shirley wrote on August 4 to El Dorado County Superior Court Judge Charles Fogerty, the same judge who made Shirley a ward of the court in October after she brought the incest charges against her father. Speaking in his thick Brooklyn monotone, Wolf read the two-page, handwritten letter to the assembled reporters.

Dear Judge Fogerty,

Hi, how's everything? I'm real upset I thought I'd write you because theres something on my mind. Remember my case with my dad? Well Kathleen Steward and Dorothy Coppings [the two Child Protective Service social workers assigned to the case] *are very sneaky. I don't mean to be rude, but I was wondering if you were aware that I tried to tell them that my case with my father wasn't true. You see my Dad did not do what he served time for. Kathleen would not let me bring it into court she held it from you. The D.A. and Dorothy and Kathleen knew about it! They threatened me that I'll go to a 'bad girls home' and I can't see my parents they won't be able to see me and that my mom can go to jail and my brothers would go to foster homes!*

Now that I'm seeing my Dad I feel wanted loved and understood. They both love me and would not hurt me and want me home. . . .

Please try to see me before the 12th and my lawyer is not so good may I please have a different one. I'd like him fired.
> *Thank you*
> *Sincerely*
> *Shirley Wolf*

P.S. You see Kathleen screwed up my head not my parents.

Wolf looked out at the reporters and began to soliloquize. "I need you to understand," he said, "why I pleaded no contest to the charges back then. I was gonna fight them and go to court to prove I was innocent, but the D.A. and my public defender told me I could get up to fifty years in jail if I pleaded innocent and the judge found me guilty anyways. So I decided the best thing for my family was to go ahead and plead no contest, and do my time in jail. Which I did — I did a hundred days — even though I had medical proof that I was impotent at the time my daughter said I molested her. I did it to save my family the publicity and pain of a court trial, and so's I could get out of jail a lot sooner."

He went on to explain how at first he had wanted to represent Shirley himself in court on the murder charges, but that he became convinced he should let an experienced attorney handle it. "I only wanted the best for my little girl," he said.

Speaking for himself and Katherine, Louis told the reporters that they both wanted Shirley to drop the insanity plea, mostly because it had been concocted out of thin air by her attorney as a ploy to get her off. Condit had already made it very clear that he planned to base the insanity plea

318

on what he called Shirley's nearly lifelong history of being sexually, physically, and emotionally abused by her father — a charge Louis Wolf disputed with angry vigor. "There's absolutely no justification for the murder, I know that," Wolf said somberly. "And I know she's sick and needs help — but I want her to be treated for what *is* wrong with her, not for what they're saying is wrong with her!" He pounded his cane on the ground for emphasis — then before anyone could throw out a question, he took his silent wife Katherine by the arm and hobbled up the concrete ramp into the courtroom.

Inside, Fred the Bailiff escorted Cindy into the courtroom for her final appearance before the Honorable J. Richard Couzens. Less than a minute later, the judge emerged from his chambers and took his seat.

"This is the matter of Cindy Lee Collier, Case Number 3912. This is the time set for the dispositional hearing.

"Cindy, I usually take the time at disposition to at least make some comments to kids that come in front of me, and I generally try to do it in a way that either helps them understand what I am doing, or hopefully in some long-term sense would be of some benefit.

"I really — even up to the point of walking up to the bench — didn't know what I wanted to say to you. I have never been confronted with a case like this before.

"I think the only thing that I want to say to you at this point is this: there has been a lot of press about this case, a lot of publicity. I suppose you're somewhat semicelebrities over at the Hall. Plus the juvenile process in these contexts is very fast, especially when compared to the adult process where it might take a year or more. But it moves so fast that it doesn't give you much time to think — and that probably won't change very much once you get to the Youth Authority. Again, you'll be something of a celebrity, a curiosity, and you'll no doubt be on an emotional high for a while.

"However, I hope at some time after all the cameras are

gone and after all the reporters are gone and time passes, that there will be a quiet moment when you're alone with your thoughts. This may be some night just before you go to sleep when you're tired and your guard is down, or maybe first thing in the morning when you're just waking up — but at some point I hope it will creep into your consciousness what you have done, and the staggering consequences of taking another life in a way that is unjustifiable in any moral or legal or conscious sense.

"If you are ever to rejoin the human race as a contributing member, obviously some things have to come from you. I hope they occur, Cindy — because if they don't, it is going to be a very long and lonely life for you."

He paused for a moment to let the meaning of his words sink in. Then his tone of voice subtly changed as he switched from his role as concerned advisor and guide to that of dispassionate jurist. "With respect to the disposition, I find that you should be placed into the care, custody, and control of the director of the California Youth Authority. Accordingly, you are to be placed there for the maximum period of confinement as currently authorized by law, which is to age twenty-seven. That would be one hundred forty months and six days from today's date." Couzens then went on to explain Cindy's right to appeal his judgment, provided that appeal was filed within sixty days.

"Do you understand these appellate rights as I have explained them to you?"

Cindy's voice cracked as she gave her one-word answer. "Yes."

"Okay, Cindy, that's it. I wish you luck down there."

Cindy Collier, still shackled and chained, shuffled out of the courtroom, head down and shoulders bowed. Her future, which almost exactly two months before had seemed so bright and full of hope for new adventures and a new life, had crumbled like the petals of a drought-scorched flower. The law had spared her life because she was under eighteen, but in her mind there was no life left. To Cindy, death might have been easier.

Judge Couzens called the Court back into session after a five-minute recess. Because the full psychiatric reports from Drs. Bromberg and French were not in yet, and wouldn't be for at least two weeks, the jurist simply needed a minute or two to allow Condit to formally enter a plea and have the hearing rescheduled. It was a simple matter that almost immediately became excruciatingly complicated.

"Your Honor," Condit began, "my client would like to make a brief statement." He looked more than mildly uncomfortable.

"Uhh, Judge Couzens, I want to cancel this insanity thing. I'm not crazy." Shirley spoke loudly and clearly, without even a trace of nervousness. "The doctor, he says my I.Q. came out above normal, and he told me himself he feels I am totally normal. What he tells you may be a different story. Plus like I said in the letter to Judge Fogerty, I would like a different lawyer. I've heard from other people that Mr. Condit's a publicity lawyer, and that he's been working for a long time to get a law passed that says you can try kids as adults. He's been using me for part of that. Anyway, I would like to have a new lawyer, and want Mr. Condit fired from my case."

"In light," Condit said when Shirley was finished, "of my client's change of heart toward me, I would request to be released from her case at this time."

Judge Couzens was clearly taken aback at this new and unexpected development. He told Shirley that he was sorry, but he just didn't agree with her about Mr. Condit. "In all honesty," he said, "I believe Mr. Condit has very ably represented you and that there are no grounds whatsoever to order that he be released from your case.

"As far as the insanity plea is concerned. . . ."

Shirley broke in. "The only reason I went along with the insanity thing was because Mr. Condit told me I could get released maybe in ninety days or a year if I went into a state hospital."

The judge warned Shirley that if she withdrew her plea of not guilty by reason of insanity, and if she was ultimately found guilty of the murder, she could be committed to the California Youth Authority until she was 27.

Shirley paused and thought for a few seconds, then glanced up at the judge again. "If they say I'm *not* sane, will I have to serve time in the Y.A. once my brain's restored?"

Judge Couzens smiled in spite of himself at her odd turn of phrase. "No, you wouldn't. However, keep in mind that it might only take ninety days for your sanity to be restored, or it might not be restored for the rest of your life. Either way, whether you are committed to a state mental institution or to the C.Y.A., you need to understand there are simply no guarantees."

Shirley and Condit huddled for a moment at the table, and then requested a short recess to discuss the matter further in light of what the judge had said.

It was twenty minutes before the pair reentered the courtroom, Condit looking far less anxious and discomfited than before. "Your Honor," he said after Judge Couzens called the court back into session, "my client has decided to continue her plea of not guilty by reason of insanity."

"Fine. Okay. Well, let's set a new date to begin the sanity phase of this hearing. We're looking at three days, I understand . . ."

"Yes, Your Honor. Three days should do it."

"Well, let's be sure and allow plenty of time for the psychiatrists to finish their assessments and get their reports in to you and the District Attorney and the Court. How about September 16?"

Condit ruffled through the pages of his date book. "September 16 would be fine, Your Honor."

"Good. Anything else to come before this Court today?"

"No, Your Honor." Condit sighed heavily and smiled.

As she walked out the small door to the left of the judge's bench, Shirley turned and grinned widely to her parents, who were seated in the third row. She waved and kissed her palm, then blew a kiss in their direction. *We'll see you soon, princess,* Wolf mouthed silently, a tiny smile playing at the corners of his mouth. Katherine simply smiled and waved back to her daughter. *At least,* she thought to herself, *one part of the nightmare is over. Let's just hope what's to come isn't even worse. I'm not sure how much more any of us can take. Or how much more my little Shirley can take.*

Before it was over a month later, Shirley would take much, much more.

The sun rose just as it had for millennia upon millennia that midsummer morning of August 24, 1983. By nine o'clock, the town was a jumble of activity — nothing out of the ordinary for a Wednesday, certainly not a thing that might make anyone take particular notice of this day among all the others. Just another scorchingly hot day in California's Sierra Nevada foothills.

Emerging through the steel door of the squatty building where she had spent the last seventy days, a young woman with dark brown hair and rock-hard eyes took a final look at the town where she was born. A few minutes later the Sheriff's car slowly pulled out of the Juvenile Hall parking lot, carrying Cindy Lee Collier toward a new life that was light-years away from the one she imagined in her golden dream of just two months before. The freedom she so desperately longed for had turned into a perverted joke.

As she stared out the window at the disappearing skyline of Auburn, Cindy knew she would never again see her hometown in the same way. When she came back — *if* she came back — nothing would be the same.

It was blessedly cool inside the courtroom building when the red-haired, freckled bailiff escorted the unsmiling teenager to her place at the long, dark table facing the bench. Once again the room was packed almost beyond capacity with the cold and the compassionate alike, all anxious to hear every sordid detail of Shirley Wolf's young life which Tom Condit said was so scarred by abuse and depravity that she had gone insane that day in June when she butchered Anna Brackett.

"All rise. Court is now in session, the Honorable J. Richard Couzens presiding." The stenographer inserted the date into the record: Friday, September 16, 1983.

From the beginning, almost nothing went smoothly with this phase of the hearing, which was designed to provide the judge with enough information about Shirley to render an opinion as to her sanity — or lack of it — on the day of the murder. First, Shirley insisted that she wanted to drop her plea of insanity. It made no difference that she had already been down this route once before and changed her mind: this time she was absolutely positive. She was *not* insane . . . not now, not ever.

This of course raised a whole new set of questions that needed to be answered before the hearing could continue, not the least of which was whether someone who initially entered a plea of insanity had the mental competency to withdraw that plea. In other words: if you admit to me you are insane, then later tell me you are *not* insane . . . how do I know if you are sane enough to determine your own sanity?

It took a full day to settle the issue — a full day of convoluted, confusing, and at times totally irrelevant psychiatric testimony from both the defense's expert witness and the doctor brought in by the court. Walter Bromberg, a somewhat renowned Freudian analyst in his midseventies, was pitted against Dr. Alfred French, a man several years younger and several inches taller than his colleague, whose clinical philosophy was poles apart from Bromberg's. Yet the two men shared some things in common, including monumental egos and attitudes that implied no one but they held the golden key to the Truth. Each one insisted he had probed the depths of Shirley Wolf's soul and psyche in two or three or half a dozen hours, and that he alone understood the person who resided there.

One of the high points — Tom Condit would have probably called it a low point — of Bromberg's testimony this first day came when he inadvertently demolished the foundation of the defense's case. "First, as to the incest and whether it was a fact or not," he began imperiously. "I investigated that fairly thoroughly, and my conviction is that it was part of a fantasy." From then on, it only got worse: the doctor's hearing wasn't what it used to be, so when the prosecutor asked him to elaborate on what he described as a bluntness in Shirley's affect, the exchange went something like this:

"Doctor, you also refer to a bluntness in her . . . is it her speech?"

"A what?"

"Bluntness."

"I don't get that word."

"BLUNT-NESS," said the judge loudly, emphasizing each syllable. "You made a statement, and you referred to *bluntness*."

"Oh: bluntness," replied Bromberg with a sage nod. "Yes, I guess I did." Incredulous heads shook throughout the courtroom.

Then Shirley demanded to be heard. Her first comment elicited a chorus of low chuckles from the spectators.

"First of all, I want to say that my psychiatrist needs a psychiatrist." After that, the self-assured teenager began to soliloquize about the accusations of incest she made earlier against her father.

"Ever since I was a little girl, I have been Daddy's little

325

girl, and my father has not committed incest."

In the front row, Louis Wolf was nodding imperceptibly at his daughter.

"He did not molest me, he did not rape me, he did not commit incest. He never hurt me; he never will. My father loves me." By this time she was smiling, although there was no emotion underneath the expression.

"But Shirley," Condit probed, "didn't you tell the police your father had been molesting you from the time you were three or something like that?"

"I have to ask you something," said Shirley with a cynical smile. "Do you really think I can remember back to three years old? Seriously?"

"I don't know whether you can remem—"

"It was too obvious that it was all a lie."

"But that night you also related about an incident in a van in El Dorado County. . . ."

Shirley's obsidian eyes snapped with anger. "I think my dad has a little more class than to screw in a van. He has a lot more class than to seduce his own daughter."

Condit bore in again, trying valiantly to shake Shirley's denial—but Shirley remained adamant. Nothing, not the threat of prison or torture or even death, would make her turn against her father now. Not when he had told her how much he loved her, how much he was counting on her, how much of his manhood it cost him to be locked up in that terrible cell because of what she had said.

By midafternoon, Judge Couzens had heard enough to rule that the insanity plea would have to stand. Although he felt Shirley *was* probably sane enough to withdraw her plea, he was nowhere near as convinced that Louis Wolf wasn't behind the scenes somehow, pulling his daughter's strings.

As the sanity hearing began in earnest — and under Tom Condit's wary guidance — Dr. Bromberg made his pitch, trying to buttress his judgment that Shirley was insane at the time of the killing. It surprised no one that Dr. French's conclusions were the absolute antithesis of Bromberg's: Shirley Wolf was as sane as she could be.

During the weekend that followed, Shirley spent most of her time wondering what the next few days in court would bring, and hoping she had the strength to make it through whatever awaited her. When her parents came to visit, her father kissed her hands and caressed her hair and pledged his undying love.

On Monday morning Tom Condit shocked the courtroom by asking to be removed from the case because of his and Shirley's irreconcilable differences regarding his handling of her defense. The judge, however, refused to dismiss the affable attorney, who he said had consistently represented his client ably and vigorously. "And," he said, "I have no doubt that will continue to be the case until we're through here, despite your differences."

Throughout the next day and a half, Condit's parade of witnesses continued, all of whom testified about the Shirley Wolf they'd known before the murder — and all of whom agreed that if Shirley was anything, she was a follower rather than a leader. A follower and a lonely, desperately needy child.

Among these witnesses were three teenage girls in brightly flowered dresses, high-heeled shoes, and gleaming hair — looking as if they belonged in a Baptist church on Easter Sunday instead of a murder trial — and a short, gray-haired woman with eyes the color of Texas bluebonnets.

Shirley looked at the foursome and smiled in recognition. She couldn't believe they were actually here to help her. For a split second she was transported back to the days at Markham when she and Christi and Tina and Christine and all the others were so crazy and alive, and the nights when Christi's kindly grandmother, Gladys Thompson, would kiss her on the cheek and tell her she loved her. She never thought she'd see any of them again.

All four had been called to testify about their individual experiences with Louis Wolf, or things Shirley had told them about her father. It was here that Cheryl "Tina" Sterling recounted the entire story of that night two years before when Louis Wolf accosted her while she was staying overnight with Shirley. As her friend detailed the attacks, Shirley sat in stoney silence, offering little more than an occasional shake of her head as the only clue to her thoughts.

Next came the testimony of the police officers who interviewed Shirley and her mother the night she confessed the incest, and the social workers who dealt with the girl and her family afterward.

Was there any time, Condit patiently asked each one in turn, that Shirley indicated to you that the history of molestation had not happened?

No, came the response from each witness.

"One thing she told me," said one of the social workers, "was that her father said he would kill her if she told about the incest. He also told her it was better if he had sex with her rather than someone outside the family." Another communal gasp of shock rippled out from the audience.

For the second time, Shirley interrupted with a request to make a statement. And for the second time, it consisted of a lengthy defense of her father, plus an entirely new story of how the murder happened, how in reality it was Cindy who stabbed Mrs. Brackett to death while she was in the bathroom fixing her makeup. The teenager's attorney did his best to hide his exasperation.

And then it was over.

Tom Condit made an impassioned plea for Shirley to be found insane, saying that his young client "simply could not hold back the rage she felt from a lifetime of abuse."

Larry Gaddis, confident that Judge Couzens could see as clearly as he that Shirley was, if not completely normal, at least not insane, responded that the issue was simply whether at the time of the crime, Shirley Wolf knew that murdering Anna Brackett was wrong. "I would submit," he concluded, "that she did know."

When all was said and done, the judge agreed.

Quietly, almost sadly, he told the courtroom that as harsh as it sounded, the one phrase which probably best described Shirley was the final line in Dr. French's report: "All the evidence points toward the most unpleasant and quite inescapable conclusion that Shirley Wolf is, at the age of fourteen, thoroughly comfortable with her role as a cold-blooded killer."

The young jurist paused for a moment, then looked directly at Shirley, sitting blankly in front of him. "That is not normal thinking . . . but it is not insanity either."

Because Shirley was a resident of El Dorado County at the time of the killing, she had to be returned there for formal sentencing. It took almost a month to schedule a court date; meanwhile, the teenager spent her days and nights writing letters and reveling in her celebrity at the El Dorado County Juvenile Hall in Placerville.

On October 13, El Dorado County Juvenile Court Judge William Byrne sentenced Shirley Wolf to the California Youth Authority for what he called the "vicious, cruel, and unheard of murder" of Anna Eugena Brackett almost exactly four months before.

Halfway through the very brief proceedings, which allowed time for oral comments from law enforcement and probation officials as well as anyone else connected with the case, Louis Wolf stood up. Methodically, he unfolded a three-page statement that accused El Dorado authorities of victimizing Shirley by removing her from her home a year before. Anna Brackett's murder, he said, could be blamed on those very authorities.

"In all due respect," he read, his thick Brooklyn accent dripping with sarcasm, "I would like to thank the leading citizens of this town for putting my little girl where she is today. They have been using my daughter, exploiting my daughter, from the very beginning." By now his voice if not his words had begun to reveal the depth of his fury, until all that was left for him to do was echo each one of his ancient accusations, each one of his bitter protestations of guiltlessness, each one of his pious statements of remorse at his daughter's role in the murder. Turning to the last page, he shook his head, unable to continue, and handed the letter to his wife to finish.

After Katherine read the final sentences, Wolf stood up once again, leaning heavily on his glossy black cane and gesturing toward the crowd with his free hand. His eyes shone with infernal hatred. "The people responsible for my baby being here today," he said in a low voice thickened by emotion, "are much more responsible for the crime than Shirley is. I know some day . . . some day these people will have to pay their dues, and all I can do is pray for them and hope that God doesn't forget them."

When Louis Wolf sat down in the hushed courtroom, it was with a carefully woven cloak of martyrdom wrapped snugly around his massive shoulders, and the faintest shimmer of a self-made halo above his head.

Meanwhile, his daughter's face was an expressionless, empty mask. For once, the twisted memories from the past had no voices with which to scourge and torture her. All that existed, for that moment at least, was something that felt like peace, and freedom from the excruciating pain.

At long last, the barren, blessed silence had returned to Shirley Wolf.

Eighteen

An attractive, dusky-haired young woman with strangely bottomless eyes sits alone in the impersonally beige room, twisting her shackled wrists aimlessly and listening to the clink of metal against metal, metal against laminated tabletop, metal against wooden chair arms. It is a sound she knows almost as well as she knows the contours of her own angular face and the shadowy gap between her two front teeth. The sound has been her companion, on and off, for the last eight of her twenty-two years. That and the silence, only newly and barely broken.

She sits and waits — something at which she has become enormously accomplished during this last near-decade — and while she waits, her mind begins spinning gently. These were supposed to be the best years of her life, or so they said. What happened? How did she end up here, locked away from love and laughter and the world outside, far from voices that care and arms that comfort when the black fog came rolling in like poison gas and the words stuck in her throat and the tears solidified behind her eyes? And what was this place, anyway: a citadel of hope, or a tabernacle for the damned?

Like blood from an old wound, the memories of the past ninety-six months come seeping back, and she finds herself drifting . . . drifting . . . into them without knowing why. When someone comes into the room and settles into the opposite chair, Shirley Wolf begins to move into that past.

The year is 1984, and the journey leads from northern to southern California, through the bleak, yawningly flat country bisected by Interstate Highway 5. Power poles on their incessant southward march stand like alien monsters as far as the eye can see, huge wasp-waisted creatures with their silver arms outstretched, casting errant shadows on the sun-scorched golden hills beneath them. Disappearing into the distance, huge viaducts slice through the rich and loamy earth, carrying billions upon billions of gallons of precious water from the snow-saturated northern mountains to quench the insatiable thirst of the once-desert southern region of the state and its three-million-plus inhabitants. Southward, ever southward, the trek continues, toward the City of the Angels.

From there, it is not far at all to Ventura. Just follow Highway 101 toward the Santa Monica Mountains, the natural boundary between the Los Angeles Basin and the more rural farm and coastal villages to the west. These undulating tracts of barren, rock-covered hills unchanged for centuries and huge vertical schist and sandstone cliffs bear mute witness to the region's untamed wildness, which stands in sharp contrast to the urban congestion of the city left behind.

Below, rippling in the warmth of the southern California sun, is a huge checkerboard of light and dark greens, soft gold and velvet black. Here brown-skinned farmworkers labor wordlessly in the loamy fields still rich with melons and ruby-red tomatoes even during these late months of fall, and wend their ways through the pregnant orchards of yellow and orange citrus. Lining the narrow

332

street leading to the Ventura California Youth Authority, giant and fragrant eucalyptus create a shady canopy for a scraggy pair of farm dogs stretched out on the dusty shoulder of the road.

Shirley peered out the window as the big car slowed and swung into a broad driveway that announced she had reached the end of another pilgrimage. Ever since she first heard it was where she was going, she'd been curious about this place, this youth prison they called the Ventura School, standing on more than a hundred lush and level acres just a mile and a half off Highway 101 and four miles west of Camarillo. Once inside, she noticed the main section was comprised of a complex of fairly nondescript, low-slung red brick buildings that reminded her of a high school campus. A wide, asphalt walkway cut through the huge expanses of lawn, crowded with trees and shrubs and here and there a rose bush in full, fragrant bloom.

Yet in spite of the apparent beauty of the place, there was something not quite right about it. For one thing, there was an inexplicable lack of the noise that seems ever present on most school campuses even during classes. The exquisitely manicured grounds appeared oddly deserted as well: not a single student wandered aimlessly toward the office or cafeteria or class with a tardy slip in hand. The buildings, too, while attractive enough, also seemed vaguely peculiar — if she had taken a moment, Shirley might have realized that part of it was that they lacked the sparkling expanses of glass which are the hallmark of many modern classrooms, and that virtually every one of the small windows lining the exterior walls was crisscrossed with a subtle web of iron bars.

Finally, she forced herself to look at the imposing woven wire fence that surrounded the buildings, and with a perceptible shudder caught the glint of the huge circular strands of malevolent-looking steel known as "razor wire" that snaked along the top of every yard, every foot, every inch of the boundary.

For all her painted-on bravado, Shirley was terrified. This was not how she expected things to turn out back on that peaceful day in June before the world went insane. She thought about the rose they gave her when she graduated, now dead and putrefying in some fetid garbage dump. For an instant, the rose was her and she the rose — and then, only darkness.

It was November when young Shirley Wolf joined her companion in crime, Cindy Collier, and some six hundred other children and young adults in the place they all call "Y.A." Many were brought there simply because there is no other. All were brought to atone for their sins, to pay their debts to society, and to somehow find a new life. Unfortunately, by the time they enter through the institution's steel doors, most are too far gone or too far down that long dark tunnel to care or even try.

Whenever anyone tried to bring up the issue of her father, or the incest and all the other craziness, Shirley snapped shut like a clam shell. She'd already learned about what telling the truth could do, and she wasn't about to be that stupid twice in a row.

By this time her family had escaped to the solitude of the Pacific Northwest, unable to cope with the endless scrutiny of a public still outraged over what little they knew about Louis Wolf's victimization of his daughter, and that same daughter's later brutal and senseless victimization of Anna Brackett. Yet despite what felt like his abandonment, the psychic link between father and daughter remained as strong as ever.

As she looked around the alternately bored, angry, and tearful faces in the group therapy session, and as she half-heard what they were saying and what the counselors were trying to get them to say, Shirley knew she simply couldn't risk losing her father's love and approval again by breaking the silence and letting even a shadow of the monsters emerge from their hiding places. As a matter of fact, there were times she could even convince herself that none of it had ever happened at all — a denial that only served to fuel the fires of her own indignation when anyone suggested that Louis Wolf might not be a candidate for father of the year.

"But Shirley," they would ask, "why hasn't he been to see you in months? Why doesn't he call? And why did they lock him up in jail for a hundred days if he didn't do anything? Tell us, Shirley."

But the boulder in her throat was too gigantic to say anything. The only response came from within, from the dark place inside that had its own voice, and spoke only to her of how worthless she was, how vile and perverted and depraved. To that, there were no answers.

Again she looked around her at the faces of the girls and the counselors, men who said how much better off she would be if she spoke the truth of what her life had been like. *Tell us, Shirley.* There was no way she would allow herself to be vulnerable enough to confess that terrible truth to a man. *Tell us, Shirley.* There was no way she could talk about the ugliness, the torture and sadism and all the rest of it, with a man. *Tell us, tell us.* No, it would never, ever happen.

Shirley was far from alone in her resistance. In the dark of night when the closeted fiends emerged to torment their victims with horrific images of the unresolved past, two or three of the girls might whisper together words of their own personal nightmares that they would never say aloud. But for the most part, each learned in her own way — Shirley included — to keep their silences, to bury their secrets even deeper, and entomb them all under an ever-thickening, impenetrable crust of caustic hatred and bitterness.

* * *

The Chairman of the Youthful Offender Parole Board sat wearily behind his desk and framed in his mind the words he wanted to say. Earlier that day, he and the Board listened in stunned silence as the details of this incredible case unfolded. Afterward, they handed down the harshest decision ever given in the history of the Youth Authority: Shirley Wolf and Cindy Collier would not be eligible for parole until the end of 1991. James Ware knew the imposition of such a lengthy sentence at an initial parole hearing would raise eyebrows from one end of the state to the other, probably even among some of the Youth Authority staff. But this case was so unbelievable, so horrible, that they all felt the most severe penalty was called for. One of Chairman Ware's comments became the highlight of the press release handed out a day later. "The brutal murder committed by these young people," it read, "shocks the conscience of a civilized society."

When she first heard their decision, Shirley felt as if someone had kicked her in the stomach. 1991. That was eight years away. And she was only fourteen. It seemed like a life sentence. Yet not long afterward, she expertly swept it away like dust under a rug, all the while smiling that empty, deadened smile.

It would be late that summer before Frank Bell, the state Public Defender, and Michael Bigelow, a private defense attorney appointed by the state, filed briefs on behalf of Cindy and Shirley with the Third District Court of Appeals. Another year would slip by before the Court ruled unanimously to uphold the original convictions. For the two hopeful teenagers there were no further appeals.

When they came to tell Shirley that her best friend had

hung herself in her cell, she felt as if a piece of her died with Melissa.

Melissa. Strange how that name kept cropping up in her life. Looking back, she realized it all started a lifetime ago with a girl in her elementary school class named Melissa. "The minute I saw her, I knew she was everything I wasn't," she said. "And I hated her for it." The object of Shirley's hatred had long blond hair, beautiful aquamarine blue eyes, skin the color of ripe peaches, and a perfect smile that showed two perfect rows of perfect white teeth. She came from a nice family, lived in a nice neighborhood, and was always dressed in nice, clean — if not new — clothes. Clearly the teacher's pet in every class and popular with almost all the students, Melissa was the exact opposite of Shirley.

If you understood Shirley at all, her loathing made sense. But in an odd twist, the young girl also later claimed the name Melissa as her own — almost as if by taking on the name she might be able to become the person. It was only coincidence — or was it? — that she had become such good friends with another girl named Melissa there at the Y.A.

After the troubled sixteen-year-old's suicide, Shirley felt herself plummeting even deeper into that ancient and seemingly inescapable pit of depression and hopelessness.

By this time Shirley was even more entrapped in the malevolent web of Satanism, a practice in which she had dabbled several years before with her cadre of curious girlfriends. But this was no childhood game: this was the real stuff. Along with a few others who latched onto black magic and Satanism as the answer to their quest for power and control, Shirley became engrossed in her new-found religion. Hardly a week went by that she didn't offer her praises to the Dark Lord, hardly a day that she didn't call on that fallen angel for the strength she so desperately needed to keep herself from ending up, like Melissa, swaying from a knotted bedsheet. She knew she had the hardness of heart to do Satan's bidding, to be a good servant — and of course, to obey without question.

There were incidents, plenty of them, which brought the young woman to the worried attention of the staff during the darkest of those days — yet even though they knew just how deeply she was involved in Satanism, unless they could catch her violating any of the institution's rules and regulations, there was little anyone could do but watch and wait to see what happened next. They didn't have to wait for long to witness something that shook even the most case-hardened among them with horror: Shirley Wolf, injecting one of the other ward's blood into her own arm with a stolen syringe.

Yet deep inside the farthest recesses of her mangled soul there remained the faintest glow of something soft and decent that struggled against the consuming evil and emptiness. As she had always done, even as a child, Shirley found the voice to tell of that struggle in writing.

When I'm alone at night I hear voices calling me,
    and I have to fight to keep my sanity.
I keep falling deeper and deeper under their spell.
    They say I have to pay the Reaper,
    but I'm not ready for Hell.
I've felt this life is pain — I've thought if
I played the Devil's game
    He might take away the pain.
    But I thought in vain.
It's been so long since I've been in the sun,
    So long since I've had any fun.
I try to slip out of His reach, but it's so hard
to stay away.

He has nothing to preach, but to be with
   Him you have to pay.
I have reasons to do the strange things I do.
   You wouldn't understand — you haven't been
   through what I've been through.
There are voices in my head
   and they're all voices of the dead.
Soon I will join them
and help torment the victims.
   Oh God, why won't they go away?

"I was already in hell, but I didn't know it." Her words
come much more easily now, punctuated at times with
something that sounds almost like wisdom. "And that
was what I gave everybody around me, too: hell. I didn't
know a thing about guilt or remorse, and what was worse,
I didn't really care. All I cared about was how to please the
devil, and how to work the system so I could get the things
I wanted and needed for myself — drugs, getting high,
you name it. It's all pretty easy to get in here. I was so sure
of myself, so convinced I was this big, badass person who
was going to show the whole world just how rough and
tough she was."

She smiles a little at the recollection of her own naïveté.
"I'm not quite sure that's how it turned out."

By January of 1988, Shirley was ready to explode.
What she wanted more than anything was to get out of
this kiddie institution and into a *real* prison, where she
could once and for all prove herself to be the biggest, bad-
dest, meanest inmate the prison system had ever seen.
Within a few short days, she was well on her way.

Were the voices there that night, reminding her again
of her own pain, her own violation? Did they shriek and
whisper and paint horrific pictures on the walls of her
mind of her father's eyes, his frozen smile, his hands
whipping at her, tearing at her, caressing her? Did they

339

fabricate and summon the cadaverous ghost of Anna Brackett to blaspheme her murderer and curse her killer's soul? Or were the voices silent, and all of it simply a part of Shirley's clever, twisted plan to recreate herself in a new image? No one knew what really happened inside her mind that evening, as she went on a rampage and savagely stabbed a supervisor in the face and head with a sharpened pencil. All they knew was that Shirley Wolf was, at least for the moment, beyond redemption.

Once again, justice was swift. Within hours the eighteen-year-old was charged and transferred to the Ventura County Jail, where she awaited her day in court. The judge showed little mercy for the unrepentant teenager who stood in the courtroom, her shoulders pushed back in a stance of utter defiance. Knowing her history, the jurist wasn't about to cut this kid so much as a millimeter of slack. To the system, she was just another in the unending parade of hopeless cases that marched through its courtrooms every year. The best you could do for people like Shirley Wolf, went the popular thinking, was to put them away — forever if that was possible — where they could do the least amount of damage to other people.

That place was the California Institute for Women, part of the state's adult prison system. The judge sentenced her to nine years and four months there.

But before Shirley could be transferred from the county jail, it happened again. The inexplicable fury, the screamed obscenities and unintelligible, random threats of hatred and violence, directed at no one and everyone. Uncertain of just how much of a danger or escape risk the young woman might be, her jailers placed her in shackles — which only served to heighten her fury. It was as if there were some maniacal force within her that she couldn't even begin to control. Undaunted, she savagely ripped a telephone off the interview room wall and smashed it to the floor, then picked up a wooden chair and began bashing it over and over against the door. The force of the hatred was so massive and overpowering that it enveloped and deadened her.

With a start, the guards rushed in and tried to wrestle her down, but Shirley was like a wild woman — thrashing and flailing and cursing at their attempts to restrain her. Some of what she said was totally foreign, as if she were speaking in the tongue of another planet, or even another universe; then in an instant, recognizable words would ricochet off the stone walls. "Leave . . . me . . . alone . . . don't . . . touch . . . hatekill . . . you . . . hatekill . . . me . . ."

A hapless deputy tried to grab Shirley's ankles. Then came a sudden stab of terrible pain, and for a moment the room swam in front of his eyes. He looked down at his hand, flopping uselessly like a sopping wet glove. A bone in his wrist had shattered.

Convicted of aggravated assault against the deputy, Shirley found herself with sixteen more months tacked onto her nine-year prison sentence.

1998, they said. Almost the new century. If she made it that long.

But as she had done ten thousand times before, she buried whatever fear was there and covered it with an impervious cloak of callous cynicism. Just before she left for the California Institute for Women, she wrote these words on the ceiling of her cell: "Down for murder, 1983. In 1988 I stabbed a cop, and I'm still not through."

Louis Wolf called his daughter sometime during that chaotic month to reassure her that she was still his princess, no matter what. A few weeks later, in mid-March, Shirley became an inmate at the women's prison in Frontera, on the outskirts of Chino, some three hours by car from Ventura.

* * *

Linda Osborne had already moved to Bakersfield to be closer to her daughter. She made the two-and-a-half hour drive as often as she could — and in a replay of many of their mother-daughter meetings in the Placer County Juvenile Hall so many years before, these visits were frequently punctuated by tears and anguished hugs when it was time to part. Despite her veneer of hardness, Cindy was enormously dependent upon her mother, and fiercely protective of her as well. Like Shirley, she remained in near-blind denial about the harsh, bitter realities of her younger years and whatever role her mother may have played in her degeneration.

Theirs was a corrosively symbiotic and codependent relationship which was only aggravated by Cindy's incarceration and internal struggles. Few people, if any, could get Cindy to acknowledge her mother's true culpability in the chaos that had swept her into the waiting darkness. Never mind Linda's apparent obliviousness to her preteen daughter's increasingly violent and antisocial behaviors; never mind Cindy's growing flirtations with alcohol and cocaine and other drugs; never mind the string of marginally or violently abusive men who drifted in and out of Linda's life over the years; never mind the countless nights she spent at the Auburn Hotel bar until it closed at two in the morning; never mind that her youngest son had joined the other two boys in jail by the time her daughter turned twenty . . . and never mind that not once in all the years her firstborn son was molesting and raping Cindy, did Linda come to her daughter's rescue or hold Keith accountable for those repeated sexual assaults against his stepsister.

Never mind any of the things that were true and clear for everyone to see. Cindy needed — or perhaps she chose — to stay outwardly untouched and unmoved by any of it. Her mother was the only source of unpolluted love she knew, and she wasn't about to endanger that for anything.

It didn't take long before an increasingly troubled Cindy, whose parole consideration date had already been extended by three months because of disciplinary problems, was taken out of the institution's general population and placed on the same unit Shirley had lived in ever since her arrival. The unit, called Alborada, was designed to house those girls with serious emotional problems. Even though the two teens now lived under the same roof, staff did their best to keep them kept separated at all times — Cindy in room 11 of one wing, and Shirley in the opposite wing.

At that point Cindy seemed to be heading for the same apocalypse as Shirley, albeit at a less hysterical pace. On the surface, each of them appeared determined to scar the institution as well as its occupants and officials with her own invidious mark of vengeance. Despite the group therapy, despite the extra time and effort the girls in Alborada received, despite the well-intentioned if ineffectual help they were offered, Cindy and Shirley seemed doomed to remain trapped forever in darkness.

However, shortly before Shirley made that pledge to etch her name in blood on the prison history books, things looked as if they were starting to change for her former best friend Cindy, who began a slow and frequently agonizing turnaround. It started when she went after her high school diploma. Later she decided that wasn't enough: I want my A.A. degree, she told her parole officer.

Lance Curtis had been with Cindy through years of tough and troubled times, and somehow she came to trust the thoughtful young parole officer where she found it difficult if not impossible to trust others. Now she was trusting him enough to admit she wanted more than what everyone expected for her, that she wanted to better herself. Taking that kind of step was a huge risk for a young woman like Cindy whose cocky, brittle demeanor was simply a cover for the raging hurricane of anguish and self-hatred that churned inside. But as Curtis knew only too well, if there was one thing Cindy Collier possessed, it was a stubborn determination to do and get what she wanted. "If that girl once gets it into her head that she's going for a junior college degree, come hell or high water, she'll find a way to do it," he'd said. By the same token, he also knew that in order to make it, Cindy would have to employ every last ounce of that drive and determination, especially when all the cards in the deck were so firmly stacked against her.

Nevertheless, by January of 1988 Cindy had already successfully completed several college-level courses. Other things were changing in her life, too: somewhere over the past four years she shed at least thirty pounds, leaving her nothing like the football linebacker she had once resembled. These days she carried herself with an easy grace, obviously comfortable inside this slender new body which gained its fair share of attention from the male wards and staff. Abandoning her trademark harsh, black eyeliner and heavy makeup, Cindy skillfully created a much more subdued look to accent her natural beauty and bring out the delicacy of her doelike eyes. Her hair, lighter now and considerably longer, framed a face which despite the years of imprisonment seemed to have lost some of its unremitting hardness — even though those lovely eyes often still burned with a fiery residue of distrust and resentment.

Especially when Shirley pulled what Cindy icily referred to as her "little stunts" like stabbing a counselor or smashing a cop's wrist — acts which, much to Cindy's dismay, only served to refocus everyone's attention not just on Shirley, but on her as well. Whenever anything happened with one of them, the spotlight washed across them both, almost as if the two were fused at the hip into some surrealistically preternatural creature known as CindyandShirley. Try as she might, that perceived connection between herself and Shirley was something Cindy simply couldn't shake.

On the other hand, that fusion effect was barely negligible on Shirley, who was intent on launching herself ever higher into an orbit of madness and destruction. By now she was clearly her own — not to mention Cindy's — worst enemy.

There is no truly "easy" way to get from Ventura to Frontera, unless you have the luxury of flying into the tiny Chino Airport. Otherwise, prepare yourself for a lengthy and sometimes harrowing journey through the labyrinth of some of the most frenetic, insane, and congested freeways in the entire nation, if not the world.

This journey east usually takes nearly three hours, but for Shirley Wolf, it had been a nineteen year odyssey.

At first she tried to fight them back, just like she'd always done. *Be strong,* she told herself. *Don't make a sound. Don't let anyone see how weak you really are.* But no matter how she tried, no matter how hard she pressed the back of her hand to her mouth, biting almost hard enough to draw blood, the raging torrent of tears would not be stopped. These were tears like she had never known before: for so many years she had learned to close them up inside where their taste couldn't remind her of just how vulnerable she was, just how hurt and frightened she was — but on this day, locked alone inside this tiny gray cell, they came without warning like a raging tsunami. Huge sobs engulfed the young woman in the hopelessness that shadowed all the years of her past; looking toward the future, she could see its curse falling like acid rain upon her tomorrows as well. The darkness, like the darkness of her cell, was almost total now.

Struggling to regain control of the tears, Shirley peered through the dimness of the evening at the icy gray walls. In time, she knew, she would come to know every crack, every blister, every irregularity of every stone like an intimate companion. This five-by-eight cell would be her hermitage for eighteen months.

An involuntary shiver danced down her spine at the thought of being trapped once again in this above-ground dungeon — especially since her time here would be much, much longer than ever before. Officially known as the Specialized Housing Unit, or SHU, everyone simply called it Greystone. The one unit on the prison grounds unlike any other, Greystone is a towering, windowless concrete maximum-security prison within a prison, housing those inmates who are violent or considered severe disciplinary problems or escape risks, and protected by its own razor-wire-topped perimeter fencing with an electronic security gate and specially trained guards who carry loaded guns by their sides twenty-four hours a day. Looming darkly above the rest of the facility with its neat, almost cheerful red-bricked buildings, Greystone seems strangely out of place, as if it had been plucked from the Dark Ages and set down here through some grotesquery of an infernal time machine. Walk inside, and the dismal impression remains.

There is little if any natural light inside these walls, and the air is thick with the odor of disinfectant and human misery. Two tiers of cells ring three walls of the boxlike structure; on the remaining wall is a bulletproof glass-walled electronic security room which controls everything from the individual cell doors to the cameras and motion detectors to the main gate outside. The center of the building, rising more than two stories, is completely open and empty, providing the ever-watchful guards an opportunity to observe each cell without leaving the safety of the security center. On one wall is a huge sign which reads: No Warning Shots Are Fired Here.

Inside the cells, most of the space is taken up with two metal beds stacked atop one another and bolted to the dingy cement wall. At one end is a stainless-steel toilet and sink; at the other end, where the beds meet the rear wall, stands a six-inch-wide sealed window, three or four feet high, so caked with dust and grime that barely any sunlight at all can penetrate.

Almost the only time inmates of Greystone are allowed outside their cells is for a brief exercise period once a day. Otherwise, they remain caged in the concrete chambers until their penance is paid, be that a week or a month or a year. On and off through the endless days and nights, the stone walls reverberate with the howls and moans and guttural mouthings of the involuntary residents, reminiscent of a scene out of *The Snake Pit*.

Shirley cringed as the loudspeaker blared it was time for lights out. The dark was no friend to her — no friend at all. It was then that the old memories came slithering back like grinning vipers. In here, there was no escape from the voices of the past. No escape from the murky, twisting vortex that was spiraling into . . . where? Shirley had never been sure.

But suddenly, that first night back in Greystone, in a moment of crystalline, iridescent clarity, she *did* know.

She knew for the first time that the vortex led into the blackness of death.

The thought was terrifying. Was this where these last twenty years had been leading? An untended grave somewhere, with not even a wilted rose to testify to the life that had been — only dust and maggots? Reaching out through the blackness of space and time, Shirley began to wonder where she had been — *who* she had been — these last many months, while she peered backward along the path that brought her to the edge of this lethal whirlpool without even knowing it.

February, 1989. Shirley Wolf was getting to be a familiar face in Greystone. An inmate at C.I.W. for only a year, she'd already spent a total of 270 days — the first time for a seven-month stretch, then a week or two here and there over the course of the year — confined inside those tomblike walls, with no human contact from the outside except for letters (which in Shirley's case were painfully few) and interactions with the guards and staff. Yet no matter the torment of the experience, she seemed incapable of freeing herself from the explosive anger and hatred that continuously put her behind those cold iron doors. Time after time she would barely catch her breath on the surface before plunging down once again into her own hell-born quagmire. Everyone feared that at some point she might never return.

By March of that year, Shirley was out of Greystone and back in the prison's general population, mixing with the likes of the Manson Family girls and others of greater or lesser fame. This part of the institution resembled the Ventura School, with its brick buildings, spreading grounds, and stately trees that brought welcome shade from the midsummer sun. Aside from the veritable plague of flies that, courtesy of the neighboring cattle farms, descended in early summer and lingered until the cooler fall weather drove them off to warmer climes or hibernation or fly heaven, the constant smell of manure, and the oppressive summer heat that gripped the tiny valley for three or four months a year, there were certainly worse places to do time.

In just a few days Shirley Wolf would complete her first year there.

One down, only nine and a half to go. *Piece of cake, ha ha*

Except for the feeling that something indescribably loathsome was sucking away. And the more and more overpowering need to be away from this place with its rules and controls and unending night terrors, to be away from everything that kept crashing in on her, to be free of all the empty loneliness and despair. She hadn't seen her family in over five years, and for the last year they hadn't even responded to her letters. Shirley was more alone than she had ever been in her life—even though she still managed to cultivate the image of someone who didn't give a damn about anything, whose goal was to put every person with whom she came into contact through a living hell. The same kind of hell she had known all her life.

Nineteen

In April of 1989, NBC News showed up on the doorsteps of the Ventura School and the Institute for Women. The network was in the process of putting together a documentary examining the issue of young women involved in violent crime and how they got there — and not surprisingly, their search led them right to Cindy Collier and Shirley Wolf. The six-page spread in *People* magazine, as well as all the other media coverage the case attracted, were like beacons for the network's research staff, who were culling every possible file for stories of girls who had killed or maimed or beaten or otherwise brutalized someone else.

Shirley's and Cindy's stories would add an important element to the documentary, the NBC representatives said, and would help illuminate the shattered pasts that all too often were at the root of these troubled girls' hatreds and violence.

At least, that was the plan. At first.

The producer and interview team spent hours with the two girls: building their trust, encouraging them to talk about things and people and events past, asking them to dig into their feelings about the murder, themselves, and their lives. Everyone seemed so earnest and concerned — before long, both Cindy and Shirley were sharing small pieces of their old torments and fears as well as their new hopes and dreams.

Cindy proudly detailed her personal triumphs at the

Y.A., including the acquisition of a junior college degree and successful completion of another degree program in culinary arts. She even managed to arrange for one of the interviews to be held at her restaurant job-training site — something, she hoped, that would prove once and for all that she really *was* trying to straighten herself out. Only because they insisted it was important for people to know what her world was like before, she also talked about the killing and the long list of other crimes she'd committed during her first fifteen years of life. Asked why she had done what she had done, Cindy replied with an odd, unself-conscious smile, "To be honest with you, I just didn't care. Not at all. I didn't care about who I hurt or what I did."

A hundred and twenty miles away, at the Frontera C.I.W. facility, Shirley also talked about many things, only one of which was the murder. She talked reluctantly about the incest and violence of her younger years, and enthusiastically about anything that might enhance her veneer of toughness. "My attitude was," she said, staring bloodlessly at the blond, blue-eyed Deborah Norville, "that if you burn me, I'm gonna hurt you. If I don't do it with my fists, I'll do it some other way." About the murder, she said it had "released a lot of old hatreds in me."

After waving their final good-byes to the news crews, both girls undoubtedly felt a glimmer of hope that at long last, someone had heard — really *heard* — their stories. Maybe at long last someone understood a little, cared a little, wanted to help a little. Maybe someone would be able to show people at least a tiny corner of the truth that for both of them lay interred under the terror and silence of the random, passing years.

But by the time the hours of interviews were edited . . . by the time the first producer was reassigned to another project . . . by the time veteran reporter Connie Chung, originally signed as the documentary's chief correspondent, suddenly left NBC for another network, only to be replaced by rising news star Deborah Norville . . . what started out as "serious journalism" had deteriorated into a one-dimensional, exploitational piece of flotsam called "Bad Girls."

The opening credits flashed across the nation's television screens on the night of August 30, 1989 — credits highlighted by a mindless rock video of leather-clad adolescent girls gleefully hurling knifelike steel combs toward a perfectly made-up, perfectly dressed, perfectly terrified blonde who somehow represented everything these "bad girls" hated. Watching in disquieted fascination, certainly Cindy and Shirley must have begun to suspect that what they'd been told by the network field crews was shaded with lies. And by the time the segment featuring them was over, whatever anticipation either young woman may have felt in the beginning was transformed into bitter rancor at what they saw as just another in a long list of betrayals. It was as if all the promises about telling the real truth, all the pledges to show more than the dark side, were simply covers for one simple, ugly fact: the only thing the network had ever cared about was making money and getting ratings — even if those ratings were earned on the blood of a handful of troubled girls.

Cindy waited anxiously for Norville or someone to acknowledge her determination and accomplishments — but all they showed were clips of her coldly talking about the murder and her other crimes. Shirley waited, too: for while she no doubt felt a thrill of self-glorification at being portrayed as so barren and cold, another part of her waited for someone to challenge that crust of toughness, to pry underneath the scab in an effort to decipher the wound tracks festering there. And so throughout the hour the two young women hoped and waited — until finally, all that was left to wait for was the eleven o'clock news.

It couldn't have been easy for either Cindy or Shirley to

assimilate what they saw and heard that night. Each in her own way, both felt utterly and savagely abused and exploited — especially when the ever-smiling Norville noted that all these young and violent women were simply "bad girls," as if that were an answer in and of itself. No need to dig any deeper . . . no need to look at the victim who might be living under the sclerotic skin of the victimizer . . . no need to listen for those echoes of pain and brutalization that might explain how someone can reach the point where other lives have no value because she's learned so well that her own life is worthless.

Cindy, for one, was infuriated by the documentary, and the people responsible for it. "I've been burned by the media before," she said with bitter acrimony, "but this was ten times worse than all the rest put together. I swear this: I will never again trust a reporter as long as I live." That winter, when she had her yearly appearance before the Parole Board to determine if she might be eligible for early release, she was convinced it was the lingering memory of that disgusting documentary that made them refuse her.

Once again, Shirley and Cindy had discovered that trusting was still a very dangerous thing, and that the only safety lay in keeping the silence.

The winter of 1989 was typical of most others the Chino Valley had seen, with days on end when the wind screamed like a banshee across the fields and dark clouds huddled conspiratorially over the nearby mountains. Walking across the grounds toward the dining hall, feeling the windswept sting of sand and grit against her face, Shirley wondered just how much more she could take before she simply imploded into nothingness. Since the documentary aired in late August, her fury and sense of impotence had been growing at a dangerous pace.

Over and over, she caressed the thought of the little .25

caliber automatic pistol that a friend said would be waiting for her the minute she broke out. In her mind, she felt its cool steel against the palm of her hand, smelled its metallic astringent sweetness, and savored the power and absolute authority its possession would confer. She had no particular desire to kill just for killing's sake — but once she was on the outside, she also had no intention of allowing anybody to pop her and bring her back. If she killed someone in the process — or got taken down herself — well, those were just the breaks. She'd felt dead for so long anyway that it didn't much matter.

The days dragged on, and the voice in her head poked and prodded at her like a child stabbing at an anthill with a wooden stick. *What's a matter, Shir-r-r-r-le-e-e-e?* it sneered. *Chi-i-i-i-cken? Don't have the balls to do it? Afra-a-a-a-id?* No way, she answered darkly. No way am I afraid. Of anything. Never. Never again.

And then it happened. A plan revealed itself to her. Like an unexpected break in a violent storm, like an answer to a prayer, it was just there. Her ticket out.

It was December 4, 1989. Only twenty shopping days left until Christmas. Shirley woke up knowing this was the day she would recapture her freedom, lost so long ago in a day of madness and blood that sometimes she could hardly believe had happened at all. Except for the dreams, where Anna Brackett's face floated above her like a huge and hungry night-moth. Maybe once she got away from here, Shirley thought, the dreams would go away, too.

Her plan was simple. She'd been doing well enough on her program lately that she had a gate pass to let her outside the main yard and into the area just this side of the maintenance section. All she had to do was get over one, maybe two, more fences — or get through them if she could find a pair of bolt cutters — and she would be out on the open road before anybody even knew she was gone.

354

All day long she looked at the plan from every possible angle, making sure it was foolproof. She ate a big breakfast and lunch — *who knows when my next meal might be?* — then went back to her room and put on several layers of clothes. No one would notice a thing, she was sure of that, because the weather had been so damn cold lately that everybody looked like six-month-pregnant Eskimos anyway.

At dinner that evening she secretly stashed some bread and meat in a plastic bag, and stuffed it into her jacket. Now all she had to do was wait for it to get dark enough.

It was six-thirty when Shirley started out. She made it through the gate with no problem at all from the guard, who simply nodded at her after he checked her pass. Under cover of the early evening darkness, she clambered up and over the interior cyclone fence, then dropped easily down into the maintenance yard. *So far, so good.* Keeping low, she began searching for bolt cutters or a hacksaw.

Nothing.

Then she spotted the brown long-bed pickup truck they used as a prison fire truck. *Maybe there's something in there I can use.* When she peered in through the driver's side window, she saw there was.

A set of keys dangled lazily from the ignition. This was a stroke of luck she hadn't counted on. Maybe things would work out after all. Without thinking, she scrambled up into the cab, pounding both door locks closed behind her. Although she'd been only fourteen years old when she was first arrested, Shirley remembered driving illegally out in the fields behind town every once in a while. She figured she knew enough to get her out of there, which was all she cared about.

She ground the vehicle into gear and floored the accelerator. The truck jumped forward like a startled elephant, pitching Shirley back against the hard plastic seat. She almost let go of the wheel in momentary panic before she realized she was actually driving.

The truck jostled off across the grounds, weaving crazily as Shirley pulled the steering wheel from one side to the other. She heard a horrible grinding of metal, and realized the truck had just sideswiped the fence. Ahead, she saw a parked car, but didn't even try to steer away from it. Another smashing, grinding noise told her she'd probably taken the car's door off.

Suddenly, a small metal building loomed up in front of her. Before she could think, the truck effectively demolished the little maintenance shed and careened onward through the gloom. She'd lost track of where she was, until she saw something that looked like one of the classroom buildings. She was headed straight for it. *So what?* said the voice in her head, and Shirley pushed on the accelerator even harder.

Suddenly a man in a guard's uniform entered her line of sight. If she kept driving in the direction she was headed, she'd crunch him like a worthless bug into the dust. At the last moment, he leapt out of her path, a look on his face of horror mixed with fury that she would actually try to run him down.

Shirley was so engrossed in watching what the guard would do — move or stay? live or die? — that she failed to notice the truck had changed course slightly and was now headed straight for the chain-link security fence. *Oh, well — it's as good a way as any to get out,* she thought. But in her inexperience, she didn't have enough speed built up to take down the fence and make good her escape. She rammed the vehicle into the heavy crisscrossed steel wires; the fence buckled and shook but refused to give way.

Adrenaline pounded through the young woman's system like molten lava, fueling her white-hot anger and rising frustration until she felt as if Shirley Wolf had simply ceased to exist; she had been changed into some sulfurous, venomous organism from the bowels of the earth. It was that creature who now gunned the engine and rocketed off down the fence line, uprooting but still failing to topple huge sections of the metal barrier that snaked its way around the perimeter of the prison.

By now the alarm had been sounded that an inmate was making an escape attempt. Men and women in the guard towers that ringed the facility went into a state of hypervigilance, alerted to the presence of the by-now-sputtering fire truck. The emergency siren blared out its strident, earsplitting wail as special security details moved into high gear, gathering up weapons and flak jackets as they headed toward the area where the chocolate-colored truck was in the process of destroying several hundred yards of cyclone fencing.

Shirley knew she was in trouble. Her new plan — such as it was — to ram through the barrier and find freedom on the open road before anybody could even pick up a phone was sinking slowly into the toilet. She wasn't sure what else to do, except to keep trying, no matter what. Her mind had shut down completely except for the primeval instinct to run, and she was totally unconscious of any pain from the brutal snapping of her neck each time she hit the fence or one of its heavy steel support poles, or even the horrendous shower of glass when the vehicle's rear window exploded behind her head.

Without thinking, she tried again to make a dead run into the center of the unyielding fence. It wasn't easy, maneuvering in the dark between huge trees that seemed to pop out of the ground like mushrooms every few seconds. Nevertheless, she was going to give it her best shot. At impact she heard a terrible screeching noise, metal smashing against metal, then watched as a thick cloud of black smoke belched out from under the hood. But still the fence stood. Not well, but it stood. Meanwhile, the truck's engine died.

Shirley fiercely turned the ignition key. The truck coughed once, tried to die again, and then sputtered into life. She gunned the engine as hard as she could, unaware that the transmission had slipped into reverse. The truck lurched backward with the force of an explosion. A huge, stately oak tree took the full force of the impact, and at the same instant the engine erupted into flames. Her head thrown against the dashboard, Shirley was only dimly aware of the acrid smell of smoke and somewhere in the far distance the scream of sirens.

The state of California tends to take a dim view of the wanton destruction of its property — especially when that property is a penal institution and the responsible party a convicted felon trying to escape. Shirley's little adventure cost the state more than forty-six thousand dollars. Retribution was swift and harsh: by now, there was no doubt in anyone's mind that Shirley Katherine Wolf was on a collision course with disaster. The best they could do was make sure she didn't take anyone else with her when she flew over that edge.

Greystone beckoned once again.

As she lay there in her cold, ashen cell that first night of 540 nights to come, her sweatshirt painted with the salt of her tears and the monsters lurking in the corridors of her mind, Shirley tried to make some sense of it all. Right now, all she knew was that she was agonizingly, overwhelmingly tired. Tired of the hellish life she'd invented for herself, tired of all the hatred and pain and suffocating darkness that always seemed to envelop her. Searching through the last half-decade, the young woman saw she was as close to going down for the third time as she had ever been, and tried to decide if she wanted to face another day of a life that had turned out to be a ghoulish, unremitting nightmare.

* * *

She couldn't even see their faces clearly. She thought one was a woman and the other a man, but she wasn't sure. She felt more than heard them, their words like jagged, poisoned spears lancing deep into the very core of her.

There was agonizing pain everywhere. Her chest, her arms, her throat, even the horrible-wonderful dark place between her legs. The word-spears were sawing at her: back and forth, in and out, violating her, tearing her apart, in a perverted rhythm of lust and blood and hate, until she was sure she would go completely insane. *Just stop!* she tried to cry out to the two faces. *Your words are killing me!* But nothing came out of her mouth.

Suddenly she felt something break loose inside of her, and all the feelings stopped. Everything stopped. Everything except her hands, which were wrapped like molten iron around the throat of first the one, then the other of her two tormentors. As the light dimmed and then finally left their eyes, she felt an incredible sense of release and freedom.

But something was wrong. Even as she looked around and realized she was alone, that no one was there to witness what she had done, the pain began to return. Only this time it was different: this time it was in a place that felt like her heart, only miles deeper . . . and the pain itself was more like a crushing weight that kidnapped her breath and brought with it a terrible, unspeakable sadness that reached like tendrils of ice-cold fog into every cell of her being. She felt something on her cheek, and reached up to find tears there.

"No," she cried softly, then louder. "No — I can't live with this. I can't handle this. It's wrong — it's wrong what I've done. I have to tell somebody, tell the truth." The tears kept coming, and the weight got heavier, and her breath came in shorter and shorter gasps, and . . .

Shirley woke up with a start to find her face streaked

with tears. For an instant she didn't know where she was — it was so dark, so closed in, more than any room she'd ever been in — until she heard a muffled moan from somewhere nearby. Oh, yes: Greystone. Her own private corner of hell, most people would say.

Except that over the last year and several months, it had also been her respite, her confessional, her university, her place of regeneration and growth. She shuddered at the memory of the dream, so much like the memory of her life with all its anguish and fury — and without even thinking, she closed her eyes and did what she had been doing almost ever since they brought her here to Greystone so long ago: she prayed. Not to Satan, but to God. To the God she once thought had forsaken her, the God whom she had scorned and cursed for years. To the God and the Christ she now fervently believed had saved her, and who forgave her.

Glancing down at her hands, bound now with metal cuffs at her wrists, she seems to puzzle over what she sees there.

"Creativity is a lot like love," she says quietly. "It gives life. I get so much joy out of being creative — writing, drawing, making little figures of animals out of soap bars, whatever. It's like I'm giving back something that I took from the world, and I'm doing it with my own hands. I know what these hands have done. I know these hands have destroyed.

"You know, when I murdered Mrs. Brackett, I didn't just murder one person. I didn't just take one victim. There were lots of victims of what I did: her family, the man she loved, her friends, the town of Auburn. So many victims . . ." Her voice drifts off, and the little smile that was there a minute before is gone.

Her visitor quietly reminds her that she, too, was a victim. Long before she spilled the blood of Anna Eugena

360

Brackett on the rusty gold carpet of a pleasant Auburn condominium eight years ago. Even long before that winter day when a five-year-old child with a fuzzy hat and a toothy grin and a floppy orange doll gripped in her arms posed in front of a New York brownstone, looking up at the camera with joy for the day and hope for the future.

Yes, so many victims.

Shirley stares out, her sable eyes still lightless and unfathomable and focused on something only she can see. Then once again she begins to talk, curling back the edges of her conscious mind, probing for the lost emotions that she hopes are buried there alive rather than dead. She speaks of sorrow at what she has done, of remorse for bequeathing such a legacy of pain and grief to those she never even knew, of the strangling tentacles of self-hatred and self-alienation that have gripped her for more years than she can count. She speaks of love, of hate, of repentance, and most of all, of God.

"It was like a miracle, that first night back on Greystone after my escape attempt," she says. "I knew I'd played myself out this time, and there was nothing left except death. I cried and cried until I didn't think there were any tears left, and then I felt something come over me and I got down on my knees. Even though I didn't feel worthy of calling on God after everything I'd done and everybody I'd hurt, I did it anyway. I told God I was recommitting my life to Him, and that I was putting myself in His hands. For the first time in my life, I think, I asked for help."

There is a hint of softness in her face as she speaks — softness and, if you stand just right, perhaps an infinitesimal gleam of light deep within her eyes.

Shirley Wolf knows all too well just how it feels to tumble off the edge of that abyss into nothingness. How it feels to grasp frantically at anything, anything at all, to stop the downward plunge.

361

Then suddenly, out of the gloom, the faint outline of something else appears. As it nears, she sees it is a hand, reaching out to her like a tangible beacon of light in the devouring darkness. Without question, she stretches out her own small hand to meet it.

"I'm not some religious fanatic," she says with a smile. "I just know what the Lord has done for me since I've been here. I know what He's helped me get through, and what He's helped me understand and learn.

"And you know what?" she asks with a knowing look. "As terrible as I feel about what I did to Mrs. Brackett and all my other victims, I'm not sorry I came to prison. I'm not sorry I got locked up, because I really think if I hadn't gotten caught, I would've ended up even worse. And I never would've learned about things that are so important, like breaking the cycle of abuse that's been in your family for generations. I wouldn't have learned about myself, or about the goodness that is in some people. Most of all, I would've never found God."

None of it has been easy to come by. Moreover, none of it is easy for her to continue holding onto. Everything she learned in twenty-two years, all the horrors that were visited upon her during her young life, are like ghouls that come in the night to disaffirm this fragile peace she has found, trying to destroy the faith on which that peace is built. But still she speaks of the hope of forgiveness and says she prays that she can one day learn to forgive herself.

She also prays that her faith will endure through the rough waters she fears are just around the next bend, slamming and crashing against the shores of her future. "I get so scared sometimes," she confesses, head bowed in shame for admitting what she believes is a weakness. "I hate feeling it, but I can't help it sometimes. And what scares me the worst is knowing that without God, I still have the potential to go backwards. Without God and

Christ, I still have the potential to go back to the place where I was hard and cold, to go out and inflict pain . . . even though I know in my heart I could never kill again."

She pauses once more, her eyes locked onto those of the listener seated nearby, while an invisible cloud appears to pass overhead. "It would be so easy to get pulled back into the past again. Back into hell."

Of all the words she has spoken, these bear the strongest imprint of emotion. Although the others are said with the utmost conviction and honesty, there is a vast wasteland between saying the words and feeling the words — and for Shirley, it is as if even she cannot be certain she truly feels them. Then, almost to herself, she admits, "I'm not sure I even know how to feel anymore."

Then she speaks once more of love and need — looking, it seems, for answers to the terrible dilemma in which she finds herself caught. She has found someone who loves her, and who she also loves. There is a gentleness to this relationship, a kindness, that Shirley has never known before — but even more, there is a profound trust that feels like soothing oil being poured on all her searing wounds.

She has never been here before, never felt this safe before. And yet every aspect of this relationship collides with her newfound faith and philosophy. It is not hard to understand how someone like Shirley, so brutally victimized by the one man in her life she should have been able to trust to care for and protect her, might find it impossible to relate to men. It is not hard to understand the depth of her feelings when she admits for the first time, "I really don't trust men at all; I never have. I'm terrified of all of them." At the same time it is not hard to understand the human need for closeness, for touch, for a way to heal and reintegrate a part of yourself blackened and twisted with shame and guilt.

Shirley has found that way, for a moment anyway, in

the loving arms of a woman. For one crystalline moment, she has found acceptance of her essential self as a female, and through that experience is searching for a way to accept that part of herself as well. This, too, is not an easy task, after so many years of denying and despising her own femaleness — if it hadn't been for that, the mind reasons, none of it would have ever happened. *In the final analysis, it was my fault after all. My fault for being born a woman.*

"I wish I knew the answers," she says. "Right now all I know is how it feels to have someone hold me and care for me and not be afraid to look at me, even when I look at myself sometimes and only see filth and sewage. She sees beyond that. Maybe someday I can, too."

As the shadows in the room lengthen into late afternoon, Shirley gazes out into a world only she can see, shifting a little in her chair as if she is searching for something.

After a long and empty silence, she smiles again, but this time it is filled with a great and plaintive sadness.

"I'm trying so hard . . . but I'm so tired. I just don't know. I just don't know if I can make it."

The room is silent now except for the lingering essence of the soft-spoken young woman who sat there only moments before. Her departure has left a deep void in the room, into which spills a lifetime of unmet need and uncharted pain which no words on earth could ever convey. The child that once lived inside her eyes now lies near death, mangled and mutilated, in perpetual starvation for a merciful touch, for tender arms to surround her when the nightmonsters come out to prey.

In one corner, the warmth of hope flickers imperceptibly against the chill of the grief that hovers near the place she had stood to walk out the door.

Yet still she searches for the peace that has so long eluded her and the many other victims gone before, alive and dead.

Still she searches for some way to end the pain, grasping for those remaining wisps of goodness and decency within herself which have not been sucked away by the darkness.

And still she searches for that lost, abandoned child whose eyes once shimmered with trust and innocence . . . hoping that the child still lives, and will live again.

Epilogue

In a perfect world, the answers to the wrenching questions of what went wrong in the lives of Shirley Wolf and Cindy Collier would be easy to discern. Of course, in a perfect world there would be no real need for answers, because their lives would have been lived out unblemished by the ravenous cancers of hopelessness and hatred.

Sadly, the world is far from perfect, and answers seldom come so effortlessly. In fact, even those first, simple questions — Why did they do what they did? How could they do what they did? — take on new and previously unimagined proportions when one stops to take a closer look, like the eye of a fly magnified ten thousand times. In the end, we discover that not only are there no simple answers, there are not even any simple questions.

The long, dark journeys of Shirley Katherine Wolf and Cindy Lee Collier began where all such journeys begin — in a place and time of purest innocence, surrounded by the redeeming light of goodness and hope. They were children not unlike the multitude that came before or followed after in the unbroken circle of infinity. Yet before the shadows of these two children's days could lengthen into springtime, each was snatched away by a malevolent undertow of family violence, sadistic abuse, abandonment and betrayal, and unrelenting despair.

366

Others have been trapped in those same or even darker waters and somehow survived; still others gasped for breath and then breathed no more, pulled to their graves by the roiling, sinister waves. There are as yet no explanations for how one child can live through the most merciless of tortures and later learn to flourish, how another dies from even lesser traumas, or how another survives, but not intact, swept into a torturous netherworld where good has no meaning and life no value. Possibly it is as simple as the battle between goodness and evil, where one side wins and the other loses. Or possibly it is as complex and unfathomable as that same battle.

We can easily stand and point an accusing finger at any number of accomplices in the destruction of Shirley and Cindy: a system that failed and allowed them both to slip through its ragged cracks; parents who should never have been parents, and in fact, never really were; teachers and doctors and police officers and social workers who could have but didn't intervene when there was still some time and hope; relatives and neighbors and friends and children who were too afraid to tell their truths; and of course, the malignant monster of child abuse itself.

But all of this seems to leave us no closer to finding answers to the "whys" hidden within the savage murder of Anna Brackett.

Or perhaps . . . just perhaps . . . there is a pattern here, a common note flowing through the sorrowful, angry requiem for her death. The writer Amos Oz says that "whoever ignores the existence of varying degrees of evil is bound to become a servant of evil." Certainly, one cannot discount the presence of evil here: the evil of the killing itself, the evil that had lain dormant and then exploded from within the two teenagers that murderous day in June of 1983. But such evil neither grows nor can it survive in a vacuum. It must first be planted, then nourished and nurtured and helped to come into its full flower by other hands, other wills. In both Shirley's and Cindy's lives, the seeds were planted early, and nurtured very, very well.

One of those seeds is named silence.

Silence is woven like a sinister web through the sagas of both Shirley and Cindy, two former innocents whose unspoken agony at their own victimization finally exploded in fury at someone just as innocent as they had been. Seeping into every crevice of their lives like cyanide gas, silence became the prison from which there was no escape, the wall through which no one could enter. Neither girl had the voice to break this silence, to tell of the demons raging within . . . while those around them were too deaf, or too afraid, to hear their muted cries. Until that bloody early summer day.

Sadly, these two were and are far from alone in their childhood despair. Child abuse is an epidemic which lies just barely contained under the onionlike skin of society. Pick any day in any month in any season, and a million children in this nation will be suffering from abuse and neglect; as many as five thousand of them will die every year, and another 25,000 will be injured for life — not to mention the tens of thousands who will be maimed emotionally and spiritually.

Yet like Cindy Collier and Shirley Wolf, most of these victims and survivors never feel safe enough to speak aloud their terrible secrets, believing that even if there were someone there to listen, no one would hear. No one would believe. No one would care.

So perhaps that is our answer, if one is to be found. That the evil which allowed two children to mercilessly rob Anna Brackett of her life is called silence. Not the renewing, peaceful silence found deep inside a greening forest, or the tender silence of a mother suckling her newborn child — rather, it is that darker and far more ominous silence we maintain about humanity's painful inhumanity toward itself. It is a silence we keep because that inhumanity touches us too profoundly, pains us too deeply, or frightens us too terribly to reveal . . . and because in confronting the truths about that inhumanity we are forced to confront our own fears — and through those fears, ourselves.

As a society and a human family, we have paid far too high a price for our deafness and speechlessness. We can no longer afford to ignore those unvoiced secrets and unseen wounds which persevere as great unmentionables and ensnare us all in that net of silence from which there is little chance for escape.

There is much we must do. We must find the courage to speak aloud those things which before were only the barest, most terrified whispers of the soul. We must find a way to acknowledge the victims who live among us, and then admit to our own vulnerability. And we must be ready to extend our compassion to the ones who suffer, to help them break the deadly circle of silence before it destroys their lives and society as well.

Finally, we must be willing to confront one last monster from the darkness: our own unspoken fear that in searching for the wellsprings of inhumanity, we just might encounter something of ourselves.

Cindy Collier spent a total of nine years at the California Youth Authority facility in Ventura. Since obtaining her junior college degree, she went on to study law at the institution under the tutelage of attorneys from the Pepperdine University School of Law. She was paroled on August 20, 1992.

Shirley Wolf was finally released from Greystone on June 1, 1991, and immediately transferred to the Central California Women's Facility near Chowchilla, in the heart of the spreading Central Valley. One of almost two thousand inmates at this prison — the world's largest women's correctional facility — Shirley continues to struggle against the darkness, and tries desperately to hold fast to her faith in God. Able finally to look toward the future with hope, she has received her high school diploma and is completing work toward certification as a dental lab technician. She is scheduled for release in 1994.

The last time Shirley saw her family was in early 1984. Since 1988, the letters she sent them in the Pacific Northwest have gone unanswered. In the summer of 1992, however, she tracked down an old telephone number through a friend, and for the first time in four years she spoke with her father. According to him, Katherine walked out on him some time before, leaving behind her three sons who now remain with their father. Shirley has no idea of where her mother is.

Less than two months after that first reunion call, Louis Wolf suddenly stopped accepting any further telephone calls from his daughter Shirley.

ABOUT THE AUTHOR

Joan Merriam holds a master's degree in communications and is currently the Executive Director of the non-profit Child Abuse Council of Place County. She lives in Auburn, California. LITTLE GIRL LOST is her first book.

*HE'S THE LAST MAN YOU'D EVER
WANT TO MEET IN A DARK ALLEY . . .*

THE EXECUTIONER

By DON PENDLETON

Available wherever paperbacks are sold, or order direct from the Publisher. Send cover price plus 50¢ per copy for mailing and handling to: Pinnacle Books, Dept. 593, 475 Park Avenue South, New York, NY 10016. Residents of New York and Tennessee must include sales tax. DO NOT SEND CASH. For a free Zebra/ Pinnacle Catalog with more than 1,500 books listed, please write to the above address.